THE ESTHER PROJECT

A BIBLICAL FICTION STORY ABOUT

LOVE,

HATE,

BETRAYAL,

JEALOUSY,

GREED,

REVENGE,

AND

GOD'S DIVINE PROVIDENCE

BY

IRENE TERRY MILLS

ISBN: 978-1-63950-196-0 (sc)
ISBN: 978-1-63950-208-0 (hc)
ISBN: 978-1-63950-197-7 (e)

Gateway Towards Success

8063 MADISON AVE #1252
Indianapolis, IN 46227
+13176596889
www.writersapex.com

CONTENTS

INTRODUCTION

This book is a *Biblical Fiction* work based on the lives of the following major Biblical Characters in the Old Testament Book of Esther; Queen Esther, Mordecai, King Ahasuerus, and Haman.

Major events in the story line follow the biblical text in the Book of Esther in that Mordecai indeed was a Jew who adopted his cousin Esther and raised her as his daughter (See Esther 2: 5-7); that the King of Persia, King Ahasuerus, selected Esther as his Queen (See Esther 2: 8, 9); that the enemy of the Jews, a man named Haman, attempted to exterminate the Jews (See Esther Chapter 3); and finally, the fact that God used Queen Esther to intercede for the lives of the Jews throughout the Persian territory and that they were victorious over their enemies (See Esther Chapter 9).

I have taken the liberty of creating characters to enhance the storyline where the scripture is silent. For example, Yara, as Esther's personal chamber maid; Zena, Esther's childhood friend, Reelaiah, Tamara and their children as Esther's Jewish neighbors. A complete manifest of fictional characters as well as Biblical characters is listed in the Bibliography Index section.

I have also added a *fictional* story line surrounding King Ahasuerus' palace lawyers. **For example, scripture does NOT record that any of King Ahasuerus' lawyers were disloyal to him in any way and that they were executed because of their disloyalty.** These story lines were included to demonstrate the frailties and sinfulness of the human soul that is not connected with God.

<u>**Also, scripture does NOT record that King Ahasuerus believed in, acknowledged and/or prayed to the God of Abraham, Isaac, and Jacob.**</u> I developed this part of the story based on Paul's letter to the Corinthians. See I Corinthians, Chapter 7 where he discusses the principles of marriage; specifically verse 14 <u>***"For the unbelieving husband is sanctified by the wife, and the unbelieving wife is sanctified by the husband: else were your children unclean, but now are they holy."***</u>

The characters permeated throughout the story demonstrate how God uses His Divine Providence in the lives of everyday people, not just prophets or priest. He uses people of all nationalities and on all levels, including servants, Kings, and Queens to fulfill His Divine Purpose.

Chapter One

ESTHER

Esther pushed back the heavy black sheep-skinned curtain that covered the opening to her and her cousin Mordecai's little hut and stood outside in the cold crisp morning air. She shivered a little and pulled her black Chador, head dress and cape tightly around her small, framed body. Her winter Chador made of double woven wool was thick enough to keep the cold Shushan winter wind out. The tan tunic over her long-sleeved white blouse and brown balloon shaped pants gathered at the ankles that she wore under her Chador made it easy to maneuver over the frozen ground. Only her large deer shaped eyes could be seen through the Chador that covered her head, nose, mouth, and ears. She was so thoroughly covered, looking at her, no one could see the beautiful young maiden underneath. This was the standard dress for all females in the village and she appreciated the covering this morning; it was wintertime and the temperature outside was about ten degrees.

Esther looked down at her feet and wiggled her toes. The heavy woolen stockings with booties kept her legs and feet warm. She was grateful that the Lord had provided enough income from Mordecai's pay to purchase a pair of thick winter sandals at the market.

It was early dawn and the sun had not risen yet. Her eyes adjusted quickly to the grayish blue hue outside. There was no movement anywhere. The village was still asleep. "Perfect," she thought, "no one else is up yet" she said quietly. This was Esther's favorite time of day, early morning with no one around. She pulled her Chador even tighter and stepped a little way out from under the extended roof and away from the hut. She looked past all the huts to the mountains that surrounded their village. A fresh snow had fallen during the night and blanketed the golden yellow and fiery red leaves that remained on the trees, but some of the leaves still poked through looking like little nuggets of golden fire speckling throughout the mountain sides. The evergreen trees stood tall like giants protecting the foliage and the dwellers from any enemies that would try to invade them. Esther felt safe and secure in this little village. Their hut was in the back of a group of 10 to 15 families that lived on the outskirts of a Persian Province called Shushan near the foothills of the Zagros Mountains.

All the huts looked the same, a one room hut made with straw mortar mixed with mud bricks and a thatched roof. The roof was extended eight to ten feet from the hut with a beam across the underside supported by two or three wooden poles. This roof extension provided a porch for families to sit under in warm weather and shelter from the snow in the winter. Hard flint stones were arranged in a circle about 12 inches high on the dirt floor in the middle of the one room hut. A fire was built inside the circle of stones which provided heat for the room in winter and utilized as a stove to cook their food on. A small hole in the top of the roof let the ascending smoke escape from the room. In the summer months, the little stove was moved outside under the extended roof.

Most of the families had sheep and goats. The women sheered the sheep, spun the wool, and made blankets, and rugs to sell in the marketplace. They used straw to make baskets and woven mats to lay on the dirt floors. Any extra rugs were hung on the inside walls of the hut in the wintertime to help keep the cold air out. The only window in the hut was on the front side two to three feet from the door and was the only source of daylight in the summertime. In the winter, it too was covered with heavy, black-skinned sheep's wool.

Colored dye was sold at the marketplace and those families that could afford it, bought it, and dyed their spun wool to give color to some of the rugs, blankets, and baskets. For her birthday one year, Mordecai surprised Esther with some royal blue, brown and gray dye which she used to make beautiful, designed blue, brown and gray blankets for them both. She had enough left over to make one big blue and brown basket. She kept extra blankets in it and set it in the corner of the room with two large fleece stuffed gray pillows leaning against it. Both items gave that area of the room a warm and welcoming atmosphere. Esther loved sitting on the pillows with blankets around her shoulders huddled in the corner near the fire, especially in the wintertime.

Their hut was closest to the mountains, and it seemed to be twice as cold there than the huts that were closer to town. It did not bother her being somewhat removed from the other dwellers. Mordecai built their hut in between two giant broad-leafed evergreen trees with an oak tree in the front and an elm and walnut tree in the back. The trees provided privacy, peace, and tranquility all year long and the walnut tree produced an abundance of nuts for the fall and winter season.

Esther inhaled a deep cold breath of air, held it for a brief second, then exhaled. She felt exhilarated, very alive, very happy and very much at peace in this Persian Country. This was the only home she had ever known. Mordecai, her cousin who was old enough to be her father, brought her to Shushan with several other Jews when King Cyprus, the King of Persia, freed the Jews from Babylonian captivity in the year 539 BC. Mordecai told her that her mother and father died in Babylonian captivity when she was only a year or so old. She had no other family, so he took her and decided to raise her as his daughter. He told her that her father's name was Abihail, the Son of Kish and that they were descendants of the Jewish Tribe of Benjamin. After they were freed, he and several other Jews went back to Jerusalem to help rebuild the temple, but moved on to Shushan when a Persian Governor named Tatnai petitioned King Darius to have the temple work stopped,

Some of the Jewish families that came with Mordecai and lived in the same village as Esther was Reelaiah; his wife Tamara and their two daughters Aisha and Shakera; Bilshan and his wife Eunida and son Motaiah.

Mordecai applied for and was hired as a Porter or Gate Keeper at the King's Palace. The work provided enough income to build their house and buy a few sheep and a horse which were corralled on the right side of the hut by the fur trees. When Esther was still a baby, Mordecai left her with their Jewish neighbor, Tamara to watch when he went to work. She grew up with Aisha and Shakera until she was old enough to stay home by herself.

Esther looked down at the new snow that had fallen overnight. The sun was coming up and the snow sparkled like tiny diamonds glittering and dancing all around her. This was her special time of the morning. "Oh God," she prayed, "it is so beautiful here! You have created such beauty for me to enjoy!" Everything was so still and quiet as if she and the Lord were the only ones on the face of the earth. "Thank you Father, for this precious peace." Esther began to pray just above a whisper, "thank you for your protection throughout the night and for a good night's sleep. Thank you for providing shelter and food for us yesterday and for what you will provide today. Thank you for our home and the animals you have given to help sustain us. Thank you for touching the King's heart to let the Temple be rebuilt. Thank you for defeating our enemies. I thank you and worship you with my life, for you are worthy to be praised for all that you do and all that you will do. For you are the one and only true God, the God of Abraham, Isaac, and Jacob. Thank you for placing Mordecai in my life, for his kindness, for his love as a father. Please bless him this day as he goes out and as he comes in. Make him a blessing to everyone he comes in contact with and protect him from the evil one. And finally, Father, please make me a blessing to you this day, that I will do and be all that you desire me to be. All praise, honor and glory be to you Most High, Amen."

This was Esther's routine every morning. She would stand outside of their little hut door and pray silently to the Lord to keep from disturbing Mordecai as he slept and for privacy with the Lord. Always after her prayer, she would just stand there quietly basking in the presence of the Lord for a few moments and then make her way over to the corral. The snow crunched with each step she took. The sheep and the horse greeted her at the corral railing. "Good morning! God has blessed us with a beautiful morning!" The sheep bobbed their heads up and down as if to answer her. The horse snorted. Esther smiled and began humming one the of the Jewish songs Mordecai taught her as she bent down to pick up straw and toss it over the railing for the animals to eat. She watched them for a few moments and then made her way back to the hut and went inside.

The fire in the center of the room was still burning brightly enough for her to see all around the room. Mordecai was still asleep in his bed roll across the room next to the wall. One of Esther's blankets was thrown over a rope which was hooked to a post and positioned in the center of the room about three feet from the fire. This separated her sleeping quarters from Mordecai's. Esther's bed roll was still unrolled and lay flat on the floor on the opposite side of the room from Mordecai's. Taking off her Chador and hanging it on the wooden peg on the wall next to Mordecai's rap, Esther thought about tidying up the room, rolling up her fleece stuffed bed, pillow and blankets and placing them in the corner, but Mordecai was sleeping so peacefully and soundly that she decided not to disturb him with movement around the room. Instead, she placed two logs on the fire, picked up a roll of yarn from the basket and sat down on the pillows and began feeding the yarn into the wooden spindle. A candle sitting on a small round wooden stump and the light from the fire in the center of the room gave off enough light for Esther to see her work clearly.

As Mordecai slept, Esther rehearsed in her mind the Jewish stories he told her since she was a child, about Father Abraham, Isaac, and Jacob. She pondered about Sarah and how badly she wanted children, wanting to bless her husband with a son, and how God waited all those years, until she was 90 before she conceived Isaac.

"Oh Father," Esther prayed silently. "I desire to have a husband and children too. A husband from Jerusalem would be wonderful. To marry a man from Jerusalem, to be able to return to my homeland, to live to worship at the Temple, to fellowship with people of my own nationality, how wonderful that would be. However, until you are ready for me to marry, I will be contented to remain here with Mordecai."

Esther had a deep desire to study the Torah and learn more of her Jewish history. Mordecai tried to teach her all he could, but working long hours at the Palace, the work at home tending to the animals, making repairs on their hut and tending to the garden in the spring and summer kept him very busy. Every Sabbath, Mordecai secretly met with Reelaiah, Bilshan and the other Jewish men assembling themselves at different locations worshiping the Lord and studying the Torah. Jewish customs prohibited women and maidens to attend these meetings. Whatever spiritual information they received, was given to them by their husbands and fathers at home. Since Esther's mother and father were dead, she had to rely on Mordecai and the Lord for any Jewish traditions and the Jewish Holy Days.

The Jewish families that migrated here from Jerusalem built their huts alongside of the Persian people but kept a very low profile. The Persian Government permitted them to live, move and work freely in all the Persian provinces, but because of past Jewish enslavement, the Jews thought it best to be discrete in their worship of God and spiritual traditions outside of their Jerusalem homeland.

Esther wondered what her mother was like and daydreamed about what she would have taught her about being a woman, marriage and bearing children. Sometimes she watched the Persian women in the village with their children, but she would never approach them for any information. She knew that the Persian culture was different from her own and that they believed in many gods whereas the Jews believed in and served only one God, the God of Abraham, Isaac, and Jacob. The women spoke kindly to her in the marketplace, and she even befriended a couple of maidens from the village, Zena and her younger sister Zoe who lived five huts up and to the left of Esther's hut. Sometimes they went to the market together and visited at each other's homes when time permitted, but she would never reveal any personal information about herself or Mordecai. Somewhere deep inside of her, she felt it was safer for her and Mordecai if they remained discrete about their heritage. Sometimes she, Aisha, Shakera, Zena, and Zoe played together in front of each other's huts, but none of the Jewish maidens divulged their nationalities to Zena and Zoe. Their parents instructed them to keep their veils on at all times and to never tell anyone they were Jews. They were told it was too dangerous.

Chapter Two

TEMPLE LETTER

Esther was lost in her own thoughts and was not aware that Mordecai had awaken, had gotten up from his bed and was standing in front of her. Mordecai was short in stature like Esther and weighed 30 pounds more than she did. His complexion was a darker brown and more olive color than Esther's with deep creased lines on his forehead and on each side of his eyes and mouth. The thick bushy eyebrows almost completely covered his eyes and was streaked with gray matching the mustache and five-inch beard that hung down to the middle of his chest. His bushy curly hair was also streaked with gray and was beginning to recede from his forehead. He was thirty years Esther's senior.

"Oh! Morde, you are up!" Mordecai looked down at Esther smiling. "Yes, I am up. What has you so deeply in thought this morning?"

Esther jumped up from the pillows she was sitting on and gave Mordecai a hug around his neck and kissed him on the cheek while tugging at his beard which was a habit she picked up when she was a baby.

"Oh, nothing much, just things."

Mordecai gently took hold of Esther's hands, pushing her away from himself a little and looked deeply in her eyes. "Uh huh, you were thinking about your mother again were you not?"

Esther dropped her head a little and Mordecai let go of her hands as she turned away from him. "Well, maybe a little" and changed the subject. "Are you hungry? Want something to eat?"

"Yes I could eat something. What do you have ready?"

"How about some rice, bread and tea?"

"That is good" Mordecai replied and walked over to the door pulling back the curtain to peer outside. The sun was rising in the sky, and everything was bright outside. "It is cold out today." He dropped the curtain back in place to keep the cold air out.

"Yes it is. I have been out and fed the animals this morning. While the tea and rice are heating up, I will roll up our beds and put them away. Would you set up the table for us?"

The table they used to eat their meals was a 36-inch long by 22-inch-wide and four-inch-thick piece of wood that Mordecai bought from the marketplace. Wooden pegs with ½ inch lips on the ends were fashioned to the walls 24 inches apart and the wooden table was secured there when it was not being used. While Esther busied herself with the bed rolls, Mordecai retrieved the table from off the wall, placed it on the mat by the fire and took a white linen cloth from the basket and laid it on top of the smooth finished table. He took the two stuffed pillows from the corner of the room and placed one on each end of the table then sat down and crossed his legs under himself. Esther placed the rice, bread, and tea down in front of Mordecai then sat down on the pillow on the opposite side of the table. They held hands as Mordecai blessed the food.

"Thank you Father for the provisions you have provided for us this day, Amen."

As Esther began sipping her tea, Mordecai pulled out a letter from his pocket waiving it in the air smiling. "I received this from the mail carrier yesterday and waited to surprise you with it this morning."

"What is it?" Esther asked very much interested. They seldom received mail from their Jewish brothers.

Mordecai opened the letter and began reading. "Shalom Mordecai and Esther. We trust that all is well with you in Shushan and that you are at peace. God has greatly blessed us and has protected us from our enemies.

You were here when Governor Tatnai challenged our rights to rebuild the temple and stabilize the wall surrounding the temple. He stopped the temple work and sent a letter to King Darius questioning our activity. In his letter he accused us of setting up a revolt against the Persian Government and that we would not pay appropriate taxes and would be a burden on the Persian Government. It took them two years to research and find the original order from King Cyrus giving us permission to rebuild the Temple in Judea.

Darius found the original order in the Medes Palace at Achmetha and commanded Tatnai to let us alone and let the Temple work continue. They were to provide us with everything we needed, timber, tools as well as return the original golden vessels that King Nebuchadnezzar took when he enslaved Israel. All our expenses are paid for. What a mighty God we serve!

We started the work again with Sanballat the Hornite and Tobiah the Ammonite attacking us on every hand. But we ignored every one of their plots and they eventually went away. God always comes through for his children. He always defeats our enemies no matter where we are. He is so good to us.

Within a few months the work will be completed, and Temple worship restored. If possible, you and Esther should come to Jerusalem to the rededication services. We would love to see you and fellowship with you. It has been reported that King Ahasuerus has ordered that the Royal Road from Shushan to Jerusalem and Juda be maintained and protected with palace guards, so it is safe to travel. If you decide to come, you could make the entire trip in seven to ten days. We will provide lodging and provisions for you both just let us know if you are coming. We pray for you constantly. God be with you, Nehemiah."

Mordecai laid the letter down on the table and looked at Esther. "This is good news" he said as he began eating his rice and bread.

"Yes it is" Esther said. "It is very good news. Every time I hear of how God intervenes in our lives; it increases my faith. Who would have believed that several Persian Kings could be so moved by God and be obedient to God to allow us to rebuild our Temple in Jerusalem! God's Divine Providence is wondrous." Esther deep in thought, continued eating her breakfast then suddenly asked, "Morde, do you regret not returning to Jerusalem to help rebuild the temple with the rest of our Brothers?"

Mordecai sipped his tea thinking for a moment. "Ah, yes and no. I think about that all the time and I know some of the brethren think that those of us who did not return to Jerusalem from the Babylonian Exodus were being disobedient to God. I have prayed about it and have peace with my decision to stay right here in Shushan and tend to the King's Gate. Being a porter is not that bad and the money is enough for both of us to live on. We live in peace and God is taking good care of us. All of our needs are being taken care of right?"

Esther, finished eating, got up and began clearing the dishes away. "Yes they are and as far as I can remember, God has always taken care of us." Esther bent down on her knees behind Mordecai and hugged him around the neck. "You were so brave to take me in when my mother and father died and raise me as your own daughter. All by yourself too!!! And allowing me to call you 'Morde' instead of father or Mordecai."

Mordecai grabbed Esther's hands and kissed them. "I permitted you to call me 'Morde' because it was too difficult for you to pronounce 'Mordecai.' Even though I have adopted you as my daughter, I liked the sound of you calling me 'Morde' and bravery had nothing to do with it Esther. God moved on my heart to do it and I am glad I did. I cannot imagine my life without you in it. Anytime God requires you to do something, He always provides everything you need to do it. This is a life principle I want you to always remember no matter what happens to us."

Esther hugged Mordecai tighter around the neck for another second then stood up and continued clearing the table responding, "Yes Morde, I will remember.

What about the invitation to go to Jerusalem, do you think we could go?" Esther thought about her prayer earlier that morning and wondered if this was an answer to her prayer to meet a potential husband from her Jewish homeland.

Mordecai looked at the letter again on the table and was quiet for a few seconds. "I had better pray on that for a while and see what God would have us do. Even though the road to Jerusalem is safe now, it is still better to be in God's perfect will. I would rather have His safety around us than to trust in man's safety." That was not exactly what Esther had wanted to hear, but she knew in her heart that if God wanted her to have a Jewish husband, she would have one weather he came from Jerusalem, Judea or Shushan. She believed God could do anything.

"I am going to share this letter with Reelaiah and Bilshan on my way home from work tonight so I will be a few minutes late for dinner. What do you have planned for today?"

Esther sat back on her pillow. "I have not seen Mama Tamara in a few days. Maybe I will stop by her hut for a visit, or I may just stay at home and work on some blankets; stay inside where it is warm."

"Whatever you decide to do, be careful" Mordecai said as he put on his wraps, grabbed his work bag, and pulled back the heavy blanket that covered the door letting in a burst of cold air.

"I will" Esther said pulling her wrap around her shoulders. Sitting in the quiet after Mordecai left, Esther decided she did not want to stay by herself today and gathered up her bag of knitting, put on her wraps and went out in the cold up the alley toward Mama Tamara's hut.

"You who, you who, is anyone home?" Esther called out standing in front of the hut door.

"Yes we are home, come on in Esther!" Mama Tamara called out. Esther pulled back the black blanket stepping inside. The warmth from the fire took the chill off as she took off her wrap and hung it on the vacant peg beside the door.

"How are you this fine cold morning?" Tamara asked Esther. "We have just finished eating, are you hungry, there is still plenty left? Here, sit down, I will pour you some tea to warm you up."

"Thank you, Mama Tamara. The tea will be fine, Morde and I have also just finished eating" Esther said sitting her bag of knitting down by the pillow then sitting down crossing her legs under herself at the table. As far back as she could remember, Esther always referred to Tamara as 'Mama Tamara.' She did not remember who instructed her to call her that, but it felt comfortable, and she looked the mothering type, short and chubby. Aisha and Shakera, her two daughters, looked just like their mother, round faced and chubby bodies with smooth brown skin and large dark eyes. They were seated at both ends of the table finishing their breakfast.

"What is that in the bag?" Shakera asked sipping her tea.

"It is my knitting. I did not feel like staying home alone today and thought I would bring my work up here for some company. Is that all right Mama Tamara?" Esther asked turning to look at her.

"You are always welcome here Esther, you know that. Our home is always open to you and Mordecai. How is he today?

"He is fine, he just left for work. He said he was going to stop by tonight after work and share a letter he received from the brothers at Jerusalem. The temple is just about completed."

"Oh that is wonderful!" Tamara said clearing the breakfast dishes from the table.

"They invited us to come to the temple dedication," Esther said with excitement in her voice.

Shakera and Aisha both sat up on their pillows at the same time. "Are you going to go?" Shakera asked looking at her mother to see how she was going to respond if Esther said yes.

"I am not sure" Esther said pulling her knitting out of her bag. "Morde says he has to pray over it first to see what the Lord would say."

"Do you want to go? Aisha asked.

"I, yes, I think I would like to go, but it is up to Morde. It would be nice to meet a nice young Jewish man, husband material" Esther said lifting her eyebrows. Everyone laughed.

"A husband, eh," Mama Tamara said with a twinkle in her eye. What do you know about husband material? All of you are too young."

"Too young!" the maidens said in unison. "I am 12 years old Mama," Aisha said. "And I am 13 and ½" Shakera chimed in. Esther sat their smiling not offering up her age just observing her two adopted sisters.

"And you?" Mama Tamara asked. "How old are you Esther?

"Well, I guess I am old enough for God to provide the right man for me. I leave it up to Him. He knows best."

"Now that is a very wise answer" Mama Tamara said as she walked over and patted Esther on the head. "Very wise, very wise indeed. Shakera and Aisha, where are your knitting bags? Get them and join Esther in her work."

"Yes mother" Aisha and Shakera said as they went to get their bags. "Esther" Tamara said turning to her, "how are you and Mordecai doing really? Do you have everything you need?"

"We are fine Mama." Esther said looking at her.

"There is plenty of room for you here if you wanted to stay with us. You would not have to be alone so much with Mordecai working all the time. I worry about you being at home alone so much."

"Oh Mama, I am fine, really. I do not mind being alone. There is plenty for me to do every day and when I need company, I can always come up here right?"

"That is exactly right child. Any time you want to come, you come and if there is anything you need, you just ask."

"Thank you Mama" Esther said grabbing Tamara's hand. "Besides I could not bear to leave Morde. We have been together for such a long time. It would break my heart to leave him. I wonder how I will be able to leave him when and if I get married. Maybe he could come and live with us?"

"That is a possibility." Tamara said laughing. Turning back to her daughters, "here, make yourselves comfortable next to Esther" Tamara said arranging the pillows in a semi-circle.

Aisha and Shakera plumped down on either side of Esther with their knitting bags and began pulling out their yarn.

"Did you see Zena outside yesterday without her veil on!" Shakera said with shock in her voice. "What is she trying to prove?"

"She is looking for a husband" Aisha said sarcastically. "She is not going to find the right kind of husband that way."

"Zena's okay" Esther said. "She is just a little flighty."

"Flighty! She wiggles around like she has ants in her pantaloons!" Shakera said laughing.

"Pantaloons!" Aisha said bursting out laughing.

Esther could not help but laugh with the way they described Zena. "Zena is her own person. She looks at things differently than we do. After all, she is not Jewish and has nothing to fear in her own home country. We cannot afford to act like she does, we must always remember who we are and where we come from."

"That is right!" Tamara said. "You must always remember who you are, where you come from and what could happen if someone decided that they did not like you for any reason. You are females in a strange country, and you are Jewish. You have two strikes against you already. Because of this, you must always be careful; that cannot be said enough. Do you understand?"

"Yes Mama" all three of them replied together. Suddenly there was nothing to laugh about and they continued their knitting in silence.

Esther spent the biggest part of the day knitting, talking, drinking tea, and eating cakes at Mama Tamara's home. As the sun went down around the ninth hour in the afternoon, Esther began gathering up her things to leave. "I must be going now; I have to build a fire and start dinner. Thank you so much Mama for allowing me to visit with you today. Thanks for the company, Shakera, and Aisha."

"You are very welcome Esther, come again real soon" Tamara said giving Esther a big hug as she lifted the blanket covering the door and disappeared into the dusk.

Esther hurried along the path toward their hut. It was getting darker by the second. She did not like being outside after dark, it was dangerous. She feared she had stayed at Mama Tamara's house way too long and walked a little faster.

"Esther, Esther, is that you?"

Esther looked around but did not see anyone and walked even faster.

"Esther, Esther, it is me, Zena. Stop. I want to talk with you."

Relieved that it was Zena, Esther slowed down a little. Zena ran up to her.

"Stop. I just want to talk for a minute or two." Zena said.

Esther looked at Zena. She did not have her veil over her face and that was not good for either of them. "Zena, I must be going, it is late, and I have to start dinner. Could we talk tomorrow?"

"I guess so" Zena said disappointed. "Is it all right if I stop by tomorrow after breakfast?"

"Yes, that will be fine" Esther said. "But I really must be going now." Esther turned and ran the rest of the way home. Reaching the door of the hut, she pulled back the blanket. It was pitch black inside. The fire and the candle had gone out. She hated going into a dark hut, especially at night. Mordecai had warned her about that all the time. The last thing he said before leaving for work this morning was 'Be careful' Esther scolded herself. "Please protect me Father" Esther said quietly entering the hut, dropping her bag by the door, and feeling her way over to the stump where the candle sat. Her fingers felt the rough top of the wooden stump, then the two flint stones that lay on either side of the candle. Putting the stones in one hand, she reached for the candle with the other feeling the top. "Good," she said, "there is still flint on the top. Taking the stones, she struck them together over and over until she got enough of a spark to ignite the candle and the little hut lit up. Glancing around the little room, everything seemed to be in order. "Thank you God" Esther said with a big sigh of relief, "now to get a fire going to heat up this place, then I will start dinner."

Mordecai said goodnight to his replacement at the king's gate and began the long walk home. The day had been slow, nothing unusual, normal palace traffic. His mind was on the temple reconstruction in Jerusalem. How amazing it would be for he and Esther to travel back to their homeland to see and worship in the temple with his brethren. Maybe if they traveled together with Reelaiah and Bilshan, they would be safer, he thought. Maybe more Jewish brothers could join them and make it a real caravan. That would be exciting. Before he knew it, he was in front of Reelaiah's hut. "Reelaiah!" Mordecai called out. "Reelaiah, are you home?"

"Yes Mordecai, I will be out in a minute" Reelaiah yelled as he put his wrap on and pushed back the blanket from the door. "Mordecai, how are you tonight? Tamara said you might stop by."

"Tamara? How did she know I was going to stop by?"

"Esther apparently spent the afternoon with her, Shakera and Aisha and told Tamara you would be stopping by."

"Oh, well, yes, I received this letter from the brethren in Jerusalem regarding the rebuilding of the temple and wanted to share it with you. Here read it" Mordecai handed Reelaiah the letter.

"Wait, I need to get a torch so I can see, wait just a minute." Reelaiah poked his head inside the hut door and Tamara handed him a lit torch which he brought out closer to Mordecai, opened the letter and read it to himself. "This is good news, very good news indeed" he said looking at Mordecai.

"What do you think? It would be great if we could go to the dedication. They will provide lodging for us if we let them know ahead of time. If several families traveled together in a caravan, it may be safer for us" Mordecai said.

"It would be good to be able to return to our homeland and worship in the temple, but I have just started this new job, I do not think it would be good for me to leave right now."

"I understand" Mordecai said looking at the letter. I am not sure if my position at the palace gate would be available to me if I left too. Maybe it is best if we do not leave right now. I am very happy that the temple is almost done though."

"Me too. Tamara has dinner ready; would you like to join us for dinner?"

"Thanks, but I am sure Esther has dinner ready for me at home."

"Okay, good night Mordecai."

"Good night" Mordecai replied as he continued walking down the path toward his hut.

Chapter Three

AHASUERUES'
104-DAY BANQUET

The light from the fireplace warmed Ahasuerus' body as he reclined on his couch in his private bed chamber. He had been up for hours; it was still dark outside. Another one of those sleepless nights that plagued him occasionally. Stroking his black beard with his right hand and watching the tongues of fire dancing in the fireplace, he reviewed in his mind, the Governor's State of the Empire Reports he had received from his lawyers the night before. Repairs on the Royal Road were complete, and Calvary Soldiers were stationed every three miles to stop thieves and robbers from raiding and killing travelers. The newest territorial lines conquered by his father Darius were holding without any rebellions or uprising. In fact, all the 127 Persian Provinces under his rule were doing well. Taxes were being collected on a timely basis without incident and all the people seemed to be contented and satisfied throughout the entire Persian Empire, including Egypt, Ethiopia, and India. Only Greece seemed to be posing a problem. Rumors were circulating that an army was secretly being assembled to overthrow Persian rule in that territory. Memucan's suggestion to send in undercover spies to infiltrate the area was a good one. A report on the activity there is expected in a month or so. In the meantime, naval ships were dispatched to monitor up and down the Mediterranean Sea all around the Greek territory. Memucan was one of seven of King Ahasuerus' top advisors or lawyers and he trusted his advice on just about every subject.

Ahasuerus thought about the people themselves that were under his rule. Great Grandfather Cyrus was a very wise man to permit the people he conquered to keep their own culture and worship their own gods. He would continue to respect all the people and not mistreat them just as his father, grandfather and great grandfather did and acquire the same respect and loyalty that they received. Why change anything Ahasuerus thought, especially if the people remained peaceful and were contented. Darius organized the empire so thoroughly; all I have to do is maintain it and enjoy the power and riches.

The stuffed purple velvet pillows upholstered to the golden couch Ahasuerus was reclined on in front of the fireplace was losing its support under his 250- pound frame. He stretched his legs toward the fire and his thigh muscles bulged through the short silk tunic that went down just below his knees. Rubbing his thighs down to his knees with both hands started the blood circulation to flow and ease the stiffness in his legs. It had been many, many years since he had trained in the cavalry or physically fought in a war, but his muscle tone and strength was still there. His physique was a little round in the middle from the rich food and drink. Vashti, his Queen, did not seem to mind his stomach; she always commented on his biceps and triceps. Was she being sincere Ahasuerus wondered, or was she just doing her duty? Lately, she had been acting as if she was doing me a favor to come to me when I call for her and when she comes, her actions seem to be rehearsed. He realized that he received more emotion out of his concubines than his Queen.

Ahasuerus' thoughts were interrupted when one of the guards stationed outside his door knocked. "Yes, what is it?" The guard opened the door and stepped inside. His 6 ft. 5 inch 200 -pound frame arrayed with shield, sword, helmet, and boots blocked the entire door.

"Your Majesty, your guests are arriving in the outer palace."

"Direct the men to my courtyard and make them comfortable, direct the women to Queen Vashti's courtyard and make them comfortable, then get Abagtha to help me dress" Ahasuerus ordered as he got up from the couch.

"As you wish Your Majesty" the guard replied as he left and closed the door behind him.

Ahasuerus' sandals made a loud clopping noise as he made his way from the couch across the purple and white marble floor to the large window overlooking two large, squared courtyards. The courtyards were decorated and displayed the lavishness and luxury of the Persian Empire. His palace was constructed similar to his father Darius' palace in Persepolis, the capital of Persia during his father's rule, shaped in a rectangle a quarter of a mile long and a mile and a half wide built on a stone platform 20 feet above the ground. Sixteen feet high carvings displayed conquered people from various Persian Provinces bringing gifts to King Darius. These carvings were chiseled on all the outside walls around the palace and the cobble stone staircase wall leading up to the inner palace. A large iron gate at the bottom of the staircase was manned by porters and guards. Large stone towers were erected on all four corners of the palace with flat areas on top of each tower for guards to patrol the area surrounding the castle.

Smaller archways were constructed on the inside of the rectangle structure to mark off the King and Queen's living quarters; storage areas, harems for the King's concubines and living quarters for the soldiers and servants. The royal throne was housed on the right side of the structure next to the staircase. On the left side of the staircase was a breezeway and on the other side of the breezeway were the King and Queen's courtyards.

According to Persian customs, women and men did not socialize together; therefore, banquets, feasts or any social events were held in their personal courtyards, men with men and women with women. When the Palace was constructed, the King and Queen's courtyards were separated by a 64 square foot flower garden. The Queen's personal quarters were located on the second level to the left of her courtyard with a breezeway in between.

From his personal quarters, King Ahasuerus could look out his window and see both his, and the Queen's courtyards as well as the Queen's window to her personal quarters. The Queen, likewise, could see the King's courtyard and his personal quarters.

Ahasuerus looked with satisfaction at the white, green, and blue hangings fastened with cords of fine linen to purple and silver rings which connected the marble pillars spaced every three feet around the courtyard. Red, blue, white, and black squared marble pavement covered both courtyards including walkways through the flower garden separating the yards.

Both the King and the Queen's courtyards were designed the same. At the back wall of each courtyard was a 16 x 10-foot platform also covered with red, blue, white, and black squared marble flooring and was elevated two feet up from the main floor. In the center of each platform was a couch 32-inches long and six-inches high. The four legs, the back and front seat of the couch were made of pure gold; the arms on either side of the couch were made of pure silver. Plush overstuffed royal blue satin pillows were upholstered to the front seat of the golden structure. Twelve more of these gold and silver couches were arranged in groups of twos and threes throughout each of the courtyards. Golden tables as long as the couches and 15 inches up from the floor were centered in between the couch groups and in front of the couches on the raised platform. Each table was covered with royal blue linen tablecloths and all the tables were set the same; a golden picture for wine, four golden wine goblets, a large golden bowel of fruit, figs, nuts, roasted lamb, rice, and beans.

A large tent was erected over top of both courtyards to keep the cold out and four golden fire pits were arranged throughout the courtyards to make it warm and comfortable. Silver lamps filled with oil were fastened to each of the marble pillars and gave the courtyard a bright festive atmosphere.

Every detail was followed to his exact specifications and Ahasuerus' eyes sparkled as he looked down on the layout. It was his third year as king of the Persian Empire, and he wanted to show off his riches to his nobles and princes throughout the 127 provinces. Invitations were sent out requiring all to come to his feasts. He was 104 days into the celebration and this week was the last seven days to host the feasts for the people of Shushan.

Ahasuerus looked across both courtyards to Queen Vashti's window. The lights were on, and he saw shadow movement on the inside. A knock at the door diverted his attention away from the window.

"Yes, what is it?"

"It is Abagtha Sire; I have come to help you dress."

"Come in" Ahasuerus replied as he turned from the window and walked toward his bed and sat down.

Sitting on a stool in front of her dressing mirror, Queen Vashti shakes her head and says "no" to her servant. "This dress is not suitable for the feast today, hand me the royal blue dress with the golden veil."

"As you wish my Queen" the servant took the dress from Vashti and handed her the one she requested.

Vashti stood up, held the dress in front of her and looked at herself in the mirror. "Yes, yes, yes, this will do." Vashti's 5'6" slender frame filled the mirror in all its splendor. The golden oil lamps on both sides of the mirror lit up her smooth golden bronze skin tone and the long black hair curled on top of her head framed her face beautifully. Her dark eyes with long eye lashes pierced to the soul anyone who dared look into them, and her nose and full lips complimented the rest of her face perfectly. This is good, she thought as she twisted this way and turned that way looking in the mirror. I will be the envy of all the princesses that come to the feast today. I am so glad this is the last of the festivities. I do not know why Ahasuerus had to have all these parties anyway. No one is challenging his riches. Vashti sighed and handed the dress back to the servant who took the dress from her, held it above Vashti's head for her to slip her arms into and pulled it down over her head. As she pulled, two of Vashti's black curls from her hair came undone. "Watch my hair!" Vashti snarled at her servant.

"I am so sorry, Your Majesty, please forgive me. Here, let me fix your hai…"

"Never mind," Vashti snapped. "I will do it myself!" Vashti pushed the servant's hand away from her head. "Go get my golden slippers from the closet and bring them here to me. Are you able to do that without any problems?"

"Yes, yes, I can do that" the servant replied. Humiliated, she hung her head, turned, and picked up the slippers from the closet, brought them over to Vashti and stood there with her head down waiting for her to take the slippers. Vashti sat down sideways on the stool and held out her feet for her servant to fasten the slippers on her feet. Once they were on and without comment, Vashti turned back to the mirror.

"I do not think I will wear my golden crown today; I do not feel it is necessary. Hand me my diamond earrings, bracelet, and my diamond ring from the box on the mantel over there." The servant gathered the jewelry and gingerly handed it to Vashti who put each peace on smiling at herself in the mirror.

Standing up and making sure everything was in place, Vashti made her way down to her courtyard where seven other servants waited for their instructions. As she entered the courtyard, all the servants bowed at the waist as Vashti walked by, stepped up to her couch on the platform and sat down. "You may open the door and let the princesses in now" Vashti instructed the servants.

As each princess entered the courtyard, she made her way to the front where Queen Vashti was seated, bowed at the waist, and greeted her with "My Queen, live forever!" waited for Vashti to nod her head then moved on to sit at one of the couches throughout the courtyard. After the twelve princesses were seated, Vashti ordered another servant to begin playing the lute and the ladies began eating, drinking wine, talking, and laughing among themselves.

Vashti sat on her couch and watched silently as the festivities went on throughout the afternoon and boredom began to set in. I do not know how many more of these festivities I can sit through, Vashti thought to herself as she put her hand over her mouth to conceal a yawn. One of the servants approached her to refill her wine goblet and Vashti waived her off shaking her head no and drifted off into her own thoughts again. Only six more days to go, she thought, and then I can go back to my regular routine of relaxation in my bed chamber or an occasional carriage ride through the countryside. It has been at least three and a half months since Ahasuerus called for me to visit him in his quarters. He is probably calling for his concubines to entertain him which is fine with me. My presence does not seem to please him anymore regardless of how I present myself to him. I perform my duties as a Queen should; stay in my place and am at his beck and call. I remember how excited and happy I was when he picked me to be his queen. Competing with all those other maidens throughout the 127 Persian Provinces was difficult; how proud my family was of me. Everything was so very exciting, especially when he called for me to come to him. But now, I am bored, especially with all these mundane feasts just to vaunt his riches and power. If someone were challenging his kingdom or his power, I could see displaying his wealth, but no one is defying him, his authority, or his power. What does he really have to be proud of anyway; he inherited the entire kingdom from his father and grandfather.

"Your Majesty," one of the servants interrupted her thoughts.

"Yes, what is it?" Vashti replied.

"The princesses would like to present their gifts to you before the evening meal, is this permissible?"

Vashti sat up on her couch and nodded for the presentations to begin. The princesses began to present their gifts of fine silk, embroidery, perfume, and oils to Vashti. The atmosphere was light and gay, and everyone was enjoying themselves; Vashti was no longer bored.

Reclining on his couch, Ahasuerus took a sip of wine from the golden goblet, patted his belly, and sighed. All his lawyers were positioned around him reclining on couches and drinking wine as well and looked up at him as he addressed them. "Ah, that is good," King Ahasuerus said referring to the wine in his golden goblet. "This is the life. Is there any other that is richer than I? Born into royalty and inheriting all this lavishness!" he waived his hand around pointing out all of the gold, silver, and fine linens on display. "All the power of my kingdom is laid in my lap to do with as I please. I am ruler over 127 Provinces from Ethiopia to India. Wealth and power, power, and wealth, that is what this feast is all about. Displaying all my wealth and riches to all my princes, servants, and all my subjects. The saying goes 'You cannot be too rich; too powerful, or too beautiful.' Even my Queen is the most beautiful woman in the kingdom." King Ahasuerus stood up too quickly and lost his balance. He was drunk with wine.

Memucan, one of the King's lawyers sitting directly in front of the King jumped up and caught the King gently lowering him back into his seat. "Careful, careful Your Majesty!!"

"Ha, ha, ha, thank you, thank you for your help Memucan," Ahasuerus slurred. "I guess I had more of this juice than I realized," holding the golden goblet up high in a salute, then took another sip. "Now what was I saying? Oh yes, my beautiful Queen. Queen Vashti!!!! How beautiful she is from the top of her head to the soles of her feet!!!! Oh my, my, my."

None of the men in the courtyard said a word, they just looked at the King who took another sip of wine and continued. "You all look at me as if you do not believe me!" Ahasuerus looked around at each of his noblemen and officials. "Hey, hey," his words became more and more slurred with each sip of wine, "hey, Mehuman, Biztha, Harbona and the rest of you servants, go to Queen Vashti's courtyard and tell her the King commands her presence at this banquet. And tell her to wear her golden crown upon her head!"

Mehuman, Biztha, Harbona, Bigtha, Abagtha, Zethar, and Carces, all of Ahasuerus' servants in the courtyard stood, faced the King, bowed then left to go get Queen Vashti.

Queen Vashti was resting on her couch with her princesses and servants all around her. They were laughing and talking among themselves, enjoying each other's company. Some of the princesses, giddy with wine, were dancing and swaying to the music that was played on the lute. All activity stopped and the princesses pulled their veils up to their faces and sat down on the couches when Mehuman and the other servants arrived to address Queen Vashti. They waited at the entrance of the courtyard until Vashti nodded granting them permission to stand before her.

As they marched in one at a time, they stood in a line before Vashti and bowed to the Queen. Mehuman stepped forward bowing again and greeted Vashti, "Greetings Queen Vashti. We have been sent to you by King Ahasuerus. He is requesting your presence at his feast."

Vashti looked startled then quickly composed herself. She never wanted any of her subjects to see her in a situation that she did not know how to handle. Still, she wondered why Ahasuerus was beckoning her to attend his feast. He had never requested her to attend any function in the presence of other men before and Vashti was frantically searching her mind to try and figure out what his motivation was behind this request. One time he had requested her presence and she went to him only to find that he was drunk with wine and the guards with him were trying to calm him down. He was ranting and raving in his bed chamber when she arrived. Thinking they were going to be alone; she learned that he wanted the guards to stay with them. The guards tactfully reasoned with him and backed out of the bed chamber closing the door. That was a very difficult trauma-filled night that was still fresh in the back of her mind. On no! she thought, he is drunk again! What would his request be tonight in front of the nobles and princes? Male and female guests did not socialize together according to Persian customs. Was Ahasuerus going to change Persian custom and make an example with her?

Vashti turned her attention back to Mehuman. Those few moments of remembering Ahasuerus in a drunken state, coupled with her boredom with the many feasts over the past three months, and just plain exhaustion, a look of disgust spread across Vashti's face as she spoke to Mehuman, "Tell the King that I am extremely involved with my banquet festivities with my guests; I cannot attend his feast at this time."

Mehuman and the other servants stiffened up in surprise. The Queen's princesses, guests and servants also looked surprised at the Queen's response and quietly put their hands to their mouths, but no one said a word. After several more minutes of awkward silence, Queen Vashti dismissed the King's servants with a wave of her hand and arrogantly turned her attention back to her party. The princesses and servants resumed their talking and laughter. Mehuman and the other servants turned in disbelief looking at each other talking quietly among themselves as they exited Queen Vashti's courtyard. Once they entered the flower garden separating the two courtyards Abagtha stopped and turned to Mehuman, "Did I hear her correctly? Did she really defy the King? What do you think the King will do? He is drunk and when he drinks, he can get really mean!"

Mehuman continued walking toward the King's courtyard and replied, "I am not sure, but we must deliver the message to the King exactly as the Queen conveyed it to us." All the servants agreed as they continued through the flower garden, entered the King's Courtyard, and stood in the breezeway waiting for him to give them permission to speak.

Ahasuerus stopped talking, looked at them and ordered them to stand before him.

In unison, all the King's servants utter, "Oh King, live forever."

"Where is Queen Vashti?" Ahasuerus asked impatiently.

Mehuman stepped forward, bowing again to the King stating, "Oh King, live forever. Queen Vashti refused to come! She said she is too busy hosting her own banquet and cannot come at this time."

Ahasuerus sat up surprised and in disbelief. In his drunken state, he became very angry, then embarrassed looking at his lawyers and princes that were seated all around him and then angry again. "Go back and tell her that I, King Ahasuerus commands her to come to my banquet immediately!"

Mehuman and the other servants bow before Ahasuerus and return to the flower garden. "What do you think will happen if Queen Vashti does not come to the King's banquet?" Abagtha asked Mehuman as they hurried across the flower garden to the Queen's Courtyard.

"I am not really sure," Mehuman said keeping his eyes straight ahead of him. "I have seen Queen Vashti defy the King a couple of time, but never in front of an audience like tonight. The King is drunk and very angry, who knows what he will do?"

They reached the entrance of Vashti's courtyard as Mehuman finished talking. Before they went in, Mehuman stopped the other servants and said, "listen, let me go in to see the Queen alone, maybe if just one of us is before her, she may change her mind and obey the King's command." All the other servants agreed. Mehuman turned and stood in the doorway of the courtyard. One of Vashti's maids pointed to him, and the Queen nodded her head for him to enter.

All the princesses stopped talking and once again took their seats and covered their faces as Mehuman walked in, stood in front of Vashti bowing at the waist. As he stood upright, Mehuman began speaking in a low soft voice, "Queen Vashti, King Ahasuerus has sent me back to you requesting your presence at his banquet and that you wear your royal golden crown. Will you please, Queen Vashti, accompany me to the King's Courtyard?" Mehuman was pleading, almost begging the Queen not to defy the King's request. The courtyard was completely silent waiting for Vashti's response to see if she would stand her ground or back down and go with Mehuman.

It seemed that Mehuman's pleading only infuriated Vashti and she glared at him for what seemed to be several minutes, but it was only a couple of seconds. Finally, in a low but forceful voice, Vashti spoke, "Tell the King that I am extremely involved in my own banquet festivities with my guests, and I cannot attend his feast at this time."

Mehuman stood there not moving.

"Did you not understand my instructions to you?" Vashti barked.

"Please forgive me my Queen, yes, I understand your instructions and will deliver your message to the King at once."

"Very good. You may go."

Mehuman bowed at the waist and almost ran out of the courtyard. A couple of the princesses giggled as he left the yard and Mehuman turned and looked at them in surprise. He met up with the other servants in the flower garden shaking his head from side to side. "She refuses to come! She is outwardly defying the King! I have never heard or seen such a thing in all my years in service to King Ahasuerus, or King Darius. Come, we must deliver this message to the King at once and see what he will do." No one else spoke as they hurried back across the flower garden to the King's courtyard. As soon as they entered the entry way, Ahasuerus spotted them and motioned to them to come in immediately.

The servants lined up in front of Ahasuerus again and began bowing, but Ahasuerus became impatient and blurted out "Where is Queen Vashti?"

Mehuman cleared his throat and gave the report, "King Ahasuerus, Queen Vashti said, 'Tell the King that I am extremely involved in my own banquet festivities with my guests. I cannot attend his feast at this time.'"

"Did you tell her, I commanded her to come into my presence?"

"Yes Sire, yes I did, and I told her you commanded her to wear the royal golden crown as well."

Ahasuerus stood up, threw his goblet of wine crashing down to the floor and began pacing back and forth in front of his couch, stopped abruptly turning to his servants, he dismissed them. "You may go. In fact, all of you may go, this feast and banquet is over! Everyone leave except my seven lawyers, you stay. Someone inform the Queen that her banquet is over as well! The servants bowed at the waist and hurried out of the courtyard as well as the noblemen and all the other servants and banquet guests.

The seven lawyers that stayed with Ahasuerus were the seven princes of Persia that over-saw the legal matters of the Empire:

Memucan, Carshena, Shethar, Admatha, Tarshish, Meres, and Marsena. Ahasuerus depended upon them to advise him in all situations, especially Memucan. He never made a decision on anything without their council. They all settled back on their couches, but none of them took their eyes from Ahasuerus, they knew he was furious as well as embarrassed.

Pacing again, Ahasuerus blurted out "What can I do about this stubborn insubordinate woman! She has the nerve to disobey my order! Not once, but twice, and in public!"

Memucan sat up in his chair and spoke directly to the King. "Queen Vashti did more than disobey your commandment King Ahasuerus, she disrespected you in front of all your princes, your servants, and your subjects. She disrespected us as well," Memucan turned and looked at all the other lawyers around him then continued, "and all men throughout the Persian Kingdom."

All the other lawyers spoke up and said "this is true" nodding and looking at each other in agreement.

Memucan continued, "all of the Queen's princesses and servants witnessed her insubordination. If we allow this behavior to go on without any consequences, this attitude will spread throughout every household in the Kingdom. Men everywhere will be disrespected in their own homes, both great and small and all women will despise their husbands!" Memucan stood and began pacing along with the King. After a few minutes, he continued, "do you know what I would do?"

Ahasuerus stopped pacing, turned, and looked at Memucan.

"I would divorce her!" Memucan stated with all the force he could muster up to make his point stand out. "Yes, I would divorce her. She would not come before me ever again! I would divorce Queen Vashti and give her royal estate to someone else more deserving. Someone who knows a Queen's responsibilities. Who knows how to treat and respect a King as great and powerful as you are! Divorce her King Ahasuerus! Let this divorcement be an example to women throughout your Kingdom! They will know, most assuredly, that they must honor and obey their husbands!"

King Ahasuerus thought about what Memucan suggested for several moments. Then slowly, he nodded his head in agreement, "you are right as usual Memucan" and called for his servant Zethar. "Zethar, go get my secretary Harbona, a new court order must be written and sent out immediately!"

"As you wish Your Majesty" Zethar bowed at the waist and hurried out of the courtyard.

"As for Vashti" Ahasuerus continued, "Memucan, draw up a divorce decree, I will sign it and seal it with my signet ring. Deliver it to her personal quarters first thing tomorrow morning, she shall not come before my face ever again. Have her clear out her personal things and be out of her palace within a week. Return her servants and maidens back into the hands of Hegai and tell him to reassign their duties. Send out a Decree to all 127 Persian Provinces stating that Vashti is no longer Queen of Persia, that she committed insubordination against the King. Hence forth, all wives will be obedient to their husbands and the husbands shall be the head of their homes."

"As you wish your Majesty" Memucan gathered up his things, bowed to the King and left the courtyard. Ahasuerus dismissed the rest of the lawyers and retired to his personal quarters weary and tired, but he was no longer drunk.

Two guards who were always stationed outside Ahasuerus' bed chambers stood to attention as he approached his door. Without saying a word, the guard opened the door; Ahasuerus walked through, and the guard closed the door behind him. It was the same room he was in earlier this morning, but it seemed different to him now. So much had happened within the space of the first and second watch and he felt empty and lonely inside. His quarters seemed much larger and empty than it was this morning. This is only my mind playing tricks on me, he thought as he walked over to the window and sat down on the window ledge. He looked across the courtyard to Vashti's window. Her light was still on he could see movement behind the curtains, she must be getting ready for bed, he thought. Why did she refuse me? If only she would have come, everything would still be the same. His anger was waning and was replaced with longing and desire for Vashti. "No, no, no" he said to himself out loud and forced himself away from the window, walked over to the couch in front of the fireplace and sat down. Suddenly fatigue swept over him, he was exhausted. Not being able to sleep the night before and the stress and tensions of the day, he yawned a couple of times and fell fast asleep.

Vashti stretched, turned over in her bed toward the window. It was daylight. What time was it, she wondered and how long had she slept. She yawned, stretched again, and sat up. It looked to be about the third hour in the morning. "Where are my maids and servants" she said out loud as if someone were standing beside her bed. Every morning without fail, her servants came to her door with a breakfast tray and awoke her if she was not already awake, helped her dress and prepare for the day. Where are they this morning she wondered. Vashti swung her feet out of bed and onto the cold white, red, and black marble floor. The fire in the fireplace was out. "What is going on?" she said out loud. "Where is everyone?" She slipped her feet into her sandals, put on her robe and was walking over to look out of the window when she heard a knock on her door. "Yes, you may come in" she replied as she continued to walk toward the window with her back to the door.

Memucan stood just inside the door and did not move. He could see that she expected him to be one of her servants.

Vashti addressed, who she thought was one of her servants, "you may place my breakfast tray on my dressing table and select a suitable dress for me to wear along with the appropriate sandals. Why are you so late this morning? And why did you let my fire go out in the fireplace? It is cold in here. Has my bath been drawn? After you lay out my clothes, build a fire!" Her voice was in her usual demanding tone. When she did not hear a reply or any movement in the room, she turned to reprimand her servant for not following her orders and was startled to see Memucan standing in the doorway with some sort of document in his hand. "Who are you and what do you want? Where are my servants?" Vashti looked past Memucan out into the hall looking for the two guards who were always posted outside her door. They were gone and terror filled her heart. "Who are you and what do you want!" she almost shrilled pulling her robe tightly against her body. What is happening! she thought, is this man going to have his way with me! Men never entered her personal bed chambers. Even the guards that protected her area stood outside the door, never stepping into her room for any reason.

Memucan put up his hand trying to put Vashti at ease. "Calm down Vashti, I am not here to harm you in anyway."

"What do you want?" Vashti demanded and "where are my guards, my servants, my maids? Where is everyone?"

Memucan did not move from the spot he was in when he opened her door, he spoke to her from where he was. "Vashti, my name is Prince Memucan, I am one of King Ahasuerus' lawyers. He has instructed me to deliver this Divorce Decree to you. As of today, you are no longer Queen of Persia. You are ordered to clear out your personal effects within one week and vacate the palace. Your servants and your maids have been reassigned as of today. Do you have any questions?" Memucan waited.

Vashti stood still as if to be in shock and began to shiver. Divorced! At first, she could not fathom what the term meant. Then speaking as if in a whisper, "Divorced! Did you say Divorced?"

"Yes." Memucan stated, "Do you understand, and do you have any questions?"

"Yes, I understand," Vashti shot back regaining the strength in her voice. "Why did he divorce me? Where am I supposed to go? How am I supposed to live? Who will help me pack my things and move me to wherever I am going if he dismissed all of my servants and maids?"

Memucan studied Vashti closely observing her shock and confusion. He did not think about where Vashti was to go and how she was to get there. All he was prepared to do was get Vashti out of the palace within the time frame that the King had given him. He turned and leaned his back against the doorway, careful not to step inside of the room. He lowered his head, folded his arms across his chest deep in thought. Vashti stood their quietly and watched him; she was still in shock. Finally, he stood straight again and faced Vashti in the doorway. "Do you have family that you could go live with?"

"Family?" Vashti snorted.

"Yes, family. Father, mother, brothers, sisters, aunts, and uncles?"

"My family" Vashti whispered. She had not had any contact with any of her family since becoming queen. For the past three years, they had tried to contact her, but only to beg from her and she sent them away. They never came back. She had no idea where they went or if any of them were still alive. "I do not know where my family is. I have not heard from them in the past three years. I... I just., what am I supposed to do? Where can I go?" Vashti looked at Memucan helplessly.

Memucan suddenly felt sorry for Vashti. Her self-centered, arrogant attitude over-powered the outward beauty she possessed. He wondered what the King saw in her besides her beauty. She was so full of herself; how could he stand to be in her presence. She had no idea of the seriousness of her actions the night before, defying the King in front of his guests. "Listen Vashti, I will go back to the King and ask him to grant you more time to get your personal affairs in order. Say, a month? Will a month be enough time?"

"A month?"

"Yes, a month."

"A month to do what?"

Memucan sighed. She had no idea how to take care of herself. "Write a note and send it by messenger to the last place your family lived. Where did your family live, where did you come from?"

"Cappadocia."

"Cappadocia? That is about 750 miles from here. It would take a runner at least two weeks to travel the Royal Road, another week to find your family and another two weeks to return with a reply. You will need at least three months to get your affairs in order. I will petition the King for a three-month extension and explain your situation to him. I will also ask if he will grant you one servant to help you, but you must move out of the palace immediately."

"Do you think the King would grant me to become one of his concubines?" Vashti said in a pleading voice.

"No, I do not. He was firm in his decision not to see your face ever again. If you became one of his concubines, there is a possibility that you could be called in to see him and he would have my head if that happened. No Vashti, you must vacate the palace. I will arrange for living quarters in the servant's area for you to stay for the three months while the runner looks for your family. You may eat your meals in your room or with the servants, but you must not enter the courtyard or the flower garden."

"Am I a prisoner?"

"No, you may go to the village, the marketplace or anywhere else you like, just not on royal palace property where the King may see you. I will also petition the King for a sum of money for you to live in some comfort. I do not know how much it will be, but I will try."

"Thank you Memucan, thank you."

"Vashti, life will go much easier on you if you treat people the way you would want to be treated. Do you understand?"

Vashti lowered her head humbly and then looked up at Memucan with tears in her eyes and whispered "yes," walked over and fell on her bed and sobbed uncontrollably.

Chapter Four

THE KING'S DECREE

Esther grabbed her chador and veil from the wooden peg beside the door, threw it around her shoulders and picked up the empty blue and brown stripped basket from the corner wall. It was market day. Mordecai had gone to work at the King's gate early today pulling a double shift to cover for another porter. This gave Esther a little more time to browse through the marketplace to see what she could see. The sunlight warmed her as the sunrays radiated through her heavy chador. It was a beautiful day. The weather was changing, and shoots of green grass pushed through the ground here and there, birds nesting in the trees were all signs that winter was over, and spring was almost here. This was a perfect day to go to the market.

Large odd, shaped gray and black stones were laid in the alley ways between the huts fashioning a zigzag pattern and made it possible to walk between the huts without getting an excessive amount of mud on her sandals. Esther made a game out of the zigzag pattern seeing how many stones she could step on without slipping and disturbing the mud. This game became more challenging to her as the ground was melting from the winter freeze.

Esther thought about going over to Aisha and Shaker's house to see if they wanted to go to the market with her but changed her mind. Mamma Tamara would want to come too and would hover too closely. Esther would not get to look at all she would like to if they were there, Mama would be hurrying them to get back home. Instead, she walked around the back way avoiding their hut and arrived in front of her friend Zena's hut and called out to her. "Zena, Zena, do you want to go to the market with me?"

"To the market? Yes. Give me a minute."

Esther stepped on a stone with her right foot and tried to see how long she could hold her balance while waiting for Zena. Within a minute Zena's tall slender frame pushed back the covering from the door of the hut and hurried toward Esther with her basket in her right hand. Her chador was black, but the veil covering her mouth and ears was a sheer blue material that some of the maidens wore in the spring season. Esther was not comfortable wearing such revealing veils. All of her veils were of black material that you could not see through. She never wanted to make herself stand out in a crowd revealing too much of herself to the public. Looking at Zena through the veil, her brown eyes and long black eyelashes sparkled with excitement. Her brown Persian skin seemed to glow as the sunlight showered down on her. Esther could see that something good must have happened to Zena because she was smiling from ear to ear. Going to the marketplace was the only time the two of them had time to talk and share anything that might be going on in their lives.

The two maidens embraced each other briefly and began leisurely walking through the pathways to the marketplace talking and laughing together.

"I have exiting news!" Zena said looking at Esther pulling out a letter from under her chador. "Look! It's an official decree from the King's Palace! Did you get one?"

"No. What does it say?" Esther asked looking down at the document.

"Here read it!" Zena said with excitement.

Even though Esther and Zena were close friends, Esther was nothing like Zena and Zena was nothing like Esther. Esther was levelheaded, wise, and conservative. Zena was flamboyant, flighty, and very excitable.

Esther took the document from Zena inspecting its front and back. "This is from King Ahasuerus' Palace!" Esther said with surprise in her voice.

"I know. Read it. Read it out loud, I want to hear it again!"

"Okay, okay! Settle down!" Esther turned the document over, opened it up and began to read. "'Hear ye, hear ye, hear ye. King Ahasuerus, King of Persia, King of the 127 Persian Provinces is seeking fair young maidens to compete for the office of Queen to replace Queen Vashti who committed insubordination against the King. All maidens must complete the enclosed application and submit it to the King's Chamberlain, 'Hegai,' keeper of the women 30 days hence. All maidens will be housed in a special palace under the guardianship of Chamberlain Hegai. Articles for purification shall be provided for each maiden and she will be presented to the King in turn at the appointed time. The maiden that pleases the King will be named Queen of Persia. This order is written under the order of King Ahasuerus, King of Persia." Esther turned the notice over. "Oh look, the King's Ring Signet! This is authentic!"

"Of course it is authentic!"

"I did not get a decree" Esther voiced returning the decree to Zena. "Maybe Morde has it. He picks up the mail on his way to work. If there is one, he might have it."

"You are probably right. Anyway, I am excited about the possibility of being Queen of Persia. I already discussed it with my parents, and they are excited too. There little maidens possibly being made queen! They said Zoe could try out too she will be 12 years old in a month." Zoe was Zena's younger sister. "What an honor for my parents if one of us wins. And look," Zena pressed her hands down both sides of her body and does a quick wiggle so no one else would see except Esther, "I have the looks and the body. I can always put on a wig to hide this hair and with a little makeup, what King could deny this!"

Esther laughed watching Zena. "An honor for your mother and father?" Esther said laughing again. "Do you know the process that each maiden will have to go through before she is even presented to the King?"

"No. But I am willing to do whatever it takes to try for that golden crown. Imagine the power, prestige and the riches that would be at my disposal if I win! My family would be set for life!" Zena sighed at the prospect of it all.

"Have you thought about what happened to Queen Vashti? I learned that all she did to get divorced was to say 'not now' to the King and all the men got scared and told the King to divorce her! Not only that, what happens to you if you do not win the 'Golden Crown?' Have you thought about that? When it is your turn to be presented to the King and he does not pick you, that is the end of it. You become one of his concubines, never to marry, never to have children of your own. Any child you may have to the King, becomes the King's property. You have no authority over his or her life. All you would ever be is 'one' of the King's concubines. He may never call for you again, ever. Can you settle for that? Can you live with that?"

"Esther," Zena said quietly, "you are forgetting one very important thing."

"What is that?"

"This is the King of Persia, and this document is a Decree from his palace. It is a command and we, you, me, all the maidens in his Kingdom must submit ourselves into the hands of this Hegai. The answer to all those questions you asked is yes, I will have to live with, settle for that and even give up my purity for that because that is the King's law. None of us has a choice in the matter."

Esther was quiet for a long time as they continued to walk to the marketplace. The thought of her having to give up her purity to a King that was not of her nationality had never crossed her mind. She thought she would be exempt because she was a Jew. But no one in her village knew that she and Mordecai were Jews, they thought they were Persians like them. Oh Father! what am I going to do? Esther prayed silently. Please show me a way out of this.

"Esther, where are you going? We are here!" Zena yelled at her. Esther was so deep in thought, she almost walked through the marketplace to the other side.

"Oh, I was just thinking about some things."

"Well, we are here. What do you need? Oh, look at this beautiful purple silk. This would be perfect to make a gown for the King's competition. Look Esther, it is beautiful!"

Esther turned in Zena's direction and nodded her head up and down then went over and picked up two pomegranates and put them in her basket. There was a sinking feeling in the pit of her stomach that would not go away. She did her shopping and walked back home in silence listening to Zena chatter away about her plans to become queen. She was glad when they reached Zena's hut and said their good-byes. Most of the time she enjoyed Zena's company but right now she needed quiet to be able to talk with her Father. For the first time in her life, Esther was not at peace living in a foreign land and she felt her happiness melting away just like the icicles melting away from the tree branches under the direct rays of the sunlight. She tried to pray but could only moan at the prospect of giving up her purity to a Persian King. What would become of her? Would she be forced to worship their many gods and not be able to serve the one true God, the God of Abraham, Isaac, and Jacob. And children, what about my children! Esther started to panic. "Calm yourself down," she said out loud to herself, "you know that God is in control of your life, he has everything under control, calm down." Esther took a deep breath in and let it out then stepped inside of their hut.

Esther took off her wrap and hung it on the peg and set her basket on the floor. "Oh no!" she said out loud looking into her basket. The only thing she brought at the market was pomegranates! "What am I going to fix for dinner?" Standing motionlessly deep in thought, she remembered, "I have some dried salmon and beans. That will do and we can share a pomegranate for dessert." Letting out a heavy sigh, she sat the basket of pomegranates in the corner, fixed herself a cup of tea and sat down in her favorite corner. That sinking feeling still in the pit of her stomach, she tried to pray again but again, nothing came out, just moans and groans. Exhausted, she fell asleep.

"Esther, Esther, wake up." Mordecai was standing over her.

"Huh?" Esther stirred and sat up. She was not aware that she had fallen asleep. "Morde! When did you get home? What time is it?" Esther rubbed her eyes, looked around and jumped up from the pillow she was sitting on.

"It is well into the ninth hour!" Mordecai answered turning to hang up his wrap on the peg. "Are you feeling well Esther? It is not like you to take a nap in the middle of the day."

"Yes, Morde, I am well. Zena and I went to the market today, and I guess it tired me out more than I realized; but I am well." Esther quickly began fixing dinner.

"And how is Ms. Zena today?" Mordecai asked as he sat down in his spot at the table.

"She is Zena. She is all excited about receiving a decree from the King's Palace about competing for the position of Queen of Persia.

"That reminds me, you have some mail today." Mordecai pulled an envelope from his shirt pocket and handed it to Esther. Esther took the envelope and sat down on the pillow opposite Mordecai. Instead of opening it, she turned it over and over in her hands looking at it anxiously. Mordecai watched Esther closely. "What is the matter Esther? You look as though you already know the contents of that envelope?"

"I do Morde; I do. It is the same decree Zena got from the Palace to compete for the new Queen's position."

"So that is what all the chatter was about all around town. All day long, bunches of young maidens with their mothers streamed past the King's gate trying to see through the bars. Such fussing and giggling. What does the notice say?"

Esther slid the envelope across the table to Mordecai. "Here, read it for yourself."

Mordecai picked up the envelop opening it while keeping his eyes fixed on Esther's. He studied her for a moment, trying to understand the look on her face. Worry, bewilderment, or fear, he could not figure it out. He had never seen her in this state before. He lowered his eyes on the notice and began reading to himself. When he finished, he looked at Esther for a long time before speaking. Finally, he asked; "what do you think?"

Esther leaned back against the wall folding her hands in her lap. "Morde, you know I am a Jew; you know my lineage. This is a Persian King, not a Jewish King. All the maidens competing will be Persian. Even if I did compete, do you know what would happen to me if I did not win? I would become one of the King's Concubines!" Esther helplessly raised her hands as if she were defeated before she even began. "What does our Jewish laws say about that?" Esther got up from the table and nervously began setting the table for dinner. Mordecai bowed his head with his hands in his lap sitting quietly as Esther began serving dinner for the two of them. After Esther returned to her seat, Mordecai and Esther held hands while Mordecai blessed the food.

"Most gracious Father, who provides for our every need, who directs our every step and whose divine plan for each of our lives is already laid out, we thank you for all that you have done for us and we thank you for all that you are about to do for us. Please let your divine will be done today regarding the King's Decree and give us your perfect peace regarding your divine will.

Thank you for the food we are about to receive for the nourishment of our bodies. Thank you, in the name of the God of Abraham, Isaac and Jacob, Amen." Esther and Mordecai began eating their dinner in silence. Suddenly, Mordecai stopped eating and looked at Esther.

"Esther, I believe you are supposed to try out for the Queen of Persia." Esther put her fork down and listened intently to Mordecai. "Do not worry about the Jewish marriage law because even if you do not make Queen, you will be legally married to the King in God's eyes. We must have faith in God. We have kept his laws all these years while living in Shushan. We have been able to worship Him in peace in the privacy of our home and I feel that He has a plan for us. However, we must be very wise and very cautious in our decision making. Do not tell anyone that you are Jewish."

"Would that be lying Morde? Would God have me to lie?"

"Of course not, Esther. Was there an application with the decree?"

Esther picked up the envelope from the table and handed it to Mordecai. "Yes, here."

Mordecai opened the application, scanned down the page then looked at Esther again. "There is no question here about nationality so do not volunteer anything about yourself that they do not ask you. Have you ever told anyone that you are Jewish?"

"No Morde."

"No one? Not even Zena?"

"No Morde, no."

"Good, do not."

"But Morde, if I compete, what will happen to you? Who will take care of you?"

"God will take care of me. He always has and he always will. As far as cooking and cleaning, I was cooking, cleaning, and taking care of you since you were a baby. I think I still know how to cook and clean for myself." Mordecai smiled and winked at Esther. With that said, Esther and Mordecai finished their dinner in silence.

That night both Esther and Mordecai tossed and turned on their bed rolls and could not sleep but neither of them said anything to the other. The blanket that was strung up between them could have been a stone wall that kept their troubled silence in their own places. Esther had prayed so much from the time she and Zena went to the market to now, that she was all prayed out. Every once and a while a tear would trickle down the side of her face which she quickly wiped away. She lay their looking up at the ceiling sighing every so often then finally drifted off into sleep.

Mordecai could hear Esther tossing and turning but remained silent. What could he say, he thought? The impression from the prayer at dinner was so heavy on him, he knew it was the Lord, but Esther was still very troubled and that concerned him. She always accepted his instructions about everything, never questioning if he really heard from the Lord on any matter. Mordecai turned on his right side facing the wall with his back to the blanket that separated his and Esther's sleeping areas. He tried to go to sleep but thoughts kept racing through his mind. No, Esther never questioned him about any decision he made regarding her and she was not questioning him now, but he knew she was very upset over the King's decree. I will stop at Reelaiah and Tamara's on my way to work tomorrow and see what they are planning to do about this decree, and he fell asleep.

Mordecai awoke at his usual time even though he did not get his normal amount of sleep. Peeking around the blanket, Esther was still fast asleep; he decided not to disturb her. Dressing quietly, he grabbed a handful of cakes, a few figs, and his work bag, put a log of wood on the fire to keep the room warm and quietly left for work. Walking down through the path he saw several of the villagers leaving their huts on their way to work. Up ahead, Zena and Zoe's dad waived to him as he passed their hut. Further down he saw Reelaiah turning the corner on his way to work.

"Reelaiah, Reelaiah! Wait for me, I need to talk to you" Mordecai called.

Hearing his name called, Reelaiah turned and saw Mordecai running up to him. "Good morning Mordecai. Is everything alright?"

"Everything is fine" Mordecai said out of breath. "I just wanted to ask you a couple of questions." Mordecai turned his head looking around discretely to see if anyone was close enough to hear their conversation.

"Is something wrong Mordecai?" Reelaiah asked noticing the caution Mordecai was displaying.

Once he was sure no one could hear them, Mordecai pulled out the King's decree and moved closer to Reelaiah. "Did you receive one of these decrees from the King about Aisha and Shakera?"

Looking at the document and then back at Mordecai, Reelaiah scanned the area to see if anyone noticed them standing there and tugged on Mordecai's arm. "Come, walk with me so we do not look suspicious. Yes, Tamara and I received one of these documents from the messengers."

"What have you decided to do about it? Are you going to fill out the application and return it to the palace?"

"We, Tamara, and I talked about it and decided that this decree was for the Persian maidens only. Up until now, we did not disclose to anyone that we were Jewish, but now," Reelaiah hesitated looking around again and then continued, "now we find it necessary to let the authorities know that it is against our religious beliefs to allow our daughters to participate in this Persian custom. That is what we wrote on that application, and I am returning it to the palace today."

"Have you talked to any of the other Jewish brothers in the area about this?" Mordecai asked looking down at the ground as they walked.

"Yes, I talked to Bilshan. Even though he does not have any daughters, he said if he had, he would not let them participate in this custom. Are you going to allow Esther to participate?"

"I am not sure yet" Mordecai replied. He did not tell Reelaiah about the prayer at dinner last night or how upset Esther was about the decree. He just wanted to know how the other brothers felt about it.

Noticing Mordecai's uneasiness Reelaiah studied him as they walked along the path. "Mordecai" he said slowly, "are you considering letting Esther participate in this ritual?"

"Well, I…"

Reelaiah stopped walking and turned to face Mordecai. "Do you know what they put those maidens through? This, this purification thing that they must go through and then be presented to the King who takes away their purity? And if he decides that he does not like them, they become his concubines forever. If they have children, they become the King's property, you will be deprived of your grandchildren! You would submit Esther to such a life?"

"Esther and I prayed about it last night and we feel that the Lord would have her to do this."

"You do?" Reelaiah asked shocked at Mordecai's response. "You really think that our God would have you submit your daughter to become married to a King who believes in many pagan gods?" Reelaiah's voice rose as he spoke to Mordecai.

"Quiet, do not speak so loudly, someone might hear you!"

"I am sorry, Mordecai, I cannot believe what I am hearing from you." Reelaiah began walking again, but more slowly, deeply concerned with what he was hearing. "We study the Torah together; you know what the scriptures say about intermarrying with the pagans of the land. How can you possibility think God would have you submit Esther to something like this? I think you need to go back and pray about it some more my friend. I really must go now before I am late for work. Mordecai, do not do this, this is not of God. Do you understand?"

"I understand what you are saying, and I will consider it. Thanks for listening to me. You have a good day" Mordecai said as he turned to walk away regretting that he decided to talk with Reelaiah about the whole subject. As he walked down the cobblestone road toward the palace gate the same feeling came over him that he experienced the night before at dinner and he knew he must allow Esther to go to the palace to try out for the queen's position. "Yes, Lord" he said in a whisper, "I will obey." With that, all the anxiety left, and he started his workday in peace.

Reelaiah worked all day long with his and Mordecai's conversation running through his thoughts. Mordecai knew Jewish law better then him. How could he even think about allowing Esther to become involved in a pagan custom. On his way home from work, he met Bilshan in the alleyway. "Good evening Bilshan."

"How was your day brother?"

"Alright I guess."

"Is there something wrong?"

"I was just thinking about my conversation with Mordecai this morning. We were discussing the King's decree about his new Queen. Do you know he is considering allowing Esther to compete for the Queen's position?"

"You must be mistaken Reelaiah. Mordecai knows Jewish law better than all of us. There is no way he would deliberately go against the law. You must be mistaken."

"No, no I am not mistaken" Reelaiah said shaking his head. He said he and Esther prayed about it last night and felt that it was God's will for her to compete."

"So, you think he is serious about this?"

"Yes I do, yes I do. If he deliberately commits this sin, we can have nothing more to do with him or Esther. I will have to instruct my family to no longer associate with either of them. This will cause them and me much sadness; however, I am not willing to risk my relationship with God because of Mordecai's deliberate disobedience. We, all of us, including all of our families must separate ourselves from both of them to keep ourselves pure and in compliance with the law."

"I am afraid you are right Reelaiah" Bilshan replied with his head down. "I have always looked up to Mordecai as one of our leaders. This is sad, very sad."

"Yes it is; however, we must spread the word to all of the other Jewish brothers and instruct them to distance themselves from Mordecai and Esther."

Reelaiah entered his hut and shared Mordecai's decision with Tamara and their daughters. They all hugged and cried together. As they saw it, they had lost a close member of their family.

Chapter Five

GOING TO THE PALACE

Esther looked around the little hut trying to engrave what it looked like in her mind so she would never forget it. It was time to go to the palace. Suddenly that sinking nervousness hit her in the pit of her stomach and she bent over a little. "Oh Father!" she prayed, "please take this fear from me, give me your strength, your peace, your power to do your will." She stood up and the fear was gone. How long will it stay gone this time, she wondered. Over the past month, since she had received the King's Decree, she had been fighting these anxiety attacks. They seemed to come on her at the oddest times, late in the night while she was sleeping, while she was fixing meals or going to the marketplace. They always seem to catch her off guard, this time was no different. Each time the attacks would come, she would pray the same prayer and the fear would go away.

Looking around, Esther had mixed feelings about leaving their little home. The last month was very lonely for her. Mama Tamera, Shakera, and Aisha would have nothing to do with her and Morde; Reelaiah would not permit it. He said Morde was breaking Jewish Law in allowing her to compete for the Queen's crown; that he, his family and all the other Jewish families in Shushan should have nothing to do with either of them. She was relieved to be leaving, but apprehensive about what she was going to encounter at the palace. She also worried about leaving Morde with no one to fellowship with, no one to study the Scriptures and worship with. "Father, I am ready to go. Please take care of Morde. Thank you."

Turning around for one last glance, she walked out the door to Morde.

"Are you ready Esther?"

"Yes, Morde, I am ready."

Mordecai looked at Esther and drew her to himself holding her closely for a long time then whispered in her ear, "All will be well with you Esther, you are in God's hands. Remember, anytime God requires you to do something, He always provides everything you need to do it. Remember Esther? Do you remember that life principal?" Mordecai pulled Esther back and looked deeply into her eyes.

Esther's eyes filled with tears that overflowed down the outside of her veil. She promised herself that she would be strong for Morde and tried to wipe the tears away. Oh how she loved him, and she knew that he loved her too. "I remember Morde. I remember everything you ever taught me. Thank you aga…"

"Hush, hush, my child" Mordecai put his hand over Esther's mouth to stop her from talking. "It is not necessary for you to thank me for anything. You are my daughter, and I am your father. There is no need to thank me for anything. Stop crying now, come, let us go." He took Esther by the arm; they began walking down the alley toward town.

The King's palace was on the other side of the marketplace. There were so many families escorting their daughters to the palace that most of the villagers walked to the palace rather than rode their horses. The only buggies on the road were from out of town. It seemed as though every household was represented in this parade to the palace except for the Jewish families and those Persian families who did not have daughters. The King granted all the Jewish Maidens exemption from this competition based on their religious beliefs. The King said he would allow any Persian citizen to worship the god of their choice in their own way and that included the Jews.

The Jewish families lined the streets watching the Persian Families escort their daughters to the palace. When Mordecai and Esther walked past, the Jews made a low hissing sound through their teeth. None of the other families walking through the streets knew what they were doing, but Mordecai and Esther did. When Mordecai decided to allow Esther to participate with the other Persian Maidens, all the Jews in the area ostracized them. Mordecai tried several times to explain his decision, but the Jewish Brothers would not accept it and separated themselves and their families from them. As they hissed at them, Mordecai pulled Esther closer to himself and moved into the center of the crowd where it was hard for the Jews to see them.

Up ahead, Esther spotted Zena, Zoe, and their parents. The whole family seemed excited and very happy. Esther wished she could muster up some excitement, but none would come. She walked along side of Mordecai silently.

As they came closer to the palace gate, Esther noticed that they were turning the parents away and only the maidens could approach the gate. This is it, Esther thought. She turned to Mordecai, embraced him kissing him on the cheek.

"Listen Esther, you know I am at the palace every day for work. I will find out where you are and come and check on you every day."

"Really, Morde!"

"Yes, every day; you will be fine. Remember, tell no one of your nationality, he whispered."

"I will remember Morde. I love you."

"I love you too. Look," Mordecai pointed up ahead where Zena and Zoe were, "Zena and Zoe are looking at you, go up and meet them so you do not have to go in alone." With that, Esther turned and ran to meet Zena and Zoe without looking back. Mordecai stood and watched Esther, Zoe, and Zena until they went through the palace gate, up the stairs and out of sight. After they were gone, he turned and walked slowly back to his empty hut.

Zena, Esther and Zoe, Zena's sister walked up to the King's gate. There were several other maidens ahead of them and they talked quietly among themselves as they waited in line.

"I am so excited." Zena said as she inched her way up the line.

"Me too." Zoe replied. "Who is that man at the Gate?"

"That must be the King's Chamberlain mentioned in the King's notice" Zena remarked. "He is the eunuch assigned to take care of us."

"A eunuch? What is a eunuch?" Zoe asked looking up at Zena.

"I will tell you later Zoe, just keep walking."

"He looks mean" Zoe commented straining her neck to get a better look. "Look at him, he does not smile or anything. All he does is nod at each maiden. He could at least smile!"

"If you knew what a eunuch was, you might not smile either" Zena said laughing to herself.

"What do you want him to do, bow and kiss your hand? We are not royalty yet?" Esther snapped and then caught herself. She did not mean to sound so harsh; it was not like her. "I am sorry Zoe; I did not mean to be harsh. I guess I am a little nervous."

Zena had been quiet for a while taking in everything around her, "How long is this purification supposed to last?"

"Twelve months" Esther replied. "Twelve months before we are presented to the king."

"Twelve months!" Zoe blurted out. "I sure hope Hegai learns how to smile before the 12 months are up." The three of them finally reached the gate. Zena went through the gate first. She looked at Hegai; he nodded his head, Zena continued to walk up the steps to the landing in the breezeway and waited for Zoe and Esther. Next Zoe approached Hegai; Hegai nodded, she walked up the steps and met Zena in the breezeway. Esther walked through the gate; her head bowed as if she did not want Hegai to look at her face. She attempted to walk past Hegai, but he held up his hand touching her shoulder lightly. She finally looked up at him. He smiled, then nodded his head, Esther walked through the gate and stopped. She could not help noticing the engravings on the palace walls lining the staircase. The staircase was made from hard gray cobblestones; the wall looked to be made from the same material but smoother. She touched the carvings with her hand. Who were these people carved in stone? Were they nobles, kings, or slaves? They all looked to be carrying some sort of gift, pottery, linen material, animals, a variety of things. These carvings were displayed all the way up the staircase. Esther looked up to the top of the stairs and saw Zoe and Zena waving to her to hurry up the stairs to meet them.

Once all the maidens were through the gate and on the landing in the breezeway, Hegai numbered them into groups of five. Esther, Zena, and Zoe grabbed each other's hands moving close together so they would all be in the same group. It worked; Zena was one, Zoe was two and Esther, number three. After all the groups were assembled, they were ordered to stay within their groups and follow Hegai. They walked down the inside hall of the palace for a long time. It seemed they walked for a mile before turning to the right. As they walked, Esther noticed the two courtyards and the flower garden in between. "Oh look, Zena!" Esther pointed to the flower garden. "Look how beautiful the flowers are!"

"Yes, they are beautiful; I wonder where he is taking us?"

"I am not sure. This is a very big palace through" Esther replied looking up at the many high archways they walked through.

The line stopped moving and they stood still for a minute or so; then began moving again at a much slower pace. Zena, Zoe, and Esther, still holding hands inched forward and finally saw what was happening. Each group of five maidens were being assigned their living quarters. As Esther's group approached Hegai, he pointed with his left hand for them to enter the next vacant quarter. It looked like a cell, a prison cell! Esther gasped. She had never seen a prison cell before, but Mordecai described them to her and she almost panicked as she walked through the archway of the door with the rest of her group. She vaguely heard Hegai giving some sort of instruction. All she heard was "Your dinner will be served to each of you in your quarters tonight."

Walking through the dark stone archway, Esther was pleasantly surprised.

"Look at this!" Zena said in a breathless whisper. "Zoe, look at this!"

"This is beautiful. It is so beautiful" was all Zoe could say.

Esther let go of Zoe's hand and clutched both her hands under her chin and took in the scene that was spread out before her. The large room about the size of one of the courtyards they passed was shaped in a round circle with three stone windows with ledges on the inside that you could sit on. Purple velvet drapes framed each window from the top of the ceiling to the red, white, and black squared marble floor softening any appearance of harshness the stone wall portrayed. Esther closed her eyes and inhaled the wonderful perfume that enveloped the entire area. She had never smelled such fragrances before and did not know how to describe them; she just kept inhaling them experiencing the effect they had on her entire being.

After several minutes, Esther opened her eyes and continued to explore the area. Zena, Zoe and the other two roommates had already selected their personal quarters running back and forth excitedly. Esther was free to leisurely walk through and inspect everything at her own pace. The quarters were large enough that each maiden could have her personal space without crowding or infringing on the other's.

In the center of the room, the floor was lower than the landing that led them into the area from the archway. It looked like a pit, Esther thought as she moved closer. Three black, white, and red marble steps with a black medal railing gave entry into the lower level where five golden-framed couches with overstuffed purple velvet pillows upholstered to their golden frames were arranged in a semicircle in the center of the pit. The purple velvet pillows matched the drapes that were hung on the windows. Four white marble pillars were spaced evenly around the circled pit. A silver lantern was fastened to each of the marble pillars. At the top of each lantern burned tongues of fire which lit up the entire sunken area. A glass lid covered the flame of fire. Esther gingerly stepped down the three steps and walked over to one of the pillars to inspect the lanterns more closely. She was not aware that there was any other way to light an area except with candles. She had seen containers of oil sold in the marketplace but was not sure what it was used for and did not ask because it was too expensive for her and Morde's household budget. The lantern had a smooth cool feel to the tips of her fingers as she glided them across its base. This key to the right must be the way to control the light, she thought. Under each of the lanterns were long sticks fastened to each pillar with velvet ties. "This is where that fragrance is coming from" Esther said out loud and inhaled the fragrance again.

Her curiosity satisfied at how the area was lighted, Esther moved over to one of the couches and ran her hand across the back of the golden frame. "Oh Father," she prayed silently, "What is this all about? Why have you brought me here? What am I supposed to do?"

"Esther! Come. Look at your bed chamber; it is beautiful!" Zena startled Esther and she jumped when she heard her name.

"Esther! What are you doing! Come!" Zena ran down the three stairs, grabbed Esther's hand dragging her up the stairs to the first landing and up two more steps to the second landing where the five bed chambers were arrayed evenly around the oval room.

"Zoe picked out this bed chamber," Zena informed Esther pointing to the center of the room. "I picked out this one to the right of her and we picked this one for you, to the right of me! The other two maidens wanted the other two rooms over there so they could be together. Do you like it Esther! Do you like it!" Zena was so excited. She pranced from one foot to the other and back again.

Esther did not mind Zena picking out her room for her. The lavishness was beautiful, but she was more concerned about why she was there rather than the riches that surrounded her. "Yes Zena" Esther answered trying to sound as excited as Zena. "I like it; it is beautiful."

Zena left Esther alone to look around. Each bed chamber was sectioned off by a stone wall and a wooden door. Looking to the left as she entered her bed chamber, Esther was stunned to see the golden framed bed with a mattress up off the floor resting on its golden frame. How was she supposed to get in and out of the bed she wondered until she walked around the other side and saw the stepping stool. Three pink velvet pillows were placed evenly across the top of the bed with matching pink woven blankets that neatly covered the mattress and hung down to the floor all around the bed. Over to the right of the bed was a large stone fireplace with a small fire burning inside. Even though it was summertime, a fire was still necessary to take off the chill from the stone walls. Over against the wall was a wooden table with legs and a wooden chair. On top of the table was another one of those silver lanterns with the glass top. This one sat on top of the table. On the other wall on the other side of the bed was a vanity with two silver lanterns on each side and a mirror in the middle. In front of the mirror was a little stool. Esther sat down on the stool and looked at herself in the mirror. She had never seen herself before and did not know what she looked like. Morde always told her she was beautiful, but she believed he was just being kind. Now she would find out for herself.

Still covered from head to toe with only her eyes peeking through, Esther unfastened the veil that covered her face from the right side, then the left and stared at herself in the mirror. The first thing she noticed was the largeness of her dark brown eyes. The dark rims around the outside of her eyes made them appear to be larger than what they were. Morde always told her she had doe-like-eyes, eyes like a baby deer. She could see it now, yes, he was right, I have doe eyes, she thought in wonderment. Her fingers explored the nose and mouth proportioned evenly and perfectly over the fair smooth face. "Oh Father," she whispered, "you have created me beautifully and wonderfully! What is it that you would have me to do?" Esther sat silently staring at herself for a few minutes and decided to remove the rest of her chador.

Removing her head dress first, she unfastened the braid that was wrapped around her head and let it fall behind her back and then unfastened the cloak around her shoulders letting it fall on the sides of the stool she was sitting on. Esther had only two sets of clothes, one set for everyday working around the hut, the other set for going to the marketplace which she wore now. The white blouse with the tie under her neck and at her wrists displayed strong but delicate shoulders and a small flat stomach and hips proportioned to her body frame. Feeding the animals, sheering the sheep and general work around the hut kept Esther's body in good shape with well-toned muscles. "Is this what my mother looked like?" Esther said in a whisper. Looking at herself for such a long time, Esther became embarrassed and picked up her cloak, put it around her shoulders, replaced her head dress and refastened her veil to her face. She did not feel comfortable going out into the lounge area without her complete chador. Moving from the mirror, she could hear the maidens assembling themselves in the lounge area and went out to join them.

Each of the four maidens were seated on a couch surrounding the little stove in the pit and waived for Esther to come join them when they saw her come out of her bed chamber. She was surprised to see all of them without their chadors and veils on out in the open. They all watched her as she made her way down the steps and took her place on the remaining vacant couch.

Zena broke the silence. "Why do you still have your chador on Esther? We are in our private lounge area, there are no men here. Why not take it off? At least take off your veil and let me introduce you to our two other roommates." Zena had been Esther's friend for many years and knew her better than any of the other maidens. When they played as little girls in front of their huts, Esther was always covered from head to toe regardless of the temperature outside. Zena could never get her to remove her veil. Some of the girls in their village dressed without veils until they reached the age of twelve. As far as Zena could remember, she never saw Esther without her complete chador and veil regardless of her age and the weather.

Esther looked around at each of the maidens. Zoe was the youngest of them, barely twelve years old but tall and rather thin; her body was just in the beginning stages of developing into a young teen. Esther wondered why her parents permitted her to participate in this competition; she doubted if Zoe had even come into womanhood yet.

"Esther," Zena said quietly and waited again.

"Alright Zena," Esther replied and unfastened the veil behind her left ear and let it fall by her right shoulder. "Please introduce me to these other young ladies" turning to look at them and smiling. Zena said nothing, the maidens said nothing, they just sat there and stared at Esther. Feeling a flush of embarrassment, Esther reached for her veil to place it again across her face when Zena jumped up and ran and sat beside her on her couch.

"No, no, Esther, keep it off. We were….," Zena stuttered, "you are just so beautiful. We did not know how beautiful you were." There was awkward silence in the room, only the crackle of the fire interrupted the stillness.

"Zena," Esther said finally breaking the awkwardness but kept the veil across her face, "please introduce me to our other roommates."

"Ah, this is Asha and her sister Ardist. They are both from Lydia close to the royal road" Zena said still looking at Esther.

"Hello Asha and Ardist" Esther said standing stretching out her hand across the pit to shake each of theirs as she spoke their names. "My name is Esther. Zena, Zoe, and I grew up together right here in Shushan. It is very nice to meet you."

"It is very nice to meet you too" Asha and Ardist both said at the same time and returned to their seats.

"What are we supposed to be doing now?" Esther said trying to strike up conversation among them.

"That Hegai man said to wait here until he returned with instructions for us; we could have our dinner in our bed chamber or go down to the dining area" Zoe said. "I think I would like to go to the dining area just to see what it looks like. If it is anything like this, it must be spectacular!"

"Me too" replied Asha and Ardist; "we like exploring. This palace is big enough to keep us busy for many, many months. We will be here for at least twelve months Right?"

"That is right" Zoe said. "At least twelve whole months. I heard one of the other maidens talking in line saying we were each going to have servants to wait on us. Can you believe it? Servants to wait on me! I am not sure I will know how to instruct them."

"Oh you will learn fast enough" Asha said, everyone giggled. With that said, Asha, Ardist and Zoe began chattering among themselves as Esther watched them smiling. Zena watched Esther.

Mordecai slowly walked back to his hut among the other parents with their boys tagging along. The mood was somber. Many of the parents were holding hands talking quietly to each other, consoling each other as they walked along. He could feel their pain; he was experiencing the same pain but there was no one he could share it with; no one he could hold hands with to help fill the emptiness in his heart. For the first time in his life, he wished he had taken a wife. He thought it too dangerous to start a family while the Jews were enslaved by the Babylonians. He witnessed first-hand the heartbreak families experienced being separated from each other, children being left as orphans just like Esther.

Esther was 14 months old when her father and mother died. Mordecai remembered seeing Esther for the first time as a chubby-faced baby sitting on the ground. His heart went out to her as he bent down and picked her up in his arms. She snuggled right up under his neck and pulled on his beard, never crying once. They bonded immediately as Mordecai walked away with her safely in his arms. The only time they were separated was when he went to work. He would get Tamara, his friend Reelaiah's wife to watch Esther for him until he returned home. That was 15 years ago. His plan was to raise her and marry her off to a nice Jewish boy so she could start her own family and have lots of children. Being one of a Persian King's concubines was not in his plans.

"Oh Father God, did I do right in letting her go? Should I have informed the authorities that she is a Jewish maiden and her status be exempt like the rest of the Jewish maidens in the village? Did I do right Father? If I have, please give me peace, I need your peace?" Mordecai prayed earnestly as he approached the entrance of his hut. Dreading going inside, he stood there for what seemed to be a very long time. Finally, he lifted the covering and stepped inside. It was dark, very dark, lonely, silent, empty; his heart broke as he walked across the room to Esther's favorite corner, fell on her pillows and cried until he could not cry anymore then fell asleep.

Esther awoke to a knocking on her bed chamber door. "Miss Esther, Miss Esther, are you awake, may I come in?" the voice spoke softly. Esther sat up in bed and pulled the blankets up under her chin. The voice was female and sounded friendly.

"Yes, come" Esther said watching the door intently. As the door opened, Esther strained her neck to see who had been knocking. A servant who looked to be about her age stood in the doorway dressed in a long black dress with sleeves that came down just below her elbows. Bunches of white towels were draped over her left arm and a basket with what looked to be different shapes and sizes of clay bottles of something, Esther could not make out what they were.

Taking two steps inside the door, the servant looked at Esther, "good morning Miss, I hope you slept well. My name is Yara; I am one of the servants assigned to you by the King to help you bathe." Yara turned and looked at the fireplace. "Oh my, I am so sorry Miss, your fire has just about gone out, I will have it going again for you in just a moment." Placing the towels across the back of the chair, Yara hurried to the fireplace, took the poker stoking the fire to bring the flames back to life then placed a piece of wood on top.

Surprised at Yara's actions, Esther jumped out of bed with the blanket wrapped around her body in protest. "No, no, you do not have to do that! I can do that myself, please, let me help you!" Esther said as she hurried to the fireplace.

Yara put the poker down turning to look at Esther and noticed she was in her bare feet. "Oh Miss, please" she begged, "you must get back in bed. I will do this, this is my job, please get back in bed!" She ushered Esther back to the bed and helped her in covering her up so she would stay warm.

Esther did not know what to make of this. No one had ever waited on her before and she felt very strange. Not knowing what to do, she sat up in bed and watched Yara go back to the fireplace, revive the fire until it was blazing hot lighting up the entire room. Once she was satisfied with the fire, Yara pulled a chair up beside the bed and sat down. Looking intently at Esther she said, "you are very beautiful." Esther felt her face get a little warm. "Oh, please forgive me for speaking out of turn" Yara continued, "but you are very beautiful compared to the other maidens."

Esther didn't respond to Yara's evaluation of her but steadily gazed at Yara with her blankets pulled up under her chin.

"You did not eat your dinner in the dining area last night did you?"

"No" Esther replied. "I requested it to be brought to my bed chamber."

"Oh, that explains it" Yara said.

"That explains what?" Esther asked.

"After dinner last night, Hegai, the Chamberlain assigned to take care of you maidens, gave everyone information on what was going to happen to them and what their duties were. You missed all of that. I think there were about seven to ten other maidens who took their dinners in their rooms last night as well. Hegai will address you this morning after you have had your bath and breakfast. Again, my name is Yara; I am one of seven servants assigned to you."

"One of seven! Why do I need seven servants?" Esther asked with shock in her voice. She was having a hard enough time accepting one.

Yara giggled. "There are seven of us and we will do everything for you that you will need done; from bathing you, your hair, your make-up, your finger and toenails, perfumes and lotions, your clothes, cleaning your personal quarters, walking with you in the garden, anything and everything you may need."

Esther was almost in shock listening to Yara with a blank stare on her face.

"Come," Yara said as she stood up picking up a pair of slippers for Esther's feet. "Swing your feet out of bed and put these slippers on." Esther obeyed. "Now, I am going to hold this very large towel up in front of you. I want you to take off your night shirt and wrap this towel around you and I will take you out for your bath; it is being drawn for you now." Esther obeyed as commanded and followed Yara out the door. To the left of her bed chamber was the bath area sectioned off from ceiling to floor with silk drapes. On the other side of the drapes was another sunken pit like the one in the lounge area, however, the center of the pit was a pool instead of couches and a stove. The area was heated by another large stone fireplace to the right of a large glass window with a grove of trees on the outside. Some type of white substance of which Esther had never seen before was floating on top of the water with a sweet-smelling steam rising enveloping the entire area.

"Come" Yara said leading Esther over to the steps leading down to the pool. "Let me help you. Hold onto the railing, sometimes the tile on the floor gets a little slippery. As you step down into the water, I will remove your towel. Do not worry, the other servants are outside waiting until you get in and I will look away to give you your privacy. Come now, go on in it is okay."

With that, Esther let Yara take away the towel, stepped down into the warm silky water letting the white substance cover her body up to her neck.

"What is this white substance?" Esther asked.

"It is perfumed bath wash. Do you like the way it smells and feels?"

As hesitant as she was to get into the pool, Esther had to admit, it smelled and felt very, very good. "Yes, it feels good."

"You relax and soak in there for a while. I will go get the other servants to wash your hair, bring your clothes and the other things you will need." Yara looked back at Esther one more time making sure she was okay then left her alone in the pool.

Whatever oils and perfumes were in the water made Esther relax. Rays of sunlight filtered through the sheer purple curtains giving off a soft pink and orange glow across the pool. Such beauty and luxury was almost too much for Esther to bear. Laying her neck against the back of the pool she closed her eyes collecting her thoughts. This was her first time ever away from home and she missed her morning routine as well as Morde. She thought about him home alone in their little hut. Their small dark little hut. Tears formed on the sides of her eyes and rolled down the sides of her face onto her shoulders. She never knew how poor she, Morde and the people in her little village were until yesterday when they entered the King's palace. Morde knew their poverty; he came here to work every day. He knew. Esther thought back to their conversations at dinnertime. He never spoke about what the palace looked like except for the prison cells he had seen when he was taken on a tour at the beginning of his employment as a porter. Never once did he mention the beauty and riches secured behind this brick fortress. And now, she was here in the middle of all this luxury and riches while Morde was at home in their little hut sleeping on a bed roll on top of a dirt floor. Hot bitter tears flowed freely down Esther's face now and she could not control them; she covered her eyes with her wet hands and sobbed into them. Her heart was breaking. She had never experienced such pain before and she cried out to God, "Oh Father" she whispered through her sobs, "Please, please help me! Is this really what you have in mind for me? Please give me the strength to do your perfect will. Please remove this pain and fear from me and replace it with faith to trust you. Please give me your boldness, your strength your peace. And Father, please, please, please take care of Morde. Father, I thank you, I praise you and I worship you with my whole heart, soul and my very being, for you are worthy to be praised. Thank you for all that you do and all that you are about to do. I offer myself to you to do with as you will. I submit myself to you, Father, not only as your child, but as your servant for you to use as you see fit. Amen."

As soon as Esther finished her prayer, a calm and peace seemed to envelope her. Her eyes were still closed, but it seemed she felt the warmth of the sun rays through the window shower down on her and she sat there not moving enjoying the peace and comfort it brought. The pain, the fear, the anguish was all gone and in its place was…, was, Joy! Yes, it was joy that she was experiencing. She removed her hands from her face putting them back into the water but kept her eyes closed trying to preserve this experience for as long as she could. Her tears were all gone. A slight smile turned up at the corners of her mouth displayed the peace and tranquility she had just come through.

"Oh, I see you have finally relaxed." Yara had come back into the area and stood beside the pool. "Good, good. May I bring in Zelda, one of the other servants assigned to you to help finish your bath, give you your facial, your hair, etc.?"

Esther looked up at Yara with that same smile on her face, with confidence and with grace nodded to Yara and replied "Yes Yara, that would be fine. Thank you for your service."

Yara did not move for a moment. She was surprised at Esther's response to her. She had been in service to the palace for the past three years; was the personal servant for Queen Vashti for a time and this was the first time anyone she served had ever thanked her for doing anything. "Oh, you are very welcome, Miss" Yara replied smiling as she left to get Zelda. I think I am going to enjoy serving this one, Yara thought as she walked away.

The two servants worked with Esther for the next hour getting her dressed and then brought her breakfast to her bed chamber. After breakfast, Yara led Esther down the hall and around the corner to a small room with a large table with ten to twelve chairs around it.

"Esther, this is where Hegai will address you and the other maidens that did not eat in the dining hall last night. Go in and have a seat." Yara looked behind her. "Here come the other maidens now; I will come back for you when your meeting is over."

"Thank you Yara" Esther responded as she took a seat close to the window.

"Your welcome Miss." Yara said smiling as she walked away.

As soon as Esther settled in her seat, all the other maidens entered the room and took their seats. They were all dressed similar to Esther with floor length pink or blue chiffon gowns with capes that went across the back and covered their shoulders. The sleeves were long and gathered at the wrists. A bow was tied at the neck; a veil made of the same material as the gown was fastened from ear to ear covering the nose and mouth. The head dress also was made of the same material and was wrapped around their heads in a decorative fashion. The only part of the body one could see clearly were the eyes.

Esther watched each maiden as she entered the room and noticed that none of them greeted each other, they seemed to have an attitude of arrogance that she had never encountered before. None of them made eye contact with her, so she folded her hands in her lap and looked out the window. Moments later, Hegai entered the room and addressed them.

"Good morning young maidens. I hope you all slept well." Hegai waited a moment and then continued. "I have only a few rules and regulations you must follow while you go through your purification process. You must obey these rules at all times."

"What happens if one or more of these rules is broken?" One of the maidens at the end of the table interjected. Everyone turned to see who this maiden was who so boldly spoke to Hegai without his permission.

Hegai raised his eyebrows focusing his eyes to where the voice came from and studied the maiden for a moment. Clearing his throat, he stared at the maiden as if boring a hole through her entire being. The maiden became uncomfortable and began twisting in her chair as if trying to get out of Hegai's penetrating gaze.

"The first thing that will happen to the maiden who breaks these rules…" Hegai began with an icy cold tone in his voice, "is they will be removed from the competition and placed into service to the palace. This service will be hard labor in the kitchen, cleaning floors, etc. The second thing that will happen to the maiden who breaks these rules is their family will be placed into servant hood, a sort of slavery position within the palace.

You are here at the King's command" Hegai continued looking around the room at each maiden, "and you must take this competition very seriously. If you become Queen, there are certain duties you must perform and you must perform them accurately and completely. Does that answer your question young maiden?" Hegai snapped focusing his attention back at the maiden who had spoken out of turn.

The maiden squeaked out a faint "yes" bowed her head and said nothing more.

Hegai looked at her again as if he were studying her to make sure he remembered who she was. He collected himself moments later and continued his speech. "Now, these rules are very simple and are outlined as follows:

1. Each of you are assigned seven personal servants to assist you with everything you need, including your personal things for purification. If there is anything special that you require, let your servants know, they will inform me, and I will make sure your request is met.

2. Every morning after breakfast, each of you will receive training on etiquette. One or more of your servants will direct you to the room where these classes are to take place. You must attend all classes unless you are ill.

3. You are never to leave your lounge area unescorted. Twice a day, I will escort all of you to the Queen's courtyard where you will be able to lounge and enjoy the flower garden. Your immediate family members may visit you at these times. Guards will always be patrolling these areas so get accustomed to seeing them.

4. You have the option of having your meals in the dining hall or in your private bed chambers; just let your servants know what your request is, and appropriate arrangements will be made for you.

5. You are not permitted to enter any other areas of the palace except those that I mentioned above and under the conditions listed above.

Does anyone have any questions?" Hegai asked and waited quietly. No one spoke. "Wait here and your servants will return to escort you back to your personal quarters" Hegai ordered and then left the room. No one moved. No one spoke a word. They all sat in silence until their servants came and escorted them back to their quarters.

Chapter Six

PALACE LIFE

Esther decided to take her lunch in her bed chamber and wait there until Hegai escorted them to the Queen's courtyard for their afternoon free time. She laid across her bed watching the fire burning in the fireplace. Before she knew it, she was fast asleep. A knock on the door woke her up. "Yes, who is it?" Esther said sleepily. She did not realize that she was tired.

"It is your servant, Yara" Yara said through the door. "May I come in?"

"Yes, yes" Esther said as she jumped up from her bed, slipped on her sandals and followed Yara out the door to the lounge area. "Thank you for awaking me Yara, I did not realize I was so tired."

"You are welcome Miss. All of this is new to you and kind of wears you out, but you will get accustomed to it. Come, the other maidens are all lined up at the door."

"Okay" Esther said as she followed Yara. Once she was outside the door, she saw Zena, Zoe, and her other two roommates at the door. It seemed like ages since she had seen them. She was about to say hello and embrace Zena and Zoe like she always did but when they saw her, they just nodded their heads toward her and turned their back to her and faced the door waiting for Hegai. Esther backed away from the maidens turned to face Yara and whispered, "What is wrong with them? Have I done something to offend them?"

"I do not know Miss. You have been eating your meals in your private quarters, maybe it has offended them?"

"Oh," was all Esther managed to get out. Hegai was at the door. Everyone filed out behind him following him to the courtyard.

Esther found a couch near a group of trees with an array of colored flowers that gave off a beautiful, scented perfume. The sun was shining high above and slivers of sunlight filtering through the trees splashed sun light spots here and there on her lap. The reception she received from her roommates puzzled her a little, but she dismissed it and planned to talk to them about it later at dinner. Maybe I will eat dinner in the dining hall with them tonight and get a chance to talk to them there. Esther sighed and looked up. Standing in front of her was Mordecai.

"Oh Morde!" She exclaimed as she jumped up into his arms. "You came. I am so glad to see you!" Esther hugged him around the neck again. "How are you, are you eating okay?"

Mordecai pulled Esther back and looked at her and smiled. "Yes, I am okay. I am eating fine. It has only been a day since I saw you."

"I know, but it seems like a week or more. I have never been away from you this long."

"I know child" Mordecai replied. "Are they treating you well?"

"Yes Morde, very well. It is going to take me a little time to get accustomed to having someone waiting on me though. Here sit beside me."

Mordecai sat down beside Esther and held her hand in his. "Living here is going to be very different than living at home and will take time for you to adjust. I believe God will give you the grace to adjust to your new surroundings."

"Yes He will, and He has Morde." Esther explained the experience she had in the bathing pool earlier that morning. Mordecai listened intently squeezing Esther's hand intermittently at the high points of her story. When she had finished, tears flowed down his cheeks. "Oh, please do not cry Morde, I am fine now, everything is fine now."

"Oh I am crying for joy, not sadness. God has answered my prayer. I was not sure I had done the right thing by letting you come here. But now I know it was the right decision. I am not sure of the outcome, but you are in God's hands now and I know you will be fine, His will be done." Mordecai leaned close to Esther and whispered in her ear, "You have not told anyone of your nationality, have you?"

Esther smiled looking up at Mordecai. "No, Morde, that is our secret."

"Good." Mordecai said getting up. "I am sorry I cannot stay any longer and visit with you. It is time for me to go to work. I will stop by tomorrow and every day after. God bless you Esther, I love you and I will see you tomorrow." With that, Mordecai hugged Esther and turned and walked away.

"Good-bye Morde, see you tomorrow" Esther said watching him leave the courtyard. After he was out of view, Esther returned to her seat and relaxed taking in the atmosphere around her. She was still at peace.

There was a low hum of chatter as all the maidens visited with their families. Scanning the crowd, Esther spotted Zoe and Zena with their parents on the other side of the yard. They seemed to be deep in conversation, so she decided to give them their privacy. Guards were posted on all four corners of the courtyard just as Hegai had said. As she looked around, Esther spotted Hegai standing off by himself watching all the activity. Suddenly Hegai spotted Esther looking at him and they held each other's gaze for a moment. It was not that hard piercing stare he had given the maiden in the room earlier so Esther nodded her head as if saying hello. To her surprise, Hegai nodded his head in reply, smiled and then continued scanning the activity in the courtyard.

Chapter Seven

PRESENTED TO THE KING

Ahasuerus jumped out of bed, ran over to his full-length mirror looking this way and that at his physique. "Today," he said out loud to himself, "Today, I am going to start getting myself fit for my new queen. Firm up my muscles," he lifted his arms up to try and make his biceps bulge. "Oh," he sighed. "I am going to need every one of the twelve months to get ready. I will start today." The weight he had lost grieving over Vashti left his stomach smaller, but he needed exercise to firm up the muscles all around his mid-section. "Hmm," he said out loud, "I wonder who I can get as a personal trainer to get me in shape. Guard! Guard!" Ahasuerus yelled.

The guard opened the door, "Yes Your Majesty."

"Have Abagtha to come to my chambers."

"Yes Your Majesty" the guard said and closed the door.

Ahasuerus went over to the window and sat looking across at Vashti's old palace. Not too much longer before my new Queen is across from me, he thought as someone knocked at the door. "Yes, who is it?"

"It is Abagtha Your Majesty."

"Yes, come in."

"You sent for me Sire?"

"Yes Abagtha, is my bath drawn?"

"Yes Your Majesty."

"Good, I will take my bath now, then have my breakfast in the King's dining hall. Have Memucan to join me."

"Yes Your Majesty" Abagtha bowed and backed out of the door and closed it behind him. Ahasuerus began to hum a song as he took his bath, dressed then went to the dining hall to meet Memucan. Knowing that the purification process was taking place with the young maidens filled him with joy and he no longer missed Vashti.

Memucan was already in the dining hall when he arrived and stood as he entered the room and bowed. "Good morning Your Majesty"

"Good morning Memucan. Please have a seat" Ahasuerus motioned for him to sit down at the table. "Have you had your breakfast yet?"

"No Sire, I have not."

"Good." Ahasuerus took his seat, clapped his hands for the servants to begin serving the meal. I have asked you here for a couple of reasons. First, I need a personal trainer. Someone from the Calvary to help get me physically in shape. The best trainer that we have. My training must be done in private. Do you know of someone?"

"Yes Your Majesty. The best trainer we have is the captain over the Calvary soldiers in Persepolis. He is an Amalekite; his name is Haman."

"Haman, huh?"

"Yes Sire; he is the best."

"Send for him immediately."

"Yes Your Majesty."

"The other item I want to discuss with you is the status and progress of the Greece situation. What information did the two spies uncover and what are their names?"

"The two spies' names are Bigthan and Teresh and it is as we suspected Your Majesty. An underground army is being formed to fight against the Empire. It is large and well organized at least 2,000 soldiers and growing. Bigthan and Teresh joined this underground army but was discovered and had to fight their way out. Being well trained Calvary Soldiers, they fought against ten of the Grecian Soldiers, overtook them and escaped on one of our naval ships patrolling the sea."

Ahasuerus sat back in his chair and looked at Memucan. "Fought off ten soldiers?"

"Yes Sire, ten."

"Were either of them hurt?"

"Bigthan suffered a couple of broken ribs; Teresh had a big bump on his head. They both had an opportunity to heal up on the journey back home."

"Ten to two, hump, that is good fighting."

"Yes Sire, I would say it was." Memucan ate in silence for a moment then continued. "Sire, it is very good to see you back to your usual self. You seem to be happy again."

"Yes I am Memucan. I think I am finally over Vashti. I am looking forward to choosing my new queen" Ahasuerus said and winked at Memucan. Memucan smiled and sat back in his chair. Having finished his breakfast, he waited for the King to finish his and dismiss him.

Esther lined up at the door with the other maidens in her group waiting for Hegai to lead them down to the dining hall. She deliberately came out early to take her place in line hoping for an opportunity to talk with her roommates; to clear the air and find out why they had acted so cold to her ignoring her earlier that day. Coming out of their bed chambers, they greeted and hugged each other talking and laughing among themselves. When they saw Esther standing at the door, they slowed their walking pace looking at each other. It was clear to Esther that they were surprised as well as uncomfortable seeing her standing there so she spoke up first.

"Good evening ladies, how have you been?"

The maiden's walking pace slowed even more, almost to a stop but none of them spoke.

"I thought I would join you for dinner this evening if it is all right with all of you" Esther continued. This was going to be more difficult than she thought. Eating her first four or five meals in her personal quarters had offended these maidens more then she had imagined. Had she offended them, or had she hurt them, she was not quite sure. She could understand Zena and Zoe being a little upset with her, having grown up with them in the same village but the other two barely knew her. Standing there waiting for a response, Zena finally spoke up.

"Hello Esther, it has been a while since we all have seen you. Seating at the dining hall has already been assigned and there is no more room at our table. There is seating in the back of the hall for the maidens who eat most of their meals in their private bed chambers. I am sure Hegai can show you where that seating area is." By the time Zena had finished speaking the maidens had arrived at the door where Esther was standing. None of the maidens embraced Esther; none of them shook her hand, and no one other than Zena spoke to her as they stood in their little group of four and began talking quietly among themselves. They were talking so low that Esther could not make out what they were saying. The line had been drawn. Esther knew she was no longer a part of this little group of roommates and the rejection stabbed her in her heart. She turned and faced the door quickly wiping a tear from her eyes so the maidens would not see them only to find Hegai at the door looking at her in surprise.

"Oh, good evening Esther, I am pleased to see you joining us for dinner tonight."

"Good evening Hegai" Esther managed to say with a smile, then "Thank you."

"Follow me," Hegai said as he continued down the hall. Esther followed but noticed that the other maidens behind her had stopped talking and were following her at a distance. As they entered the large dining hall with rows and rows of tables and chairs, all the maidens ran to their seats and left Esther standing there alone looking around not sure what to do. Hegai had already taken his seat at the officer's table when he noticed Esther standing alone in the doorway of the dining hall. The room became deathly quiet when Hegai stood up. He left the officer's table and walked over to Esther. All eyes were on him as he approached Esther and escorted her over to the tables in the back of the room where no one was sitting.

"Esther" Hegai said quietly, "Unfortunately this is the only seating left in the dining hall, but the servants will serve you here just as well. Will you be all right here? Hegai asked with sympathy in his voice.

"Oh yes" Esther replied trying not to let the hurt show through; "this will be fine." Esther took her seat, folded her hands in her lap and smiled, determined not to let anyone see any tears or discomfort in any way.

Hegai looked down at Esther and smiled with satisfaction, folded his hands behind his back and walked back to the officer's table and ate his dinner occasionally looking up to check on her.

All the other maidens noticed the attention Esther had received from Hegai and a low hum resumed throughout the hall as they finished eating dinner.

After dinner was over, the maidens lined up at the door of the hall ready to be escorted back to their private quarters. Esther waited until everyone was in line and made sure she was the last one in line. By the time she reached her quarters, Zena, Zoe, Asha and Ardist had already settled in the pit. They were seated on the couches with wigs, makeup and raiment spread out over the couches. There was no place for Esther to sit even if she had wanted to. Observing the situation for a few minutes and not ready to go to her bed chamber, she walked over to the window, sat on the window ledge focusing her attention outside at the landscape. It was still the middle of summer. The trees were displaying themselves in all the glory that God had created. Esther studied the blend of colors in the mix of trees, the evergreen trees dispersed among the oak trees mixed with splashes of red, yellow, and green flowers planted at the base of the trees. She longed to be out there among them in the cool of the day. As she watched the birds, squirrels and the bees going about their business, she thought about Morde. If she were at home, they would be sitting out under their extended roof, Morde would be smoking his pipe and she would be spinning wool or knitting a blanket or sweater for winter. I wonder if Hegai would allow me to have some yarn, needles and such to make some blankets for Morde for the winter, Esther thought. I will put in a request through Yara tonight she decided. She spent the remainder of the evening on the window ledge.

From that day on, Esther ate all her meals in her bed chamber. She had her personal time with God in the early morning hours before her servants came for her with her breakfast, to bathe and dress her. Yara bought her a little basket which she carried her sewing supplies in. She took that basket with her when she went to the courtyard everyday making blankets, sweaters, and socks while she visited with Mordecai. She decided to give some of the items she made as gifts to her servants. It helped her to pass the time and kept her from being lonely. She adjusted very well in keeping to herself.

"Your Majesty," the guard said knocking on the door, Captain Haman is here for your morning workout. Shall I show him in?"

"Yes, let him in" Ahasuerus said getting up from his couch.

"Good morning Your Majesty. Are you ready for your workout this morning? I have some exciting new exercises for you to try out" Haman said in a cheerful, jovial tone coming through the door with his hands full of strange looking objects.

"Good morning Haman" Ahasuerus replied. I am feeling very well and unusually full of energy. Is this normal?"

"Yes it is Your Majesty, yes it is. You have adapted extremely well to the routine I have charted out for you. Your body is strong and tone; just like the Calvary Soldiers I train every day!" Haman was exaggerating and smiled to himself as he said it. He knew the King was in his late 30's and could not compete on any level with the soldiers, especially a Calvary Soldier.

"Haman, you make me feel like a 20-year-old boy! Do I look like a 20-year-old- boy?" Ahasuerus asked fishing for a compliment.

"Yes you do Your Majesty, yes you most certainly do." Maybe I should not over do the compliments, Haman thought to himself, he might catch on to my plan.

"You know, Haman, I am in the process of picking out a new Queen and my energy level is very high. I think I owe it all to you and your exercise program." Ahasuerus strutted over to the mirror and profiled himself in his full-length mirror.

"A steady routine of daily exercise does wonders for the body," Haman replied as he put the exercise equipment down on the floor, walked over to the window ledge and watched the King prancing in front of the mirror. "I stress this point to my Calvary Soldiers in training every day. It certainly made a difference with the two spies we sent into Greece last month. They were my top two soldiers, and they did an excellent job."

"Yes, I heard about them, what were their names?" Ahasuerus asked turning his attention from himself and focusing on Haman.

"Bigthan and Teresh."

"Yes, Memucan gave me a report on them a few weeks ago. He said they did very well despite being hurt. You trained them?"

"Yes Your Majesty, as I said before, they are two of my finest soldiers. I understand that they are now in your employ here at the Palace as special guards for your throne room."

"Yes they are. I need only the best soldiers around me at all times. Memucan was the one who suggested sending in the spies. Do you think that was a good strategy?" Ahasuerus moved from the mirror back to the couch and sat down. He motioned for Haman to sit in the chair next to the couch. "Have a seat Haman, let's talk a little before we begin my workout."

Oh this is easier than I expected, Haman thought to himself as he sat down in the chair pointed out by the King. All my hard work is finally paying off for me. Striving to be the best soldier in every event; becoming the top trainer for the elite Calvary Soldiers was extremely difficult but the hard work has given me the opportunity to train the King himself. Being in the right place at the right time for Memucan to observe me at the height of my training; this is almost too good to be true. I must choose my words carefully to continue to gain the King's trust in me.

"Sending spies in was one way to handle the situation, but it just confirmed what we already knew, the Greeks are displeased being under Persian rule and are planning to rebel. Not only that, confirming what we already knew almost cost us two of our best soldiers. What I would have done was to strike first and ask questions after. That way the underground Grecian Army would have been caught off guard and defeated; and fear of additional strikes would keep future underground armies from forming. This is the action I would have suggested to you had you asked me." Haman sat quietly waiting for his words to sink in.

Ahasuerus listened to Haman and observed him closely as he spoke. "That is good sound reasoning. I will think on this," Ahasuerus paused in mid-sentence then continued, "maybe there is still time to execute your plan," he stated as he got up from the couch and began his workout.

Haman remained seated for a moment with a slight smile on his face. He was extremely satisfied with himself. I cannot wait to get home and tell my wife about this.

Chapter Eight

QUEEN ESTHER'S ROYAL BANQUET

Summer ended, winter had come and gone. The blankets, sweaters and socks Esther made were given to her servants who were very surprised and appreciative when they received them. She had found favor with everyone around her, except her roommates. She knew they had grown to hate her, but she did not hate them. She always spoke kindly to them whenever she saw them, but she did not try to make conversation with them.

The twelve months of purification were just about up. Esther noticed that the number of maidens that came out to the courtyard everyday was getting smaller. Two of her roommates were already gone and only she, Zena and Zoe remained. Tension between them was even higher with the other maidens gone. Esther made a point of staying out of their way as much as possible. She sat in her special window looking outside and knitted. Zena and Zoe sat in the pit whispering between themselves when the guard announced that Hegai was at the door, then let him in. He called Zoe out into the hall to speak with her privately. Esther and Zena did not move from their seats but waited quietly. A few moments later, Zoe reentered the lounge area with her head hung low with tears streaming down her face and ran into her personal chamber. Zena ran after her and closed the door so Esther could not hear their conversation. Looking back at the opened door, Esther saw Hegai and the guard standing quietly outside. Neither of them looked Esther's way or spoke to her but they were aware of her presence in the lounge. Ten minutes later, Zena and Zoe emerged from the bed chamber. Zoe was carrying the bag she had when they first came to the palace. Zena had her arm around her shoulders trying to console her as they both walked to the door of the lounge where Hegai and the guard were waiting. Zena hugged Zoe then stood back as she left with the two men then closed the door and ran into her personal bed chamber and closed the door. Esther could see that Zena was extremely upset and longed to go to her and try to comfort her even though she did not know what had happened. Moving from the window ledge, she slowly walked over to Zena's door and lightly knocked.

"Zena, Zena, may I come in?"

"Go away!" Zena shouted through the door.

Esther backed away from Zena's door, picked up her knitting basket and went into her own bed chamber closing the door softly behind her. Setting her knitting basket down by the table, Esther sat on the couch in front of the fireplace as sadness filled her heart. She greatly missed her childhood friend and tears streamed down her face knowing that her friend was in pain, and she could not comfort her.

"Miss Esther, may I come in?"

"Yes Yara."

"Are you ready to go to bed?" Yara asked.

"Yara, what happened to Zoe today?"

"She was sent back home to her parents."

"Sent back home? Why!"

"You know that Hegai is responsible for all of you maidens while you are going through your purification process. Part of his responsibility is to give monthly reports to the King on each maiden's progress. Zoe was rather young when she first came to the Palace. Everyone commented about it. The King said to give her a chance, she may mature within a year's-time. I do not think she matured enough, and the King ordered her to be sent back to her parents before her turn came to be presented to him."

"That was probably the best thing that could have happened to her" Esther commented.

"I thought so too. I do not believe she or Zena feel that way though. Would you like me to draw a bath for you tonight? You look a little tired?"

"Yes, I think I would like that. Thank you Yara?"

"You are most welcome Miss Esther."

Zena and Zoe were on Esther's mind as she bathed and dressed for bed. As she crawled into bed, she prayed for her two childhood friends then fell asleep.

Esther ate her breakfast and lunch in her personal chambers as usual but decided to go outside in the courtyard in the early evening and wait for Mordecai's daily evening visit. Tonight, Zena sat by herself across the yard from her and stared at her. Esther turned her body changing her position on the couch diverting Zena's direct glare when she noticed Hegai approaching her. He spoke to her then led her through the flower garden back to her personal chamber quarters. Esther and all the other maidens left in the yard watched until they were out of sight.

Esther was settled in her heart, mind, and spirit about her time to be presented to the King. Her daily time in prayer and meditation with God had given her the inner peace she needed. Not knowing what or how things were going to go, she trusted God that He would help her and that everything would be done decently with patience and gentleness when the time came. Yes, with all the training classes and the time with God, she felt ready and confident; ready to accept whatever God had planned for her.

Standing up from her couch, Esther turned facing the opposite way and saw Morde standing in the archway. She went over to him and visited with him until Hegai returned to escort the remaining maidens to their personal quarters.

Being the only one left in her quarters, Esther sat down on one of the couches in the pit and invited her servant Yara to sit with her.

"Are you all right Miss?" Yara asked. "Is there anything I can get for you?"

"No thank you Yara. I am fine. It is just strange being the only one left."

"Are you lonely? Will you be all right being the only one left in your quarters tonight?"

"No, I am not lonely, I have adjusted to being alone. I think I will just sit here for a little while before getting ready for bed."

"Very well Miss" Yara said and left.

Esther went to bed a couple of hours later and slept soundly.

The next day seemed to fly by quickly. With so few maidens left and no more classes to attend, more time was given to the remaining maidens to relax in the courtyard visiting with each other and their family members. Esther continued to keep to herself, and the remaining maidens still had no interest in befriending her. She always looked forward to her visits with Morde and he came as often as he could.

It was early evening and Morde normally would have come and gone by this time, but he did not show up this night. There was nothing for her to do but sit on her favorite couch under her favorite tree and enjoy the outdoors. As she changed her position to get more comfortable, she noticed Hegai walking toward her. It was her turn. She suddenly felt a flutter of nervousness in the pit of her stomach. "Oh Lord," she prayed silently. "It is time, please be with me, help me and do not let me be afraid. Thank you Father. Amen." Esther took a deep breath and let it out just as Hegai reached her.

"Good evening Miss Esther." Hegai greeted Esther in a calming voice. "Tonight is your turn to be presented to the King. Are you ready? Is there anything that you need?"

"Good evening Hegai. Yes, I am ready, and no, there is nothing that I need."

"Very well, I will escort you back to your personal quarters where your servants are waiting to help you with your bath and dress. Will you please follow me?" Hegai turned and led Esther back to her quarters.

There was no conversation between the two of them as they walked down the long hall to Esther's quarters. She appreciated the silence. She used the time to try and figure out how she was feeling. It was not fear. It was not exactly peace; however, it was not dread either. She seemed determined to be obedient to God, to do his perfect will and there was not, at least not at this time, any emotion in it. She was just walking to her quarters.

Once they reached her door, Hegai finally spoke. "I will return to escort you to the King in two hours," then waited until Esther went inside before walking away.

Yara was waiting for Esther on the other side of the door with towels draped across her arms and Esther was relieved to see her.

"Good evening Miss" Yara greeted and studied her face to see how she was feeling.

"Good evening Yara. Is my bath ready?"

"Yes Miss, it is. Come I will help you get prepared."

Esther followed Yara. All the preparations that night seemed to go by in a blur and before she knew it, Hegai was leading her toward the King's personal quarters.

Standing outside of the King's door, Esther still could not figure out how she was feeling. The guard knocked on the door and announced Hegai and Esther then opened the door. Hegai stepped inside first and announced Esther, then reached back for her hand and led her inside and introduced her to the King.

"Your Majesty, may I present to you Maiden Esther, Esther, this is King Ahasuerus."

Hegai placed Esther's hand into the King's hand, bowed at the waist and backed out and closed the door.

Esther stood there with her head bowed. She did not remember what she was wearing, she only knew that she was covered from head to toe in a chador with only her eyes exposed.

Ahasuerus just stood there holding Esther's hand in his without saying a word for the longest time. Finally, he took his other hand, put it under Esther's chin and lifted her face so her eyes would meet his. When her eyes met his, a peace came over her and she could feel herself breath again.

Finally, Ahasuerus spoke. "Good evening Esther. How are you this evening?"

"I am fine Your Majesty."

"Would you like to come and sit by the fire with me?"

"As you wish, Your Majesty."

Ahasuerus led Esther to the couch by the fire. A table was set up in front of the couch with a bottle of wine, wine goblets, bread wafers, fruit and cheese placed on top.

"Would you care for a glass of wine or some refreshments?"

"No thank you Your Majesty." Esther said in just above a whisper.

"Have you ever tasted wine before Esther?" Ahasuerus asked looking into her eyes.

Esther lowered her eyes before responding. "No, Your Majesty."

"Would you please try just a sip for me?"

"As you wish, Your Majesty."

Ahasuerus poured a little wine in the goblet and gave it to Esther. "May I remove your veil Esther?" he asked very patiently waiting for Esther to give him permission.

"As you wish Your Majesty" Esther replied softly.

Slowly and carefully, Ahasuerus unlatched the veil from the left ear and let it fall to Esther's right shoulder and stared at her face for a long time.

Esther held his gaze. She was not afraid to look at him and she smiled.

"You are so very beautiful Esther. I have never seen anyone as beautiful as you." He looked at her a while longer before moving the wine goblet up to her mouth so she could take a sip.

Esther took a sip of the wine. The sweet grape wine on her tongue gave her a warm sensation down her throat and into her stomach as she swallowed it and she noticed that she became more relaxed. She sat the goblet back on the table without taking another sip.

Ahasuerus watched her closely, held her hand and they made themselves comfortable on the couch quietly watching the fire. After a time, Ahasuerus began to tell Esther about his father, grandfather, and great grandfather; how the Persian empire came to be. Esther listened and asked questions and laughed at the funny stories he told about incidents in war. He did not share any gory battle stories though. They talked and laughed well into the night until Esther became sleepy at which time, Ahasuerus picked her up and carried her to his bed.

Ahasuerus lay beside Esther watching her sleep until the sun rose. She was like no other he had ever met. Beautiful, intelligent, and very kind. She is the one, he decided, that will take Vashti's place. At that, Esther stretched, yawned, and turned over to discover Ahasuerus looking at her.

"Oh, good morning Your Majesty."

"Good morning Esther. Did you sleep well?"

"Yes, thank you."

Ahasuerus smiled. "You are most welcome. I will have the servants to come and draw a bath for you with appropriate attire for you to wear back to your palace after you have had your breakfast. Are you hungry?"

Esther pulled the blankets up around her. "Yes, I am hungry" she said in surprise.

"Very well" Ahasuerus said smiling pulling on his robe and walked to the door. "Guard, have the appropriate servants come for Queen Esther and have them bring breakfast for both of us as well.

"As you wish Your Majesty" the guard replied and closed the door again.

Esther was still sitting on the bed with the blankets around her and waited until Ahasuerus walked over to her side of the bed. "Did I hear you refer to me as 'Queen Esther?'"

"Is that all right with you?" Would you be my Queen?" Ahasuerus asked, pleadingly.

All Esther could do was nod her head yes. Ahasuerus reached over and kissed Esther.

A knock on the door interrupted them.

"Yes, who is it?" Ahasuerus answered.

"Sire, your Queen's servants have arrived. May I show them in?" the guard yelled through the door.

As the door opened, Esther was greatly surprised and very pleased to see Yara and the other servants that attended to her in her personal quarters the night before. Watching the delight across Esther's face, Ahasuerus motioned for the servants to line up and stand in front of them at the bed side. "These, your servants, are you pleased with their service Esther? Would you like to keep them in your employ, or should I arrange for a different group?"

"Oh yes, Your Majesty, I am very, very pleased with their service, they have taken great care of me over the past year. I do not wish to replace or substitute anyone."

Smiling from ear to ear, it surprised Ahasuerus that he found so much satisfaction in pleasing her and with such a small thing as servants. He had questioned Hegai about all the maidens before they were presented to him, about their character, how they treated each other, their servants, and what types of articles they requested from Hegai while they went through their purification process. Hegai's report on Esther surprised and intrigued him. She was the only maiden who requested yarn to make blankets, sweaters and socks and then gave them away. All the other maidens requested jewels, makeup, hair pieces, expensive silks from India which they instructed the seamstress to spend hours upon hours creating fancy gowns for them to wear when they were presented to him. It was so refreshing seeing Esther standing in the doorway in a simple sheer white chador with golden borders on the edges. Her grace and presence, even the self-confidence she displayed overwhelmed him last night when he delicately undressed her and found nothing fake. Just pure natural beauty. He was glad when she fell asleep; he did not want her to see him watching her all night long as she slept next to him, he could not take his eyes off her. Now, she was his. He asked her to be his Queen and she accepted. If she had asked him for anything, he would have granted it to her, even up to half of his kingdom. He watched the happiness spread across her face as she looked at each of her servants.

"As you wish, my Queen." Ahasuerus stood and kissed Esther's hand. "I will leave you with your servants. After you have dressed, would you join me in the Royal Dining Hall for breakfast, or would you prefer to have your breakfast set up in your Queen's quarters?" Ahasuerus was hoping she would join him, but he was not going to make it a command. He thought she might want some time to herself after being presented to him last night.

"I would be pleased to join you for breakfast Your Majesty" Esther said smiling.

Still holding her hand, he bent down and kissed her on the forehead, "until then," he said and turned to the servants. "Has Hegai instructed you about Queen Esther's quarters? Has everything been moved from her old quarters?

Yara stepped forward bowing. "Yes, Your Majesty, everything has been arranged for Queen Esther according to your instructions."

"Very good" Ahasuerus replied and left Esther in the care of her servants.

As soon as he was gone, Esther jumped up from the bed, ran over to her servants and hugged each of them.

"Queen Esther, Queen Esther!" Yara said as tears rolled down her face. "I knew he would pick you; I just knew it!" All the other servants chimed in agreement. "Now, our instructions are to address you as 'Queen Esther'."

"You may address me as 'Queen Esther' if someone is around, but when we are alone, you may call me 'Esther' or, 'Miss' just like you did for the past year."

"Oh, no, we cannot call you 'Miss' any longer, you are married now! It would have to be 'Mrs.!'" They all laughed and hugged each other again. "Come" Yara ordered just as she did that first day Esther met her in her room. "We must get you ready to meet the King for breakfast. Hegai ordered these dresses for you." Yara held up several dresses as they walked to the bathing pool. "Which one would you like to wear this morning?"

Esther looked at each dress; they were all beautiful. "I will wear this one Yara." She pointed to the soft light green chiffon dress with the dark velvet green cape.

"As you wish, Your Majesty" Yara said smiling and draped the dress across the chair.

After Esther was dressed, the guard announced that Hegai was there to escort her to the Royal Dining Hall. When the door opened, Hegai stood there smiling at her extending his arm out to her. "Queen Esther, King Ahasuerus has sent me to escort you to the Royal Dining Hall."

"Oh, thank you Hegai" Esther replied taking his arm as they walked out the door. Just as the night before, neither of them said a word as they walked down the hall, but each of them knew that the other was pleased and happy with the outcome.

"Hegai," Esther broke the silence. "There were several other maidens who did not get a chance to be presented to the King. What will happen to them?"

It was just like Esther to be concerned about the other maidens, Hegai thought to himself. "They have a choice to become one of the King's concubines or they can be returned to their families; it is their choice."

"If they are returned to their families, will they be given any type of stipend to help their families to live?" Esther looked at Hegai hoping something would be done for the maidens and their families. She knew the ones that had been presented to the King would be well taken care of as concubines, but it would be very difficult for those maidens that choose to go back to their families and live in poverty after living a life of luxury for a year.

"I had never considered their fate. Would you like me to speak to the King about this?"

"Would it be appropriate for me to speak to him about it at breakfast? Esther asked still looking at Hegai.

"Hmmm," Hegai said as they approached the doorway of the dining hall. "You ask very difficult questions Queen Esther. He is your husband, and you have audience with him this morning, I do not see any harm in your request."

"Thank you Hegai and thank you for all of your help and teaching throughout the past year. You have made this experience a pleasant one. Thank you." Esther squeezed his arm as the door opened.

"King Ahasuerus" Hegai announced. "Your Queen is here to join you for breakfast."

Ahasuerus stood as Esther was escorted to her seat at the table. They ate in silence.

"Your Majesty." Esther broke the silence.

"Yes, Esther, what is it?"

"I asked Hegai what would happen to the other maidens who did not get an opportunity to be presented to you. He said they would be sent back home or could choose to be one of your concubines. If they choose to go back home to their families, it will be very difficult for them adjusting to a life of poverty again after living in such luxury here at the palace for a full year. Would it be permissible to send them home with a monetary stipend to help them and their families?"

Ahasuerus stopped eating, sat back looking at Esther in amazement. For a moment he did not speak. "I do not see any harm in that request. How much do you suggest we give them?" He waited to see what Esther would say.

After thinking for a moment Esther replied, "I think Hegai would have a better idea what to extend to each maiden. He has watched and observed them for a whole year; I am sure he would make an appropriate amount for each one."

She is intelligent, diplomatic, and caring all at the same time. "As you wish, my Queen." He replied. Will this one never cease to amaze me, Ahasuerus thought as he continued eating.

"I have arranged to have a Royal Banquet in your honor announcing your appointment as the new Queen of Persia. It will be held one month from today. After that, you will begin to perform your royal duties. Hegai has informed you about these duties has he not?"

"Yes Your Majesty."

"If there is anything that you need, let your servants know and they will provide it for you." They ate the remainder of their meal in silence at which time, Hegai escorted Esther to her new personal quarters, the Queen's Quarters.

"Your father is here to see you. He is waiting for you in your courtyard" Hegai informed her as they walked. "Would you like to visit with him there or would you prefer to visit in your personal lounge?" Hegai asked as he escorted Esther down the hall. They would pass the Queen's courtyard on their way to her personal quarters.

Esther stopped walking. "Hegai, I think I would like to visit with him in my personal lounge area. Is this permissible?"

"Yes Your Majesty."

"It was not permissible before." Esther stated. "I do not wish to break any of the rules."

"Yesterday you were not Queen Esther" Hegai said smiling down at her. He had become quite fond of Esther and appreciated that she still sought instruction from him about proper etiquette even after becoming Queen of Persia. Once she understood what her Queenly duties were, she did not have to ask him anything. What an honor, he thought, to have a friend in the Queen. "The fact that he is your father and not some strange man makes it proper."

"I would rather see him in my private lounge area. He is waiting for me in the courtyard. Is there another way we could get to my personal quarters without passing him in the courtyard?"

"Yes there is" Hegai said and turned left down the very next hall. "This is a short-cut."

Within minutes, they were at the Queen's personal lounge.

Two large Calvary Soldiers stationed on each side of the door stood to attention and bowed at the waist as Hegai and Esther approached. The guard to the left opened the door for them to enter. Hegai let Esther go through, but he stopped at the doorway and asked, "Shall I bring your father to you now, or would you prefer to settle in for a few minutes?"

"Please give me fifteen minutes and then bring my father to me."

"As you wish Your Majesty." Hegai bowed to Esther and turned to leave.

Having Hegai bowing to her made Esther feel a little strange. She was now royalty, and she knew she would have to get use to the protocol, but it still felt strange. Quickly glancing around the lounge area, she was pleased with its layout and colors. The lounge area itself was as big as her old personal quarters' lounge area and all five bed chambers put together. The outer wall was shaped in a round circle just like the old quarters; however, there was no sunken pit. Instead, several luxurious couches were arranged in various positions throughout the lounge all on one floor. Seven windows spaced evenly around the outer walls let in the morning and afternoon sunlight. All the windows were open. A gentle breeze caused the purple velvet drapes to dance in the wind. A strong smell of fresh flowers filtered through the air and Esther went to the window to see where the fragrance was coming from. To her amazement, outside her window was a large lavish rose garden with trees, benches and stone walkways designed throughout. She was caught up in the fragrance of the perfume and the atmosphere itself until she heard the guard knock on the door.

"Your Majesty, your father is here, shall I show him in?"

Esther moved from the window to the center of the room. "Yes, you may show him in."

As the door opened, Esther could hardly control herself from rushing into Morde's arms. She waited until he was in the room and the door was closed before running over to him and embracing him.

"Good morning Morde" Esther finally said pulling herself back from him.

"Good morning to you Queen Esther" Mordecai replied in proper decorum smiling with tears in his eyes. "Is everything all right?" he asked searching her face to see if there was any evidence of trauma.

"Everything is fine, Morde, just fine. God has answered all my prayers, every one of them and everything is fine. Come and sit down with me. Have you eaten, are you hungry? I could have one of the servants bring you something to eat."

"No, no, no, I am not hungry. I just want to sit here with you for a while. They are treating you well then"

"Yes Morde. They treat me very well. The King graciously returned the same servants to me that served me while I went through my purification. The only thing I must get use to now is being addressed as 'Queen.' The King is throwing a Royal Banquet to announce me before Persia in a month. Will you come?"

"Oh, I, Esther, I think I would feel better at my post as porter."

"Morde," Esther began slowly, "are you all right? Do you need anything?"

Mordecai patted Esther's hand and smiled at her. He understood what she was asking now that she was Queen, did he want to live in the palace or be elevated up to a higher position. He was satisfied right where he was. "No, child, no. I still believe I am where God would have me to be. I am comfortable at home, I still miss you, but I have adjusted. If the Lord wants to make a change in my living situation, I trust He will do it in His time; until then, I am fine right where I am.

"Okay, I just had to offer. God has been so good to me here, but I still do not know why He has placed me in this position?"

"He will let you know in His time Esther; you relax and wait on Him."

Esther nodded her head in agreement and she and Mordecai talked for an hour longer about the villagers, the sheep, the horse and if he had heard any news from the brothers at Jerusalem, but he had not.

After their visit was over, Esther went into her bed chamber and found it to be just as exquisite and luxurious as her personal lounge. Lying across her bed, she fell asleep.

Chapter Nine

....

PLOT TO KILL THE KING

Bigthan and Teresh were finally released from the naval ship infirmary and reassigned to the royal thrown room as guards. Before going on guard duty, they reported to the officer's training camp for their daily physical exercise.

"Have you noticed Haman leaving the training yard every morning about this time? I wonder where he goes?" Bigthan asked Teresh. The two of them had become very close after going undercover in Greece and having to fight off ten enemy soldiers to escape once their mission was revealed.

"I overheard Haman talking to one of the other trainers. He said the King himself requested Him to personally train him and that they had become very close. He said the King even solicits his advice on war strategies."

"Where did Haman come from? What is his nationality? Bigthan asked.

"I think he is an Amalekite."

"An Amalekite!" Bigthan said in surprise. "How did an Amalekite rise up to the top ranks in a Persian army? Do the officials know that he is an Amalekite?"

"I am not sure" Teresh retorted. "He is siding up too close to the King as if he thinks the King will elevate him to a high command. I heard that the King does not seek Memucan's advice on war strategies or legal advice like he did before."

"I wonder what the King is planning?" Bigthan said half to himself and half to Teresh. The two men continued their workout.

The Queen's Royal Banquet began well into the ninth hour. Ahasuerus along with his lawyers, princes and other official guests were all reclining on couches surrounding him. "I have a new Queen. You all were right; she is much, much better than Vashti. I have sent presents to all the Persian citizens and have declared this banquet in honor of Queen Esther. To Queen Esther!" Ahasuerus raised his golden goblet in a salute to the new queen. All the lawyers lifted their goblets high and in unison repeated, "To Queen Esther!"

After the salute to Esther, Ahasuerus looked to his right at Mehuman and beckoned him to come close to him. "Mehuman, go get Queen Esther and bring her to the Royal Feast. Make sure the Royal Crown is upon her head."

Mehuman stood and bowed before the King. "As you wish Your Majesty."

Esther was entertaining her own guests in the Queen's courtyard and sat on her couch with her princesses and servants around her. Zena was among them. Esther spotted her; she was seated among the concubine's way in the back of the yard. The front seating was reserved for the princesses from the various provinces. All the princesses were presented to Esther with their gifts and then seated. The concubines were escorted to the back and seated there.

Zena watched Esther from where she was seated in the very back. When she learned that Esther made queen, sadness filled her heart as she remembered how she, Zoe and the other two roommates treated her during the purification period. She wondered if Esther could ever forgive her. After the greeting period was over, everyone was seated. As they began eating and socializing among themselves, Zena beckoned for one of the servants to deliver a note to Esther.

Opening the note, Esther read, "Esther, may I have a word with you, your friend Zena." For several minutes she did not look up. She just held the note in her hand. She still cared about Zena as a friend; after all, they grew up together. But she was very surprised when she and Zoe turned on her throughout the last year. Even with her flighty character, she would have never believed Zena could have treated her the way she did. Esther prayed silently, "Father, please give me the ability to forgive Zena and treat her the way you would have me to treat her." With that, she raised her head and made eye contact with Zena across the courtyard, smiled, nodded her head instructing the servant who had not left her side, to bring Zena to her.

Esther watched Zena as she left her seat and made her way up front. None of the other guests seemed to notice. Standing in front of Esther, Zena bowed her head. She was too ashamed to look at Esther now that she was standing in front of her. She just stood there until Esther called name.

"Zena," Esther said softly. "Zena, look at me."

Zena finally looked up at her with tears in her eyes. "Can you ever forgive me Est., um."

Esther could see that she was not sure how to address her. Should she say 'Queen' or could she address her as her friend 'Esther.'

"You may address me as 'Queen Esther' Zena" Esther instructed her in a soft warm tone. She was not angry with Zena; she felt empathy for her because she knew this was humiliating, humbling and very difficult for her. "You may call me 'Queen Esther' and yes, I forgive you, Zoe, and all of the other concubines. Will you let them know that I forgive them?"

"Yes, yes, I will" Zena replied bowing her head again.

Esther's heart was breaking. It was very difficult for her to stay seated; she wanted to stand up and embrace Zena like they did when they were kids but knew it was inappropriate for her to do so as Queen. Instead, she held out her hand to Zena. Zena took her hand and squeezed it tightly, bent down and kissed it, let it go and quickly walked back to her seat. Tears filled Esther's eyes as she watched her go. It would be a long time before she saw or spoke to Zena again.

Esther's attention was drawn away from the ladies to the activity at the door. Mehuman, and the other King's servants waited for her to give them permission to enter the Queen's courtyard. Esther nodded her head and the King's servants entered and bowed before her.

"Greetings Queen Esther" Mehuman spoke as he bowed before her. The King has requested your presence at the Royal Banquet and that you wear the Royal Crown."

Hegai was standing close enough to Esther to hear the King's request and immediately retrieved the Golden Crown and placed it on Esther's head.

"Thank you Hegai" Esther responded as the crown was placed upon her head and they left the courtyard heading toward the King's banquet. At the door of the hall, Hegai and Mehuman traded places. Mehuman took Esther's arm and led her up to Ahasuerus. Everyone stood as Esther entered the hall. They all bowed as King Ahasuerus escorted Esther to her seat right next to his.

After Esther was seated, King Ahasuerus picked up his scepter and began to address all the guests in the banquet hall. "Citizens of Persia and in all of the 127 Provinces, from Ethiopia to India, I introduce to you the new Queen of Persia! Queen Esther!!" All the people stood, clapped, and cheered. The crowd was divided into two sections with an isle down the middle. As they continued to clap and cheer, King Ahasuerus took Esther's hand and paraded her up and down the aisle, then returned her to her seat on the throne.

The banquet was over, and Esther was fully engaged into her Queenly duties. Sitting at her desk writing thank you notes for the many gifts she received, she was interrupted by the guard's knock at the door.

"Queen Esther, your father is here to visit with you. May I show him in"

"Yes you may." Esther put her papers aside and stood to greet Mordecai. He came every day at this time before going to the gate.

"Good morning Morde!" Esther greeted him in her usual warm manner hugging him around the neck. She still tugged at his beard like she did when she was a little girl.

"Good morning Esther" Mordecai replied. Even though Esther had been queen for several months now, Mordecai still searched her face to make sure she was treated well. He never saw any evidence of abuse. Esther always stood quietly smiling as he conducted his checkup on her. When the inspection was over, they sat down and had tea; fruit, bread and talked until it was time for him to go to work.

"How is Zena? Her parents ask me of her welfare every time they see me.

"The last time I saw her was at my Royal Banquet. Hegai told me that she is doing well as the King's Concubine; she is being well taken care of, but I have not seen nor talked with her. Are her parents and Zoe living better since she became one of the King's concubines?"

"Not really. They are surviving like the rest of us. Not much has changed. The refreshments were good as usual, but I must be going now, I cannot be late for work even though my daughter is the Queen of Persia." Mordecai winked at Esther as he stood up to leave. He took Esther's hand in his and kissed it again as he bowed to her. "Until tomorrow my lady."

Esther held her hand out and giggled at Mordecai as he left the palace, she was full of joy and peace.

Only an hour left before Mordecai's workday was over. He worked a double shift again and was glad to be going home soon. Toward the end of the ninth hour, not too many people were entering and leaving the palace. He opened the King's gate to let a visitor go through and closed the gate behind them then settled himself down on a makeshift seat a little lower than the gate on the right side. The thick black iron bars were cold against his back, but it did not bother him. His tunic was thick enough to keep the chill away and the bars made for a good back support as he sat in between opening and closing the gate for visitors. Hearing the palace doors open, he peered through the iron gate and saw two men come out. Getting up to open the gate for them, he noticed that the men walked away from the gate toward the big oak tree on the side of the palace. They looked behind them as they walked to see if anyone was watching and hid themselves behind the big tree. They appeared to be in deep conversation. When they did not come toward the gate, Mordecai returned to his seat, but he kept watching them. It was Bigthan and Teresh, two of the King's top guards. Mordecai recognized them because he had opened the gate for them to enter the palace several times during the day and night. The two men were not aware that he was there and that he could hear and see them through the gate bars. The two torch lights on both sided of the palace door reflected on the palace's blue and white marble walkway illuminating the area. Mordecai could see the two men clearly. "Did you see how Haman sat close to the King at Queen Esther's banquet?" Bigthan asked Teresh leaning his hand against the tree. "The King had to ask him to move away from him to make room for Queen Esther to attend the banquet! The King keeps him at his side day and night now and some of the servants say Haman gets the King drunk quite often."

Teresh looked around to make sure no one had walked up on them. "Yes, I saw them, I hear it is pretty much settled that the King is going to elevate him to top prince, second in charge of the entire empire. We have been serving this King and the one before him for 20 years or more. That position should rightfully go to one of us! If not us, one of his lawyers like Memucan who has been very faithful to him. Elevating an Amalekite over faithful servants is very, very foolish. Especially when that Amalekite only has a year and some months in service duty. Who knows what he has planned for Persia?"

"The King is a fool!" Bigthan blurted out angrily. "He cannot see the type of man Haman is? All he does is flatter the King every chance he gets, then offers him wine to drink and the King eats it up like honey. Flattery and drink, flattery, and drink!"

"He is sneaky, arrogant and greedy" Teresh retorted. Harbona told me the King and Haman have spent thousands of dollars drinking up the King's wine supply. How can he rule properly if he stays drunk all the time?"

"Who is Harbona?" Bigthan asked.

"He is the King's secretary. He should know, he keeps the books."

Bigthan sighed in disgust, threw his hands up in the air and continued. "The King is a fool!" He said again, this time with more force and volume. "He does not have the experience necessary to govern a kingdom this large. The Grecian Navy is preparing an all-out attack against the empire and this King spends his time getting drunk day and night. He has never worked for anything in his life; King Darius just handed everything into his hands, so it stands to reason that he does not have the ability to manage all the wealth and power that was laid into his lap. And if he is entertaining the likes of Haman, an Amalekite, it shows that he is not a good judge of character as well."

"You are right" Teresh said in agreement. "This King is a fool. We need to get rid of him for the kingdom's sake as well as our own sake."

"Get rid of him?" Bigthan asked. "How?"

"Kill him."

"Kill him?"

"Yes, kill him" Teresh said with hatred in his voice. "This could be accomplished very easily. We are the King's top guards and know all the guard's schedules. We can arrange for the two of us to guard him at the same time and kill him any time we choose and get away without anyone witnessing anything. If we get caught, we fight our way out. Remember we just healed up from fighting off ten Grecian Soldiers." Teresh raised his hand, then stood there letting the idea sink into Bigthan's mind.

Bigthan thought about Teresh's suggestion. Both he and Teresh were big, strong, and very muscular. They both graduated at the top of their training class as official officers and were two of the first officers hired by King Darius; and they did indeed fight off ten soldiers by themselves. None of the other officers could defeat either of them in competition. "Okay" he finally said. We just have to decide when and where and how we will do it." Teresh nodded his head and the two men walked back into the palace.

Mordecai remained very still and quiet as the two men finished their conversation and left. He breathed a heavy sigh of relief after he made sure he was alone again. Kill the King? This must not happen. His night shift would be officially over very soon. It was now very close to the end of the ninth hour. He wondered if Esther would still be up by the time he reached her palace. This was too important to wait until his shift was over or to wait until morning. He gathered up his things and rushed back to Esther's palace.

When he arrived, he was out of breath from running. The palace torch lights were burning all around the palace door as usual. The guards patrolling on top of the towers recognized Mordecai as he approached and permitted him to approach the door. At this time of night, the personal guards remained inside of the palace doors and relied on the tower guards to patrol the outside of the palace. As Mordecai continued to size up his surroundings, he thought about waiting until morning to reveal the plot against the King to Esther, but Bigthan and Teresh's conversation flooded back into his mind and he went up to the palace door and began banging on it and yelling 'Open up, open up. I must see Queen Esther! Open up!"

The guards yelled from inside the door, "Who goes there?"

Mordecai yelled back, "It is Mordecai, Queen Esther's father. Please open the door, I must speak with her at once, it is very important, a matter of life and death. Hurry, you must open the door!"

The guard opened the door. Hatach stood behind the guard dressed in his night clothes with a helmet on his head, a sword in his right hand and a shield in his left. Hegai was right behind him in his night clothes, but fully armed with weapons and in a stance ready to attack an enemy if necessary. The strange ensemble of night clothes accessorized with armor took Mordecai aback for just a second. He quickly collected himself and continued. "I am Queen Esther's father. It is important that I speak with her immediately, it is urgent, where is she?"

Hegai relaxed and walked up to Hatach. "This is Queen Esther's father. If he is here at this hour, it must be important. Come." Hegai motioned for Mordecai to follow him, "I will take you to her." Hegai led Mordecai to the door of Esther's private chamber and the guards stood to attention as they approached. "Tell the Queen her father is here with important information" Hegai ordered.

The guard knocked on the door, "Queen Esther, Hegai, Hatach and your father are here to see you. They say it is urgent. May I show them in?"

"Yes, show them in."

The guard opened the door and Mordecai rushed in. Hegai and Hatach remained in the doorway. Mordecai went over to Esther grabbing her hand. "Esther, the King's life is in danger. I heard Bigthan and Teresh, two of the King's personal guards talking inside the palace gate tonight while I was at work. They were not aware that I was there. They are planning to kill him. You must get word to the King tonight! I do not know when they plan to do it, but they are definitely making plans."

"Why would Bigthan and Teresh want to kill the King?" Esther asked.

"They think the King is going to promote this fellow named Haman over them to First Prince. They said that Haman is spending a lot of time with the King getting him drunk and spending up the kingdom money on wine. They said Haman is an Amalekite and they would kill the King if he even considered promoting an Amalekite over them; that they served in the King's army for over 20 years, first under King Darius and now King Ahasuerus! Esther, you must get word to the King! You must do it now!"

Esther patted Mordecai's hand trying to calm him down a little. "Yes, yes Morde, I will get word to the King." Esther looked up and saw both Hatach and Hegai standing in the doorway. Getting up from her chair she went over to her writing table and began writing a note, then handed it to Hegai. "Hatach, Hegai, both of you, please see that the King gets this note immediately. If he is asleep, wake him up. Do not leave him until you see him read the note and take some sort of action, then return to me and let me know what was done. Do you understand?" This was the first official order that Esther had ever given to either of her personal servants. The boldness and authority in her voice as she gave it surprised everyone in the room, including herself, but she did not let the others see it. Hegai took the note from Esther's hand and both he and Hatach bowed at the waist, backed out of the room, and ran to the King's palace. Mordecai sat with Esther in silence as they waited for the men's return. After a few minutes Mordecai got up from his chair and began pacing the floor deep in thought. Esther watched him pacing but said nothing. Finally, Mordecai broke his silence. "Esther, Bigthan and Teresh said that Haman was an Amalekite. The Amalekites have always been enemies of the Jews."

"Our enemies? Why Morde?"

"The hatred between Israel and the Amalekites started hundreds of years ago after God delivered us from Egyptian slavery while we were wondering in the wilderness." Esther sat up straight in her chair listening intently to Mordecai's every word. This part of her Jewish history was not familiar to her. Mordecai continued. "The Amalekites came out against us in that wilderness. Moses told Joshua to pick out capable men to fight. He, Aaron, and Hur went up on a hill to watch the fight. When Moses held up his arms," Mordecai held up both of his arms to demonstrate the action for Esther, "we, the Israelites prevailed in the battle. When Moses' arms got tired and he put them down," Mordecai put his arms down, "the Amalekites prevailed. So, Aaron and Hur stood on either side of Moses and held his arms up until we, the Israelites won the battle."

"Wow!" Esther said her eyes glued to Mordecai.

Mordecai hesitated for a moment. "All through history, the Amalekites have hated and warred against us Jews. One of my favorite stories my father told me when I was a child was the one about Gideon. Gideon was threshing wheat and hiding it from the Midianites who also enslaved Israel at one time. An Angel of the Lord appeared before him and told him he was going to save Israel from the hands of the Midianites. Gideon told the Angel that he was the least, or the smallest child in his father's house and that his family was very poor. How was he going to free Israel from slavery? The angel told him God would be with him and he would take out the Midianites as though they were one man. Well, Gideon's faith was less than low. Gideon's father told him of the miracles God had performed for Israel in the past, but he had not seen or experienced any of them himself. So Gideon said if you are really an Angel, show me a sign. The Angel said, "Stay here. Do not leave. Bring me a gift and sit it here and wait for me; I will be back."

Esther was mesmerized with Mordecai's story. She did not take her eyes off him.

Mordecai continued, "Gideon went into the house and fixed a meal for the Angel to eat. He fixed some bread and meat in a stew pot and set it for the Angel to eat. The Angel came back and told Gideon to take the bread and the meat and lay them on a rock and pour the broth from the stew over them. Gideon obeyed. Then the Angel took his staff and touched the bread, meat, and broth with the end of it and fire came up out of the rock and burned up everything." Mordecai waived both his hands in the air as if acting out the Angel's actions. "You know, that would have been enough for me to believe that this was an Angel from God" Mordecai said.

"Yes, but what does that have to do with the Amalekites?"

"I am getting to that point in a minute. I just wanted to give you some background history. Anyway, Gideon is now captain over the army of Israel. They are camped outside of a city called Manasseh. The Amalekites teamed up with the Midianites to war against Israel. Gideon was beyond scared. Most of his soldiers were scared too. So Gideon asked God to give him a sign that He would deliver them from the Amalekites and the Midianites. God told Gideon to send all the soldiers home that were scared and that lapped up water from the stream like dogs. Gideon sent those soldiers home. God told Gideon not to worry, that He would be with him. So Gideon told the few remaining soldiers that he had left to do exactly what he tells them to do. He told each of them to get a trumpet, a glass water pitcher and a torch and do exactly as he does.

The Amalekites and Midianites had Israel surrounded and were ready to descend upon them. Gideon blew his trumpet loud; his soldiers blew their trumpets loud. Gideon smashed his glass water pitcher with a loud noise and blew his trumpet loud again. His soldiers smashed their glass water pitchers with a loud noise and blew their trumpets loud again. Gideon raised his torch in his free hand and yelled 'The Sword of the Lord and of Gideon!' and blew his trumpet loud again; his soldiers raised their torches in their free hand and yelled 'The Sword of the Lord and of Gideon!' and blew their trumpets loud again. Suddenly, the Amalekites and the Midianites became confused. They pulled out their swords and began killing each other! The Israelites stood in the midst of their camp and watched them. They did not have to lift a finger to physically fight their enemies! God did it for them!" Mordecai walked back to the chair and sat down, exhausted from acting out the story before Esther.

Esther was spellbound. After a few seconds she whispers half to herself and half to Mordecai sitting next to her. "God sure does take care of his own!" Mordecai nodded his head in agreement but remained silent.

"Morde, if the King does promote Haman as his highest official, we and all of us Jews could be in real danger! We have got to do something to stop this, but what?"

"I am not sure Esther; but I know God has a plan. His Divine Will is already laid out. We must trust Him. Believe in Him. Have faith in Him. He will show us what to do, if we are to do anything, and He will show us when to do it."

Hegai and Hatch rushed through Esther's door out of breath startling both of them. "My Queen, we delivered the note to the King as you commanded. He read the note; sat quietly for several minutes, looked to his left and then to his right. Bigthan was standing by his right arm and Teresh was standing by his left arm. The King called for extra guards. Bigthan and Teresh asked the King if there was a problem. King Ahasuerus said nothing but sat quietly until the reinforcement guards arrived, then he read the note out loud. Bigthan and Teresh slowly began backing away from the King, but he ordered the guards to take both of them out and hang them from the gallows and record the whole matter in the Book of Chronicles."

Esther gasped in horror placing her hand over her mouth. Mordecai put his arm around her shoulders to comfort her. Hegai and Hatach waited there until Esther dismissed them.

Chapter Ten

HAMAN PROMOTED TO FIRST PRINCE

After the attempted assassination on Ahasuerus was foiled and the two perpetrators were hung, palace activity returned to normal. It was in the middle of winter and Ahasuerus sat at the head of the table in one of the conference rooms waiting for the arrival of the governors, princes, and lawyers. Haman was sitting at his right hand. They talked quietly between themselves as the men filed in.

"How do you think your nobles, princes and lawyers are going to respond to my promotion?" Haman asked Ahasuerus.

"What or how they think, or feel does not concern me. They are here to serve me. You have proven to be a wise and valued counselor as well as a friend to me Haman. Over the past year, you have gotten to know me quite well, how I think, what my goals are and how to meet those goals. I used to think that Memucan was the wisest of all my officials, but you have surpassed even him. You have earned this promotion, please accept it graciously."

"As you wish Your Majesty" Haman said smugly sitting back in his chair watching the men file through the door and take their seats around the table. He was very satisfied with himself and his accomplishments. It had only taken him a year and six months to work his plan of advancement starting with the lowest rank as soldier all the way up to top instructor of the Persian Army. It was a lot of hard work, but the hard work had paid off as well as being in the right place at the right time. The easiest part of all was befriending this King. Haman turned and looked at Ahasuerus and smiled. Ahasuerus returned the smile and directed his attention back to the men seated at the table. Yes, Haman continued his thoughts; getting close to this King was easy, all I had to do was become his drinking companion. He is a drunkard and a fool. Haman slowly looked around the table making eye contact with each man as Ahasuerus called the meeting to order and the reports were read.

At the end of the reporting, the men began talking quietly among themselves eating and drinking as was the custom at all their meetings. Ahasuerus stood up and called the meeting back to order. "Gentlemen," he began. All the men turned their attention back to the King. "I am giving notice to all of you today that I have promoted Haman, Son of Hammedatha," Ahasuerus turned and acknowledged Haman sitting in the chair next to him, "I have advanced him and set his seat above all other princes in the entire Persian Empire. As of this day, you will bow and reverence him just as you bow and reverence me as well as respect his authority. Notices about his promotion have already been sent out to all the provinces and it has been officially recorded in the books. If there are no other reports, this meeting is adjourned."

The room was completely silent as Ahasuerus turned shook Haman's hand and returned to his personal quarters. Haman stood up with a satisfied superior look on his face, scanned all the nobles and princes in the room. No one said anything to him, they slowly gathered up their documents, put on their wraps and made their way out of the room and out of the palace. Only Memucan, Admatha, Tarshish, Carshena and Meres, five of the King's lawyers remained behind and walked out of the palace with Haman. As they walked out the door from the palace and onto the top landing that led downstairs to the gate, Haman could not contain himself any longer and shouted out loud, "King Ahasuerus has just promoted me above all of his princes, nobles, and lawyers. I am the most powerful man in the whole Persian Kingdom! except for the King himself, of course. Not only that, he has commanded that all men, young and old, women and children must bow down before me. Even you lawyers!" Haman cocked his head sideways and stared at Memucan until he dropped his head and bowed at the waist. All the other men surrounding Haman imitated Memucan bowing at the waist. "That is right, you must bow down before me!" Haman laughed out loud and began flicking his hand in the air for the men to move out of his pathway and proceeded down the stairs.

Mordecai was at his post at the gate. He heard and observed Haman's arrogant display of his new authority. At the beginning of his shift, his superior advised him and all the other porters of Haman's promotion and was instructed on how to address him. So, it has happened, Mordecai thought to himself and sighed. The King did promote this Amalekite, an enemy of the Jews to the highest position in the land, requiring all men to bow down to him just as Esther and I feared. Father God, you are the only one that I will ever bow my knee to, Mordecai prayed silently. I worship and reverence you and only you regardless of the outcome.

Mordecai watched Haman run down the stairs to the gate where he was standing. Haman threw his purple and royal blue wrap around his shoulders with a flourish then gave Mordecai a nod of his head indicating that he was ready to exit through the gate. Mordecai witnessed the humiliation the King's lawyers and servants were subjected to by Haman. Determined that he was not going to be humiliated into bowing to him, Mordecai looked directly into Haman's eyes as he opened the gate for him to walk through.

Haman waited for Mordecai to bow before him before walking through, but Mordecai did not bow, he just stood there looking at him waiting for him to exit so he could close the gate behind him. All the King's lawyers and servants stood back and watched to see what Haman would do; they wanted to see if Mordecai's humiliation would be worse than theirs. After all, he was just a lowly porter; they were the King's top official lawyers. They expected Mordecai to be fired and jailed for insubordination. He could even have Mordecai put to death if he desired. They stood back in silence and watched to see the outcome.

Haman could feel all the lawyers' eyes on him. He knew he had to do something especially after the way he had acted just moments ago, but what? What should he do? He was not prepared for this type of disrespect from anyone right after his promotion. He could not believe he would have to defend his title and authority to a lowly porter, a gate keeper. After several awkward moments, Haman walked through the gate, walked a little distance away from the gate and stopped. Mordecai closed the gate behind him and walked over to his seat to sit down. Before he could sit, Haman turned around, walked back to the gate, stopped just to the side of the gate staring at Mordecai again, trying to stare him down, to humiliate him. Mordecai stood up strait, glared back at Haman and without taking his eyes from him, he reached over, opened the gate, and stood back for Haman to walk through. Haman walked through the gate and over to the group of men standing in the corner of the courtyard.

"Who is that porter?" Haman barked at Memucan. "Does he know who I am?"

Memucan stuttered a little, clearing his throat and answered Haman nervously. "His name is Mordecai; he is a Jew. He has worked in the King's court as a porter for the past 10 years now. He and all the Jews have been dispersed throughout the entire Persian Kingdom for the past 30 or so years under King Darius."

"Humph, a Jew huh?" Haman turned around and approached the gate a third time, waited for Mordecai to open the gate, but he did not make eye contact with him. As soon as Mordecai opened the gate, Haman stumped through and kept walking. Mordecai closed the gate and walked back to his seat and sat down. Memucan and the other lawyers watched Haman as he walked away. Admatha, one of the lawyers that was in the bunch walked up to Memucan. "Did you see that!"

"Yes" Memucan said looking at Mordecai. "I saw it. I am going to have a word with that porter. The rest of you go on home." As the lawyers approached the gate, Mordecai stood up and opened the gate letting the men go through. Memucan was the last to go through and waited as the gate was closed.

"Mordecai" Memucan began, "your name is Mordecai is it not?"

"Yes," he said looking into Memucan's face. "May I help you with something?"

"Yes you may. Are you aware that the King has just promoted Haman, the man that walked back and forth through the gate; do you know who he is?"

"I do not know him personally" Mordecai retorted as he leaned his back against the gate.

"I thought everyone on the King's staff was made aware of the change in authority. Has your superior advised you and the other porters of the proper way you are to respond to Haman when you open and close the gate for him?"

Mordecai was wearied with this line of questioning and wanted it to be over. Looking away from Memucan, he sighed, then replied in the same formal tone that Memucan was speaking to him. "Yes, I and the other porters have been advised as well."

Memucan was silent for a moment trying to decide whether to address Mordecai's sarcasm as insubordination or to ignore it. Deciding to ignore it, he asked, "if you are aware of his promotion and you have been advised of the proper way to address him, why are you disobeying the King's direct command that everyone everywhere is to reverence Haman and bow before him; it is the King's law!" Memucan reinforced his statement with authority in his voice.

Mordecai was silent and did not respond to Memucan's question.

"The next time Haman approaches this gate; you are to respect and honor him according to the King's law. Do you understand Mordecai?"

Mordecai remained quiet.

Memucan looked at him for a few more moments, turned and walked away.

Mordecai did not stop in to see Esther before going to work the next day. She knew him too well and would know that something was troubling him so he went directly to his post in front of the gate. The porter that Mordecai was to relieve was a Jew like himself. As he approached the gate, the porter stood up with his personal things in his hands ready to leave.

"Anything going on that I should know about?"

"Yes" the porter said. "Everyone is talking about you."

"About me?"

"Yes, about you and your insubordination against Haman. Why are you breaking the King's law? We have it nice here Mordecai. This King does not bother us, we are left alone to live and follow our religious customs. They do not interfere with us. Why would you disobey the King's law and bring attention to us? You always seem to do things to trouble our people!"

Mordecai did not expect to be questioned from a fellow Jew about bowing to and reverencing a man when the Jewish Law forbade it. "You are aware of our Jewish Law are you not?" He asked the porter as he turned to face him. "Why would you ask me such a question? Did you bow down to Haman?"

"Yes, I bowed down to Haman. If it keeps the peace, if it allows us to continue to live in peace and worship God and keep His laws, yes, I bowed to Haman and will continue to bow down to him."

Mordecai could not believe what he was hearing. "So," he began slowly looking at the man. "In order to live in peace, you would compromise your belief in God. Do you fear man more than you fear God?" he asked. "Have you not learned anything about our God? What do you think our last Babylonian enslavement was about? Why did God permit Nebuchadnezzar to enslave us? Do you know our Jewish History? Do you remember the law that Moses handed down to us, the one that says 'Thou shalt have no other gods before me?' Do you not realize that bowing down to this Haman is reverencing him as God? I tell you this, my friend, I am more afraid of what God would do to me if I bowed down to Haman rather than what Haman himself would do to me. The God I serve and worship is more powerful than

Haman and the King himself. No, I will not bow down to Haman or any other man."

The Jewish porter dropped his head in shame, turned and walked away from Mordecai. Father, Mordecai prayed silently, please help me this day to stand on your word, to be obedient to your word. Please keep Haman away from me. There are plenty of other gates leading into the palace, please let him use the other entrances. Thank you. Amen. As soon as he finished his prayer and sat down on his seat, he heard the palace door open and got up to open the gate. It was Haman. To his surprise, Haman descended the stairs and approached the gate; however, he deliberately ignored Mordecai. He kept his eyes straight ahead and waited for him to open the gate. Mordecai opened the gate, Haman walked through and kept going never saying a word, never acknowledging Mordecai in any way. Mordecai closed the gate behind him, walked back to his seat and sat down. He was not aware that Memucan was observing him from the top of the stairs and waited until Haman was out of sight before coming down the stairs to the gate.

Thank you Father for answering my prayer so quickly, Mordecai prayed within himself to the Lord. You have a unique way of answering prayers, he thought to himself as he sat down on his stool deep in thought. Mordecai heard someone clear his throat and stood up to get the gate. "Oh, I am sorry, I did not hear you walk up" he said as he opened the gate for Memucan.

"Mordecai" Memucan spoke slowly and distinctly, "I thought we had an understanding after our discussion yesterday. I thought we agreed that you would obey the King's law regarding Haman. I observed you just now not bowing to him as he approached the gate. Just what is the problem with bowing to this man? He is the second most powerful man in the Persian Kingdom. He can have you dismissed from your post here; he can even have you hung for insubordination. All you have to do is bow to the man. Set your pride aside and bow to the man." Memucan let the words sink in hoping he had made his point to Mordecai. He stood there silently watching him, waiting for Mordecai to respond.

During Memucan's silence, Mordecai silently prayed, Oh God, please give me the right words to say to this man. Let me speak your words to give him a good understanding of who I am, who I serve and who I honor.

"Memucan," Mordecai began slowly, "I am not trying to be difficult, insulting, or full of pride. I am a Jew. King Ahasuerus has given us the freedom to worship and serve the God of our choice and to observe our religious customs. To bow down and worship or reverence Haman goes against my religious laws and beliefs. I bow down worship and reverence the one true God, the God of Abraham, Isaac, and Jacob. Do you understand this?"

The authority with which Mordecai spoke his words startled Memucan. He had never heard Mordecai speak more than a few words in his 10 years of service at the King's gate. Those words were 'good morning sir,' 'good evening sir,' or 'how are you today sir.' His articulation, his philosophy, his intelligence very much surprised Memucan. He looked at Mordecai for a brief second more and in an almost whisper he said, "I fully understand Mordecai; however, I do not know what the consequences of your defiance will have on you and your people." Memucan turned and walked away.

Chapter Eleven

HAMAN'S PLOT TO KILL THE JEWS

Haman leaned back in his office chair running his fingers over the studs that fastened the leather padding on the armchair. He loved his new office. Being the King's number one Prince provided him with luxuries he never dreamed of. The long oak desk he sat behind was supplied with everything he needed to do whatever work he wanted or needed to do. The office itself was lavishly decorated. Long purple velvet drapes pulled back and tied with velvet cords let in the morning sunlight. He had a beautiful view of the countryside with a manicured flower garden and groves of trees in the distance. On the opposite wall was a large stone fireplace where the servants built a fire for him every day. The purple and white marble floor reflected the tongues of fire as they flickered in the fireplace. Two plush leather-back chairs were evenly placed in front of the fireplace. Most days, that was where he sat sipping his tea and reading a book, but not today. Today he was at his desk drumming his fingers first on the side of his armchair, then on top of his desk. The atmosphere in his office did not comfort him today. Today he could not be comforted. He could not stop thinking about that Jew at the gate yesterday; Mordecai was his name. The man infuriated him. Was it really that the man did not bow before him? Was that it or was it because Memucan told him that he was a Jew. Haman got up from his desk and began pacing back and forth in front of his desk. The more he thought about Mordecai, the more anger built up in him. Was it anger, or was it hatred? Why do I hate the man, Haman thought? I do not even know him. Haman stopped his pacing in mid stride at the corner of his desk and said out loud. "He is a Jew!" A knock on his door interrupted his thoughts. "Yes, who is it?"

"It is Memucan Sir; may I enter my lord"

"Yes, come in." Memucan entered and stood waiting for Haman to offer him a seat.

"What can I do for you Memucan?"

"I just wanted to report to you about the Jewish Porter at the King's gate yesterday."

"Yes, you spoke to him then?"

"Yes I did."

"I would like to hear about it. Here, sit here" Haman motioned for Memucan to sit in one of the chairs in front of the fireplace. He sat in the opposite one, crossing his legs and pressed his fingers together, finger on finger making a tent with both hands together and gave Memucan his full attention.

"I approached Mordecai yesterday after the incident he had with you. I asked him why he was disobeying a direct command, a court order from the King? I told him that you were a very powerful man and that you could take his job and even his life in an instant if you wanted to."

Haman adjusted his position in his chair with a slight grin on his face at Memucan's description of him as a "powerful man." He liked the sound of it and he liked the way it made him feel.

Memucan continued. "I really thought he was going to ignore me and walk away. He turned his back to me for a moment, then looked me square in the face and said, 'Listen Memucan, I am not trying to be difficult, insulting, or full of pride in not worshiping Haman. To bow to him is worshipping him and I do not worship any human being. I worship and bow my knee to the one and only true God, the God of Abraham, Isaac, and Jacob. Do you understand this?" Memucan sat straight up in his chair. "My lord, the man spoke with such authority and power, I was left speechless! In all the 10 years of his employment with the King, I never heard him say more than three or four words, 'Good morning, good evening, or how are you today.' I never paid any more attention to him than a rock lying next to the gate. But, when he spoke, he was articulate. He is his own person, knows what he believes and the way he spoke about his religious philosophy, he seemed determined to stand by it regardless of who was in opposition to it. Even you!"

"What was your reply to his statement?"

"To be honest with you my lord, I was so stunned by him, all I could say was 'yes, I understand Mordecai; however, I do not know what consequences your defiance will have on you and your people.' Then I walked away."

Haman got up from is chair making a hissing sound through his teeth then said in a disgusting voice, "that blasted Jew. I hate him. I hate all of them!" He stood in front of the fireplace and leaned his elbow on the fireplace mantel with his hand supporting his head.

Memucan watched him closely. He saw Haman's fury and his hatred. It seemed to consume him. This one man. A Jew, no doubt, but one little old Jewish man. Why did Haman hate him and all the other Jews? His curiosity got the better of him and he asked, "My lord, why do you hate Mordecai?"

"He is a Jew!"

"What have the Jewish people ever done to you? I understand Mordecai's disrespect for you, his insubordination, but is that a cause for you to hate all Jewish People?"

Haman stiffened up and glared at Memucan. "Do you dare question me!"

Haman settled himself down and went back to his chair and sat down and began talking to Memucan as though telling a story. "Before you knocked on my door, I was sitting here trying to make sense of my feelings about Mordecai myself. I could not figure out at first why I had such hatred for the Jews. Then it all came back to me. I can remember when I was a little boy, my father, grandfather, and my uncles telling me stories of the different battles my people fought. I am an Amalekite. All through history, the Amalekites warred against the Jews."

"Why, what did they do to your people?" Memucan asked.

"It is not exactly what they did, it was how they lived. They were enslaved by the Egyptians for many, many years. A Hebrew man named Moses went up against an Egyptian Pharaoh and told him to let the Hebrew slaves go. He, this Moses, used some type of magic to try to influence the Pharaoh. With each magic trick Moses performed, the Pharaoh had his soothsayers to perform the same trick. The Pharaoh would not let the slaves go until Moses performed the best magic spell he had on the Pharaoh and on all the Egyptian people. Using his special magic, he killed all the first-born males in every Egyptian household throughout the whole Egyptian Kingdom. This included all the livestock as well. Not a hair was harmed on any of the Hebrew slaves though. It was reported that Moses and the Hebrew priests splashed some magical tonic on the door posts of their homes which kept them alive. Even the Pharaoh's own son was killed. After that, he let the Hebrews go."

"Where did this god get his power from?" Memucan asked.

"I do not know. You see, that is what is so strange about these people. They seem to have all types of magic tricks up their sleeves and no one, other than themselves, know what it is and how it works! I remember my uncle telling me about the Amalekite-Medianite war against the Israelites. After they left Egypt, they changed their name from Hebrew slaves to 'Israelites.' I am not sure why they changed their name. Anyway, they settled in one of our little villages. Everything was fine at first. I mean, we tried to be friendly, get to know them a little, but we noticed that they were not hospitable. They would not socialize with us; eat our food, would not let their sons and daughters marry our sons and daughters. They would not worship our gods or participate in any of our customs. Our people talked it over with the Midianites and we decided to kill them and get them out of our country. They figured that the two armies together could conquer them easily. There were not many of them in the camp, so we surrounded them on all sides and at a certain time, had planned to descend on them and kill them all. Memucan, my uncles told me that suddenly, they heard all this crashing noise, they saw fire all around them. Out of nowhere, it seemed these Israelites multiplied into a huge army. Our army became confused and turned on each other!"

"Why in the world would they turn on each other?"

"It sounded preposterous to me too. It does not make any sense at all! But that is what they did. They kept fighting until they destroyed each other." Haman sat up in his chair and slowly shook his head, then continued. "I kept asking my father and grandfather about this story. They swore that it was true. My grandfather told me that this god that the Israelites worshiped vowed that He would continue to wage war against the Amalekites forever. Every time my people waged war against these Jews, these Israelites, as they like to call themselves, we lost." Haman became quiet for a moment. "Humph, these Jews are scattered throughout the Persian Kingdom now are they not?" Haman asked.

"Yes. A lot of them are. A lot of them went back to their homeland which is Judea and Jerusalem, but when King Nebuchadnezzer conquered and enslaved them, they and their home-land are now under Persian rule."

"Is that right? Haman asked surprised. They are in our land, but do not follow our laws, do not follow our customs, and do not worship our gods. What good are they to us? What good are they to the King? It seems to me that they are nothing but a burden to us."

Memucan studied Haman's face intently. "Where are you going with this my lord?"

Haman got up from his chair and stood facing the fireplace. Without looking at Memucan he said in an icy, low, steady voice. "Now that I know who Mordecai is and who his people are, I realize that they are my worst enemy. This enemy has been right under my feet all this time and I did not know it. The beautiful thing about it is that I am now able to do something my father, grandfather and my great grandfather could not do. I am going to get rid of these

Jews, these Israelites, or Hebrews, whatever they call themselves. I am going to kill all of them, their priests, their men, women, boys, maidens and even their infant babies. I am going to wipe them off the face of the earth. Eliminate any trace of them, as if they never existed. I am not only going to do this because of Mordecai, I am going to do it to avenge my people! The Amalekites!" Haman threw his hands up in the air to emphasize his point.

"Ah, er, do you not mean the Persians?"

Haman blushed, then replied, "Well, yes, you are right."

"How do you plan to accomplish this enormous task?"

Haman looked at Memucan again. "You let me worry about that. Do you know of any soothsayers in the area? I mean really good soothsayers, someone who really knows their craft."

"Yes. I know of a good one. I have seen his work personally."

"Good. Go and bring him here to my office immediately."

Memucan immediately got up from his chair, bowed to Haman and backed out of his office. While Memucan was gone, Haman rearranged his office. He moved the two chairs that were in front of the fireplace and set them on the side of the room. He removed the baskets and the fireplace utensils from in front of the fireplace and placed them on the side of the fireplace to make a clean space in front so dice could be thrown easily and could be seen easily. By the time he finished, he heard a knock at the door.

"Yes, who is it?"

"It is Memucan and the soothsayer. May we enter?"

"Yes, come in."

Memucan and the soothsayer entered Haman's office. The soothsayer stepped inside and was overwhelmed by all the luxury in Haman's office. Haman cleared his throat to get his attention. Memucan introduced the soothsayer to Haman.

"My lord, this is Baylacka, the soothsayer."

Baylacka looked in Haman's direction, but did not look him in the eyes, he just bowed at the waist. After several seconds in the bowed position, he stood up and waited for further orders from Haman.

"I have a matter of great importance" Haman said. I want to know which of the twelve months of the year would be the best month to carry out this important matter. Entreat the gods for me, then cast the lots everyday of each month for the 12 months and let me know the month the lot falls on for this matter to be carried out."

Baylacka turned from Haman and Memucan, walked over and stood in front of the fireplace and bowed his head for a few moments, then stepped back, pulled out a set of die from his inside pocket and began throwing them against the little step that separated the fireplace from the floor. Haman and Memucan watched as he threw the die over and over and over until every day and every month was accounted for. After the last throw, Baylacka picked the die up. He waited for a moment, then turned to face Haman and Memucan. Baylacka looked in Haman's direction, but again, he would not look him in the eyes. He focused his eyes on Haman's chest and held out his hand and placed the die in Haman's hand.

"The lot has fallen on the twelfth month, the month of Adar, on the thirteenth day of the month of Adar."

Haman took the die from Baylacka. "Twelve months from now, huh? That gives me plenty of time to plan this task right down to the last detail. Good. Before you go, set those two chairs back in front of the fireplace and the utensils back in their proper places."

Memucan and Baylacka put Haman's office back in order, bowed at the waist and backed out of his office closing the door. Haman went back to his desk, sat down, and poured himself a goblet full of wine and drank it all in one gulp. The wine tingled and warmed his insides as he gulped it down. After a few minutes, he got up and left his office walking through the courtyard to the King's Palace and stood in the outer court. Carces, one of the King's officials was sitting at the King's feet and noticed Haman in the outer court. Ahasuerus followed Carces' attention to the outer court and saw Haman standing there.

"Haman! How good to see you!" Ahasuerus held his golden scepter out to Haman who then approached him and touched the top of the golden scepter, then bowed at the waist.

"Come, come, sit, sit. Make yourself comfortable!" Ahasuerus continued. "Carces, you may leave us now" Ahasuerus commanded.

Carces got up from his seat, bowed to both Ahasuerus and Haman and backed out of the King's Palace. After he left, King Ahasuerus turned his full attention to Haman.

"How are you my friend?"

"I am fine my King. Just fine. May I pour you a glass of wine?"

"Sure, sure. Pour one for yourself as well."

Haman poured wine for Ahasuerus and one for himself.

"Do your office quarters meet with your approval? Do you have everything you need?"

"Oh yes, Your Majesty, my quarters are quite comfortable." They both took another sip of wine. "You know King Ahasuerus," Haman began slowly. "There are certain people scattered abroad and dispersed among the people in all the provinces of your Kingdom. Their laws are different from our laws and they do not keep the King's laws nor do they follow Persian customs. If we do not keep them in check, they could spread their customs, philosophy, and laws to the Persian Citizens, which could eventually cause a rebellion; an up rise against you and your Kingdom just like Greece is doing." Haman was silent for a moment, took another sip of his wine and waited for the "rebellion" statement to sink into the King's mind. After a minute or so, he continued. "I do not see any profit that they bring to you or to your Kingdom. They roam from city to city like vagabonds. A lot of them end up in prisons which puts a financial burden on the King's treasury to house and feed them. They are a dangerous people and I do not think it wise for us to harbor them. If it pleases you, let it be written that they be destroyed, and I will pay $5,230,000 in silver to hire the people to carry out the order. After these people are destroyed, all of their money and goods could be added to the King's treasury." Haman paused again, taking another sip of his wine. He watched the King out of the corner of his eyes. The King took another sip of his wine too, trying hard to concentrate on what Haman was saying. Haman noticed that the King's wine goblet was empty and picked up the wine bottle. While he poured the King another helping of wine, he asked. "What do you think about this Your majesty?"

Without saying a word, Ahasuerus took off his ring and handed it to Haman. "Here, take my ring, the money and the people also and do whatever you think is good. I trust you."

Haman had a hard time containing himself. A sinister smile spread across his face as he settled back in his chair, took another sip of wine, and whispered to himself "this is good. This is very good." He looked over at Ahasuerus sitting in his chair. His head was hung low in his chest and the wine goblet in his right hand fell empty to the floor with a clatter. Haman looked at him in disgust shaking his head. He got up and called for Harbona, the King's Secretary.

Harbona stood in the breezeway of the palace waiting for Ahasuerus to hold out the golden scepter to him but noticed that the King had his head down. Not knowing what to do, he stood there waiting until Haman spotted him standing there.

Haman stood up waiving his hand to him. "Come, come here!" he shouted at Harbona.

Still not sure that it was appropriate, Harbona approached the King's throne cautiously and stood in front of both men looking at the King first, then Haman, then back at the King. "May I be of service to you my lord?"

"Yes, I have a court order that needs to be written and submitted to all of the King's Lieutenants in all of the 127 Provinces in King Ahasuerus' Persian Kingdom."

Harbona looked at Haman, then back at the King sleeping on his throne.

Haman became agitated that Harbona did not follow his orders immediately and barked at him. "I gave you a direct order, do you question me? I have everything I need to implement this court order." Haman raised his hand up to Harbona's eye level and twisted the King's ring on his ring finger. Harbona looked again at the sleeping King, then sat down at the desk with his pen and pad and took Haman's dictation.

After the dictation was completed, Haman sealed the order with the King's ring and gave Harbona the following instructions. "I want you to make sure your fastest messengers in every Province delivers this court order post haste. Spare no expense. I expect every area to have this order and begin preparations to carry it out within the month. I want all Persian Citizens to be ready when the appropriate day arrives. Is that clear?"

Harbona got up from the desk, collected his supplies, bowed at the waist replying "Yes, my lord" and backed out of the room. Standing out of sight of Haman in the King's breezeway, Harbona felt sick to his stomach and leaned against the wall to steady himself.

Abagtha, one of the King's servants saw him across the breezeway and ran to him. "Harbona, are you all right? Are you sick? Can I help you?"

"I will be fine. Come, I want to show you something but not here." Harbona staggered down the steps and around the corner into a little room from the King's Palace. Once the two men were in the little room and lit a candle. Harbona pulled out the decree that Haman had dictated to him and let Abagtha read it out loud.

> To all lieutenants and to all governors that are over every province and to the rulers of every people of every province, to every people after their language, in the name of King Ahasuerus:
>
> UPON THE THIRTEENTH DAY OF THE TWELFTH MONTH, WHICH IS THE MONTH OF ADAR, ALL PERSIAN CITIZENS ARE TO KILL AND CAUSE TO PERISH ALL JEWS BOTH YOUNG AND OLD, MALE AND FEMALE INCLUDING INFANTS IN ONE DAY, EVEN UPON THE THIRTEENTH DAY OF THE TWELFTH MONTH, WHICH IS THE MONTH OF ADAR. YOU ARE TO TAKE THE SPOIL OF THESE JEWS AS PREY WHICH WILL BE ADDED TO THE KING'S TREASURY. THIS

ORDER IS GIVEN BY HAMAN, FIRST PRINCE OF THE 127 PERSIAN PROVINCES IN KING AHASUERUS' RULE.

"We must kill all of the Jews? Even the women and children?" Abagtha asked.

Harbona nodded his head with tears in his eyes. "He sealed it with the King's ring. I must get this out as soon as possible or Haman will have my head." He rushed out the door and left Abagtha standing in the middle of the room in a daze.

Haman sat back in his chair and watched Ahasuerus in a drunken sleep. "You sleep on, you drunken fool. Before you know it, I will have your crown and your kingdom" he whispered low so the guards could not hear him. Satisfied that his plan was in action, he decided to go home and share the news with Zeresh, his wife. He was so full of exhilaration over his accomplishments that he ran down the stairs to the gate only to run into Mordecai. Stopping just in front of the gate, Haman scowled. Mordecai opened the gate, stood back letting Haman exit as he had done in the past, but he did not bow to him.

Haman could see that Mordecai was not intimidated by him and anger welled up in him as he stomped through the gate and walked home.

Having finished his dinner, Reelaiah remained seated with his legs folded under himself and his head hung down.

"Reelaiah" Tamara called as she cleared the evening meal from the table. "Reelaiah, what is wrong? Why are you so sad? Do you still miss Mordecai? It has been almost a year and a half now since Esther was made Queen of Persia. Do you and the brothers still hate him?"

Reelaiah looked up at Tamara and sighed. "I miss him. I miss fellowshipping with him."

"We miss him and Esther too papa. Shakera and Aisha interrupted.

"Quiet children" Tamara scolded. "Why not go and talk with him?

"You make it sound so simple Tamara."

"What is so difficult about mending fences Reelaiah? Is it your pride? Mordecai said he felt that God would have him to allow Esther to compete for the Queen's position. It looks to me like he was right. God wanted Esther to become Queen and she is Queen."

"There is more to it than that. Mordecai is still making trouble for us Jews."

"What has he done now?"

"Reelaiah looked at Tamara for a long time trying to decide if he should share the latest news about Mordecai. He did not want to upset his wife and daughters. "I was talking with Bilshan last night. He told me that Mordecai was causing trouble at the King's gate. He refused to bow to the King's first prince, a fellow named Haman the King had promoted. The porter Mordecai replaced last night on duty told Bilshan that Mordecai refused to bow to this Haman. Mordecai told Memucan, the King's top lawyer, that he would not bow his knee to any man, that it went against his religious beliefs as a Jew to worship only the one true God, the God of Abraham, Isaac, and Jacob!"

"This is the truth is it not! This is what we Jews believe. We live and obey the law that Moses handed down to us. Why is this causing trouble for you and Bilshan and the other Jewish brothers?

"It is causing trouble because it is bringing attention to us. Why does he always have to do things and say things that bring attention to the Jews!" Reelaiah was upset and angry at the same time. "Why is he not like the rest of the Jewish men and stay in his place? We live in peace here in Shushan and throughout the Persian Provinces. It seems he wants to cause disruption or be noticed, or…, I do not know. I just feel that something bad, very bad is about to happen. I do not know when, where or how it is going to happen; I just know something is about to happen."

Watching her husband from across the room, Tamara finally understood his sadness. Before she could walk over to comfort him, there was a tapping outside the door. Tap, tap, tap. Someone was posting a note on their door post. Reelaiah went to the door and pulled the notice from the post and read it. Tears welled up in his eyes and he turned his back to his wife and daughters trying to conceal his emotions and fear.

"What is it Reelaiah?" Tamara rushed over to him. He did not turn around, he just handed her the notice. After reading the notice, Tamara let out a horrific cry, ran over to her daughters and hugged them as she continued to sob. Reelaiah turned and looked at his family crying openly now. He felt helpless. How could he protect his family? All the strength left his legs and he crumbled to the floor and wept bitterly.

It had been hours since Haman had gone through the gate, but Mordecai was still agitated within himself and decided to go straight home instead of stopping off to visit with Esther. She seemed to be well adjusted to her new position as Queen of Persia. Everyone appeared to be treating her very well, he saw no signs of abuse anywhere and determined it was not necessary to check on her everyday as he had over the past year and a half.

As he left the palace grounds, he noticed people looking at him in a strange way. There…, there it was again, a man just passed him with a scowl on his face. Mordecai looked back at him and tried to speak, but the man just walked past him and hissed at him. What is going on? He thought. As he turned the corner to go down the alleyway between the huts, he saw his neighbors standing outside of their huts talking. As he walked pass, they all stopped talking and turned to look at him. He was about to say hello when they all turned their backs to him. These were his neighbors! What is wrong? Stopping to look around, he did notice that the only neighbors that were out were Persians. All the Jewish neighbors were in their huts with their heavy black sheep skinned curtains pulled down. It was the middle of summer. It was too hot to have the curtains in front of the doors and windows. Mordecai apprehensively walked up to Reelaiah's hut, stopped in front calling out to him hoping he would answer. Since he escorted Esther to the King's palace Reelaiah, Tamara and their daughters completely ignored him. When they saw him in the streets or marketplace, they would walk away from him. Standing in front of his hut, he hoped Reelaiah would come out and talk to him.

"Reelaiah, Reelaiah, please come out. I need to talk to you. Please come out" Mordecai pleaded.

Reelaiah poked his head outside the curtain that covered his hut door. "What do you want Mordecai, what do you want!"

"I.., I just need to talk to you for a minute. Would you please come out, or could I possibly come in? Just for a few minutes?"

"Come out to you! No! And you are not welcome in my home ever again. You have done enough damage to us. Go away. I do not want to talk to you about anything!"

Something was drastically wrong. Fear suddenly pierced through the pit of his stomach as he turned from Reelaiah's hut and ran through the alley to his hut behind the village.

As he reached his porch out of breath, he saw a document tacked to the side of his hut door. Bending over to catch his breath, he reached up and took the document down, unfolded it as he walked inside and lit a candle. As he read the decree, Mordecai heard a high-pitched scream penetrating the quietness of his hut, and throughout the village before he realized that the sound was coming from inside of himself. Unbearable pain cut through his very soul. He could not contain the whelps and screams that emanated from his body. Reaching up with his hand, he tore the mantle that he wore and fell face down in the ashes and dirt in the middle of the floor. Continuing to scream, he got up, ran out of the hut down through the alley and back up to the palace gate. The porter on the King's gate, who was not a Jew, would not let him in. It was against the law for anyone dressed in sackcloth and ashes to enter onto palace property, so Mordecai laid on the street outside the palace gate crying bitterly and moaning, "no, no, please God, no" over and over and over. No one came to try and console him. Word had spread about his defiance against Haman. Now everyone knew that he was a Jew and knew of the King's Decree to kill all the Jews on the thirteenth of Adar.

Yara, one of Esther's personal servants, was walking down the courtyard. Hearing the crying she went to the gate to see what was going on. A man dressed in sackcloth and very dirty was on the ground crying and moaning. "What is wrong with that man?" she asked the porter.

"It is just that Jew, Mordecai. Since the King put out the new decree, a lot of them have been yelling, screaming, and crying. Not to worry, when he gets tired, I guess he will go on home."

Yara studied the man in the street a little longer and then gasped! "That is Queen Esther's father!" she said to herself. "I must go and tell her." Yara ran all the way to Esther's personal quarters. Running up to the door, the guards stepped in front of her and blocked Esther's door with their spears not letting her in. "Oh, please, please, I must see the Queen, would you please announce me to her? Please, it is very important!" Yara pleaded.

One of the guards looked closely at Yara. "Are you not one of her servants?" he asked.

"Yes, yes. I am Yara. I am her personal servant. Please, I must see her immediately."

The guard knocked on the door, "Your Majesty, your servant Yara is here to see you. Shall I show her in?"

"Yes, of course." Esther said sitting up on the couch as the door opened.

"Yara, what is it? Why are you upset?"

"Your father is outside of the palace gate on the ground in ragged clothes crying."

"Crying? Why is he crying? Why is he wearing sackcloth with ashes on his face?" Esther knew that something was terribly wrong for Mordecai to be dressed in sackcloth with ashes all over him. This kind of behavior in Jewish customs signified danger and disaster for the entire Jewish race and it grieved her to know something this dreadful had somehow affected Mordecai's well-being. "Yara, go get Hatach, have him get appropriate raiment for Mordecai to put on and then bring him here to my quarters."

"Yes, as you wish Your Majesty" Yara replied and ran out the door. Meeting Hatach, one of Esther's chamberlains in the hall, they both retrieved proper raiment and took them to the front gate where Mordecai was still laying in the street crying.

"Mordecai, Mordecai!" Hatach called from inside the gate. "Here, Queen Esther has sent this raiment for you to put on. Here, take them." Hatach handed the articles through the gate.

Mordecai lifted his head and looked to see who was calling him. He recognized Yara, Esther's personal servant. Through his tears he shook his head no and laid back down in the street and continued to cry and moan.

Hatach told Yara that he would go back to Queen Esther's quarters alone. The guards showed him in, he told Esther that Mordecai refused the raiment.

"Go to the gate and ask him what has happened to cause him to be vexed."

Hatach ran to the street where Mordecai was lying. "Mordecai, the Queen wants to know why you are troubled. What has happened to cause you to wear this sackcloth and ashes and to refuse her raiment that she sent for you to wear; what is wrong?" Hatach came outside of the gate, sat down on the ground beside Mordecai and helped him to sit up.

Wiping his tears with the back of his hand, Mordecai told Hatach of the King's decree sent out by Haman to kill all the Jews twelve months hence and the large amount of money Haman promised to add to the King's treasuries from killing all the Jews. "Here." Mordecai said to Hatach handing him the copy of the King's decree. "Show this decree to Queen Esther and tell her to go to the King and make an appeal to him for our people."

Hatach took the decree from Mordecai and showed it to Esther.

Taking the decree from Hatach's hand, Esther sat down on the couch, opened it up and began to read. Hatach stood silently waiting for further instructions as Esther read the document.

What she and Mordecai had feared had come to pass. Haman proved to be the enemy Mordecai said he was. He had moved up in power so quickly and now threatened to wipe out the entire Jewish nationality. Esther stood, walked over to the window sitting on the ledge looking outside as she contemplated Mordecai's request for her to petition the King on behalf of her people. Everyone knew, including Mordecai, that anyone approaching the King without him requesting their presence was put to death. Anyone. Ahasuerus had not called her to his personal chambers for 30 days and she knew she could lose her life instantly.

"Hatach, tell Mordecai that according to the law, no one is permitted to go in to see the King unless he calls for them personally. If anyone attempts to see him without his calling, they will be put to death." Esther turned to look at Hatach and nodded her head for him to go.

Mordecai still lay in the street as Hatach approached him again and delivered Esther's message to him.

"Tell Esther that even though she is Queen, she is still a Jew and will not escape being killed like the rest of us. Tell her that if she holds her peace, God will raise up someone else to deliver the Jews, but she and her father's house will be destroyed. Tell her that this may be the reason that God permitted her to be made Queen. Tell her!" Mordecai blurted out to Hatach.

Back in Esther's quarters, Hatach delivered Mordecai's message. He is right Esther thought. Mordecai is right. We were wondering why God had placed me here and this is the reason. "Hatach, tell Mordecai to go and gather all of the Jews in Shushan together. Tell them to fast for me. That they should neither eat nor drink for three days. I and my staff will also fast for three days, neither eating nor drinking. On the third day, I will go and see the King. If I perish, then I shall perish."

The porter that manned the gate watched Hatach go and come over and over delivering messages and taking messages back. He did not ask any questions, he just watched. This time was different through; when Hatach came and delivered the last message, he watched in surprise. Mordecai got up and walked away from in front of the palace back toward the village.

The first hut Mordecai stopped at was Reelaiah's. "Reelaiah, Reelaiah, come outside; I want to talk with you. Reelaiah, I know you hear me; it is urgent that I speak with you. Come out now!" Mordecai yelled with authority in his voice.

Reelaiah pulled back the curtain from the door and poked his head out.

"Come out here now!" Mordecai demanded.

Hearing the authority in his voice, Reelaiah came out and stood in front of Mordecai. Before he could open his mouth, Mordecai held up his hand. "Listen, I know that you and all of the brothers in Shushan are angry with me. Some of you even hate me. That is not important now. I have spoken with Queen Esther. She has instructed me to gather all the brethren together. The Queen instructed us to fast and pray for her for three days. On the third day she will go to the King and ask him to change the decree that Haman published to have us killed on the thirteenth of Adar. You, your family, and all the Jewish families must fast and pray. Our very lives depend upon it. Will you do this?"

Reelaiah stood there amazed at the authority with which Mordecai spoke.

"Reelaiah, did you hear me! Will you do this? We must all agree and become as one as we fast and pray. Will you do this? Will you gather all of the other Jewish families together and fast and pray?"

"Ah, yes Mordecai, yes. I…, we, I will gather everyone together starting tonight and we will do as you and Queen Esther have commanded us."

"Good" Mordecai replied and walked away. Mordecai knew that the Jews were all angry with him. News had spread around the village that all of this came about because he would not bow down to Haman. Mordecai explained himself to them; reminded them of Moses' law and told them what Queen Esther had commanded them to do. They all agreed and in one accord fasted and prayed for three days.

Esther called for all her servants to stand before her. When they arrived, she commanded them to neither eat nor drink anything for three days. They asked no questions, just bowed before her saying, "As you wish your Majesty" and she dismissed them.

On the third day, Esther put on her royal apparel and stood in the breezeway next to the King's royal throne. The King was sitting on his throne with the royal guards on either side of him when he spotted Esther standing in the outer court.

Ahasuerus looked at Esther and his heart warmed inside of him. He held out the golden scepter to her and Esther came forward and touched the scepter and bowed to him.

"Esther!" Ahasuerus said warmly. You have come to see me; do you have a request? Whatever your request is it shall be granted to you even up to half of my kingdom; it is yours if you request it."

Standing in front of Ahasuerus, Esther was surprised at how calm she was and how pleased the King was to see her. "Your Majesty, if it is pleasing to you, would you and Haman come this day to a banquet that I have prepared for the two of you?"

"As you wish my Queen" Ahasuerus said calling for the guard to instruct Haman to join them in Esther's personal quarters for a banquet in an hour.

Esther bowed before Ahasuerus again and left to prepare the banquet.

An hour later, Ahasuerus and Haman approached Esther's personal quarters and sat down at the table that was prepared before them. During the wine portion of the banquet, Ahasuerus asked, "now that we are here, what is your petition of me Queen Esther. Ask anything of me, even up to half of my kingdom and I will grant it to you." Ahasuerus watched Esther closely wanting to do anything to please her.

Looking at Haman then back at Ahasuerus, Esther took a sip of her wine. She was not sure how to phrase her request and a little nervousness came over her. "If I have found favor in your sight," she said as she sat her wine goblet down, "and if it pleases the King to grant my petition and to perform my request, would you and Haman come to a banquet that I shall prepare tomorrow; I shall reveal my request to you then."

"As you wish, my Queen" Ahasuerus said. They finished their dinner and he and Haman left Esther's quarters.

Ahasuerus and Haman went their separate ways. Ahasuerus went back to his personal quarters and Haman left the palace to go home. Happiness overwhelmed him as he went down the stairs to the gate. He could not wait to get home to share with his wife and friends that he and only he and the King were summoned to Queen Esther's quarters for a banquet. As he approached the gate, all the joy and happiness disappeared when he saw Mordecai tending the gate. This time Mordecai did not stand up and open the gate for him at all, he ignored him completely. Anger and indignation welled up in him, but he did not address Mordecai. Infuriated, he opened and closed the gate behind himself and walked home.

Zeresh, Haman's wife, his ten sons and several of his friends were all waiting for him when he reached his house. He told them of the glory and all the riches that he had acquired with his new position. "I have everything I could possibly want. My office is lavishly designed and very comfortable."

Parshandaltha, Haman's eldest son stood up, walked over to his father hugging him. "I am so proud of you father. When can we come and see your new office and tour the palace?"

Haman looked up beaming at his son. "Wait until I take care of a few things in the palace. There are some changes that need to take place before I have all of you as my guests." Haman looked all around the room at everyone smiling at him and continued telling them about his success. "All the servants I need or could ever want are at my beck and call. I am the only man, other than the King himself, that was beckoned to Queen Esther's quarters for a private banquet. Tomorrow, she has invited me and the King again for another private banquet" Haman boasted and then was quiet for a moment. "The only thing that concerns me is this Jew named Mordecai who sits at the King's gate."

"Did you not petition the King to have all of the Jews killed?" Zeresh asked.

"Yes, I did, and the decree has been sent out, but it will not take place until next year, Adar thirteenth" Haman replied sighing. "I have to put up with that Jew for a whole year!"

"Why not have gallows built 75 feet in the air and tomorrow ask the King for permission to hang this Mordecai early. He is a Jew and will be killed eventually anyway. Tell the King how he disrespected you and does not follow the King's law. Then you can enjoy the Queens banquet in peace knowing that that Jew will no longer be tending the palace gate; you will never have to see him again."

"That is an excellent plan" Haman exclaimed as he walked out the door of his house and summoned one of his servants appointed to him by the King giving him instructions to begin building the gallows. "Here," Haman said pointing his finger to the area out in front of his door. "Build it here so I and everyone in the area can see when we hang that Jew. We are going to let his body hang there for a while for all the other Jews in the area to see what is to befall them. Right there, yes, right there" Haman pointed again making sure his servant completely understood his instructions.

Satisfied with his plans, Haman walked around his house with his hands behind his back watching the gallows being built. When can I go in and get permission to kill Mordecai, he thought? Early tomorrow morning. The King is usually in a good mood then, yes, I will ask tomorrow morning. With one last look around, Haman went back into his house and went to bed.

Chapter Twelve

HAMAN'S PLOT EXPOSED

Ahasuerus walked around his bed chamber during the second watch of the night. He could not sleep. 'Oh no, he thought, I cannot sleep again!' It had been a while since he had had a sleepless night. I wonder what is on Esther's mind, what her request is going to be. She never asks anything for herself, it is always for someone else. I hope I have been giving her enough attention Ahasuerus thought. He walked over to his window and looked across both courtyards to Esther's private window. All of her lights were out. What kind of banquet is she preparing for us? And why? She never ceases to amaze me; I love that about her though. "Oh, I wish I could sleep" he said out loud and walked over and opened the door. "Guard!"

"Yes Your Majesty."

"Have the book of records brought to my throne room, The Chronicles" he commanded.

"As you wish Your Majesty" the guard replied and closed the door.

Ahasuerus put on his royal robe and the guard followed him down to his throne. Moments later the door opened. A servant carrying the Book of Chronicles came in, sat down, and began reading the history for the past three months. By the time the servant read where

Mordecai revealed Bigthan and Teresh's plot to have the King killed, it was daylight.

"What honor did we give this Mordecai for saving my life?" Ahasuerus asked.

"Nothing was done for him Your Majesty" the servant replied.

"Nothing huh?"

"No sir, nothing."

"Is there someone in the outer court?" Ahasuerus asked.

The servant got up and went to the door and opened it; it was Haman.

"It is Haman" the servant replied turning back to the King.

"Show him in."

Standing up straight with his shoulders back Haman marched into the throne room confident that whatever he requested was going to be granted to him. "Good morning Your Majesty! How are you this fine morning?" he said cheerfully.

"I am fine Haman. I have a question for you. What should be done unto the man whom the King delighteth to honor?"

To whom would the King desire to honor more than me Haman thought as he stood there looking at Ahasuerus. What else could I possible want? he asked himself; then, "for the man in whose honor the King delighteth, I would dress him in the royal apparel that the King wears; set him on the horse that the King rides on and place the King's Royal Crown upon his head. I would have all of this done unto the man by the King's most noble prince, then have that prince parade that man throughout the city streets on horseback and the noble prince leading him on foot telling everyone that this man is the man in whom the King delighteth. That is what I would do for that man your Majesty." Haman strutted back and forth before Ahasuerus proclaiming the honor he thought King Ahasuerus was going to shower on him.

"Yes!" Ahasuerus said. "Yes, Haman. Quickly, get the apparel, the horse as you said, everything that you said; have it all prepared for Mordecai, the Jew that sits at the King's gate. Put the royal apparel on him, the royal crown upon his head, set him on my horse and you,

you Haman, parade him throughout the city streets and proclaim him to be the man in whom I, King Ahasuerus delights in because he saved my life."

Haman could not believe what he was hearing. "Who, uh, who," he stuttered then tried to speak again. "Your Majesty, whom did you say?"

"His name is Mordecai, the porter that sits at the royal gate. I know you have seen him. He opens the gate for you every day. Him. Now go quickly and do as I have commanded you."

Haman was breathing heavily as he left the throne room and walked out to the breezeway to the top of the steps that led to the royal gate. Stopping at the top of the stairs, he took one last breath to give him the courage to do as the King ordered him. Maybe I could get one of my servants to get Mordecai for me, dress him and...., "no," he said out loud, "the King would find out if I do not do as he commanded. This is so humiliating, but I must do it." Stepping down one step at a time, Haman stretched his neck to see if Mordecai was at the gate this morning. He entered the palace through another gate upon arrival to the palace to avoid the possibility of seeing him before getting permission to have him killed. He thought he might not be working this shift and he could report back to the King that he was not there. But to his dismay, Mordecai was at his post.

Sitting with his back against the iron gate, Mordecai wondered who was stepping so slowly down the stairs. "Click..., click..., click." The sandals seemed to echo with each step. Getting up from his seat, Mordecai turned and looked through the bars, then sighed heavily, "Oh no, it is Haman again" Mordecai said to himself. Opening the gate, he waited for Haman to walk through. Why was he walking so slowly; he wondered if he was sick. Mordecai looked at him closely as he approached him; he appeared to be fine. Should I ask him if he is okay, he thought to himself. Just as Mordecai opened his mouth, Haman spoke.

"Mordecai, follow me."

"What?"

"Follow me."

"Where are we going?" Mordecai asked "and who will relieve me of my duties?

Haman sighed again. He had not thought about having someone to replace Mordecai at the gate. "Wait here, I will have your superior order one of the servants to replace you. After you are relieved from duty; join me in the King's royal throne room just up the stairs to the right. Do you understand?" Haman asked looking back at Mordecai as he started to climb the stairs again.

Trying to grasp what had just taken place, Mordecai did not answer Haman he just looked after him as he climbed the stairs.

When Haman did not hear a response from Mordecai he stopped, turned around on the stairs, and asked Mordecai again barely above a whisper, "Do you understand my orders to you Mordecai?"

"Yes" was the only reply Mordecai could manage. What is going on? Father, do I need to be concerned about following Haman's command? He prayed silently. As quickly as he prayed, a calm came over him and he felt at peace following Haman's orders. As soon as his replacement came, he joined Haman in the King's throne room as he was instructed.

Two servants stood beside Haman who was sitting on a stool by a table. Mordecai noticed some sort of raiment draped over the back of a chair. Haman motioned for Mordecai to come over to them.

"The King has ordered that you wear his royal raiment; his golden crown and for you to ride on his royal horse throughout the streets of Shushan. I am to lead you on foot and proclaim throughout the city that you are the man in whom the King honors and delights in for saving his life. These servants will help you to dress. When you are finished dressing, the King's royal horse and I will be waiting for you outside." When he had finished speaking, Haman turned and stomped out of the room slamming the door behind him.

As the servants dressed Mordecai, he marveled at everything that was happening. Somehow the King must have found out that it was me who foiled the assassination against him. Maybe this will help the King to see that it is wrong to kill all the Jews. Hope filled his heart. He remembered Esther telling him on one of their visits that once the King makes a law, that law can never be undone. Those decrees were sent out a month ago. Father, he prayed silently as the servants finished dressing him and were leading him outside to Haman, I know that nothing is impossible for you, and you have everything under control. Amen.

Haman stood beside the King's horse with his head down waiting for Mordecai to mount. Once he was firmly in the seat Haman led him through the city gates crying with a loud voice, "Hear ye, hear ye, hear ye. Here sits the man in whom the King honors and delights. This man saved the King's life." He repeated this saying over and over, up and down the city streets.

Reelaiah, Tamara and their family were eating breakfast talking among themselves when they heard the proclamation outside.

"What is happening now!" Reelaiah asked getting up from the table. Gingerly he moved toward the door and moved the curtain back ever so slightly peeking out to see what was going on. Most of the Jewish neighbors stayed indoors after the King's last decree against them and Reelaiah did not want to bring any attention to himself or his family regardless of what was happening in the alleyway. "Oh, oh my! Tamara come! Come and see this!" Reelaiah turned beckoning to Tamara. "Hurry! I do not believe my eyes! That is Mordecai sitting on the King's horse is it not! Do my eyes deceive me! Look!" Reelaiah stepped away from the door allowing Tamara space to look out.

"Oh, you are right Reelaiah! That is Mordecai. Why is he dressed in the King's raiment? He is even wearing the King's crown! Look, everyone is outside of their huts. Can we go out to see and hear what is going on?" Tamara asked looking back at her husband. Shakera and Aisha ran to the door begging to go outside.

Reelaiah pulled back the curtain from in front of the door looking up and down the alleyway. Everyone was out. "It looks to be safe enough; come, we will all go out. Who is that leading Mordecai's horse? Tamara, look! That looks like Haman. It is Haman! Listen, what is he saying?"

Just as Reelaiah and his family stepped outside, Haman and Mordecai made their way in front of their hut. Mordecai looked at

Reelaiah, Tamara Shakera and Aisha, nodding his head to them as Haman proclaimed "Hear ye, hear ye, hear ye, here sits the man in whom the King honors and delights. This man saved the King's life."

"Mordecai saved the King's life? How did he do that!" Reelaiah asked looking at Tamara in amazement.

"I do not know Reelaiah" Tamara replied shaking her head from side to side as she watched the two men going thought the alley. "I thought Haman was Mordecai's biggest enemy! How did his biggest enemy end up parading him throughout the street and alleyways of Shushan?"

"How did Mordecai save the King's life! Something drastic always seems to be happening to Mordecai" Reelaiah said as he ushered his family back inside. "Does the King know that Mordecai is a Jew and that he signed an edict to have all of the Jews killed? Haman is the man that influenced the King to have us killed! This is strange. Very strange indeed" Reelaiah replied returning to his seat.

"It sounds to me like God is at work" Tamara said as she began to clear the dishes from the table. "Esther instructed us to fast and pray for three days which we did and now this. Yes, I believe God is working things out for his children."

"I believe you are right Tamara. I wish I knew how He planned to work them out" Reelaiah said as he leaned back against the wall and finished his tea.

It took five hours for Haman to cover all the streets and alley ways throughout Shushan. By the time they returned to the palace, Haman was exhausted. His throat was sore from yelling the King's Proclamation. He did not wait for Mordecai to dismount the horse. As soon as they reached the palace gate, he dropped the horse's reigns and ran home through the back alleys with his head covered so no one would recognize him. He felt so degraded.

Mordecai marveled at the way God worked as he watched Haman run down the back streets of Shushan with his head covered. "Father, you are an awesome God, there is no other God like you" Mordecai said out loud as he dismounted the King's horse. His heart was full of praise and thanksgiving, and he sang songs to himself as he returned to work.

Reaching his house, Haman rushed in and fell on his couch with his hands covering his head. Zeresh his wife, his sons, his wise men, and his friends were all at the house waiting for him. They heard his proclamation and saw him leading Mordecai on the King's horse throughout all Shushan. They all rushed over to his house to ask Zeresh what he was doing?

"I went to the palace early this morning to ask the King for permission to hang Mordecai as we discussed last night. Before I could ask him, he asked me what I would do for the man in whom the King delighted, the man that the King Honored. I thought he was talking about me!" Haman lifted his head and pounded on his chest. "Me!" he cried through the hoarseness of his throat. "So I told him I would dress him in the King's royal apparel, place the King's golden crown upon his head and ride him on the King's royal horse throughout the city streets proclaiming him the man whom the King honored. I really thought he was talking about me!" Haman sobbed. "Here he was talking about Mordecai, that Jew! Sometime ago, Mordecai apparently overheard two of the King's guards plotting to kill him. He told Queen Esther about it who informed the King who had the guards hung. For some reason, the King choose to honor Mordecai for his actions today." Haman got up from the couch and walked over to the table and sat down with his head hung low.

Zeresh sat down at the table with him and held his hands in hers. "If this Mordecai is a Jew, your plan to destroy him and his people is going to fail. You will never succeed against him!" Zeresh looked at Haman with worry. Haman's wise men agreed with her saying, "the King rarely bestows that type of honor on anyone" one of them said. As they continued talking, the King's chamberlain knocked at the door.

"Yes, who is it?" Haman yelled.

"It is King Ahasuerus' chamberlains, to escort you to Queen Esther's banquet."

"I will be with you in a minute" Haman replied as he got up from the table and splashed cold water on his face. Looking at his wife and friends, Haman did not know what to say. He hung his head and left with the chamberlains.

Esther stood in the lounge area of her personal quarters making sure that the seating for the banquet she was preparing for Ahasuerus and Haman was appropriate. The back of her couch was to the fireplace, Ahasuerus' couch was to her left and Haman's couch was in front of them both with the banquet table in between. Fresh cut roses from the flower garden outside of Esther's palace were place on stands by each couch filling the room with a sweet fragrance.

Yesterday, I was not sure how to phrase my request to Ahasuerus, Esther thought; but today, "Lord," she spoke out loud, "I believe you will put the correct words in my mouth and at the right time with the right emphasis. I am ready" she said as she walked over to the window and looked across the meadows.

"Queen Esther," the guard called through the door; "the King and Haman are here.

"Please show them in." Esther replied.

The guard opened the door and Ahasuerus walked over to Esther, embracing her as he kissed her lightly on the lips. "How are you today Esther?" he asked as he led her to her couch and helped her to sit down.

"I am very well, Your Majesty," Esther replied.

After the King and Queen were seated, Haman bowed at the waist and said, "Good evening Queen Esther."

"Good evening Haman" Esther replied and motioned for him to take his seat on the couch on the other side of the banquet table. As soon as everyone was comfortable, Esther clapped her hands for the servants to begin serving the wine.

Ahasuerus picked up his goblet full of wine and raised it up in a toast to Esther, "To my beautiful and gracious Queen Esther" he said.

Haman joined him in raising his goblet, drank, but said nothing; he was still exhausted from his earlier activities of the day.

Ahasuerus sipped more of his wine as he looked at Esther. "Now that we have returned to your banquet, what is your petition of me Esther? What is it that you wish for me to do for you? Whatever it is, it will be granted to you even up to half of my kingdom. What is your wish?" Ahasuerus waited patiently for Esther's response.

"Your Majesty," Esther began, "if I have found favor in your sight, and if it pleases you, let my life be given to me as my request and the life of my people as well. For we are sold, I and my people, to be destroyed to be slaughtered and to perish. If we would have been sold into a service of slavery to the King for some offense that we had committed against your government, I would not be making this request. This request for the destruction of me and my people is made by one man and for no other reason than his own personal greed. He would have you believe that the amount of wealth you would gain by destroying me and my people would increase your treasuries three-fold. However, by killing us, the amount of currency you would lose in taxes alone would decrease your wealth because you would no longer have those individuals paying taxes into the kingdom's treasuries." Esther could see that Ahasuerus was a little confused and paused a moment to give him time to think.

"Kill you! Kill your people! Esther, what are you talking about? Why would I kill you or your people?" Ahasuerus moved from his couch and sat beside Esther holding her hand. He could see she was very upset and that caused him to be upset as well.

Haman sat on the couch listening to Esther's petition, but she phrased her request in such a way that he had no idea she was talking about him. He did not know who Esther's people were and he sat there sipping his wine in silence trying to keep from yawning.

"Esther," Ahasuerus continued, "tell me who are your people?"

"My people are the Jews dispersed throughout your kingdom Your Majesty. We have lived happily and peacefully among you since King Cyrus freed us from the Babylonians many years ago. We lived peacefully with you until now."

Haman sat straight up on his couch; she is a Jew! He thought. No, no, no, how could a Jew be made Queen of Persia! His mind was racing, what had he done, what could he do to save himself.

Ahasuerus stood up looking down at Esther and asked, "who is he that would dare touch you and any of your people? Who is he Esther!"

Esther pointed her finger at Haman, "it is this evil man Haman!" she cried.

Ahasuerus whirled around and glared at Haman sitting on the couch then stormed out of the room to the palace garden pacing up and down.

Haman got up from his couch and fell at Ether's feet leaning against her couch pleading for his life. "Queen Esther, please, please forgive me. If I had known that your people were the Jews, I would have never, never..." he reached up to try and grab Esther's hands pleading his case just as the King returned to the room.

"What! Will you try to take my wife right before my very eyes!" Ahasuerus screamed! "Right in front of me! Guards! Guards!" Two guards broke through the door and dragged Haman away from Queen Esther tying his hands behind his back. After the guards had subdued Haman, Ahasuerus walked over to him and wrenched his ring off Haman's hand putting it back on his ring finger. Harbona, one of the King's chamberlains standing behind the guards spoke.

"Your Majesty, Haman just had a 75-foot gallows built in front of his house last night. He had it in his mind to ask permission from you to hang Queen Esther's father, Mordecai, who looked out for you and saved your life from Bigthan and Teresh's plot to kill you."

Ahasuerus stepped back and looked at Haman in disgust. How could he have ever befriended such a man. "Take him and hang him on his own gallows!"

Hearing the King's command, Haman began screaming and kicking trying to get away from the guards, but they had a good grip on both his arms. They drug him out of Queen Esther's palace, down the long hall and to the top of the stairs leading to the gate. Haman did not have very much voice left after leading Mordecai through the streets earlier that day and by the time he and the guards reached the top of the stairs, all Mordecai heard from the King's gate were muffled sobs and intermittent "no, no, please no." Looking through the bars of the gate he saw two guards holding a man thrashing back and forth sobbing, trying to free himself from the guards. As the men came closer, he recognized Haman. "What, what is happening?" Mordecai asked as he opened the gate for the guards, Haman and Harbona to walk through.

"This is Haman" Harbona said watching the guards struggling with him. "The King has ordered him to be hung on the very gallows he had built to hang you on!" Harbona stated as a matter of fact then followed the three men to Haman's house.

Mordecai watched as the men drug Haman through the street toward his house in amazement. Hearing the commotion, people began gathering around the men and followed them as they made their way through the city streets. Mordecai did not follow them but watched as the mob flooded the streets yelling, screaming, and raising their fists in the air. Word spread quickly that Haman, the King's number one Prince was to be hung.

Closing the gate, Mordecai was about to go back to his seat when Reelaiah approached.

"What is happening Mordecai! We were about to go to bed when we heard people running through the alleyways toward the main street. I told my family to stay inside and to keep the window and door covered."

Mordecai turned to face his friend. "Our God works in wonderfully mysterious ways. That mob is following the King's servants who have orders to hang Haman."

"Hang Haman! He was leading you around on the King's horse as you wore the King's crown this morning! What happened from this morning until now?"

"Harbona, one of the King's servants who received orders to have Haman hung told me as he went through the gate that King Ahasuerus ordered Haman to be hung on the very gallows he had built to hang me on."

"I do not understand. Did he not petition the King to have all of us killed? Why would he build gallows to specifically hang you?"

"I am not sure. Esther commanded us to fast and pray four days ago. I believe God is answering our prayers. When I know more, I will let you and the others know." Mordecai sighed, turned, and sat down on his makeshift stool. With all that had taken place earlier in the day; fatigue was washing over his body. Reelaiah could see the exhaustion overwhelming his friend and sat down on the ground beside him.

"Mordecai" he began slowly, "I.., I am so sorry for the way I treated you. Can you ever forgive me and the other brothers for the way we treated you? I.., we, all of us believed that what you were doing went against our teachings. We did not believe you were hearing from God when you allowed Esther to compete for the Queen's position. Even after she was made Queen, we still did not believe it was of God. Now...,"

Mordecai held up his hand. "You do not need to say anything more Reelaiah. I forgive you and all the brothers. I understand. If the situation were reversed, I probably would have acted the same as all of you. Of course I forgive you. I forgive all of you." The two men sat quietly for several minutes listening to the crowd.

"What do you think will happen after Haman is dead?"

"I am not sure. I will have to wait and talk to Esther in the morning. She will let me know what is to be done."

"I should be getting back home. I know Tamara must be worried." Reelaiah stood up and began to walk away but stopped and came back to Mordecai. "Mordecai, thank you for all that you and Esther have done for our people. Thank you."

"You do not need to thank me, thank God. It is not all done yet. Haman's decree has not been canceled yet; we must continue to pray. I know God is at work and everything will be alright eventually. Go home to your family and have a good night's rest."

"Goodnight Mordecai" Reelaiah replied and turned and walked away. Mordecai continued to watch the crowd of people running toward the gallows.

By the time Harbona, the servants and Haman reached Haman's house, the crowd surrounded the front of the house where the gallows was erected. Haman would no longer walk and the guards drug him up the steps where the rope was thrown over the beam.

Seeing the crowd assembling in front of her house, Zeresh, her family and friends peered out the window. "Who is that!" Zeresh yelled. Then she recognized Haman's raiment. "No, no, no!" she screamed and tried to run outside and up the steps of the gallows, but Haman's wise men grabbed her and pulled her back into the house.

The guards finally reached the top of the gallows and moved Haman to the center where the trap door was. Haman would not stand up. "Let him lay there!" one of the guards said out of breath. As long as he is over the trap door, we can put the rope around his neck, step away and unlatch the door. He did a good job in building this gallows 75 feet in the air; there is plenty of space down below to do the job effectively."

All around the gallows the people were whispering quietly asking "Who are they hanging and why?" One man answered, "That is Haman, you know the man King Ahasuerus just promoted above all his other princes. They told me he tried to have his way with Queen Esther!"

"Really?" The man asked.

"No!" another man said. "He did not try to have his way with her, he tried to kill her and all of her people. She is a Jew, and no one knew it! Remember the Decree the King sent out to everyone that all Persian countrymen should be prepared to kill all the Jews on the thirteenth of Adar and take all their wealth? Well, I heard that this Haman fellow was the one who convinced the King to issue that decree."

"What is going to happen to the Jews now?" another man in the crowd asked. No one answered.

"Everything is ready!" the guard yelled standing up from putting the rope around Haman's neck and stepped away from him standing on the solid part of the platform. "Pull the latch! He yelled. The guard on the ground pulled the latch and the trap door opened with a loud clank as the trap door hit against the post underneath the platform. Haman's body fell through the floor with a thud and all the people gasped. His feet jerked and swung from side to side it seemed forever before his body became still. One by one, the crowd dispersed and went to their own homes.

Zeresh jerked away from one of Haman's wise men who was restraining her from going outside to the gallows and fell in one of the chairs at the table wailing and sobbing. "You could have stopped him from trying to kill those Jews! You could have advised him that it would be a trap that could get him killed. You are his wise men! You did not do your job! Now he is dead!"

All ten of Zeresh's sons were in the room crying. One of them bent down on his knees in front of her trying to console her.

"Mother, you know how adamant father was about the Jews; he hated them with a passion. No one could have persuaded him not to do what he did. He would not listen to anyone, not even his wise men!"

"What is going to happened to us now?" Zeresh asked looking up at the five wise men standing by the door.

"Nothing I hope" one of the wise men said. "Hopefully the King's wrath will be appeased by Haman's death. I strongly suggest that all of you, especially the ten of you sons, keep a very, very low profile."

"A low profile?" The son who was on his knees in front of Zeresh asked as he stood up drying his tears. "What do you mean a low profile?"

"What I mean is that all of you must stay away from the palace, avoid the marketplace. If you must go out, go out at night. If you encounter any Jews, do not let them know you are Haman's sons, do not tell them what your name is. Do not go to work."

"No work?"

"Do not go to work! You should have enough money from Haman's estate for all of you and your mother to survive on. Stay inside during the day. Let one of your friends go to the marketplace and buy the supplies you need and bring them to you. But all of you must stay inside at least until the King's wrath subsides.

One of Zeresh's other sons walked over to the window and looked out. His father's body still hung from the gallows. There were only three or four people standing around; the guards had left Haman's body hanging at the end of the rope.

"How long are they going to let father's body hand there?" he asked with tears streaming down his face. "I am going to go out there and get him and give him a proper burial!" he blurted out as he quickly moved toward the door.

One of the other wise men stood in front of the door blocking him.

"That is not a wise thing to do. Unfortunately, your father's body will hang there until the King decides to have it taken down. If any of you approach the King requesting a proper burial, his anger may be rekindled, and he may give the order to have all of you hung! Is that what you want?"

All the sons shook their heads no and looked down at the floor.

"I know this is very difficult for all of you" the wise men said looking at Zeresh and the ten sons. "Keep all of your windows and doors closed. Do not let any of your neighbors in and none of you go out until the King has the body removed. The palace guards will remove your father's body when the King orders them to do so. Until then, stay inside and keep a very low profile as I advised earlier. This is all the advice we have to offer you. Now that Haman is dead, we will be leaving this area to seek employment in another city. Remember all that we have said to you. We are sorry for your loss; may the gods be with you."

The wise men stood silently looking at Zeresh and her ten sons then left them alone.

Zeresh sat at the table quietly. "The wise men said we must stay inside until the King removes your father's body. I suggest we leave and go to Haman's homeland; go to his people, the Amalekites."

"Do you know where his people are mother?"

"Yes, I know. We cannot leave this place yet, but we can send a messenger to his homeland explaining our situation. Maybe they will allow us to join them."

"How are we going to get a messenger? We cannot leave this house!"

Zeresh looked around at each of her sons. "After dark, one of you put on all black raiment, sneak out the back door and meet up with one of the messengers at the palace. Be very discrete, surely there is someone who will be sympathetic to our situation. Take these 50 pieces of silver" Zeresh took the top off one of the clay jars sitting on top of the table and placed them in her son's hand. "If they are not sympathetic with us, this will persuade them. While we are waiting until it gets dark, I will write a letter to the Amalekites in Canaan. Make sure all of the windows and doors are shut and locked securely."

Zeresh walked over and sat down at Haman's desk and began to write the letter. Her sons went into every room closing and locking all the windows and doors as their mother instructed them.

Esther and Ahasuerus were alone in the lounge after the guards took Haman out to the gallows. Still very much upset, Ahasuerus stood at the window looking out over the courtyard.

"Your Majesty," Esther said softly to get his attention. "Our people are still in danger. The decree that Haman put on the books to kill all the Jews on the thirteenth of Adar is still in effect and on that date me and my people will be massacred. If I have found favor with you and if you think it seems good to you, could letters be written to reverse Haman's decree?"

Turning from the window, Ahasuerus rejoined Esther sitting beside her on the couch. "It shall be reversed this very night Esther. Here," he handed her a goblet of wine, "have a couple of sips of wine, it will help to relax you."

Esther accepted the wine as Ahasuerus lifted the goblet and handed it to her. Drinking two or three sips she sat back against the couch folding her hands in her lap.

"Esther," Ahasuerus asked, "who is Mordecai? Is he related to you in any way?"

"He is my father" Esther replied, "well, my adopted father. My real father and mother died when we were in captivity in Babylon. Mordecai is really my cousin; our family is from the tribe of Benjamin. After my parents died, he saw me sitting on the ground by myself, picked me up and decided to raise me as his own daughter. We have been together ever since."

"Guard!" Ahasuerus yelled; Esther flinched. She was not expecting him to call for the guard. "Oh, I am sorry my dear, I did not mean to startle you."

Opening the door and poking his head through the guard asked, "May I be of assistance to you Your Majesty?"

"Yes, the porter at the King's gate, his name is Mordecai. Go and escort him here to Queen Esther's quarters immediately and inform the scribes to report here with their supplies."

"As you wish Your Majesty" the guard replied.

Feeling quite warm on the inside from the wine, Esther sat up and began eating a piece of bread and fish and served some to Ahasuerus. Moments later, Mordecai and the scribes stood in the doorway being announced by the guard.

"Ahasuerus walked over and met Mordecai at the door, shook his hand and led him to the couch and had him to sit down while directing the scribes to set up their equipment behind the couches. "I understand that you are Esther's father" he said as he sat down beside Esther again.

"Yes, Your Majesty, I am Esther's father."

"First, I want to thank you personally for all that you have done for me in preventing the plot for my life. Today, I have turned over the entire household of Haman into Queen Esther's hands to do with as she pleases." Ahasuerus took off his ring, stood up and motioned Mordecai to stand also, then continued, "I am giving you my ring," he placed the King's ring on Mordecai's hand. "Do you understand what I have just done?" he asked.

Mordecai looked down at the ring on his finger and then back at Ahasuerus. "I am not sure Your Majesty" he said looking at Esther for help.

"All of the power and authority that was granted to Haman is now granted to you by your acceptance and wearing of the King's Ring."

After Ahasuerus placed the ring on Mordecai's finger, Esther stood, "Mordecai, father, as Queen of the 127 Provinces of Persia, I hereby place you as the head of Haman's household and all of his riches to go along with the King's authority and power." Esther walked around the table to where Mordecai stood, hugged, and kissed him on the cheek then returned to her seat as Ahasuerus continued.

"My scribes are here. Prepare a decree that all Jews throughout the Persian Kingdom are to stand and defend themselves on the thirteenth of Adar in the King's name and seal it with the King's ring. No one can reverse any document that is written in the King's name and sealed with the King's ring," Ahasuerus concluded and sat down beside Esther.

It took Mordecai a few moments to gather his thoughts together before dictating the reversal letter to the scribes. Once he began to concentrate, the words flowed smoothly.

"TO ALL JEWS, LIEUTENANTS, DEPUTIES, SOLDIERS AND RULERS THROUGHOUT THE 127 PROVINCES OF PERSIA FROM INDIA UNTO ETHIOPIA; UNTO EVERY PEOPLE AFTER THEIR LANGUAGES: ON THE THIRTEENTH DAY OF ADAR, ALL JEWS IN EVERY CITY ARE TO GATHER THEMSELVES TOGETHER AND STAND FOR THEIR LIVES, TO DESTROY, TO SLAY, AND TO CAUSE TO PERISH ALL PEOPLE IN EVERY PROVINCE THAT WOULD ASSAULT THEM, MEN AND WOMEN, YOUNG AND OLD ALIKE. ALL JEWS SHOULD BE READY ON THAT DAY TO AVENGE THEMSELVES OF THEIR ENEMIES."

Mordecai sealed the decrees with the King's ring and instructed the scribes to immediately send the letters with the King's swiftest messengers on horseback, camels, and young dromedaries or camel runners. When the dictation was completed, Mordecai joined Esther and Ahasuerus and the three of them ate the banquet dinner Esther prepared for Haman, and the King.

After dinner, Ahasuerus and Esther stood as they instructed the servants to prepare personal quarters for Mordecai somewhere close in proximity between Queen Esther's and the King's quarters. "You will serve and honor Mordecai just as you serve and honor the Queen and me" Ahasuerus commanded. While those preparations are being made, draw a bath for him and prepare royal raiment for him to wear. Do you have any questions?"

"No, Your Majesty" the servants replied. "If you are ready Sire, I will escort you to your personal quarters." Mordecai looked at Ahasuerus waiting for him to follow the servant.

"Mordecai," Ahasuerus said smiling, "I think the servant was addressing you. You will have to adjust to being treated like the royalty you are now." He and Esther looked at each other and smiled. Mordecai blushed lowering his head saying "goodnight Your Majesties" and followed the servant out the door.

Esther and Ahasuerus sat back down on the couch. "It is getting late," Ahasuerus said. "I think I should be going as well."

"Do you really have to go?" Esther asked looking at him.

Ahasuerus looked at Esther quietly studying her face. He knew it had been a month or more since he had called her to his bed chamber but considering everything that had happened tonight, he thought she might want to be alone. "You want me to stay with you here, tonight?" he asked in amazement. He was not use to anyone desiring his presence out of affection. Whatever he wanted, he always had to demand it. This was new to him, his Queen wanting him to stay with her. When Esther did not respond to his question, he looked down at her face.

"Do you really have to go?" Esther asked again looking at him.

"No….," he hesitated studying her face. "I can stay if you want me to."

"I want you to stay" Esther said as she reached up putting her hands around his neck kissing him passionately.

Following the servant down the hall, Mordecai looked at the ring the King placed on his finger. It was made of solid gold. He felt the weight of it as he held his hand up to his face. To his surprise, the ring fit his finger perfectly. The King's seal on top of the ring was set in bold type symbolizing the power and authority the jewelry possessed.

Turning the corner, the servant led Mordecai into the bathing area and attempted to remove his clothing. Mordecai put up his hand and stopped him. The servant looked to be about 30 or 35 years of age and Mordecai asked him, "What is your name?"

The servant stepped back, bowed at the waist then stood up, "my name is Zethaiah my lord. I was one of Haman's servants ordered to serve you. Please forgive me if I have overstepped my authority but bathing you is part of my duties."

"Well…, Zethaiah, thank you for your service. We need to come to an understanding."

"As you wish my lord" Zethaiah said bowing at the waist again.

"First Zethaiah, it is not necessary to refer to me as 'my lord,' you may address me as 'Sir,' is that understood?'

"Yes my lor…, ah, yes Sir."

"Second, do not bow down to me or to worship me in any way. Is that clear?"

"Yes sir" Zethaiah responded being very much surprised by his new orders

"Finally, it is not necessary for you to dress, undress or actually bathe me. I am capable of doing these things for myself; is that understood?"

With a smile on his face, Zethaiah responded loudly, "Yes Sir!"

Mordecai looked at Zethaiah, smiled, then held out his hand to shake Zethaiah's hand. Zethaiah did not know how to respond so Mordecai grabbed his hand and shook it. "It is going to be a pleasure working with you Zethaiah" he said while shaking his hand. "Now that we have a good understanding of what is expected of each other, will you please show me where the raiment is that I shall wear; the towels I will need to bathe with. I will take my bath in private. Oh, where will you be when I am finished bathing, I do not know where my bed chamber is located?"

"Ah, your, ah, your raiment is laid out here on this chair, Sir, your towels are folded and are placed on the edge of the pool. I will be right outside in the hall waiting for you. When you are ready to go to your quarters, just call. Is there anything else that you think you will need Sir?"

Mordecai looked around the room then back at Zethaiah, "No," he said slowly, "I think I have everything I need. Thank you again for your service Zethaiah."

"You are most welcome kind Sir" Zethaiah replied, turning leaving Mordecai alone in the room. As he stood in the hall waiting for Mordecai to finish his bath, Abagtha walked up to him. "Why are you standing here in the hallway instead of helping Mordecai with his bath like the King instructed you?"

"He, Mordecai, would not let me bathe him or undress him, or help him in any way with his bath. He said he could do all of that by himself. He also told me not to address him as 'Sire, my lord' or for me to bow down to him and worship him. He told me to address him as 'Sir' and only 'Sir'" Zethaiah said raising his eyebrows and his voice. "He shook my hand and said, 'thank you for your service! He thanked me for serving him!'"

Abagtha shook his head in awe, "Yara, Queen Esther's personal servant said she was very pleasant to work with too, nothing like Queen Vashti. She too thanked Yara and all her other servants for serving her and even made gifts for them, sweaters, blankets, and socks. Yara said she really enjoyed serving her and was very happy when the King re-assigned Queen Esther to her again."

Both Abagtha and Zethaiah were quiet standing in the hallway both thinking about the changes in the royal palace. "Things are changing around here, Zethaiah" Abagtha said. "I think they are changing for the better for us and all of Persia."

"I think so too" Zethaiah replied. "Where are you off to?"

"Home." "I am going home. The King and Queen have given me the night off."

"Have a good evening then," Zethaiah said sitting down on the marble floor crossing his legs under himself with his back against the wall.

"I will. I most certainly will" Abagtha said as he walked down the hall whistling a tune.

Mordecai disrobed and cautiously stepped down into the soapy water. The water was at just the right temperature, not too hot and not too cool. He felt his entire body relax as he sat down and leaned his back against the tiled ledge inside the pool. Having never experienced being totally submerged in a warm soapy bath, he moved his arms and feet around splashing in the water like a little child at play and was glad no one was around to witness this activity.

Finally becoming adjusted to the water, he began to reflect on all that had taken place during the day beginning with the King honoring him with his royal apparel, his crown and being led throughout the entire city by his number one enemy, Haman, proclaiming how the King favored him. God's Divine Providence, he thought. He remembered he and Esther sitting in their little dirt hut discussing God's Divine Providence regarding the rebuilding of the temple in Jerusalem. I never imagined you found Esther and me worthy enough to work your Divine Providence so intimately in our lives to influence the outcome of the Jewish Nation.

While he lay there in the pool, Mordecai remembered the words that King David penned in the holy writings. How he praised God for delivering him from his enemies. "Lord, you have done the same for me, Esther, and all of your people! How I love you. I will praise your name forever" Mordecai whispered.

I know that these Holy writings were referencing King David, Mordecai thought, but I can also see how they apply to me in a lot of respects. "I am not a warrior as King David was, a Priest from the Levitical Tribe, or a Prophet," Mordecai said a little above a whisper so Zethaiah could not hear him. "However, I did have an enemy in Haman." Changing his position in the water, he continued thanking and praising God for all He had done that day as streams of tears flowed down his face. "Oh Father," Mordecai prayed out loud, "now that you have placed Esther and me in these high positions, please guide our feet and light our path as we walk day to day careful to be mindful of your will, that we continue to obey you and your laws all the days of our lives. Thank you Father, thank you. I pray in the name of the God of Abraham, Isaac and Jacob, Amen."

Zethaiah was not sure if he heard Mordecai call him or not and yelled from the hall, "is there something that you need Sir?"

"No, I am fine. I will be ready in a few minutes" Mordecai yelled back, washed off and dried quickly putting on his clothes. "Zethaiah, I am ready."

"Yes Sir" Zethaiah replied getting up off the floor and entering the pool area.

"How do you let this water out of the pool?" Mordecai asked.

"Oh Sir, you do not have to trouble yourself with that, I and the other servants appointed to you will take care of this as well as the maintenance in your personal bed chamber." Zethaiah delivered his answer in such a tone that Mordecai knew there was no arguing with him to change his mind.

"Come," Zethaiah said. "I will escort you to your bed chamber."

Suddenly feeling the stress of all the activity of the day on his body, Mordecai realized that he was emotionally drained as well as physically exhausted. "How far is my bed chamber from here?" he asked.

"Not far Sir, just around this corner."

Turning the corner, Zethaiah opened the door to a large lounge area. "This is your private lounge area. "Over here," pointing across the large room to the other side as they continued to walk, "here is your personal bed chamber." Zethaiah opened the door, walked over to the bed turning down the covers. The fireplace was burning, but Mordecai did not notice. He followed Zethaiah to the bed, sat down swinging his feet up on the bed and under the covers, laid back on the bed and mumbled "Thank you Zethaiah."

Zethaiah smiled at him, covered him up and said "You are most welcome Sir" in a whisper and walked toward the door. Looking back to make sure his master was all right, he was surprised; Mordecai was asleep. He closed the door softly and left.

Mordecai awoke early in the morning before the sun arose. Sitting up, he slipped out of bed, put on a robe that lay across the foot of the bed, slipped his feet in the sandals on the floor and walked around his bed chamber. The fire from the fireplace was burning brightly and lit the room enough for him to see the lavish furniture, drapes, and fine linen bed clothes. This is the way Esther has been living since she left our little hut back in the village, he thought. I remember her telling me how long it took her to adjust to living here. Walking over to the door, he listened to see if there was anyone out in the lounge area before opening the door. Hearing no movement, he opened the door and walked around his personal lounge area. His area was designed the same as Esther's lounge area with the same exquisite furniture made of gold and silver and another large fireplace with a fire burning on the far wall opposite his bed chamber.

He felt well rested even though he had slept in a strange bed in a strange room. Sitting down on the over-stuffed chair in front of the fire, he thought about the events of the previous day and again, bowed his head in thanksgiving to God for His goodness and His Divine Providence.

Wide awake, Mordecai opened the door that opened to the hall and was startled by the two guards standing on each side of the doorway.

"May we be of service to you Sir?"

"Oh, I did not expect anyone to be out here" Mordecai said looking at the guards.

"We were assigned to stand guard for you by the King Sir."

"Oh," Mordecai replied. "Am I free to walk throughout the palace?

"You are free to go where you please Sir. The King provides security for you because of your high rank in the Persian Empire, however, it is at your discretion. We stand guard at your personal quarters for your security during the evening hours and while you sleep during the night until breakfast is served in the morning."

"What time is breakfast usually served?"

"What time would you like your breakfast to be served Sir?" the guard asked.

"Can you tell me what hour of the morning it is now?"

"It is the first hour, sunrise, Sir."

Mordecai thought for a moment. The first hour is quite early to bother the staff for breakfast. Looking back at one of the tables in the lounge area he spotted a bowl of fresh fruit and some nuts. "Would you please have my breakfast served here in my lounge area at the end of the first hour?"

"As you wish Sir. Is there anything else we can arrange for you? Would you like to have your bath drawn before breakfast or after?"

"If you could have Zethaiah bring my raiment for today after breakfast, that is all I will require. Thank you."

"As you wish Sir" the guard replied and closed the door after Mordecai returned inside.

Mordecai took the bowl of fruit and nuts off the table and set them on the table beside the chair in front of the fireplace. Walking over to the window, he tied back the drapes with the velvet cord, sat down in the chair eating the fruit and nuts and watched the fire in the fireplace. Fifteen minutes later, he was fast asleep again.

Feeling something warm across his face, Ahasuerus opened his eyes and realized it was the sun shining through the window onto the bed. For a moment he did not know where he was. The sun never filtered through his windows in his personal bed chamber. He sat up and looked around the room then down at the bed and saw Esther sleeping soundly next to him. "I slept here with Esther last night" he said softly to himself. He was strangely happy as he lightly laid back down trying not to awake her as someone knocked on the door.

"Queen Esther, Queen Esther, are you awake, may I come in?"

It was a female voice and Ahasuerus did not recognize it.

Esther sat up answering "Yes Yara, you may come in" before she remembered that Ahasuerus was in bed with her. "Oh, wait!" but it was too late, Yara opened the door and was already inside tending to the fire with towels and dresses hung over her arm. Her back was to both Esther and Ahasuerus as she went about her morning duties. Neither Ahasuerus nor Esther said a word. They both sat up in bed with the blankets pulled up around their necks and watched Yara.

The fire finally stoked to her liking, Yara turned around and was about to say good morning but gasped and dropped the things she was carrying on the floor. "Oh, Oh, Your Majes... Oh, I am sorry.... I did not know...."

Esther and Ahasuerus looked at each other and laughed out loud for several minutes. Yara ran out of the room and Esther called behind her. "Yara, Yara, it is alright, please come back. Everything is fine."

Yara returned to the room with her head down too embarrassed to look at either of them. "Please, please forgive me Your Highnesses. I was not aware that the King was here. If I had known, I would not have come in, please forgive me."

"There is nothing to forgive..., Yara...? is it?" Ahasuerus asked looking at Esther.

"Yes, her name is Yara" Esther said still smiling. "The King is correct, there is nothing to forgive, we are married!" Esther said and burst out laughing again falling back in the bed. With that, Ahasuerus began to laugh again and Yara joined in.

After regaining their composure, Ahasuerus looked at Esther, "My lady, what is your pleasure, shall we bathe, dress then have breakfast, or should we have breakfast, bathe and then dress?"

"Esther looked at him with a twinkle in her eye. "Could we have breakfast in bed, sleep some more, then bathe and dress?" she asked with laughter in her voice.

"You never cease to amaze me Esther" he said looking down at her as she laid back in the bed. This is almost too good to be true, he thought to himself. Someone like her in love with me. "Well," he began slowly and looked up at Yara who was picking up the dresses and towels from the floor. "Yara,"

"Yes Your Highness" Yara replied standing still.

"Would you please have Abagtha to locate Memucan and have them both meet me here in Queen Esther's lounge area, then order our standard breakfast and have it delivered to the bed chamber here? Also, have Abagtha to bring my robe and raiment from my personal quarters with him."

"As you wish Your Highness" Yara said as she turned to leave.

"Oh, and thank you, Yara."

Yara stopped and turned to look at the King, "You are most welcome Your Highness" and walked out the door with a smile on her face.

Esther lay in bed with a big smile on her face, then pulled the blankets up over her head. Ahasuerus laid back down and met her under the blankets giggling like two children.

Chapter Thirteen

THE GREEK REBELLION

Memucan sat at his desk reviewing the latest reports from the Greek uprising. The information was not good. Haman's suggestion to militarily strike the Grecian people before they fully rebelled only infuriated them more and they joined up with a Spartan army from the South of Greece and became extremely strong overtaking our Persian Navy. Several of the Persian boats were sunk and many of them were returning home. This was an ominous report to have to deliver to the King, but he had no choice. Things did not look good for Persia as far as Greece was concerned.

Getting up from his desk, Memucan walked over and sat on the window ledge looking over the palace courtyard trying to think of a solution he knew the King was going to ask of him. Now that Haman was dead, the King will be asking my advice and I want to be ready he reasoned. It is strange, he thought, how quickly Haman rose in the ranks to become the highest-ranking officer or prince in the entire Persian Kingdom only to fall back down through the ranks even more rapidly to the point of being put to death. "Life sure has a lot of twists and turns," he said out loud, "and this turned for the better for me. I am glad Haman is dead. His arrogant, condescending ways got him killed. Now the King should elevate me back to my original position." Memucan rubbed his hands together with a satisfied smile on his face. He is gone and I did not have to lift a finger to do it. "Yes, life sure has a lot of twists and turns" he said out loud again as someone knocked on his door.

"Yes, who is it?"

"It is Abagtha."

"Come in."

"Good morning Memucan. The King is requesting your presence in Queen Esther's personal lounge area in 30 minutes."

"Queen Esther's personal lounge area?"

"Yes, Queen Esther's."

"Why would he request me to meet him there?"

"He did not say. He just requested your presence" Abagtha replied as he turned to leave.

Memucan gathered up the reports from his desk. "I think I should take these reports with me anyway, just in case he asks for them. It is better to be prepared" Memucan said to himself.

"Your Majesties!" Yara yelled from outside Esther's bed chamber. "Your breakfasts are here. Would you like me to bring the table in or set up your breakfasts in the lounge area?" Yara waited for an answer to come through the closed door.

"What would you like Esther, this is your bed chamber."

"Well, you do not have your raiment here yet; I suggest we have the food brought in here and we eat in bed until Abagtha brings your robe."

"As you wish" Ahasuerus said sitting up in bed.

"Yara, you may have the breakfasts set up in here."

Yara opened the door. Three servants followed her carrying trays of food. They placed the trays of food on tables and moved the tables by the bed and left.

Esther and Ahasuerus ate their breakfast sitting on the side of the bed. Neither of them spoke much, just smiled at each other occasionally between bits of food. They both were extremely hungry.

They had just finished eating when Abagtha arrived with the King's raiment

"I must have a brief meeting with Memucan to get an update on a matter. After that, we can spend the rest of the day together if you would like" Ahasuerus said to Esther as he put his robe on heading for the lounge.

"As you wish Your Majesty" Esther replied. "I will have our bath drawn.

Memucan was waiting for the King when he entered the lounge area and was surprised to find him in his bath robe, but he did not comment on it. "Good morning Your Majesty."

"Good morning Memucan. Please, have a seat" Ahasuerus motioned for him to sit on the couch across from him. "I see you have some documents in your hands, what are they?"

"This is a report on the recent Grecian rebellion Sire."

"Good, good, what is the status?"

Memucan gave the King the report and watched as the King's pleasant countenance instantly change to somber. "The orders that Haman gave seemed to have agitated the Grecian people more than quiet them into submission. Shall I order more Soldiers to the front Sire?"

"No. I want to discuss the matter with Mordecai before further action is taken.

"Mordecai?" Memucan asked raising his eyebrows.

"Yes, Mordecai. I have placed Haman's household, authority, and his power into the hands of Queen Esther, who transferred it into the hands of Mordecai. He has taken Haman's place. I want you to provide all documentation pertaining to the Grecian uprising and anything else Haman was working on to Mordecai as soon as possible."

Memucan sat silently and motionlessly on the couch.

"Was there something else Memucan?" Ahasuerus asked standing up.

"Ah, no Your Majesty."

"Very well, you may go."

Memucan stood up and bowed at the waist still stunned at the King's instructions. Regaining his composure Memucan turned and left the lounge area.

Leaning against the wall outside Queen Esther's lounge area, Memucan's thought were racing through his mind. When was Mordecai placed in Haman's position? Why was Mordecai placed in Haman's position? Where was I when all of this took place? His confusion turned into anger as he walked down the hall back to his office.

By the time Esther and Ahasuerus had their baths and dressed, it was well into the afternoon. They took a leisurely walk through the courtyards stopping to look at the flowers. The guards and the servants hid behind pillars and doorways watching them. Never had they seen the King and Queen walking and talking together in public without it being an official affair of some sort. Watching them now caused the entire palace to ignite with excitement.

"Would you like to take a ride through the countryside Esther?" Ahasuerus asked holding her hand as they walked.

"Yes, I would like that very much." Esther had not been off palace grounds since she left her little hut by the mountains. She did miss being out among the trees and seeing the wildlife.

"Guard!"

"Yes Your majesty."

"Have my royal chariot made ready with appropriate security. We are going to take a ride through the countryside, southeast of the palace. Send out scouts immediately to survey the area making sure it is secure."

"As you wish Your Majesty."

"I have never ridden in a carriage before."

"I think you will enjoy it."

Esther looked up at Ahasuerus and noticed that he had been deep in thought all afternoon. His mood had changed after having his meeting with Memucan. Something was wrong. Something had happened to upset him, but she knew it was not her place to ask what it was. Her etiquette instruction taught that as Queen, she was never to ask the King questions pertaining to official matters, so she remained quiet sitting beside him. Esther's thoughts were interrupted by the approaching guard.

"Your Majesty, your chariot is ready and waiting for you at the palace gate."

"Very good." Ahasuerus replied standing up placing his left hand in the small of Esther's back guiding her to the breezeway descending the stairs. Four guards followed behind them. Esther could see the chariot through the gate bars as they walked down the stairs. She had never seen anything like it before in her life. In front of the gate stood a cabin-like structure supported by four large golden wheels being drawn by four white horses with golden harnesses connecting the chariot and horses together. Each horse had golden hats tied to their heads with golden tassels hanging down the sides and stood at attention at the hand of the attendant standing in front of them. The carriage itself was made of some sort of white material with a golden trim outline. One of the attendants opened the carriage door for Esther and helped her up the golden steps into the red plush pillowed seats. She ran her hand on the soft velvet as she slid over to make room for Ahasuerus to sit next to her.

The seating was so very comfortable that Esther rested her head on the back pillow with her hands folded in her lap and looked out the window as the carriage smoothly made its way down the cobblestone road.

"Are you comfortable?" Ahasuerus asked.

"Yes."

Ahasuerus put his arm around Esther's shoulders and drew her close to him. Esther laid her head against his chest; he smelled like lavender. They traveled the road in silence for a long time. It was peaceful and each of them seemed to be consumed with their own thoughts. After a while, Ahasuerus sighed and looked down at Esther to see if she was asleep.

"Are you awake?"

"Yes, I am awake" Esther replied looking up at him. "May I ask a question?"

"What is it you wish to know?"

"Something seems to be troubling you. May I ask what it is?"

"Yes, Esther, I am troubled. I was thinking about Haman, how my putting trust in him effected the Kingdom. I misjudged his character giving him so much authority. I thought he was a good friend, a confidant; but all he was, was a drinking partner. Now I can see how he deliberately got me drunk so he could maneuver his will over mine. What a fool I was."

Esther sat quietly listening while Ahasuerus revealed his inner thoughts to her and finally asked, "Have you learned anything from that experience?"

"Yes, I have. I will no longer permit myself to get drunk or stay in a drunken state of mind. The consequence of my irresponsibility may have caused me to lose the Grecian territory my grandfather acquired for the Persian Kingdom. What a heavy price to pay for foolishness."

Esther sat quietly resting her head on Ahasuerus' chest. After several minutes, she spoke softly saying; "everyone has some type of weakness in their character. No one does everything right or always makes the right decisions or choices. Everyone makes mistakes from time to time. I think that if one looks at themselves in the mirror recognizing and owning the mistakes he has made; that person is in a great position to change themselves and not repeat destructive behavior. The person that cannot see their mistakes themselves are clearly the ones destined to repeat those mistakes and are doomed for failure. Yes, one must suffer the consequences of their actions. In this case, for example, the possibility of losing Greece. However, you still have a vast Persian territory under your rule. You made a mistake; recognize the mistake, learn from the mistake, forgive yourself for the mistake and move on.

Ahasuerus looked down at Esther as she finished talking with tears in his eyes. He could not hide them. No one had ever encouraged him like she just did. He was overwhelmed as the tears flowed down his face.

Seeing the tears falling on his shirt, Esther pulled a handkerchief from her sleeve, reached up and dried his tears then laid her head back on his chest.

"How did you become so wise in your young age?"

"I believe the God that I serve provides whatever we need to live successfully, that includes wisdom." Ahasuerus did not reply; he looked outside as they rode along the countryside in silence.

Once they returned to the palace, Ahasuerus escorted Esther back to her personal quarters. "Thank you my Queen" he said smiling. "I really enjoyed our time together today as well as last night. You have helped me in ways you will never know."

"I have greatly enjoyed myself also, Your Majesty."

"Is there another name you could call me instead of 'Your Majesty?' It sounds so formal when we are together. You are a part of me now; we are one."

Esther looked at him and smiled. "We will have to come up with something. Until then, I will call you 'Dear' because you are dear to my heart; is that suitable to you?"

"It most certainly is" he replied smiling down at her hugging her tight. "I would love to spend the night with you again, but I have pressing affairs that I must attend to."

"I understand." Neither moved from their embrace.

"I really must go" he said finally pulling away from her turned, smiled, then left.

Walking back to his personal quarters with his personal guards behind him, Esther's words rang out in his mind; "Everyone has some type of weakness in their character. No one does everything right or always makes the right decisions or choices. Everyone makes mistakes from time to time. But, if one looks at himself in the mirror recognizing and owning the mistakes he has made, he is in a great position to change himself and not repeat the same destructive behavior. The person that cannot see himself and his mistakes clearly are the ones doomed for failure. Yes, one must suffer the consequences of their actions, in this case, Greece; but you still have a vast Persian Territory under your rule. You made a mistake, recognize the mistake, learn from the mistake, and move on." What sound advice she has given me. It is amazing how comfortable she is to be with so pleasant, warm, and inviting. Vashti was nothing like Esther, he thought. I doubt if there was any wisdom in her whole being. What was I attracted to?" he asked himself. She was just like Haman, superficial and phony. I guess I was phony and superficial as well to be attracted to such people, he thought.

Reaching his bed chamber, he walked over to the mirror and studied himself. "How did she say that 'look in the mirror, own the mistakes that I made, decide to make a change in the behavior and never make the same mistake twice.' Well, that is what she meant. I was a drunkard, a wine bibber. I have decided no longer to allow wine to control me. I was superficial, phony, egotistical and selfish. I have decided to no longer overindulge myself in any area of my life. She mentioned that she received wisdom from the god she serves. I do not know her god. Maybe sometime I will ask her about him."

The fire was burning bright in the fireplace as usual as he sat down on the couch. Looking around his bed chamber, he suddenly felt loneliness creeping up on him. He missed Esther already and he just left her chambers. Maybe, he thought, they could combine their living quarters together in the same location instead of all the way across the double courtyard. Knowing she would be just down the hall or in the very next room as she was earlier that morning was very comforting. His love for her was growing stronger and stronger and it frightened him just a little, he did not want to do anything to cause her to be unhappy and turn into another Vashti, just performing her Queenly duties. He decided to talk to her about the move in the morning. "Right now," he said out loud, getting up from the couch, "I must focus my attention on Greece and what action should be taken against them. Guard!" he called out walking over to his desk sitting down.

"Yes Your Majesty" the guard said poking his head in the door.

"Have Harbona bring the royal books; I want to review them."

"As you wish Your Majesty."

Esther sat on the window ledge looking out over the palace rose garden happy and fulfilled. She extremely enjoyed the time she had spent with Ahasuerus.

"Queen Esther" the guard called through the door.

"Yes, what is it?"

"Your father is here to see you; shall I show him in?"

"Yes, you may show him in" Esther replied moving over to the couch.

"Morde! How good to see you" Esther said hugging him around the neck. "I hope you slept well last night. Was it difficult sleeping here at the palace rather than on your bedroll at home?"

"I did not have any difficulty sleeping last night. With everything that took place yesterday, I was extremely tired. I think I was asleep before my head hit the pillow. You know, we must start to think of the palace as home now. There are a few things I would like to retrieve from the hut though. I will ask one or two of the servants to bring them to me. Is there anything from the hut you would like Esther?"

"Yes. I would like our large pillows and the baskets with the blankets in them."

"Esther, you want the pillows and blankets from home?"

"Yes, Morde. They will always remind me of where we came from, our heritage."

"I understand" Mordecai replied. "The Lord has elevated us Esther."

"I know, it is wonderful."

"Have you eaten dinner yet?"

"No, not yet."

"Do you have plans to eat with the King?"

"No. I think he prefers to eat alone tonight. He has some things to work out."

"Would you have dinner with me?" Mordecai asked. "Just the two of us like old times."

"I would love to Morde! We could have the table set up on the floor in front of the fireplace, sit on pillows and eat dinner just like we did at home, or, back at our hut" Esther said with a smile.

Mordecai looked around the room. "Do you have any pillows in here Esther?"

"No," she said. "There are no pillows in here except the pillows on my bed and they are not large enough. I am sorry Morde. We will have to eat our dinner on tables, but when we get our pillows from home, I will arrange for us to have dinner in front of the fireplace."

"That will be fine Esther, just as long as we are together. Once we get what we want from the hut, what do you suggest we do with everything that is left?"

"I wonder if Zena's family would like to have them. I will ask her."

"Do you get to see her often?"

"No. The last time I saw her was at my royal banquet when the King announced me as the new Queen of Persia. She asked to see me and apologized for the way she, Zoe and the other roommates treated me when we were going through our purification."

"They treated you badly?" Mordecai asked in surprise.

"Well, yes. I think they were trying really hard to compete for the King's attention and looked at me as the enemy."

"The enemy! But the three of you grew up together. They would turn on you like that!"

"Oh, it is fine now Morde. After I became Queen, Zena asked to see me, and I forgave her and all the other maidens for their behavior. Everything is fine now, and I think I would enjoy seeing how she is doing. They sent Zoe home. I thought she was a bit young to be going through the purification process. After my visit with Zena, I will let you know if they are interested in our hut."

"As you wish, Esther. It was difficult for you here. Why did you not tell me?"

"It was not that bad Morde. I was a little lonely, but I looked forward to our visits together, my servants were more like friends and sisters to me, and I used the lonely times to talk with the Lord and make blankets and things for you and the servants. I became quite contented. Besides, this is God's will for us right?" she said with a big smile on her face.

"Yes you are right" Mordecai replied smiling back at her. With that said, they ate their dinner and talked well into the night.

....

Chapter Fourteen

CONCUBINE ZENA

Ahasuerus sat on his throne staring across the room at nothing. He still had not made up his mind what to do about Greece. Maybe losing Greece is as Esther had said, a loss due to foolish decisions made on my part. I should just let them go and not lose any more soldiers to them. Abagtha had read him the status of the war and the Greeks were winning.

"Guard."

"Yes Your Majesty."

"Have Harbona stand before me."

"Yes Your Majesty."

"You called for me Your Majesty?" Harbona said bowing at the waist.

"Yes. Arrange for all of my lawyers and Mordecai to meet with me after lunch."

As you wish Your Majesty" Harbona said and backed out of the palace door.

"Your Majesty, would you like to have your lunch in your lounge area?" Yara asked poking her head through Esther's bed chamber door.

"Yara, do you know all of the King's concubines?" Esther asked.

"I know some of them. Sometimes when I am not serving you, I am requested to wait on one or two of them if their servant was sick or something."

"Do you know of the one named 'Zena?'"

"Yes I know Zena. I have waited on her a few times."

"Would you take this note to her and then escort her here to have lunch with me?"

"As you wish Your Majesty. Shall I serve something special for lunch?"

"Something special? Is there a reason I would serve something special?"

"Well, yes there is. Zena is with child and not everything she eats agrees with her. Sometimes we cannot get her to eat anything. She sips on mint tea most days."

"She is with child!" Esther whispered half out loud. The thought had never crossed her mind. "With child! With the King as the father." Esther felt a sense of jealousy come on her. It felt strange to her, she had never experienced this before and did not know what to say or do. Yara watched her closely and went to her bending down on her knees in front of her.

"Esther" she said quietly.

Esther looked down at her with tears in her eyes.

"There is no need to be sad or jealous. You know the King has concubines and what they are for do you not?"

Esther wiped the tears from her eyes. "I know Yara. I know. I was just caught off guard that is all. I did not expect to hear that news. Do you know when the baby is due?"

"She is about eight and a half months along now" Yara said still watching Esther closely. "Esther, I can tell you this. Zena has only been in to see the King one time. That was the night Hegai presented her to him. He has never called for her or any of the other concubines since making you Queen." Yara waited for her words to sink into Esther's mind. "You have nothing to be sad about Esther. Everyone knows that the King is madly in love with you. All of his concubines know it too and they are very unhappy; but there is nothing they can do about it."

Esther got up from her chair and walked over to her favorite window ledge and sat down. "Do you still want me to give this note to Zena and escort her here for lunch?" Yara asked quietly.

"Yes Yara. Yes, please deliver the note and escort her here." Turning to look at Yara, she continued. "What do you suggest I order for lunch?"

"I would suggest mint tea, fruit, and wafers. No fish or caviar or anything spicy."

That sounds good. Will you take care of this for me?"

"Yes Your Majesty." Yara said trying to comfort her.

Esther looked at Yara, smiled and said, "Thank you" in a whisper; "I will be alright."

Yara smiled and left the room.

Esther turned her attention back outside and prayed. "Father, please forgive me for being jealous. I have no right to be jealous of anyone after all you have done for me, Mordecai, and the Jews. Please give me only love and help me to support Zena in every way possible. You see, I know you are in complete control of my life and if it is your will, you will bless me with a child. Until then, I again, place myself totally in your hands to do with as you please. Thank you for hearing my prayer, Amen."

After her prayer, Esther was suddenly drained. She went to her bed chamber, laid across the bed and fell fast asleep.

"Queen Esther, Queen Esther!" Esther was startled out of her sleep. She thought she heard her name called, sat up on the side of her bed and listened. "Queen Esther, Queen Esther!" Then the usual knock at her door. "Queen Esther, are you awake, may I come in?" It was Yara.

"Of course Yara, come in."

Yara poked her head through the door. "Your lunch is here, and Zena has been seated at the table waiting for you. Are you alright?" Yara asked concerned.

"Yes Yara, I am fine. Please tell Zena I will be with her in a moment."

"As you wish" Yara said closing the door and walked over to the table where lunch was set up. "Zena, are you comfortable, is there anything I can get for you?"

"No, I am fine" Zena replied looking around the room.

"The Queen will be with you shortly" Yara said and took her place standing by the door waiting for Esther to come out of her bed chamber.

Zena did not reply but continued looking around the lounge area. Everything was magnificently laid out from the draperies, couches, the gold and silver wine goblets, plates, and silverware. She thought she had seen all the beauty the palace had to offer, but nothing prepared her for the luxury that was displayed in Esther's personal quarters. There were no flowers around and she was grateful. These days the perfume they expelled caused her to become violently ill. As she continued viewing the lounge area, she fought off the pangs of jealousy. Before she saw Esther without her veil, she always thought that the King would have preferred her instead of Esther. "It is strange how things turn out" Zena said to herself.

"Is there something I can get for you Zena?" Yara asked.

"No, no, I was just thinking out loud; I am fine."

"Zena, it is good to see you again." Esther said as she came out of her bed chamber.

Zena attempted to get up and bow before Esther, but Esther put up her hand stopping her.

"This is not necessary Zena, please do not attempt to get up."

Zena sat back down but did not look Esther in the face.

Esther took her seat at the table. "Yara, you may leave. I will serve the lunch."

"As you wish Your Majesty," Yara replied and left them alone.

"Zena, Zena, please look at me."

Zena lifted her head and looked at Esther with tears in her eyes. Seeing her tears, Esther got up from her seat, took Zena by the hand leading her to the couch and they sat down together. "Zena, what is wrong? Why are you crying?"

"Oh Queen Esther."

"We are here alone Zena; you may call me Esther. What is wrong? Why are you sad?"

Zena sat up and dried her eyes. "Esther, remember when we were talking about what would happen to us if the King did not pick us as his Queen?"

"Yes I remember."

"Remember when I said I would not mind being a concubine?"

"Yes, I remember that too."

"Well, I do mind. I did not think it would be like this. I am so lonely. I thought it would be great having someone to wait on me all the time, but there is nothing to do. I sit all day long and cannot sleep at night because I am not tired."

"Zena, when the baby comes, you will have plenty to do."

"No, the servants will take the baby to the King's nursery and raise it as the King's child. They even have wet nurses to take my place. It is too hard for me to accept having my baby taken from me.

Esther was silent for a moment. "Does your family come to see you?"

"They use to come visit me every other day. Now, they rarely come once a month. It is like being in prison. I am to sit here and be made beautiful waiting for the King to call. He has never called for me since the night I was presented to him, now I am with child, and that will eventually be taken away from me."

Esther was quiet again. "Zoe has not come to visit with you either?"

"Not since she went back home with our parents. I wish I could go back home as well. The King is not interested in me or any of the other concubines."

Hearing this news caused Esther to be troubled but she was not sure she could do anything about it. "Zena," Esther said slowly, "what would you like to see happen to you if you had a choice in the matter."

Zena sat quietly for a long time before answering Esther's question. "First, I would like permission to help raise my baby. To nurse him, have him sleep with me in my personal quarters and sometimes be with him when he is taken to the King for visits. This way he will know me as his mother and the King as his father. Second, I would request that the King release all the concubines from his harem that he is not interested in so they could meet someone, marry, and have a life of their own. That he allow those concubines to leave the palace if they are willing to leave their children behind with the King."

"You mean the mother is released, but the child stays within the palace with the King?"

"Yes."

"Would you really be willing to leave your child here and start a new life without him?"

"Me, no. I could not do that."

"How many of the concubines are with child?"

"There are about five of us that I know of. Esther, all of us know that the King has greatly favored you and desires you above all of us. He has not called for any of us since making you Queen." Zena broke down and cried again.

"Zena, Zena, come, get a hold of yourself. Everything is going to be alright. God has a way of fixing things for his children."

Zena sat up and dried her eyes again. "Esther, word is going around about the letter your father has sent out regarding the thirteenth of Adar. Do you think me and my family could become Jews? Could we believe in and trust in your God?" I do not want anything to happen to them."

"Yes it is possible Zena. Do you remember the family that lives right across from your mother and father's hut?"

"Yes I remember them."

"They are Jews. Tell your mother and father to go over to their hut and ask them how to become a Jew. They will help them."

"They really will help them?"

"Yes Zena, they will tell them everything they need to know and what to do."

"Esther?"

"Yes Zena."

"All those years we spent growing up, you never told me you were a Jew. Why?"

Esther looked at Zena surprised at her question and searched her heart to find the right words in which to answer her. "My people, the Jews," Esther began slowly, "were sold into bondage by the Babylonians. When the King's grandfather, King Darius the II, freed us from bondage and gave us permission to rebuild our temple in Jerusalem, he also gave us freedom to live and serve our God throughout all the Persian Provinces, which was a blessing. Because we had been in slavery so many times, we decided to be discrete with our nationality, not to draw any attention to ourselves so we could live and worship our God in peace. That is why I never told you I was of Jewish descent. That is why I always wore my chador and never let anyone see my face."

"You were living in fear?"

"To a certain degree, yes, we lived in a certain amount of fear, but we learned to replace that fear with faith and trust in God. We have learned through all our troubles to believe and trust in God. He proved himself to us over and over by defeating our enemies. The last enemy He defeated for us was Haman."

"Do you think I could become a Jew?"

"Why would you want to become a Jew Zena? No one would hurt you here?"

"It is not that. You seem to have such peace. When we were going thought our purification, I watched you closely. When all of us maidens turned on you, you seemed to be contented within yourself. You seemed to possess an inner strength. I always wondered how you could have that inner strength being by yourself all the time. When the rest of us requested gowns, makeup, jewelry, and hair pieces to try and make ourselves beautiful; you requested yarn and a spindle and made blankets and sweaters and things for the servants! None of us could understand your behavior. We were glad we did not have to do manual labor, but you seemed to thrive on it. We...., I could not understand. Now I know it is because of the God that you serve. For the first time in my life, I am afraid." Zena looked down at her stomach and tenderly patted the baby inside. "I am afraid for myself, and I am afraid for my baby. If the God you serve took away your fear and replaced it with courage and peace, I want to serve a God like that too. I need His peace, His protection, and His love. Esther, do you think I could have that too?"

"Of course you can Zena. Just believe that God is and do what is right in your heart."

"Believe that God is? What do you mean believe that God is?"

Esther got up from the couch, took Zena by the hand and led her over to the window. "Look outside Zena, what do you see?"

"I see flowers, fields of trees, grass and off in the distance, I see the mountains."

"Who do you think created the trees, the flowers, the grass and those mountains?"

"The gods!" Zena replied. "The god of the sun, the god of the moon. We were always taught as children that there were many gods."

"Have you ever prayed to those gods and have they ever answered your prayers?"

"Yes, we prayed to them all the time, we made idols of them, worshipped them and sacrificed to them."

"Can you tell me of a prayer that they answered for you?"

Zena was quiet for a long time. "No, Esther, I cannot."

"Zena, our sacred writings in the Torah tell us that in the beginning, God created the heavens and the earth. God created all of it; the trees, grass, sun, moon, stars, mountains, you, me, and all the animals. He created all of us, everything. To get to know Him, you must believe that He created all of this and that He will reward those who believe in, rely on, and trust in Him completely. This is how you become a Jew. Trust in, rely on and believe in the one true God, the creator of the whole world and stop worshipping those other false gods.

"Wow, is that all there is to it? It is that easy?"

"Well, sometimes it is easy and sometimes it is difficult. It is easy if you just surrender yourself to Him as He instructs us to. It becomes hard when we want to do things our way, with our own understanding, without fear and reverencing Him."

Zena continued to look outside. "Esther, there is so much to learn. Will you help me to learn about your God?"

"I will share with you everything I know. I will ask Morde for help as well. I am sure he would not mind explaining the Torah to us so we both can learn and understand it together. Would you like that?"

"I would love it" Zena said with a smile on her face. "Esther, would you entreat your God for me now? I mean if you would not mind?"

"Come Zena." Esther said leading her back to the couch sitting down holding Zena's hand in hers and began praying. "Father God, thank you for this time of fellowship with Zena who desires to become one of your children. As she seeks you with her whole heart, please give her your peace, let her experience your love and show her that you are indeed in control of her life as she surrenders it to you and the little one she is carrying. Please lead her and guide her in the way you would have her to go. We ask blessings on her mother, father, and Zoe back home. We ask that as they too seek you with their whole heart that they too will find you. We thank you and praise you Father and pray in the name of the God of Abraham, Isaac and Jacob, Amen."

"Why did you pray in the name of the God of Abraham, Isaac and Jacob?"

"Morde will explain that to you when we start studying together."

"Am I a Jew now?"

"Do you believe?"

"Yes!"

"Then you are now a Jew, one of the family of God. Now come to the table and eat your lunch, I am getting hungry." As they sat down at the table, Esther told Zena why she requested to see her. "So, do you think your parents would be interested in our little hut and what is left inside of it, including the animals?"

"Yes, I think they would be interested. What should I tell them?"

"Tell them to request a visit with my father. He will see that everything is transferred."

"Thank you Esther; you are still a great friend."

"You know Zena, now that you have become a Jew, we are now Jewish sisters!"

Zena, overcome with emotion, grabbed Esther's hand squeezing it. They finished their lunch talking about old times when they were children. Before long, Yara returned and escorted Zena back to her quarters. They agreed to meet again for lunch in a week. After Zena left, Esther picked up her yarn and began knitting a sweater, for whom she did not know, she was heavy in thought about all that she had learned that afternoon and how she could possibly help the King's concubines. "What should be done about them Lord," she prayed out loud. "They are most miserable.

FINAL DECISION OF GREECE

All the King's lawyers and Mordecai were seated around the table in the King's conference room. Ahasuerus called the meeting to order and asked for the latest progress report from the battle with Greece. Memucan stood up and gave his report.

"Your Majesty, we have been in battle with Greece for the past ten years. As you know, some of the battles we have won and some of them we lost. They always seem to get help from other soldiers in various parts of Grecian territory. One thousand, four hundred Spartan soldiers from the southern part of Greece fought against our soldiers in the Thermopylae Mountain Pass leading into the Greek Cities and defeated us. However, one of the Greek soldiers turned traitor to his countrymen and led our army through another passageway which allowed us to surround them and defeat them."

"Did we take the city?" Ahasuerus asked.

"Yes. We infiltrated Athens and burned the city to the ground."

"Good! Good. That is very good. My grandfather would be very pleased." Ahasuerus replied slapping his hand on top of the table. All the other lawyers repeated, "very good" parroting the King. Mordecai sat quietly listening and observing.

"But that is not the end of the report Your Majesty" Memucan interrupted. "Yes, we were victorious over Athens, but the Athenian Navy struck against us a few days later tricking our navy into following them in the narrow straits of Salamis. Our navy ships were so large that it was difficult to navigate the narrow strait and the Athenian boats sank all of our large navy ships."

"How many ships did we lose in this strip?"

"We had a fleet of twenty with 100 men on each ship" Memucan reported.

"Is that the end of the report?"

"No, Your Majesty, it is not."

"Continue" Ahasuerus replied flatly with a big sigh.

"The last battle to report is the Battle of Salamis."

"Please tell me we defeated them there" Ahasuerus pleaded.

Memucan looked at the King shaking his head sadly. "I am sorry Your Majesty, but unfortunately, we did not. The Greek army is a well-organized unit of soldiers and defeated our soldiers at Plataea. We lost another 12,000 Persian soldiers. This is the end of the report" Memucan said quietly and took his seat.

Everyone was quiet reviewing Memucan's report. Finally, Ahasuerus spoke, "Well gentlemen, what do you suggest we do about Greece? Should we continue to pursue them, try to re-conquer them and keep them part of the Persian Kingdom?"

No one spoke; everyone's head was bowed except Mordecai's and the King's. They looked around the table at each of the men but none of them spoke.

"Memucan, what action do you think we should take?" Ahasuerus asked.

"We have been fighting Greece for more than ten years as I said earlier. If we continue fighting, we may wear them down until they become weaken and submit their territory."

"You think we should continue fighting then.?"

"Yes Your Majesty."

"Is there anyone else that agrees with Memucan? Speak up" Ahasuerus looked at each man and called their names, "Carshena?"

"Fight!"
"Admatha?"
"Fight!"
"Shethar"
"Fight."
"Tarshish?"
"I agree with Memucan Your Excellency."
"Meres?"
"Fight!"
"Marsena?"
"I too agree with Memucan Your Excellency."
"Mordecai?"

Mordecai looked intently at each of the men around the table. He could see that the men answered out of loyalty to Memucan not considering or thinking through any of the facts that had been presented to them. Finally, he asked, "Has anyone recorded the total number of soldiers and their names that were lost over the past ten years up until now? How many Persian Soldiers were killed altogether in this war?"

"Memucan, do you have those figures and the soldiers' names?" Ahasuerus asked.

"Ah," Memucan looked through his documents. "Ah, no, Your Majesty, I do not have the total figures nor the total number of soldiers' names."

"Is there any way we could find this information?"

"Ah," Memucan did not know where to begin to look for the information the King was requesting. "Haman, ah, when Haman was in charge, he never requested that such a list be maintained Your Majesty. I am sorry, I could check with all the captains in our 127 provinces. They may have a manifest of all of the soldiers that perished and their names."

"Would you like to have an official manifest drawn up Mordecai?"

"It may be comforting to those families that lost their husbands, fathers, and sons who gave their lives for Persia to be honored by having their names on a roll where everyone could see. If we had such a list, we could see how much it has cost Persia in human lives as well as the cost on the King's treasury over the past ten years of fighting Greece. If Greece was not a part of the Persian Kingdom, would our strength or wealth be drastically reduced?"

"Memucan," do you have our financial status reports?"

Memucan ruffled through his stacked papers again. "I, ah, I would have to research that information for you as well Your Majesty" he said turning red in the face.

Seeing that Memucan was uncomfortable and ill prepared, Mordecai finished his comment. "Why beat a dead horse. We should cut our losses and leave Greece to themselves."

Memucan eyed Mordecai closely as he spoke and was again surprised by his speech. He hated to admit it to himself, but he made sense. How did this Jew acquire such wisdom, he thought to himself as he studied Mordecai. He could see that the King too was impressed with his strategy.

"Memucan, send letters to all 127 provinces and gather the information that Mordecai has requested. As for the matter of the Grecian people, let them have their independence. This matter is closed. Have the minutes written up and placed in the Book of Chronicles. This meeting is over" Ahasuerus said. Standing up, he shook Mordecai's hand and the two of them left the room together. The other lawyers stood up as the King stood but remained silent and did not move from the table until the King left the room.

Memucan gathered up his documents, placed them under his arm and briskly walked out of the room. All the other lawyers followed him silently. When they were outside of the conference room, Memucan stopped the men. Looking around to make sure no one could hear him, he said, "meet me in my office in fifteen minutes. Do not let anyone follow you or see you coming."

"Why?" Meres asked? "Why are you whispering?"

"Just do as I ask Meres!" Memucan stated in a commanding voice.

Meres did not respond. He just looked at Memucan for a moment and eventually agreed with the others. The men separated and went their separate ways.

Ahasuerus and Mordecai walked down the hall toward the King's courtyard.

"Have all of the notices retracting Haman's decree been sent out with my seal to your satisfaction Mordecai?"

"Yes they have. The runners and messengers have gotten the message out quickly and my people are preparing against the thirteenth of Adar. I have heard that many of them are having feasts and worshipping the Lord. Many of the Persian people who lived around my people watched the agony the Jews suffered under Haman. They also observed God's rescue of His people and decided to become Jews themselves and serve the one true God. However, I believe some of them committed themselves to Judaism to escape the retaliation of the Jewish people on the thirteenth of Adar."

Reaching one of the couches in the courtyard, Ahasuerus motioned for them to sit. "Esther has talked to me about your god. Can you tell me more about Him?"

"What would you like to know?"

"Everything. Who is he, where did he come from? Everything."

"Our God is the creator of the whole world and everything in it. You, me, the animals, all nature itself. He created man in His image and commanded us to worship and obey Him. If we were obedient, He promised that He would be our God and we would be his people. Over the years, we have not always obeyed Him, and He allowed our enemies to conquer and enslave us. But when we repented and turned from our wicked ways, He took us back and restored a right relationship with us because of the agreement He made with the Prophet Abraham. He told Abraham to leave his own country and He would lead him to a new land and make his name great that he would become the father of many nations. If Abraham would believe Him and obey Him, He promised never to forsake Abraham or any of his descendants. Abraham believed God and God maintained His agreement or covenant with us even to this day. The outward sign of the covenant between God and Abraham was that all the men and boys in the Hebrew community were to be circumcised. All male children must be circumcised eight days after their birth. This is an outward sign of the Covenant God made with Abraham and all his seeds after him. This is the God we Jews serve. Over the centuries, He has shown us His greatness in defeating every one of our enemies in a mighty way."

"He fights your battles?" Ahasuerus asked intrigued.

"Most definitely."

"This is most interesting. I think I would like to know more; however, it is dinner time. Would you like to have dinner with me? I will check and see if Esther can join us."

"I would very much enjoy dinner with you and Esther."

Chapter Sixteen

KING'S LAWYERS ARE DISSATIFIED

Fifteen minutes later Memucan met Shethar, Carshena, Admatha, Tarshis, Meres and Marsena in his office. "Did anyone see you or follow you?" he asked.

They all shook their heads no.

"Have a seat, gentlemen," Memucan said with a tinge of command in his voice. All of them sat down in chairs around his desk. "All of us have served the King since he took over the throne from his father. We know him better than he knows himself in many respects."

"Yes, you are right Memucan" Carshena said. "He is very easily influenced."

"Yes he is" Memucan replied looking at each of the men. "Look at how he promoted that Haman over all of us. The man came from nowhere and the King promoted him over all of us."

"You were the one that introduced Haman to the King, Memucan" Carshena retorted.

"Yes, yes, I know. I thought he was a good trainer, and the King would promote me for finding Haman for him. Little did I know that the fool would promote him over me. Before Haman was promoted, the King consulted me on every situation. I hated that man with a passion. He always belittled me."

"He belittled all of us Memucan" Carshena replied letting Memucan know without a doubt that he was not the only lawyer that had been offended by Haman.

"Now," Memucan continued, "the King has a new 'best buddy,' this Mordecai. A gate keeper if you will. He promoted a gate keeper over me who has been with him and loyal to him for years.

"He promoted him over all of us Memucan," Tarshis said exasperated. "Not just you! You are beginning to sound like Haman now and you know what the King did to him. Do not make the same mistake he made."

"Yes, yes, yes, I know. I must control myself, not make any public displays of dissatisfaction about anything. I know, but we cannot just sit still and do nothing! The King is now being indoctrinated into the Jewish religion because the Queen turns out to be Jewish! The guards have confided in me that the King and Mordecai sit up late at night discussing the Jew's God! What is to become of Persia if this continues?" Memucan got up from his chair and looked out the window.

Meres sat quietly listening and watching his fellow lawyers. What has happened to these men? He thought to himself. When did they become so bitter and disloyal to our King? The King has a right to appoint whom he wants to whatever position he desires. I am satisfied with where he has placed me. I am going to be quiet and see where this is going. So he continued to watch and listen to the men.

"You are aware," Admatha said, "that the King repealed Haman's decree to destroy all of the Jews on the thirteenth of Adar."

"Yes, so!" Memucan said looking at him.

"You also know that the Jews are training themselves to fight against that day."

"Yes, I am aware of that also."

"If we could figure out a way to secretly ambush Mordecai in the fight, we could get rid of him while the others are fighting for their lives. If we destroy their leader, we may have a chance to take Persia back and make it like it was before."

"You may have something there Admatha. You may have something there" Memucan said running his hand through his hair. "Listen, the Jews are having secret meetings preparing for the fight. Each one of you discretely talk to the servants and the towns people. See where their loyalty falls. If it is with us, invite them to a secret meeting we will have next week. I will arrange a discrete place for us to meet that will be safe. If their loyalty is with the Jews, act like you agree with them, but do not mention anything about our meeting. Does everyone understand?"

All the men agreed.

"Good" Memucan said. "As you leave my office, make sure no one sees you. I will let you know when I have found a suitable place and the exact day we will meet.

The five men lined up at the door and left one at a time making sure no one saw them. Memucan went to his desk and began writing letters to the captains of the 127 Provinces as the King had commanded him.

As Meres took his turn to leave, he walked silently down the palace hall with his head down and his hands folded behind his back. He was so deep in thought that he did not see Hegai walk up to him and stop right in front of him. Hegai and Meres had become friends while servicing the various Kings throughout the Persian Kingdom. Many times they sat talking about the events of the day in the King's courtyard when time permitted. Seeing Meres so deeply in thought, Hegai decided to stop and find out what was so heavily on his mind.

"Meres" Hegai said getting his attention.

"Oh, Hegai, how are you today?"

"I am not so deeply in thought to the point that I do not know where I am walking!" Hegai said with a smile on his face. "Is there something troubling you?"

Meres stood there looking at Hegai for a few minutes. "Do you have a few minutes to talk?" he asked.

"I could spare a few minutes for you my friend. What is on your mind?"

Meres looked around. The palace halls were busy with servants walking here and there. Guards were around every corner standing guard or escorting palace visitors to various locations. "Is there somewhere private we could go to talk?"

"This sounds serious" Hegai said looking at him. When Meres did not reply, Hegai said, "my personal quarters are right around the corner. We can talk there."

Both men entered Hegai's quarters and sat down. "What is on you mind my friend."

Meres leaned forward resting his elbows on his knees folding his hands together in front of him. "Hegai, would you say the King and palace life is better since he made Esther his new Queen?"

"Yes, very much better. Queen Esther has a very positive effect on the King.

"What do you think about her father Mordecai?

"I think is he very good for the Kingdom; where are you going with this Meres?"

Meres sat back in his chair and stared down at the floor. "Hegai, you are a man with a gift to be able to judge good character."

Hegai sat back, still not sure of where Meres was going with his questions and comments. He was intrigued so he said nothing and waited for him to continue.

"What do you think of Memucan? What type of a man do you think he is?"

"What type of man do you think he is Meres? You have intimately worked with the man for over ten years. You should know him much better than I. What has happened to cause you to ask these questions?"

"You are right; I have worked with him for over ten years. I thought I knew him well, but now; I am not so sure about him. Listen, Hegai, will you keep my confidence if I share something with you?"

"Of course Meres! We have been friends for a long, long time.

"All of the King's lawyers were in a meeting with the King and Mordecai after lunch discussing what should be done about the Grecian uprising. Memucan gave the report of the status, which was not favorable to Persia. King Ahasuerus asked what advice Memucan would take regarding Greece. Memucan said he thought we should send more military over and continue fighting for the territory. It sounded like a good strategy to me, so when the King polled all the other lawyers, we all agreed with Memucan. In the past, he always seemed to give the King good advice, so we all agreed with him. When the King asked Mordecai for his advice, he asked a couple of questions which Memucan could not answer. The King told Memucan to do the research, draw up a report and submit the findings to Mordecai. This infuriated Memucan. We all saw it, even the King, but no one acknowledged it or commented on his reaction. When the meeting was over, King Ahasuerus and Mordecai left together talking about something personal between the two of them. All of us lawyers waited until they left, then we left through another door. Once we were outside, Memucan looked all around to see if anyone could hear him and then told us to meet him in his office in fifteen minutes and to make sure no one saw where we were going. I asked him why and he said just come. So, I discretely went to his office with the others as he requested."

Hesitating for a moment, Meres sat back in his chair and continued. "When we were all seated around his desk, he started talking about how long we all had been loyal to the King; how the King promoted Haman over all of us and how he, Haman, belittled all of us. Now that Haman was gone, instead of promoting one of us who had been loyal to him, he promoted Mordecai over all of us. Memucan and all the rest of the lawyers resented the fact that the King was asking Mordecai questions about the god that he and Queen Esther served. They feared that she and her father would influence the King with their religious customs and turn the Persian Providence into a Jewish territory. Admatha reminded us that the King had repealed Haman's decree to kill the Jews on the thirteenth of Adar. He said that at that time, if we organized ourselves like the Jews were organizing themselves; we could set up an ambush and kill Mordecai. That if we kill the Jews' leader, then we could take control back and return Persia to the way it was before. This does not sit right with me Hegai. When I saw you in the hall, I wanted to know what you thought."

"You asked me what I thought about Memucan. I watched him at a distance when King Ahasuerus promoted Haman over him. He did have a difficult time with it and tried to hide his feelings but if anyone watched him, studied him closely, one could see him seething inside every time the King went off with Haman, spending quality time with him, drinking with him. Meres, human nature dictates that anyone will become disloyal against their leader if they are not secure within themselves. They measure their personal value on whatever position and power that they hold and not on the content of their character or skill level. They will do anything, even kill, to get what they think is rightfully theirs, regardless of how it affects others around them. That person is dangerous and is not good for a King or for his Kingdom."

"I think you are right my friend. Should we advise the King of this plot?"

"How does Memucan plan to carry out his plot?"

"Right now he has ordered us to talk to the towns people to see whose side they are on, the Jews or the Persians. If they say they are on the Jew's side, we are to act like we agree with them and walk away; if they say they are on the Persian's side, we are to inform them of a secret meeting Memucan is going to organize to fight against the Jews."

"You do not have any factual evidence against Memucan and the others yet. I would suggest you do as Memucan says until you find out exactly what, where, and when his plan is to be played out. When you get the information, let me know. I will make an excuse to meet with the King regarding his concubines which will not raise suspicion and report your findings to him."

"That sounds good to me" Meres said standing up shaking Hegai's hand. "Give me five days. By that time, I should have more information for you. We could meet again by accident in the palace hall at noon."

Esther was still at a loss to help the King's concubines. She was not sure if Persian law would allow any changes to be made to the concubines' circumstances. She was not even sure if Ahasuerus would want any changes to be made with the women in his harem, but she knew they were very sad and that made her sad as well.

"Guard!" Esther called from her couch.

"Yes Your Majesty!"

"Is Hegai around? Would you please find him for me?

"As you wish Your Majesty."

Ahasuerus offered Mordecai a seat and some wine when they reached the King's lounge area, but Mordecai refused. "I will wait until dinner if that is alright with you."

"Fine, So, in order to worship your god, one must become circumcised?"

"Yes, that confirms the covenant God made between himself and Abraham."

"And there are no other gods beside him?"

"No. He is the one and only true God. He is the God of all creation. He created everything for himself and for his good pleasure. He created man in his own image."

"Do you believe this god had anything to do with my choosing Esther as Queen?"

"I most certainly do. I prayed earnestly to the Lord before allowing Esther to compete for the Queen's position. As Jews, we were not to participate or marry into other cultures but after praying about the decree you sent out looking for another queen to replace Vashti, God impressed upon me to trust him and allow Esther to participate."

"Do you believe that your god controls everything that happens to you, his people?"

"Yes I do."

"Why did he allow your people to be sold into slavery so many times? If he loves you, the Jews, why would he permit you to be enslaved and all that goes with slavery? That seems to be rather cruel to me. Is this your god's type of love? I do not understand."

Mordecai shifted his position in his seat becoming a little uncomfortable. These were difficult questions the King was asking. 'Lord help me to give the King the right answer in the right tone to give him your understanding to change his life,' Mordecai prayed silently. "Your question is a good one" Mordecai said sitting up in his chair resting his elbows on his knees while folding his hands together under his chin. "Do you know anything about Hebrew history?"

"Hebrew History?"

"Yes. Do you know anything about the Jews being enslaved by the Egyptians?"

"Yes, I vaguely remember something about that. The Pharaoh had the Hebrews enslaved and did not want to let them go. I had heard from my grandparents that a lot of strange things happened to that Pharaoh before he let the Jews go. They told me that most of those stories were made up, just myths."

"Well, they were not myths, my friend, they were true."

Ahasuerus sat up in his chair looking directly into Mordecai's eyes. "You say they were true? All of them?"

"All of them" Mordecai replied.

"How do you know they were true?"

"They are written in our sacred writing, the Torah. All of the accounts that the Prophet Moses recorded in the sacred writings have been proven by eyewitness accounts handed down from generation to generation and proven to be true."

"This 'Moses,' he came after Abraham?"

"Yes. After the covenant God made with Abraham, the people that descended from him became a mighty nation over several hundred years. God watched over them and protected them. Then one year there was a famine in the land and the Hebrews migrated down into Egypt to survive the drought. For many years, the Pharaoh welcomed the Hebrews to live peaceably among them.

After several years a Pharaoh arose to power that did not favor the Hebrews and enslaved them. God used Moses to lead them out of this slavery and into the wilderness for 40 years. While we were there, God gave Moses the laws that the Hebrew people were to live by and obey. Over and over the Hebrews broke those laws. As a result, God permitted them to be enslaved by the enemy as chastisement. Our God is a God of love, Ahasuerus, but He will chastise us when we refuse to be obedient to Him; however, He will never forsake us or turn His back completely on his people because of the covenant he made with Abraham."

A guard at the door interrupted Mordecai and he stopped talking as the King's attention was drawn away.

"Yes, who is it?" Ahasuerus asked.

The guard opened the door and announced the servant Abagtha.

"Show him in" Ahasuerus said.

"Your Excellency," Abagtha stood in the doorway bowing at the waist. "Please forgive me for interrupting you. Where would you like to have your dinner served?"

"In the dining room. Ask Queen Esther if she would like to join us for dinner."

"As you wish Your Excellency" Abagtha replied, bowing at the waist closing the door.

Turning his attention back to Mordecai, Ahasuerus was quiet for a moment before speaking. "Your god is very interesting; you have given me a lot to think about. Would it be possible for us to speak on this matter again? I would very much like to learn more."

"Of course it is possible Ahasuerus. We can continue the discussion whenever you like.

"Very well. Come, dinner is being set up in the dining room."

As the two men moved from their couches, Ahasuerus questioned Mordecai again about the status of Haman's rebuttal decree and if the Jews were ready against the thirteenth of Adar.

"As a matter of fact," Mordecai said as they walked together down the hall, "there is a meeting set up tonight with the Jewish brothers to help them get prepared."

"If there is anything that you need from me, just ask."

"Thank you" Mordecai said as they entered the hall and sat down in the two chairs positioned in front of the fireplace.

Esther picked up her knitting again as she waited for Hegai to come. He surely would know how to advise me about the concubines' situation, she thought.

"Queen Esther," the guard called through the door, "Hegai is here as you requested."

"Thank you, please show him in."

Hegai stood at the door bowing to Esther and smiling at her at the same time. He was delighted to see her. Now that she was Queen, he rarely had opportunities to talk with her.

"Come in Hegai, come in and have a seat." She showed him to the couch directly across from hers. Would you care to have some tea?"

"No thank you. I am pleased that you have called to see me; I miss our conversations."

"Oh so do I Hegai. I have a question concerning the King's concubines."

Hegai raised his eyebrows at hearing Esther's words. "The King's concubines?"

"Yes. I know it is probably very unusual for the Queen to ask about the King's Harem."

"Yes it is Queen Esther. In all my service at the palace, no Queen has ever inquired about the King's concubines. What is it that you wish to know?"

Esther lowered her eyes a little embarrassed but felt she had to press on for Zena and the other concubines' sake. She just did not know how to approach the subject with Hegai to ask his advice. "Hegai, I was talking with one of the King's concubines, the one I grew up with in the village. I called to see her because my father and I thought that her parents might be able to use our old hut and the supplies and animals that we no longer needed."

"Is this the same Zena that was your roommate when you were going through your purification?" Hegai asked surprised.

"Yes, yes it is" Esther responded slowly realizing that Hegai was aware of how all her roommates treated her during that process. "I have forgiven them for their actions at that time; I understand why they acted that way."

Hegai sat there with his hands in his lap and nodded his head. This Queen is very gracious indeed he thought to himself but said nothing out loud. He just nodded his head and waited for Esther to continue.

"When Zena came to me, I noticed a couple of things about her. First, I noticed that she was with child; and second, I noticed that she was extremely unhappy."

"Why does Zena's or any of the concubines' state of being concern you Queen Esther?"

Esther was quiet. She was not prepared to answer this type of question. Getting up from the couch, she walked over to the window looking out searching for the answer. Hegai waited patiently in silence as he watched her.

"The only answer I can come up with, Hegai, is that if I were in their situation, I would want someone to be concerned about me if I were extremely unhappy and miserable" Esther said still looking out the window.

"The King's concubines are unhappy and miserable?"

Esther turned from the window, walked back sitting down on the couch. "Yes. They are all very unhappy and very miserable."

"Queen Esther, you know that the King has placed me in charge of the concubines. If they are this unhappy, why have they not informed me. What do they need that I have not provided for them? They have very comfortable quarters to live in with the finest foods and raiment with personal servants to wait on them hand and foot. What else do they need?"

"The way Zena explained it to me was they need a purpose?"

"A purpose?" Their purpose is to always be ready if the King calls for them. The King has already granted your request to allow those maidens that were not presented to him to return to their families with a monetary stipend to help their families and to have a life of their own. What more can he do for them?"

"Zena has informed me that the King never calls for them since he made me Queen" Esther said lowering her head feeling uncomfortable about what she had just said, however she had to say it. "I asked Zena what her petition would be to the King if she could make one. She said she would ask that the King would allow her to have an integral part in raising her child after it was born instead of the child being taken away from her and placed in the palace infirmary to be raised by servants; that she would be able to visit the King with the child on some occasions so the child would know his mother as well as his father, and finally, if the King would release the concubines that he has no delight in, does not want to see again. That he would release them back to their families so they could make some sort of life for themselves if they were willing to leave their children here in the palace. That is what she requested." Esther sighed and sat back down on her couch. The guard knocked on the door.

"Queen Esther."

"Yes?"

"The King's servant Abagtha is here with a message for you. Shall I show him in?"

"Yes you may."

"Your Majesty" Abagtha said bowing at the waist. "The King has sent me to ask if you would like to join him and your father for dinner in the royal dining room?"

"Tell him I will join them. Thank you."

"As you wish Your Majesty" Abagtha said bowing at the waist again and turned to leave.

Hegai sat watching Esther in silence as she dismissed Abagtha, not sure what to say. He was caught off guard regarding the concubines and thought he was doing what was expected of him in supplying their every need. To be informed of their dissatisfaction and unhappiness concerned him greatly. If the King found out about their complaints, he could lose his life.

Esther turned her attention back to Hegai and saw the worried look on his face and immediately understood his concern. "Hegai, none of this is your fault! You have done your job and I am not complaining about you in anyway. I called to ask your advice on how to ease the unhappiness of the concubines. Is there anything in the law that we could use to maybe change things for these ladies in any way? Would you investigate this for me and advise me how or if I should even approach the King about this matter. I am not accusing you of not doing your job."

Hegai took a deep breath and smiled. "Your Majesty, that makes me feel much better. I will certainly look into this matter and get back to you as soon as possible."

"Thank you so much Hegai and we will keep this between the two of us alright?

"As you wish Your Majesty" Hegai said bowing at the waist. "Your Majesty, would you give me the honor of escorting you to the royal dining room to meet the King and your father?"

"I would love for you to escort me Hegai. It would be like old times" she said smiling. Just give me a minute to freshen up and I will be right with you" Esther said as she went to her bed chamber. Moments later she came out in her royal apparel and the two of them walked down the long hall toward the royal dining room arm in arm talking quietly between them.

Chapter Seventeen

THE BABY

"Tamera, could you hurry with dinner!" Reelaiah called out entering their hut. "The brethren will be meeting at the hall at sunset. I do not want to be late."

"Dinner is on the table Reelaiah. Sit down and we will serve you."

Reelaiah grabbed his pillow, sat down folding his legs under him, blessed the table and began sipping his tea.

"You have found a room to have the meeting then?"

"Yes. One of the King's servants came to me secretly wanting to become a Jew after he read Mordecai's decree. After we explained who God was and the commandments handed down by Moses, we circumcised him and now he is a believer. He told us there was a large vacant room in the back of the palace that was not being used by anyone. Not even the guards went back there. He said we would not be disturbed and could have our meeting there."

"Do you trust him Reelaiah? It may be a trap?"

"I thought of that too. But after we circumcised him, I checked with Mordecai about it and he approved the plan to meet there. He said he may even attend and address the brothers and give us instructions."

"Do you think the brothers will listen to him?" Tamara asked setting his dinner plate down in front of him. "It was just a week ago that they wanted to stone him to death."

"They will listen to him now! Everyone knows that the King has made Mordecai the most powerful man in the Kingdom, next to himself. After the King hung Haman, he gave him Haman's title and all the power and riches that Haman had. Mordecai even has the King's ring! The King's ring! Can you believe that?"

"So…, then., Mordecai was right in his actions with Esther?

Reelaiah put the bread down he was holding in his hand, leaned back against the wall looking at Tamara. "Yes," he answered slowly, "he apparently was correct in the choice he made even though it seemed to go against everything that we believed in as Jews. God's Divine Providence. Our God moves in mysterious ways. His ways are not like our ways. Yes, I am glad Mordecai was able to stand up against us and dared to believe what God was telling him and Esther to do. As it turns out, it is saving our lives and the lives of Jews everywhere."

"I am glad too. The girls and I miss spending time with Esther, and I know you miss visiting, worshipping, and studying the Torah with Mordecai."

"Yes, you are right my dear. I miss them enormously. When this is all over, maybe we could visit them at the palace."

"That would be wonderful" Tamara said hugging Reelaiah around the neck. "Eat, eat so you will not be late for the meeting."

Reelaiah finished his dinner, picked up his bag with the official documents from the palace and other papers of instruction for the brothers. "I will be back in a few hours Tamara" he said and kissed her on the cheek.

"Go with God and be safe" Tamara said as she sat down beside their daughters and began spinning wool from the sheered sheep.

"I do miss Esther and it will be good to see her again" Aisha said.

"I do too" Tamara said. "I bet she has changed a lot since we last saw her; being Queen can change a person."

"Do you think she has any children yet? Shakera asked?"

"I do not know. No one in the village has heard anything about her except Zena's mom and dad. When Zena's father, Taziah became a Jew, he told your father that Esther and Mordecai had given their old hut and everything they left in it to them, but he did not say anything about how Esther was. We will find out soon when all of this is over" Tamara said. They continued their work in silence.

Reelaiah walked down the alley and met Taziah. "All ready for the meeting tonight?"

"Yes. Wait, do not walk so fast. I am still a little sore."

"Oh, I am sorry brother; I forgot. How are you feeling?"

"I am healing up pretty fast, I just have to remember not to move so fast that is all. Reelaiah, I have been talking to some of my friends and they too want to become Jews. Do you think it will be alright for them to attend this meeting?"

"I do not see any harm in it. Tell them to come."

With that, Taziah turned around and yelled, "Come on, he said it is okay!"

Reelaiah turned around to see who Taziah was yelling to. To his surprise, the alley filled up with at least 50 to 100 men who fell in line behind them.

"What is this?" Reelaiah said turning to Taziah. "Who are all of these men?"

"They all want to become Jews" Taziah said. I told them what I experienced with you and the other brothers, even about the circumcision and they all want to become Jews."

"Are you sure that is it or are they afraid of being Persians because of Mordecai's decree?" Reelaiah asked looking intently at Taziah.

"I cannot see into their hearts Reelaiah. I guess some of them are afraid, but some of them may truly want to become Jews. Only God knows the truth."

"Yes, I guess you are right. Who am I to judge?" With that, Reelaiah waived his arm in the air and yelled, "okay, brothers, follow us!" and they all walked to the palace to the place Mordecai designated for them to meet.

Ahasuerus and Mordecai both stood as Hegai escorted Esther into the dining room and to her seat. Before sitting down, Ahasuerus took her hand and kissed her lightly on the mouth. Every time he saw Esther, it surprised him how much he missed her when they were apart. As she hugged Mordecai, Ahasuerus decided that he would ask her about moving her personal quarters closer to his after dinner.

The love and affection Esther felt for these two men as she sat down to dinner overwhelmed her. Ahasuerus was to her right at the head of the table and Mordecai was to her left at the other end of the table. The table had been shortened so that all three of them were within reach of each other's hands. After the three of them were seated, the servants began to pour the wine. Esther looked at Mordecai, then at Ahasuerus, then back at Mordecai.

"Is there something wrong?" Ahasuerus asked looking at the two of them.

"Would you mind if my father blessed the table before we begin eating our meal?"

"Oh" Ahasuerus said clearing his throat. "I do not mind at all, please Mordecai, bless the table according to your tradition."

Mordecai took hold of Esther's hand who took hold of Ahasuerus' hand. They bowed their heads and Mordecai began to pray. "Dear Lord, thank you for all that you have done for us. Thank you for your peace, your love, and your protection. Thank you for this King and Queen and for the fellowship that we have. Please bless the food that we are about to receive, please bless the hands that have prepared the food for the nourishment of our bodies in the name of the God of Abraham, Isaac, and Jacob, Amen."

"Amen" Ahasuerus said. Mordecai and Esther looked at Ahasuerus and smiled as they picked up their wine and took a sip.

Esther had gotten use to the effect of how the wine made her feel, that familiar warm sensation that went down to her stomach. She decided to take another sip and leaned back in her chair as the servants served the caviar and crackers. Ahasuerus and Mordecai were deep in conversation about Greece as Esther picked up a cracker to spread it with a dab of caviar. The smooth textured food slid down her throat and into her stomach. Suddenly her head began to spin, and she felt weak. Pushing her chair back from the table, she attempted to stand but fell back into her seat. Her stomach was churning. She was about to be sick.

"Esther, Esther! Guard, Guard! Get the palace doctor! Hurry!" Ahasuerus yelled.

The guard ran off to find the palace doctor as Ahasuerus gathered Esther's limp body up in his arms; she had fainted. The two men were both horrified as Ahasuerus took Esther over to the nearest couch and gently laid her down. Grabbing a chair from the table, Ahasuerus sat down next to her as she lay on the couch. After a few minutes Esther began to stir.

"What happened?" she asked trying to sit up but her head and stomach started spinning around again and she quickly laid back down.

Just then the palace doctor came in. The Queen was lying on the couch. "What happened?" he asked moving Ahasuerus out of the way looking down at Esther.

"She fainted" Ahasuerus said. "What is wrong with her, she was fine a minute ago?"

"What did she have to eat?" the doctor asked.

"Just a sip or two of wine and a bite of caviar with a cracker!" Mordecai blurted out; "then she tried to stand up and fainted."

"Hmm" the doctor said feeling Esther's forehead. "Are you sick to your stomach?"

"Yes" Esther said. "When I try to sit up, I get dizzy, and my stomach is nauseated."

"What did you have to eat earlier today?"

"Just a little mint tea and a little fruit. That is all."

"Oh" the doctor said raising his eyebrows. "I think I would like to examine the Queen privately. Would you have her moved to her personal quarters?" he asked looking at Ahasuerus.

"I would prefer you to examine her in my personal quarters. It is closer and she would not have to walk so far. I would like to carry her there myself" he said as he picked Esther up holding her close and walked down the hall toward his bed chamber. Mordecai, the doctor, and the guards followed close behind.

Esther laid her head against Ahasuerus' chest. She felt better in his arms, her head was not spinning as much, and her stomach seemed to quiet down. She could hear his heartbeat. It seemed to be racing rather fast and she realized that her husband was upset and afraid. She looked up at him, put her hand up against his check and whispered, "I will be fine Ahasuerus, there is no need to worry; this will pass."

Ahasuerus looked down at her and kissed her forehead as he laid her down on the bed.

"You all may leave now" the doctor said in an authoritative tone. "I will do my examination now. Please close the door behind you."

Ahasuerus and Mordecai looked at Esther.

"It is alright; I am in good hands" Esther said reassuring the two men.

With that, both men left and waited in the King's lounge area right outside of his bed chamber door. The guards took their standard positions in the hall outside of the lounge.

Mordecai looked at Ahasuerus, "Would you mind if I used your desk to write a note?"

"No. Feel free to use whatever you need" he replied not taking his eyes from the door.

Mordecai walked over to the desk, wrote a note, folded it up and handed it to the servant standing by the door. "Please deliver this to a man named 'Reelaiah.' He is hosting a meeting in the back of the palace over against…"

"I know where it is being held Sir. I will deliver it immediately."

"Thank you" Mordecai said handing the man the message.

"You are welcome Sir." The servant quickly left the King's lounge area. Mordecai walked over to the window and waited for the doctor to come out.

"Esther," the doctor said pulling up a chair beside the bed and sat down. "How long have you been feeling ill?"

"I have been feeling fine until just now."

"Have you been having any headaches?"

"Yes. A little one this morning; I just ignored it."

"Have you been feeling tired more than usual?"

"Yes. I have been having to take naps in the afternoons for the past couple of weeks. I just thought it was because of all that had been happening around the palace lately. Do you know what has been happening?"

"Yes, yes, I know about Haman and his evil deeds."

"Well, I thought it was due to the stress of that activity."

"I see" he said patting her hand. "Have you missed any of your monthly cycles?"

"Yes, I thought that too was a result of the stress as well and dismissed it."

"Hmm."

"What is it doctor?"

"How many times have you missed your cycle in a row?"

"Three, maybe four."

"Do you know precisely how many, three or four?"

Esther thought for several seconds. "Four. It has been four months."

"Judging from all of your symptoms, I would say that you are going to have a baby."

"A baby! Really!"

"Yes. You are about to become a mother in about four or five months from now depending on the number of cycles you missed. You rest now, everything will be fine. I want you to refrain from drinking wine, or any strong drink. Do not eat any spicy foods and get as much rest as you can. I will come back and see you in a few days. Would you like me to inform the King and your father, or would you prefer to tell them yourself?"

"I would like to tell the King myself. Would you inform my father so he does not worry any longer than necessary?"

"As you wish Your Majesty" the doctor said smiling as he opened the door and turned to leave. As soon as he turned around, he came face to face with Ahasuerus.

"Well!" Ahasuerus asked anxiously. "Is she alright? What was wrong?"

"Your Majesty, your Queen wishes to see you now" the doctor said stepping aside looking for Mordecai who was standing by the window.

Ahasuerus rushed past the doctor to Esther's bedside. Esther had propped herself up with pillows with a light blanket thrown over her legs. The dizziness had stopped and the nausea in her stomach had settled down; she felt much better and managed to smile at Ahasuerus trying to ease his anxiety.

Looking down at her lying on the bed, Ahasuerus pulled up a chair and sat down. "Are you alright Esther?" he asked with extreme concern on his face.

"I am fine dear; I am fine. We are going to have a baby" she said taking his hand in hers.

Ahasuerus did not move; he just looked at her with tears in his eyes. "A baby!"

"Yes, a baby. I know you have had several children and ..., I ..., someday, if it is alright with you, I would like to meet them."

Ahasuerus still sat there quietly looking at her, the tears now falling down his face. He made no attempt to wipe them away, he continued holding her hand.

Esther did not know what to do. She was not sure if he was happy or upset. "Ahasuerus" she finally said. "Are you alright?"

Without saying anything, he sat beside her on the bed, put his arms around her and held her tightly in his arms. "I am fine Esther, I am fine. I was not expecting this. I was so frightened when you fainted, I thought I was going to lose you. I have only just found you; I love you so much and the thought of losing you now, I know I would not be able to bear it." Pulling her back from himself and looking at her again he asked, "are you sure you are fine?"

"Yes Ahasuerus, I am fine."

"This is good. This is very good. You are fine" he said holding her close again.

"The baby" We are having a baby, does this make you happy?"

Ahasuerus laid her back on the pillows placing his hand on Esther's stomach. "Yes, yes, yes, I am very happy about our baby. I have never been so happy in my life. Esther, you have made me very happy. After dinner, I had planned to ask you if you would like to move your personal quarters closer to mine, right next door so we would not be so far part physically." Waiting a moment for the words to register in her mind he studied her face then continued; "and now with the baby coming, I just want to be near you even more, that is if it is agreeable to you. I never want to force you to do anything you do not want to do. If you would be more comfortable in your own quarters, I would understand…., I…"

"Hush, hush now" Esther said pulling him down to her and kissing him. "I would love to move in with you right here in your private bed chambers and be close to you all the time. I miss you so much when you must leave me or when you send me back to my personal quarters after calling for me. Yes, I would love to move in here with you. Here," Esther moved over on the bed, "please lay beside me and hold me."

"As you wish, my Queen" Ahasuerus said smiling and wiping the tears away from his face. He laid down beside her holding her in his arms as Esther continued talking.

"Maybe we could have our separate lounge areas for me to visit with my servants and friends and you to have your meetings in."

"That sounds good, very good to me. I will give the servants instructions to make the move."

"No, you have enough to do. I will have them move my things over in the morning."

"As you wish, my Queen" Ahasuerus replied. They both laughed.

Esther felt so comfortable, contented, and peaceful lying in his arms. She felt like she could tell him anything, whatever was on her mind. She thought about the conversation she had with Zena earlier that day and wondered if it was the right time to broach the subject with him. She told Hegai she would wait for him to get back with her on the matter; but now, she felt she could tell her husband whatever was on her mind and in her heart. As her head rested on his chest, she could hear his heartbeat and his heavy breathing. "Are you awake?" she asked quietly.

"I most certainly am. Do you think I could sleep at a time like this?" he said looking down at her and kissing her gently on the lips. "No, I am not asleep. What is on your mind?"

"I had lunch with one of your concubines this afternoon."

"Yes, the one called Zena."

"Yes, how did you know? Esther asked in surprise.

"I know everything that goes on in and outside of the palace dear. It is my responsibility to know what is always going on. Was it not Zena and your other roommates that treated you so badly when you were going through your purification?"

"Yes, but I forgave her and all the rest of them. I understood why they were acting the way they did."

"Why?"

"They thought I was a threat to them. They thought that if they ignored me, they would cause me to feel insecure, inadequate, and afraid when it was time for me to be presented to you. They were acting out of fear."

"You must know Esther, none of them could come close to competing with you. When you walked through my door, you took my breath away. I could not take my eyes off you. Your natural beauty was breath taking. Even now, when you walk into the room, I am still affected the same way. It is not just your outward beauty. You have a unique inner beauty that is difficult to describe. Self-confidence mixed with grace and love for everyone. I have never experienced anyone like you before."

"That self-confidence, self-assurance, grace and love comes from the God I serve."

"Ah, yes," Ahasuerus said kissing her forehead. "That god of yours. I was talking to your father about the god you serve. We have planned to speak more about him."

"This is good. But I was talking with Zena. She is having your baby, as well."

"Yes, I am aware of this. She should be ready to give birth in a month or two. Does this upset you Esther? If she and all the other concubines upset you, I can have them housed in another facility outside of the palace and you will never have to see them ever. Whatever your wish is just say the word and I will do it."

"It does not upset me that she is with child" Esther said slowly. "When I saw her, she was so very unhappy and when I asked her why she was so unhappy, she told me that she and all of the concubines were miserably unhappy because they never get to see you. That since you made me your Queen, all they do is sit around all day and are waited on. And those of them that are with child or have given birth; the babies are taken away from them and are raised by the palace wet nurses. They have nothing to do with their child or with you and they are very unhappy.

Esther stopped talking and waited for a response from her husband, but he was quiet. When he did not respond, Esther began to worry and wondered if she had overstepped her boundary with the King. Not being able to read Ahasuerus and figure out what he was thinking, she lay quietly in his arms and did not move.

Ahasuerus got up from the bed and walked over to the window looking out. Esther looked after him as fear gripped her in the pit of her stomach and she felt like she was going to be sick all over again, but she took a deep breath and forced her stomach to settle back down, got up and walked over and stood beside him looking up at his face. "Ahasuerus, if I have spoken out of turn, please forgive me. I know that concubines should not be any of my concern and that I should focus my attention on the things I am obligated to do and be as Queen of Persia. Please forgive me for overstepping my authority, I am sorry" Esther said lowering her head turning to walk away from him, but he reached out and took her arm pulling her back to himself holding her close to him again.

"Esther, my beloved Esther. I am not upset with you, and you have not overstepped your authority. It just never occurred to me that my concubines could be unhappy. I thought I provided everything that they could possibly need or want. That was the reward, I thought, for being a King's concubine. To be waited on hand and foot with servants and provide everything they needed. No one has ever told me that they could possibly be unhappy. What more could I do for them?"

"I asked Zena what she would request if she could make any request of you."

"You did?"

"Yes. When we first received the palace letter that you were looking to replace Queen Vashti, Zena and I talked about what might happen to us if we did not make Queen. That we may end up being one of your concubines and what that would mean, not having a life of our own, only being available to you when you so desired. She said she could accept being waited on every day and not having to work. Now that she is in that position, she is finding it difficult to live from day to day. I told her that when her baby arrives, she will have plenty to do. She reminded me that after she delivers the baby, the servants take the baby to the palace nursery and she has no more contact with him, no input in the raising and nurturing of the baby at all. She said she and the other mothers would ask if they could raise their babies themselves instead of sending them to the nursery. They said that since you made me your Queen, you no longer call for any of them to come to you and that if you are no longer interested in any of them, they are requesting to be released from your service to try and make a life for themselves."

"They want to leave the palace altogether and take my children with them?"

"No. The ones that want to leave, if they have children to you, they will leave their child within the palace and try to make a life for themselves because you are no longer interested in them. The ones that do not have any children are requesting to leave because you do not have any interest in them, but then, the ones like Zena, who will be delivering their babies soon and desire to stay within the palace request that they be able to raise their child and visit with you with their child so the child will know both their father and their mother. That was her request."

"Esther, how would you feel about me visiting with my sons and daughters and their respective mothers? Would that upset you?"

"Being an orphan myself, I think that a child needs both parents in their lives. I am secure in myself and can share the love that God has given me with whomever he desires to have it. I know that you love me, and you love our baby. Our son or daughter will have sisters and brothers and that is a great thing. If you desire one of the concubines, as King, that is your..."

Ahasuerus lifted her head putting his hand over her mouth to stop her in mid-sentence. "I love you Esther, and you love me. I want you to know here and now that I do not and will not desire another woman in my life. You are all that I want. Do you understand me? I do not want anyone else, just you. Whatever you decide to do with the concubines is fine with me as long as I have you" and he kissed her long and passionately then picked her up and carried her to his bed.

Chapter Eighteen

JEWS PREPARE FOR ADAR 13

Mordecai stood over by the window waiting for the doctor to come out from examining Esther. Fear gripped the pit of his stomach as he looked outside over the palace grounds. What would he ever do without Esther, he thought? She was the only family he had, and he loved her dearly. He began to pray silently in earnest to the Lord as he waited. 'Lord, please let her be alright. Touch her body and make it whole again and give her back to her husband and to me. But your will be done, Amen.' The door opened and the doctor whispered something to Ahasuerus and he rushed inside the room and closed the door behind him. Mordecai looked at the doctor and decided to wait by the window, not sure if he was to be briefed on Esther's condition.

Looking around the room, the doctor noticed Mordecai watching him, so he walked over to him. "You must be the father" he stated.

"Yes, I am. Is the Queen alright?"

"Yes, yes, you need not worry. She has instructed me to let you know she is fine; she is going to have a baby and that was the result of the fainting spell. She had not eaten properly, and the wine and spicy food did not agree with her. She will be fine you need not worry."

"A baby?" Mordecai said in awe.

"Yes, a baby. You are going to be a grandfather!" replied the doctor smiling broadly.

"A grandfather! Are you sure?"

"Yes, yes, I am very sure."

"And she is alright; everything is alright?"

"Yes, she is alright. She wanted to tell the King herself but instructed me to let you know so you would not worry. You know, I like this new Queen. She seems to be very thoughtful and considerate of everyone."

"Yes, she is very kind and thoughtful. She always has been. Thank you doctor for letting me know. There is nothing for me to worry about, but I have a lot to rejoice about. Thank you again."

"You are very welcome my friend." The doctor shook hands with Mordecai and left.

"Thank you, Father," Mordecai said as he looked out the window again. "I am going to be a grandfather! What a blessing!" Mordecai said out loud. No one was in the lounge area, and he felt free to praise the Lord by lifting his hands and waiving them in the air. "Thank you, Father, for this special gift, this child, thank you, praise your holy name."

Knowing that Esther and Ahasuerus would want to be alone for the rest of the evening, he decided to attend the meeting that Reelaiah was moderating. He put his royal robe around his shoulders, his golden crown on his head and left the King's lounge area. A cold wind whipped around him blowing his robe open and caused a chill to come over his body as he walked down the hall toward the back of the palace. Winter would be here soon the thirteenth of Adar is only a couple of months away, he thought to himself as he turned down around to the right of the palace. He was amazed at the large group of men that had assembled there. They were standing shoulder to shoulder, row after row. It was impossible for Mordecai to make his way through the crowd to the platform where Reelaiah was standing without physically pushing his way through, so he stood in the back and observed. Reelaiah was calling the meeting to order with his opening remarks.

"Men, Jewish brothers. We are gathered here tonight in the name of God. The God of Abraham, Isaac, and Jacob. The God we serve is a good God, the only true and faithful God."

All the men shouted "Amen!" and raised their hands in the air. Reelaiah continued.

Since the beginning of time, God called Father Abraham and told him he would make him the father of many nations, that He would be our God and we would be His people if we would obey Him, serve, and worship Him. He said He would always fight our battles and defeat our enemies. And He has!"

Again, all the men shouted "Amen!" and raised their hands in the air. Mordecai too shouted "Amen" and raised his hands in the air. One of the men standing in front of Mordecai turned around to see who was standing behind him and recognized Mordecai dressed in royal apparel with a golden crown on his head. Tapping the men on both sides of him, he whispered, "Look! That is Mordecai is it not? The man that King Ahasuerus just promoted! That is him. Look, he is wearing royal apparel!" The three men began tapping the men around them whispering that Mordecai was in the back. As they began to recognize him, they opened an isle from the back all the way up to the platform. Hearing the whispering in the crown and seeing the isle opening, Reelaiah recognized that Mordecai had arrived.

Reelaiah shouted, "The man God has used to help us defeat our enemies is here tonight! Mordecai, please come to the platform and address this assembly!"

At the mention of his name, all the men began cheering "Mordecai, Mordecai, Mordecai!"

Hearing his name being chanted, Mordecai was overwhelmed as he made his way to the front of the crowd and onto the platform where Reelaiah was standing. The two men embraced each other.

"I am so glad you were able to come. Is all well with you, the Queen, and the King?"

"Yes, all is well. You received my message then?"

"Yes, I did, but now that you are here, would you do me and all of these men the honor of addressing us?"

"I will say a few words at the end of your address if this is permissible. You already have your speech prepared do you not?"

"Yes, but I think the men would prefer to hear from you. Please," Reelaiah stepped back from the platform and directed his hand motioning Mordecai to move to the front of the platform. As he did, the crowd erupted again chanting "Mordecai, Mordecai, Mordecai." Mordecai bowed slightly to Reelaiah and stepped to the front of the platform and the crowd quieted down to hear what he had to say.

"Brothers, as you know, God has been good to us as He always has. His Divine Providence always permeates throughout His people whether we are enslaved or free. He blessed us with Kings who favored us in allowing us to rebuild the temple in our homeland of Jerusalem."

The crowd erupted in "All praise to the God of Abraham, Isaac, and Jacob! All praise to the God of Abraham, Isaac, and Jacob! All praise to the God of Abraham, Isaac, and Jacob!"

"Yes!" Mordecai continued. "All praise to the God of Abraham, Isaac, and Jacob, for He has touched the heart of this King to allow us to worship our God and not the pagan gods of this land. We are free to worship our God and to even travel to our homeland and worship God in the restored temple!"

Again, the crowd yelled All praise to the God of Abraham, Isaac, and Jacob!"

"Because we worship the one true God, I would not bow my knee to any other god, including the man 'Haman!'"

The crowd began to hiss and stomp their feet at the mention of Haman.

"We no longer have to fear this man Haman!" Mordecai shouted. "God delivered him and his entire household unto the King, who delivered it to Queen Esther, who delivered it to me! Then the King hung Haman on the very gallows he built for me! We no longer need fear this man! This is God's Divine Providence at work gentlemen, all praise to the God of Abraham, Isaac, and Jacob!"

"All praise to the God of Abraham, Isaac, and Jacob! All praise to the God of Abraham, Isaac, and Jacob! All praise to the God of Abraham, Isaac, and Jacob! All praise to the God of Abraham, Isaac, and Jacob!" The men shouted, clapped their hands waiving them in the air.

Mordecai raised his hands to quiet the crowd down again. "Yes gentlemen, God has indeed delivered our enemies into our hands once again, but there is still work to do. Have all of you received the latest Decree from the palace with the King's official sealed ring reversing Haman's plot to kill all the Jews on the thirteenth of Adar. If you have your decree, waive it in the air!" Mordecai shouted.

Throughout the entire room, there was a sea of white documents waved in the air.

"This decree gives us the right to defend ourselves against our enemies on the thirteenth of Adar. We must prepare to fight. All the Jewish men in all the Persian Provinces are preparing to fight. We have captains here to train you in military warfare to defeat our enemies. Captains, would you please come up on the platform."

Twenty Persian military captains climbed the stairs to the platform dressed in military attire and stood at attention.

"These soldiers will train you in the art of combat and help get you ready to defeat our enemies. You will take instruction from them; learn from them. They will instruct you as to when and where you are to report for training. After your training is complete and when the time is close to the thirteenth of Adar, we will meet again for further instructions. Now, will you please line up. The captains will take your personal information and give you your instructions. God be with you!"

The crowd returned the shout "God be with you!" then lined up in front of the captains.

Mordecai turned to Reelaiah and embraced him and shook his hand.

"That was a very inspiring speech Mordecai. Thank you."

"Praise God, Reelaiah, praise God. Without Him we could do nothing."

"You are right about that" Reelaiah retorted shaking his hand again and the two men left the platform and left the men in the hands of the captains.

Chapter Nineteen

CONCUBINE DEMANDS

Hegai sat at the library table pouring over law scrolls. "Concubines" he said to himself. "Do Concubines have any rights?" What he read in the law surprised him as he re-rolled the scrolls replacing them on their shelves and made his way down the corridor to the concubines' personal quarters. The guard stationed outside concubine Zena's door acknowledged Hegai as he approached.

"Would you like me to announce you to the concubines?"

"Yes. Please knock and make sure they are presentable."

The guard announced Hegai's presence and asked if the ladies were presentable.

"Yes, please show him in" Zena called out.

Opening the door, Hegai stepped in. Zena, Arwa and Orit, three of the King's concubines that were with child were all seated on couches facing each other and stood to greet Hegai as he entered their chamber area. There was a warm fire burning in the fire pit in the center of the lounge making the room warm and inviting.

"Come in Hegai, please sit down" Zena said moving to the couch where Arwa was sitting and motioned for Hegai to take her couch. "How are you today?"

"I am very well, thank you" Hegai replied. "How are the three of you doing? Is there anything that you need? Have the midwives or the palace doctor been in to see you lately?"

"The palace doctor was in yesterday and examined each of us; he said everything was fine with all of us" Arwa replied looking at the other two ladies.

"Everything is fine then?" Hegai asked again looking at each of the women. "There is nothing that you need? You are all contented and happy?"

None of the women answered Hegai. All three of them looked to the floor.

"Ladies, is there something wrong? It is my duty to make sure all of you are comfortable, satisfied, and happy. If you are not, you must let me know."

"It is not that we are uncomfortable or that our basic needs are not being met Hegai" Zena answered slowly keeping her eyes to the floor. "Our personal quarters are comfortable; our servants do a good job of taking care of all our physical needs. We are just unhappy being the King's concubines. He never calls for us." The other three ladies nodded their heads in agreement to what Zena was saying.

"There is nothing for us to do here. We are with child, but when our children are born, they will be taken away from us. All we do all day long is sit around being waited on to look beautiful for a King that does not have any delight in any of us. What kind of a life is that Hegai? Would you like to sit around all day doing nothing?"

Hegai sat quietly looking at each of the ladies in his presence. "It is my responsibility as keeper of the concubines to make sure that you are well taken care of. If you are unsatisfied or unhappy in any way, I must try and change your situation so that you become and remain happy and contented. What can I do for you three and the rest of the concubines to change your situation?"

"The three of us have been talking about our situation and have come up with a few ideas. Would it be permissible with you if we met with the other concubines to get their input?" Arwa asked looking to the other two ladies for support. Zena and Orit both nodded in agreement.

"I do not see any harm in that. After dinner tonight, I will arrange for all of you to have a meeting; list your ideas and we will discuss them. I will have one of the servants go to each of the concubines' personal quarters to let them know about the meeting, that they must eat their dinner in the main dining room tonight and for them to submit any ideas they may have at that time" Hegai said standing to leave.

"In an hour or so we will go to the dining hall" Zena said looking at Arwa and Orit after Hegai left their chambers. "The major complaint, as I see it, is we want to have a life of our own, right?"

"That is only part of it" Arwa said. "Those of us that are with child would like to be involved in raising our children here in the palace and continue living in the palace to be close to them; those of us that are not with child would like to leave the palace altogether to make a life for ourselves. Then there are those who desire to leave their children within the palace but want to leave to make a life for themselves."

"Arwa" Zena asked, "could you really leave your child here in the palace letting the palace servants raise him, never to see him again?"

"Arwa looked down at her stomach and sighed, "I…, no Zena, I could not; but what is the alternative? I would have to accept living here within the palace walls and be satisfied with raising my child, that is if the King grants our request. I know I could never leave my baby."

"I could never leave mine either" Zena replied. "What about you Orit?"

Orit looked at both of her fellow concubines and then down at her own stomach. "I am not sure" she said slowly. "I would have to wait until the baby is born, then I will make up my mind. After all, I am still young, and I could have other children with a husband of my choice and make a life for myself. If I left my baby within the palace, I know he or she would be well taken care of." Orit looked at both ladies intently, then continued. "If the King grants our petition, and if I decided to leave my child here, would the two of you look after him for me?"

All three were silent. None of them had thought about taking care of someone else's child. After a long period of silence, Zena asked.

"Orit, would you trust us to raise your child?"

"Why not? We have lived together within the palace walls for more than a year now. I think I know both of you well enough to trust you. I know that neither of you would intentionally do anything to harm my child, that you would love him or her as you love your own. Is this not true?" Orit asked looking at each of them intently.

"Yes, it is true" Zena said. Arwa nodded her head in agreement.

"We were Just surprised that you trusted us to raise your baby" Arwa said looking at Zena. "If this is your choice, do you think the King would allow you to come to the palace occasionally and visit with your child?

"That is a very good question" Zena said. "We should write these questions down and have them ready for the meeting after diner. Here, I will get some paper and a pen" Zena got up from the couch, went into her bed chamber and came out with her writing utensils. "Now, what was that request?"

"First" Arwa said, "We request that the King release any concubine that he is not interested in; that is not with child and desires to leave the palace to make a life for herself."

"Second" Orit stated, "we request that the King release any concubine that he is not interested in that is with child if the mother agrees to leave the baby here at the palace.

Third, we request that the King allow the mothers of the children to come and visit the children left behind as often as she requests. The mothers, however, will not remove the children from palace grounds."

"Fourth," Zena piped in as she continued writing; "We request that the King allow the mothers of the children born of concubines and wish to remain within the palace even though the King has no interest in them, to raise their respective babies within their private quarters."

"That is good, that is very good" Arwa said smiling.

Zena finished writing and looked up. "Is there anything else we wish to ask of the King?"

"Zena, are you really willing to live here at the palace with your child never to have a husband of your own; never having any other children of your own?"

"At this time Arwa, I really do not desire to have a husband of my own. I am not sure if I will always feel this way. At this moment, I am satisfied and content right where I am. If my desires change later and if the King grants all our petitions, then I will make a change.

"How can you be so sure of yourself?" Orit asked. "How can you live your whole life here within these walls. It is like a prison here! Sure, all our material needs are met, but life is nothing without freedom. Do you not want freedom for yourself and your child?"

Both Zena and Arwa noticed the agitation in Orit's voice as she got up from her couch and walked over to the window.

"I hate it here and I hate being with child. I cannot wait until this child is out of me!"

Zena and Arwa went over and stood beside Orit at the window. Zena reached out and put her arms around Orit's should and held her close. "I know this is difficult Orit, but we have each other to help us through this stressful time. We are here for you and if the King grants our petitions, it will not always be like this."

"If we stay here after we have our babies, do you think the King would give us permission to go into the marketplace?" Arwa asked. "Do you think that should be one of our requests? What would be the harm in allowing us off the palace grounds?"

Orit dried her eyes as they went back to the couches and sat down.

"Oh, I could think of a couple of problems with that request Arwa."

"What?"

"Well for one, we are the King's property, and he has enemies. What if one of his enemies grabbed one of us and held us for ransom while we were in the marketplace? For another, what if we met someone while we were in the marketplace… a man!"

"If we meet someone while in the marketplace," Orit interrupted, "we could request to leave and make a life for ourselves if we agree to leave the baby behind. We could also request that the King provide a guard to accompany us when we leave the palace grounds; we have escorts within the palace, why not outside of the palace as well?"

"Hmm, those are good arguments Orit. What was the next number?" Zena asked.

"I believe it was 'Five,'" Orit said with a smile.

"Okay, fifth, we request permission to leave the palace grounds with a security escort from time to time. Did we cover everything?"

"Yes" Orit said.

"Yes" Arwa agreed. "We finished just in time to go down to the dining hall." The three put their wraps around their shoulders and opened the door.

"We are ready to go to the dining room for dinner, would you please escort us?" Zena asked looking up at the guard standing beside their lounge door.

The guard held the door for them to walk in front of him.

"Oh wait!" Zena said turning to go back into the lounge. "I forgot the list!"

"We must not forget the list!" Arwa said laughing. "The most important part of dinner."

They all laughed then continued their way to the dining hall.

Esther lay quietly in Ahasuerus' arms listening to him breathe.

"Are you asleep?" she asked quietly?

"No."

"I am hungry."

"You are?"

"Yes, our dinner was interrupted remember?"

"Oh yes, something about a baby, yes?"

"Yes." Esther replied Laughing sitting up in the bed. "Can you believe it? We are going to have a baby! God has answered all my prayers. Every one of them"

"He has? What did you ask of Him?"

Esther pulled her knees up to her chest with her arms wrapped around them. Her white night gown covered her knees and only her arms and feet could be seen. "It is hard to explain. I remember waking up every morning in the village. I had a daily routine. I would get up early being very quiet not to awake Morde; put a log on the fire, put on my chador, go outside of our hut standing underneath the porch. I loved getting up early, the village was still asleep and there was a peace and calm everywhere. In the summertime, the cool morning dew moistened my face." Turning to look at Ahasuerus who was propped up on one elbow looking up at her, she continued. "I would make sure no one was around and remove the veil from my face to let the morning dew fall on it. Being a Jew, I was very, very careful to always have my face and body totally covered whenever I was out in public.

In the wintertime, the cold air caused my whole body to awaken and become energized. This time in the morning was so special because it seemed that only God and I existed in the whole world. This is when I talked with Him, and He talked with me."

"Your God talks to you?" Ahasuerus asked sitting up in bed beside Esther.

"Yes. I talk to Him, and He talks to me."

"What does He say?

"I say, 'Good morning Lord' and He says 'Good morning Esther.'"

Ahasuerus began to laugh putting his robe on as he got out of bed. Pulling up a chair, he sat down facing Esther directly as she continued talking.

"Why do you laugh?"

"You speak as though your god knows you personally!"

"Oh, He does Ahasuerus, He does! He knows me personally and I learn more about Him every day. Back at the hut in the village, every morning I would look around and thank Him for all that He had done for me and Morde. For providing a home for us to live in, for food to eat and for protecting us during the night from our enemies and for taking care of the animals He gave us."

"Now wait a minute, Esther. I am the one who allowed you to live in Shushan, who protects you from your enemies and provides food for you. I.., me…., the King of Persia provides all these things for you, your people and all the people of Persia. How can you give this credit to your god!" Ahasuerus got up from his chair and stood in front of the fireplace with his back to Esther.

Esther detected a little agitation in his voice as she watched him standing in front of the fireplace with his hands jammed into the pockets of his robe.

"Yes, Ahasuerus, by your hand, all these things were provided for me, my people, and the Persian people. By your hand, you permitted our Temple to be rebuilt in Jerusalem and Temple Worship restored. By your hand, we are free to worship our God in freedom and peace. By your hand, you have allowed us to avenge our enemies; however," Esther hesitated, got out of bed and met Ahasuerus at the fireplace turning him to her so he could see her face, then continued, "but, God touched your heart and your father's heart and your grandfather's heart to first free the Jews from Babylonian slavery, to allow us to live here in Shushan, Jerusalem, and anywhere else in the Persian Providence in peace. God touched your heart to allow us to exist. Do you see, many times, God uses man to do his bidding and He used you and your forefathers to protect and provide for His Jewish children. It is called 'Divine Providence.' He used His 'Divine Providence' to bring the two of us together."

"You really believe this?"

"I most certainly do. Who would have arranged for a Jewish maiden to become Queen of Persia? How many other Jewish maidens tried out to become Queen?"

Ahasuerus took Esther in his arms and held her close. "You and your father have given me a lot to think about. Your god is a very interesting god." Pulling her back, he looked at her and asked, "did you ask your god for a husband and for a baby?"

"I most certainly did."

"And you believe he answered your prayers?"

"He most certainly did. I am waiting for him to answer one more prayer request though."

"What is that?"

"I think I will wait for Him to answer it before I share it with you. Right now, I am hungry. It is not too late, do you think we could get one of the servants to bring us something to eat, or could we go down to the dining room ourselves?"

"Go down to the dining room?"

"Yes, why not? The guards can escort us; we will be alright. Put on your royal robe, I will put mine on. We will be alright."

"Are we going to the royal dining room?"

"No, why not go to the other dining room where the others eat?"

"You never cease to amaze me Esther, but alright, we will go. Make sure you wrap up good, the halls are drafty this time of year."

"I will dear. Come let us go." Esther took the King's hand, opened the door greeting the guard. "We will be going down to the dining room to get something to eat."

"Would you like me to have one of the servants bring a diner tray to your quarters?"

"No," Esther replied. "We will go to the dining room."

"To the royal dining room?" the guard asked.

"No, the other dining room" Esther replied.

The guard looked at King Ahasuerus for permission to follow Esther's command. Ahasuerus nodded his head and the three of them walked down the long hall toward the servant's dining area.

Dinner had already been served. As the King, Queen and guard entered the dining hall, everyone stopped eating and stood to their feet. Hegai also stood at his elevated table, but no one knew what to do or say, they just stood there and looked at the three of them quietly.

"Please sit down and continue your dinner" Esther said waiving her hand. "Hegai, do you think there is enough room for the King and me to sit with you and have some dinner?"

"Oh, oh, most certainly Queen Esther. Here, take my seat."

No, you sit and continue your dinner. Guard, please have the servants to set a place for the King and me at Hegai's table. We will wait here until it is set up. Thank you. The rest of you, please be seated and continue your dinner." At Esther's command, everyone returned to their seats and slowly began eating.

"What do you think this is all about Zena?" Arwa whispered as they sat back down.

"I am not sure. Queen Esther may want to make an announcement, or she may only be hungry and want something to eat."

"But they have their own royal dining room. Why would they want to eat with servants and concubines? Do you think Hegai told them of our meeting?"

"Hegai said he would allow us to address him with the other concubines after dinner. Besides, look at him, he is just as surprised as we are."

"You are right."

"Knowing Queen Esther as I do, she probably was hungry and did not want to bother the royal servants to fix them something to eat and came to where dinner was still being served. I think that is all there is to it."

"I heard that you and the Queen grew up together in the same village. Is this true?" Orit asked sitting down on the other side of Zena.

"Yes, we did."

"Well, I guess you know her pretty well then."

"Yes, I do. Now eat your dinner."

In minutes, the servants had two extra place settings set up; the King sat beside Hegai, and Esther sat next to him on his left. All three of them sat facing the servants and concubines on the lower floor.

Hegai tried to continue eating his dinner as usual, but it was hard for him to control his nerves and his hands shook as he tried to lift the food to his mouth. His mind was racing. Why were they here, had he done something wrong; did someone make a complaint against him? He took a deep breath and sat back in his chair looking out over the group of people eating in the dining room trying to see if anyone looked suspicious. Everyone had their head down eating avoiding the platform where he, the King and Queen sat.

Ahasuerus noticed that Hegai was not eating and that he was nervous. Leaning over, he whispered in his ear. "Relax Hegai. You are not in any trouble. The Queen was hungry and decided she wanted to get something to eat here instead of the royal dining room. We normally eat our dinner earlier then you. Our dining room is closed, and she did not want to disturb the servants. You are not in any trouble so relax and eat your dinner."

"Thank you, Your Excellency." Hegai said and began eating his dinner again.

"Your Excellency," one of the servants addressed Ahasuerus. "What would you and the Queen like to eat. The cook is prepared to fix anything you wish."

"I will have what everyone else is eating. The Queen will have tea, biscuits, and fruit."

"Would you care to have wine with your dinner Your Excellency?"

"Is everyone else drinking wine?"

"No, Your Excellency, they are drinking tea."

"I will have tea as well."

"As you wish Your Excellency" the servant replied and backed away from the table.

Ahasuerus looked around the room. Everyone had their head down fixated on their dinner. "Esther," he whispered in her ear. "Maybe this was not a good idea. They are all so uncomfortable with us here. We should leave."

Esther noticed it too; everyone was very uncomfortable. She spotted Zena at one of the tables in the middle of the room, but even she did not look up at them. Esther was at a loss for words as she sat back in her chair and began to pray silently. Father, did I make a mistake in coming here and bringing the King with me. Everyone is so tense and uncomfortable with us. Should we leave as Ahasuerus suggested? If I was wrong in coming here, please forgive me and show me what to do. Thank you, Lord, Amen.

"What do you think Esther, should we leave?"

The servants brought their dinner and set it down in front of them.

"Can we eat first? I am so very hungry."

Ahasuerus looked at her remembering that she was with child. He discretely placed his hand on her stomach smiling, "of course Esther, we will eat first then we will leave.

As they began to eat, everyone else had finished eating but continued to sit quietly at their tables. No one moved. Hegai knew the concubines were waiting to have their meeting with him but was not sure if it was appropriate with the King and Queen in the room.

"Your Excellency."

"Yes Hegai, what is it?"

"The concubines and I had planned on having a meeting after dinner to discuss some issues they have raised. We were not aware that you and the Queen were going to grace us with your presence tonight. We can reschedule the meeting."

No, no. Do not change your plans because we are here. Carry on as you normally would. What are the issues about?"

"Uh, er, they are about the concubine's rights Sire."

"Concubine's rights?" Ahasuerus said putting his eating utensils down. He and Esther had been discussing that earlier that evening. "Esther, Hegai planned a meeting with the concubines tonight after dinner to discuss what we were talking about earlier. I told him to go on with the meeting."

Esther nodded her head in agreement.

"Go ahead and start your meeting Hegai, the Queen and I will continue to eat our dinner."

"As you wish Your Excellency." Hegai stood up and addressed the group of servants and concubines. "We will now begin our meeting with the King's concubines. Everyone else is excused from dinner and may resume your regular duties. If all the concubines would turn their chairs to face the front of the platform, we will begin."

All the concubines turned their chairs to the front as Hegai commanded and sat down.

"I was not aware that the King and Queen were going to have dinner with us tonight, but he has instructed me to continue with our meeting as we had planned. Zena, did you draw up a list of suggestions as we discussed earlier?"

"Yes, Hegai here they are. These are some of the ideas we came up with," she said handing the list to Hegai.

"Thank you, Zena. I will read these suggestions out loud. If anyone has any other requests or suggestions, you may submit them after I finish reading."

"Hegai began reading the list that Zena handed him. With each of the requests, they all were quite impressed with the details of the five items.

"Does anyone have any other suggestions, requests or comments regarding this issue?" Hegai asked as he laid the list on the table in front of him.

None of the concubines replied or even looked up at Hegai. They were intimidated by the presence of the King and Queen. Hegai knew what they were feeling.

"Your Excellency, do you or the Queen have any comments regarding the concubines request at this time?"

Ahasuerus stood up looking at each of his concubines. "The Queen and I discussed this matter earlier this evening. The requests that you have raised were very well thought out and sound very reasonable to me. However, I suggest that Hegai submit these requests to my staff of lawyers for review. If your requests fall within Persian law; I will meet with Hegai and give him the final decision regarding your requests." When he finished speaking, Ahasuerus looked down at Esther to see if she had finished her dinner. "Are you ready to leave Esther?"

"Yes" Esther replied.

Ahasuerus held out his hand to help her up from the chair and escorted her to the door. All the concubines stood and bowed at the waist as they left the platform. The guards met them at the door and followed them back to their personal quarters. Neither of them said anything about the meeting as they walked through the halls. Esther was not sure how Ahasuerus was feeling about the meeting and decided not to ask. Thank you, Father, she prayed silently as they entered the door of their bed chamber.

Chapter Twenty

MORDECAI SHARES HIS FAITH

"Raise those arms up high! Hold your swords securely! Come on men, you must show better skill than this if you plan to subdue your enemy! the Persian Captain yelled at the group of men paired off in groups of two. Clink, clink, clink, ugh! ugh! The sounds of the swords clashing together and the men sighing kept Mordecai's attention as he watched from the side lines. He could clearly see that these men were not professional soldiers. Father, God, he prayed silently, please make us ready for the thirteenth of Adar. I know these are not fighting men but strengthen us to defeat our enemies. Be with us just as you were with Moses when you parted the Red Sea; and as you were with Gideon when he fought against the Midianites and defeated them, please be with us on the thirteenth of Adar.

Two trainees fighting close to where Mordecai was standing scuffled against each other with their swords clanging this way and that. The other trainee next to Mordecai raised his right foot and wrapped it around his opponent's left leg knocking him off his feet causing him to fall flat on his back in a vulnerable position. The trainee stood over his make-believe enemy with his sword held high in the air ready to cut off his so-called enemies' head with one smooth swoop when the captain yelled at him. "Stop!" and came running over to them.

The trainee stopped in mid-air.

"That was an excellent display of skill soldier, but please do not kill him; he is not your real enemy. Stand down!"

"Yes sir! The trainee that was standing replied as he offered his hand to his opponent helping him from the ground.

"Soldiers gather around!" the captain shouted. He walked over to the two trainees pulling them into the center of the men. "I want the two of you to re-enact the fight up until the time I shouted for you to stop so the men can copy your strategy. Go!"

The two trainees approached each other just as they had earlier, the one wrapping his foot around the other's leg throwing him off balance and again he landed on his back in a vulnerable position.

"Stop!" the captain yelled again, and the two trainees stopped.

"Did everyone see and understand the moves these two trainees displayed?"

"Yes Sir!" all the men replied together.

"Go back to your training stations and practice those moves to perfection."

"Yes Sir!" the men replied again and went back to their fighting stations.

Reelaiah walked over to Mordecai and the Captain.

"What do you think Captain? Will the men be ready? We only have a few weeks left."

Turning to face Reelaiah and Mordecai the Captain bowed at the waist and looked both men in the eyes before replying. "Considering that these men are not really soldiers but everyday farmers, they are doing very well. Also, the fact that most of their enemies will be just like them is a good thing; I believe they will be ready. They will not be fighting real Centurion Soldiers. The King has ordered all military in every rank to assist you in your fight. So, yes, I believe they will be ready in a few more weeks."

"This is good news!" Reelaiah said turning to Mordecai who stood quietly taking in every word of the captain and watching the men continue to train.

"God's will be done" Mordecai said turning to walk back to the palace grounds. Reelaiah walked with him; the captain turned his attention back to the training soldiers.

"You do not seem pleased Mordecai, what is on your mind?"

"Oh, I guess I have been waiting for this day for so long, I will be glad when it is over, and our people will be avenged of our enemies."

Reelaiah walked along side of Mordecai quietly until they reached the palace.

"I must be going home now. Tamara has dinner waiting for me. Oh, she wanted me to ask you how Queen Esther is doing?"

Mordecai had not thought about Esther in a few days. Knowing that she and the baby were fine and in the palace doctor's care; his mind was consumed with the up-coming fight. He was not sure if she wanted him to tell anyone of her condition, so he gave Reelaiah a general greeting. "The Queen is fine and sends her love."

"Tamara, Shakera and Aisha miss her and have asked permission to come and visit her at the palace when the fighting ends and things settle down."

"I think that can be arranged" Mordecai said shaking Reelaiah's hand. "I will give the Queen your greeting. Tell them we said Shalom and I will meet up with you tomorrow. Have a good evening Reelaiah."

"The same to you Mordecai" and the two men went their separate ways.

Walking through the gate and up the stairs, Mordecai stopped at the top trying to decide where he wanted to go; back to his personal quarters or to visit with Esther. Several days had passed since he learned of her condition, and he wanted to see how she was feeling. He turned left at the top of the stairs and walked down the long hall to Esther's personal quarters. This was strange, he thought. Normally there was a lot of activity up and down the halls. Servants going and coming during their daily chores whatever they were, but the halls were empty. There was no activity at all. The echo of his sandals ringing against the marble floor bounced off the stone walls as he reached the end of the hall and turned right approaching Esther's door. There were no guards posted in front of Esther's lounge door. Mordecai stood in front of the door for several minutes trying to make sense of what he was seeing. Clip, clip, clip, the sound of footsteps echoed from somewhere; he could not tell the direction. He waited hoping the steps would come close to him.

"Your Majesty!"

The greeting echoed from behind him and startled him. He turned to see Hegai walking toward him from the end of the hall.

"Your Majesty, may I be of service to you?" Hegai asked.

"Yes." Mordecai said relieved that there was another living soul in the area. "Where is everyone? Where is Queen Esther? Where are her guards?"

"Oh, Your Majesty, please forgive me. No one informed you that the Queen had her personal quarters moved into the King's personal quarters a few days ago. The King had this section of the palace closed until further notice. All the servants have been transferred to the King and Queen's personal quarters. Please forgive me for not reporting the change."

"Not to worry, Hegai. I just thought I would stop in and visit with her."

"If you wish, I will accompany you to her new quarters?"

"Her quarters are right beside the King's personal quarters?" Mordecai asked.

"Yes sir."

"I know where that is. Thank you for the information."

"You are quite welcome Sir." Hegai replied and continued walking down the hall.

Mordecai walked the opposite direction toward the King's personal quarters. Hegai quickly disappeared down the hall and around the corner; Mordecai again, was left alone in the hall and again heard the echo of his own steps on the marble floor. The oil lamps on the walls were set very low casting eerie shadows down the long corridors and Mordecai picked up his pace walking past the

Queen's and King's courtyards. Finally, he reached the breezeway and stopped. Voices were coming from the King's throne room. They seemed to be coming closer to him, so he waited. Two guards and Ahasuerus meet him in the breezeway.

"Mordecai, how are you this evening?" Ahasuerus greeted extending his hand to him.

"I am fine Ahasuerus. How are you and Esther?"

"Esther is fine. I believe she is resting now."

"I will not disturb her then."

"Have you eaten your dinner yet?"

No."

"Come, join me for dinner in the dining room. Guard, have the servants prepare dinner for Mordecai and me. Check with the Queen's servant to see if she has eaten and if she would like to join us for dinner."

"As you wish Your Excellency" the guard replied walking down the hall.

The two men continued to walk toward the dining room with the guard following behind.

"How are things going with your people Mordecai? Are they ready against the day?"

"I was just coming from the soldiers training session. They will be ready according to the captain's report. He informed me that per your orders, all the Persian soldiers will be involved in this revenge."

"Yes, I gave that order. I have given you and your people permission to stand for their lives and destroy anyone who comes against you, whether men, women boys and girls and my soldiers will assist you. You have permission to slay them and take their spoil. Does this please you Mordecai?" Ahasuerus asked looking at him.

"Yes, I am very pleased Ahasuerus. I was trying to picture in my mind how the fight was going to play itself out."

Turning the corner, the two men entered the dining hall and sat down.

"I have heard rumors that Haman's wife Zeresh and her sons are planning to leave town. That they have contacted their people, the

Amalekites, and have arranged to leave Shushan before the thirteenth of Adar."

"May I pour your wine now?" the servant asked holding the wine bottle.

"Yes, that will be fine" Ahasuerus answered. "Yes, I heard that also. I have stationed guards around her home in plain apparel. They will deter them if they try to escape."

"That is good" Mordecai replied sipping his wine.

"Your Majesty, Abagtha is here with a message from the Queen."

"Show him in."

"Your Majesty, the Queen says she is not feeling up to having dinner tonight and sends her apologies to you and her father."

"Thank you Abagtha."

"You are welcome, Sire" Abagtha replied and backed out of the dining room.

"I have not seen Esther since she fainted during dinner last week. How is she doing?"

"She is doing as well as can be expected. She gets tired and sleeps a lot. Sips mint tea and biscuits with a little fruit. The doctor says she is fine, and the baby is fine."

"Your Majesty, Memucan is here with a report he says you wanted as soon as possible. Will you see him now, or should I have him wait until after dinner?"

"You may show him in now. Memucan, you have the report I requested?"

"Yes, Your Excellency."

"Tell me what you have found."

Memucan walked over to the table pulled out the report and began to read. "The laws on the books state that if you take a concubine as your wife and find that you have no pleasure in her, you may give her a paper of divorcement letting her go where she desires to go. However, any children that she may bare to you belong to you and must remain in the palace."

Mordecai sat quietly listening to the report not sure what it was all about. Ahasuerus sat back in his chair carefully listening to Memucan's report.

"Is that all there is to the report?"

"Yes, Your Excellency. You may divorce them, send them back to their families if that is where they wish to go but the children must stay within the palace."

"Arrange for letters of divorcement to be drawn up with that stipulation and that anyone requesting a divorce will be provided with a monitory stipend to help them rebuild a life for themselves. Also include that any concubine that wishes to continue to remain within the palace with their children are free to do so; that they will have the right to raise their children in the palace. If they decide to stay, they will continue to receive the care they currently receive. They will be provided with the appropriate security when they leave the palace grounds to visit their family or to go to the market. Did you get all of that Memucan?"

"Yes, Your Excellency."

"Very good. Have the documents drawn up and bring them to me in the morning. Also, have Hegai accompany you in the morning with the documents."

"As you wish Your Excellency" Memucan replied, bowing at the waist as he backed out of the room. As he left, the servants served Ahasuerus and Mordecai their dinner. Both men began eating in awkward silence.

He could have had this meeting in private Mordecai thought to himself as he put another biscuit in his mouth. He apparently wanted me to know that he is going to be faithful to Esther. This is good. This is very good Mordecai thought smiling to himself slightly.

"Mordecai, tell me more about your god" Ahasuerus said breaking the awkward silence.

"Where would you like me to begin?"

"Esther mentioned something to me about your god's divine providence. She said that it was your god's divine providence that brought the two of us together, that it was his providence that freed your people from slavery permitting you to live here in Shushan and throughout the Persian Provinces. How could all of this be? I have my own mind and make my own decisions. So did my forefathers. Explain this to me."

Mordecai sat back in his chair, took a sip of wine thinking for a minute. "Divine Providence is God moving upon man's heart to make decisions that would benefit the lives of His people according to His Divine Purpose. In this case, His people the Jews."

"So, you are saying that your god touched the hearts of my father, grandfather as well as me to act favorably to your people, the Jews, to free them from slavery; give them safe haven in Persian territory and allow them to freely worship your god?"

"Yes. That is exactly what I am saying."

"Esther also says that your god talks personally with her. Is this true?"

Mordecai smiled. "It sounds like Esther has spoken to you at length about the relationship she has with God."

"Yes, she has. I find it intriguing that one could possibly have a personal relationship with a god that speaks personally with you and seems to be concerned about every aspect of your life. If this is indeed true, I would like to know that god for myself. How can I find out if your god is real?"

"You really want to know if God is real?"

"I most certainly do. Prove it to me!"

Mordecai got up from his chair and walked over to the window beckoning Ahasuerus to follow him. He pulled the drapes back from the window. It was dark outside. A full moon was rising in the sky with bright stars twinkling on either side. "Look at that!" Mordecai said. "Who could create something that beautiful! Look how the trees stretch their bare branches up toward the heavens in praise to the God that created them. Look how the seasons stay in their routine, spring, summer, fall and winter; each in their personal cycle's year in and year out. Can you tell me who or what holds the sun and the moon up in the sky and has them rotate around the earth in perfect intervals? He is God my friend. God who created the heavens and the earth. This same God created you and me. Look how wonderfully our bodies are created. How self-sufficient they are with the ability to heal itself. There is your proof Ahasuerus. If you want Him to talk to you personally, I suggest you get up early in the morning, go over to your window, look up and say 'God, if you are real, please show me. Give me the faith to believe that you are the one and only true God.'"

"Is that all I have to do? Is that all God would want from me, just to believe that he is? No gifts, no sacrifices? It sounds too easy."

"There are sacrifices to be made for atonement for sin, but the Levitical Priest take care of that, that has to do with Temple Worship. There is the Circumcision performed on all males as an outward sign of the Covenant that God made with Abraham that He would always be with him and protect him because he, Abraham, believed and trusted Him. When all this fighting is over, if you like, we could take a trip to Jerusalem to the Temple, offer sacrificial gifts to the priests for atonement for our sins. Until then, get up early in the morning and pray to God."

"Pray?"

"Yes. Praying is just talking to God. You want to know if he is real, ask Him? You can talk to him about whatever is on your mind. Pray in faith believing that He hears you."

"Hmmm. This is interesting, very interesting indeed" Ahasuerus said walking back to the table with Mordecai following behind.

"Your Excellencies, would you like me to warm your dinners? They have gotten cold" the servant asked.

"No, I am fine. What about you Mordecai? Would you like your dinner warmed?

"No thank you; I would like a cup of tea if possible?"

"Yes, me too" Ahasuerus said as the servant walked away. The fire crackled in the fireplace drawing the men's attention in that direction.

"Come, we can have our tea by the fireplace."

The two men sat by the fire sipping their tea. Mordecai shared stories of how God intervened in the lives of the Jewish people. He told about the Jew's first king, King Saul, how he was disobedient to God and how God dethroned him. Ahasuerus was fascinated with the stories; he asked questions here and there. The two men sat talking way into the wee hours of the morning.

Chapter Twenty-One

MEMUCAN PLOTS TO KILL MORDECAI

Memucan tossed and turned in bed. It was late in the evening, and he could not sleep. Rather than disturb his entire household, he rolled out of bed careful not to awake his wife sleeping soundly by his side, slipped on his clothes, and eased out of the house. The moon was full. Moonlight reflections bounced off the cobblestones and lighted his pathway so he could clearly see where he was stepping. He could hear the echo of his sandals ring out in his ears as he walked down the cobblestone street. No one was around. He felt a strange sense of peace as he walked toward the palace. Oil lamps positioned all around the palace always burned providing the necessary light for the guards to provide effective monitoring. It is good that I am unable to sleep he thought to himself. This is the perfect time for me to scout out a place for us to hold our meeting. "With the King's loyalty to the Jews, our meeting place should be off palace grounds" he said quietly to himself and turned to the right and walked down a big hill away from the palace. After reaching the bottom of the hill from the palace, he walked a mile and a half more before he saw it. "What is that!" he said to himself as he slowed his pace. Something was glowing in the distance. It appeared to be a bright yellow glow down over a little crevice toward his right. He was no longer on cobblestone roads, so he quietly inched up to the top of the little crevice on ground that was not hard and not soft, but firm. It was just right for him to sneak up without being heard or seen. The yellow glow turned out to be an open fire surrounded by three stone walls. Each wall looked to be six feet tall.

Deciding to get closer, he put his right foot over the top of the crevice feeling for something, a twig, or an exposed tree root to support himself. Finding what he thought was a solid tree root, he swung his left leg over, but the root did not hold him. He slid halfway down the hill with rocks and dirt rolling down in front of him making a rustling sound. Fear gripped him in the pit of his stomach, and he dug his fingers into the dirt trying to find something to stop his fall. Dirt, grass, and mud covered his face and went in his mouth prohibiting him from crying out as he continued to fall. Finally, he came to a stop at the bottom of the crevice and laid there motionlessly for a few minutes before trying to move. Raising himself up on his hands and knees, he wiped his face with his hands, spit out the mud from his mouth and stood up brushing off the dirt from his clothes. When he turned around, he stood face to face with three large men who had surrounded him. The six-foot stone wall shielded the firelight, but the moonlight shining down on the three men gave them a menacing appearance and fear gripped him again.

"Who are you! What are you doing out here?" the big one in the middle demanded.

"I, ah, I am..." Memucan looked at each of them trying to find the right words to say that would not get him killed. These three men looked like vagabonds that roamed the outskirts of the city. Realizing his foolishness in coming out by himself in the middle of the night, he was at a loss for words.

"Come!" the big one in the middle said grabbing Memucan by the arm. His shoulders were at least four to five inches above Memucan's head. As the four of them walked toward the fire, Memucan kept stumbling; he had broken his sandals in the fall down the hill. Seeing him tripping, one of the other men, big, but not as tall as the first, grabbed his other arm and they lifted him up causing his feet to dangle touching the ground here and there as they walked.

"I, ah, listen, I am… I have silver!"

The men stopped and looked at Memucan.

"Where is it!" the big one barked.

"I do not have it on me, but I can get it for you if you do not kill me. I promise I will get it for you if you do not kill me!" Memucan pleaded.

The big man grunted, and they continued around the brick wall where the fire burned. Spaced around the fire were three wooden crates with bed rolls, swords, knives, shields, and helmets placed on the ground in between each crate. A small tree branch was positioned over the fire with a rabbit pierced through roasting.

Dragging Memucan closer to the fire, the big one shoved him down on one of the crates. The other two sat down on the other two crates while the big one grabbed a crate over by the wall that held other supplies. Dumping the supplies on the ground, he turned the crate upside down and sat next to Memucan with his sword drawn.

"Who are you and what are you doing out here!"

"My name is Memucan," was all he could manage to eke out.

"What are you doing here?" the big one continued.

"My name is…."

"You already told us your name, what are you doing here? Where is this silver!"

"I am a member of King Ahasuerus' court. His top lawyer."

The smallest one of the men jumped up from his seat, pulled his sword out of its' sheath and ran over to where Memucan sat. "He is one of them responsible for killing our brother Haman!" he yelled. The other two men jumped up and positioned their swords for attack as well.

Memucan fell backward on the ground yelling "Wait! Wait! Wait!" Scrambling to his feet, he backed away from the three men with his back against the six-foot wall. He was trapped and he knew it. "Wait, please wait a minute! Let me explain!"

You have three minutes to tell us why we should not cut your head off right now and throw your body out for the jackals to eat!" the big one said in a low controlled voice.

Memucan caught his breath, swallowed trying to explain. "Yes, I am one of the King's Court, his First Prince, but I had nothing to do with the killing of your brother...., ah, Haman? Was that what you said his name was?" Memucan knew very well who the men were talking about, but he was trying to distance himself from the King and his actions.

"Yes, his name was Haman. Our kinfolk here in Shushan wrote to us telling us that he was hung because of a Jew named Mordecai. Are you sure your name is not Mordecai?"

"No! no, no. My name is not Mordecai, no, no, no. Gentlemen, please, if we could just sit down, I will explain everything to you. Please believe me, I did not kill your brother, but I know who did. If you give me a chance, I will tell you all about it. Could we sit down? Please?"

Memucan looked at each of the three men pleadingly, trying to save his life.

"Sit!" the big one said. All four men pulled their crates back around the fire and listened as Memucan began to tell his story. He told how he was the one who introduced Haman to the King, how the King befriended him and gave him the highest power in the land, apart from the King himself. He told how all men everywhere were to bow down and worship Haman.

"He had that much power?"

"Yes! He was the most powerful man in all the 127 Persian Provinces."

"Why did he not tell us?" the little one asked.

"I do not know" Memucan said hunching his shoulders and continued his story. "As I said earlier, all men were to bow down to Haman and worship him like he was a god. Everyone did, me included. But there was one man who refused to bow down. That man's name was Mordecai. He refused. After Mordecai's continual refusal to bow down to your brother, he asked me to find out who

Mordecai was. I told him he was a Jew. When your brother found out that Mordecai was a Jew, he became enraged!

"Yes, all of our people hate the Jews!"

"Who are your people?" Memucan asked.

"Amalekites. We are Amalekites and we have warred with the Jews almost since time began" the little one said.

"That is what Haman told me. Finding out that Mordecai was a Jew, your brother went to the King to asked him for permission to exterminate all the Jews from Persian territory and the King granted him his petition."

"The King agreed!" the big one blurted out.

"Yes, he did. So, Haman sent out a decree throughout the 127 Persian Provinces that said that on the thirteenth of Adar, the Persian citizens were to slaughter every Jewish man, woman, and child, even babies throughout the providence."

"The thirteenth of Adar? That is just about a week and a half away!" the big one said.

"Yes, it is. However;" Memucan held up his hand and continued, "Mordecai deceived the King. The King replaced his old Queen and searched the 127 Persian Provinces for another one. This Mordecai submitted his daughter not disclosing that she was a Jew. No Jewish maiden should have ever entered the contest to become a Persian Queen, but Mordecai did not tell anyone that his daughter was Jewish. Well, when Mordecai received his decree that he and all his people were to be exterminated on the thirteenth of Adar, he went to his daughter, whom the King had picked to be his Queen, and asked her to intercede for him and his people. She did. She told the King that your brother had deceitfully tricked him into killing all her people. The King became irate and killed your brother. He hung him on the gallows right in front of your brother's house where his wife and ten sons could see. That is who killed your brother, not me!" Memucan sat quietly watching the effect his story had on the three men. "So, the three of you have come here from where?"

"We have come from Canaan."

"Canaan? That is a long way. Did you come to avenge your brother?"

"Our sister wrote to us asking permission for her and her sons to come home. We have come to assist them in the move. She did not tell us all that had happened to Haman, just that he was dead, and they needed to leave Shushan and return home immediately.

"Does she know that you are here?"

"No. We did not tell her."

"Do you want to avenge your brother?"

The three men looked at each other. "How could we accomplish that? You say this man Mordecai is the next to the most powerful man in the kingdom. He would always have all kinds of security around him. There are only three of us" the big one snorted.

Memucan sat quietly his mind racing. How can I use these men to help me get rid of Mordecai? There must be a way. It would have to be done on the thirteenth of Adar he thought running his hand through his hair.

"What are you thinking so hard about?" the big one asked.

"I was thinking of a way you could avenge your brother. Listen, when King Ahasuerus elevated this Mordecai into your brother's position, he gave him the power to rescind the decree Haman sent out to destroy all the Jews on the thirteenth of Adar and gave the Jews the right to fight back and kill anyone who challenged them. I was thinking that on the twelfth of Adar, I could sneak the three of you into the palace and show you where Mordecai's personal quarters are." Memucan looked at each of the men again. "You all look like strong warriors. Could you overtake two or three palace guards?"

"Humph!" the big one grunted. The three of us could handle ten to fifteen palace guards." The other two men shook their heads in agreement.

"Fine, I will meet you right here in the middle of the second watch on the twelfth of Adar and lead you up to the palace and sneak the three of you in. I know a lot of the back secret passages that has little to no guards. I will lead you to Mordecai's quarters and you can take care of him. Does this sound like a good plan to you?" Memucan asked.

"It sounds good" the big one said. "But this is some story you have told us. How do we know that we can trust you? For all we know, you could be this Mordecai trying to save your own life?"

Memucan had not thought about that, and he sat quietly staring into the fire. "You asked me what I was doing out here in the middle of the night all by myself, right?"

"Yes, that is right."

"Well, I was looking for a secret place to organize the local Persian villagers to fight on the thirteenth. Would you allow me to use this place to have our meeting? If so, there will be several people attending the meeting who could vouch for me, that I am not Mordecai; that I am Memucan, the King's First Prince. If I do not attend the meeting with the other villagers, you will know that the story I told you was a lie, that you should immediately go get your sister and her sons and leave Shushan as quickly as you can. But when I show up here with a large group of villagers seven days from now, you will know that I was telling you the truth and the three of you will have an opportunity to avenge your brother."

The three men sat quietly digesting Memucan's words. "What do we really have to lose?" the big one said. His two brothers nodded their heads in agreement. "Alright, Memucan, we will let you go. You arrange to have your meeting here in seven days; we will be waiting for you. But know this, if you do not show up, we will track you down and kill you and your whole family. Do you understand?" the big one said standing up looking down on Memucan.

"Ah, yes. I understand" Memucan said becoming a bit nervous again. The other two men stood up as the big one told Memucan to go. Standing up, Memucan offered his hand to shake the three men's hands, but they just stood there staring at him. He turned and quickly walked away from them stumbling on his broken sandals. Kicking them off, he quickly began walking home in his bare feet. Climbing back up the same steep crevice he had fallen down earlier proved to be easier without his sandals, but the dirt, sticks and rocks hurt his feet tremendously. He tried to ignore the pain, grateful that he had gotten away from those men and was able to make it home with his life.

Chapter Twenty-Two

THE ROYAL'S PERSONAL STRUGGLES

Ahasuerus rolled over on his right side, stretched out his arm to feel if Esther lay beside him. Her side of the bed was empty. He missed her at dinner last night and wondered if she was be feeling better this morning. As he lay in bed, the conversation he had had with Mordecai the night before played through his mind. He said all I had to do was ask this god if he were real and wait for an answer. It sounded simple enough, too simple. Mordecai and Esther talked as though he were real, like a real person they could talk to, almost touch. None of his ancestors talked of such a god. Turning over on his left side, he tried to dismiss the conversation and go back to sleep; it was very early in the morning, and he had only been to bed for five hours. "Go back to sleep" he told himself and closed his eyes, but the words kept ringing through his mind, 'you must believe that God is, believe that he created everything in the world, this is called faith. Try Him Ahasuerus. Get up in the morning when everyone else is asleep. Get quiet and pray.' Groaning to himself, he lay back flat on the bed, stretched his arms and legs looking up at the ceiling. 'Believe that God is, believe that he created everything in the world, this is called faith. Try Him Ahasuerus. Get up in the morning when everyone else is asleep. Get quiet and pray.'

"This is foolishness" he said to himself. "It is foolish to talk out loud to someone or something that is not there."

"To whom are you talking to when you talk to yourself and no one else is in the room?"

Ahasuerus sat straight up in the bed looking around to see who was talking to him. He heard someone, but no one was there. Feeling a bit unnerved, he rolled out of bed and went over to the window pulling back the drapes to look out over the landscape. It was early dawn. The only movement going on were the guards walking through the courtyards doing their scheduled patrols, no one else was stirring. As he sat there on the window ledge, a sense of peace overwhelmed him, and he understood now what Esther said to him several days ago about this being her favorite time of the day.

"God?" he said softly. "God of Abraham, Isaac, and Jacob. Esther's and Mordecai's God. If you are real, please show me. I would like to get to know you just as they do. Amen." The peace remained as he sat there on the window ledge looking out over the courtyards and watched the dawn turn into the morning light.

As the servants began to awaken and go about their morning chores, Ahasuerus got up from the window and put a log on the fire to keep the fire going. He no longer felt tired. As the fire crackled and sparked, he remembered that Esther said she too felt alive, energized, and refreshed after spending time with her God. "This is real. It must be real" he said to himself and jumped when he heard a knock at his bed chamber door.

"Your Excellency." It was his personal guard at the door.

"Yes, come in."

The guard opened the door and poked his head through. "Are you ready for your morning bath or would you prefer to have breakfast first?"

"I will bathe first."

"As you wish Your Excellency" the guard replied and closed the door.

Ahasuerus walked over to the door that connected his personal bed chamber with Esther's. Quietly opening the door, he poked his head through and saw that Esther was still asleep. He closed the door just as quietly, put on his bath robe and went down for his morning bath. The peace that he experienced earlier was still with him along with, with, what was it that he was feeling now? He thought to himself. He felt happy, joyous, and energized. Had Mordecai's God revealed Himself to me, Ahasuerus wondered.

Slipping out of his robe and into the warm bath, the peace still seemed to envelope him. Everything seemed to be bright all around the room, but the sun had not risen. It was a cold cloudy day outside; however, he felt warm, bright and joy as he took his morning bath.

Esther opened her eyes. What time is it she through? The fire in the fireplace spread a warm glow throughout her room so she knew Yara had already been in to check on her. She still had not gotten use to her new personal quarters. The sun did not seem to flow through her window in the morning as it did in her old quarters, but she adjusted to the changes. Most of the time she figured she would be waking up in Ahasuerus' room anyway. Pulling the covers back and sitting up on the side of the bed, dizziness and a nervous stomach descended on her along with that annoying headache. Esther groaned and laid back down in the bed pulling the covers up under her chin.

"Queen Esther, Esther, are you awake, may I come in?" It was Yara.

"Yes Yara, please come in."

"How are you feeling this morning Esther?" Yara asked coming over to her bed.

"I have felt better" Esther said not moving and not sitting up. "Yara, I feel so sick. How long does this sickness last?"

"It varies from individual-to-individual Esther. You are about five and half to six months along now. By your sixth month, you should be feeling a lot better. Would you like me to draw your bath for you?"

"No, the smell of the bath salts makes me sick to my stomach. If you fix the water for me, I will take a sponge bath right here."

"Very well, I will put the chamber pot beside you just in case you need it."

"Thank you Yara" Esther said and tried to lay as still as she could so her stomach would settle down. "Yara, you are a midwife are you not?"

"Yes I am."

"Is there something else I could drink or take to calm my stomach down? Something other than mint tea?"

"There is an herb that I think will help you; however, I must check with the palace doctor first and get his permission to give it to you."

"Please check with him."

"I will Esther. Everything is going to be fine; you just rest there; I will be right back. Yara stood outside of Esther's door thinking for a long time before walking away. She had been a midwife for several years and delivered many babies at the palace and in the village. In all her years of experience, there were only three times she saw mothers as sick as Esther was in their fifth and sixth months. Out of the three, only one baby was born healthy and strong, the other two babies did not survive and one mother of the two babies died in childbirth. Esther must be feeling very sick to ask for something to relieve her symptoms. In the past, she always seemed to work through whatever was ailing her on her own, never calling for the palace doctor. Sadness and grief overcame Yara as she hurried down the hall toward the palace infirmary. Turning the corner, she saw Dr. Kazim, a doctor from India sitting at his desk.

"Doctor," Yara called. "May I speak with you?"

"Yes, please come in. You are Queen Esther's personal servant and midwife, yes?"

"Yes I am."

"What can I do for you?"

"I was in with the Queen this morning and she is very uncomfortable, very sick to her stomach, dizzy with headaches."

"How many months is she into her pregnancy?"

"About five and a half to six months. She has asked me for something to curb her upset stomach. She barely eats anything and has been staying in bed for the past few days. I thought I should report her condition to you."

"Yes, you did right. At five and a half to six months along, morning sickness should not prevent her from getting out of bed and having a normal day. Has the King seen her?"

"I do not think so. She has been taking what little she eats in her personal bed chamber and has not received any visitors, not even her father."

"Wait here while I get my medical bag and I will go with you to see her."

Esther lay in bed trying to lay as still as possible, but it did not work. Her stomach took over and she bent over the bed and was sick in the chamber pot. She grabbed a towel and wiped her face and eyes. Warm tears were flowing from her eyes in a steady stream, and she did not understand why she was crying. "This is not like me" she said to herself. "This is not like me at all! Why am I so sad!" Esther rolled over on her side and sobbed uncontrollably. Drying her eyes again, she began talking to herself. "Come on Esther, get a hold of yourself! You have been sick many times before, wipe your eyes, sit up, take a deep breath. Oh Father, please help me to feel better. Thank you, Amen." After drying her eyes again, she propped herself up on her pillows and watched the fire burning in the fireplace as she waited for Yara to return.

Yara waited by the door; the doctor joined her and the two of them hurried down the hall to Esther's quarters. No one was around as they walked down the corridor and Yara was glad. She did not want anyone to see the doctor going into Esther's personal quarters. The guard stood at attention as she and Dr. Kazim approached the door. He looked at Yara, then the doctor in surprise but did not say a word; he just opened the door for them.

"Do you want me to go into her room with you doctor?"

"Yes, please come in with me; you may be of some assistance."

As they entered Esther's room, they found her sitting up in bed. Her eyes and face were red and a little swollen. Yara moved the chamber pot away from the bed and set a chair in its place for the doctor to sit down.

"Queen Esther, how are you feeling today?"

"How long is this going to last doctor? Give me something to make me feel better."

"What is it Esther, nausea, headache and dizziness?"

"Yes, tiredness, sadness; why am I so sad doctor? I have nothing to be sad about?"

Doctor Kazim looked at Esther and smiled a little. "Esther, did your mother tell you anything about childbearing?"

"My mother died when I was a child. I never really knew her. I was raised by my cousin who treated me like his daughter."

"Oh, I see" the doctor replied opening his medical bag pulling out a small round bag with what looked like a small bag of rice to Esther. "Yara, bring me a cup of water and something to stir with please."

Yara brought the cup over, the doctor opened the small round bag with his fingers and took three small spoons of the substance; dropped them into the cup and stirred it around until it was completely dissolved. Handing the spoon back to Yara, he turned toward Esther and held the cup up to her mouth and told her to drink all of it.

Esther took a sip and pushed the cup away with her hand. The liquid was bitter and had a burning sensation as she swallowed it.

"No, no, no, Queen Esther, you must drink all of it at once. Come, drink it all!" the doctor said pulling her hand down and pushing the cup back up to her mouth.

Esther quickly drank the mixture down, laid back on the pillows and took a deep breath. The burning lasted for a few seconds.

"In a few minutes you will feel much better. Here Yara, please wash this out immediately. Make sure everything is washed out of this cup before returning it to the table. Do you understand?"

"Yes doctor, I understand" Yara said as she took the cup and left the room.

"Esther, what you are feeling and experiencing is all a part of having a child. The sickness, the tiredness, the headaches, nausea, even the sadness that you are feeling is a part of childbearing. The medicine I gave you will settle your stomach giving you a desire to eat again which will give you more energy as well as take away your headache. These symptoms you are experiencing are normal and they may come back. However, if they do, I want you to try and deal with them without this medication. Drink your mint tea, force yourself to eat fruit, biscuits, and some meat. If you throw it up, eat again to keep your strength up and remember; this too will pass."

"Does everyone experience this when they are having a child?"

"Some women have no symptoms at all; others have sickness as soon as they know they are with child for the first three to four months and then the symptoms go away, still others are sick for the full nine months of childbearing. Everyone is different. The important thing to remember is that all of this will pass, and you will feel happy again after your baby is delivered and you are holding him in your arms. How are you feeling now?"

"I am feeling much better, thank you doctor."

"You are most welcome Queen Esther. Now, I want you to get washed and dressed and eat some breakfast. Have Yara come and get me if the symptoms return as severely as they were earlier."

"Yes, doctor I will."

Dr. Kazim gathered up his medical bag, looked back at Esther one more time smiling and left. Yara was just returning from cleaning out the cup that the medicine was in and met him in the lounge.

"Doctor, may I ask you a question?"

"Yes, of course, what is it?"

"I am aware of an herb that helps with those symptoms, but none that work that fast. What was the herb you gave to the Queen? I have been a midwife for many years, have delivered many babies and have seen at least three patients in the same condition as the Queen. Two of the three mothers as well as the babies died in childbirth."

"Ah, yes I too have seen these severe symptoms. In India, my homeland, scientists have discovered fast working herbs to help these symptoms. When you have some time, stop by and I will explain the new developments in medicine which should be shared among the other midwives."

"Thank you doctor."

"The Queen is feeling better, get her up bathed and dressed. Have her breakfast fixed. It would be better if she had her breakfast in the royal dining room to get her out of her room. It may be a good idea to have her eat with the King and her father. Can you arrange that?"

"Yes, doctor, I can."

"Very good."

After the doctor left, Yara went over to Esther's desk and wrote two notes; one to the King and one to Esther's father stating the Queen is requesting them to have breakfast with her in the royal dining room. Folding up each note, she opened the door and asked the guard to have messengers deliver each of the notes for the Queen.

Esther was sitting on the side of the bed with her bath robe and sandals on her feet as Yara entered her room. "It is good to see you up; would you like to take your bath now?"

"Yes. I am feeling better now."

"What do you think about having breakfast in the royal dining room with the King and your father?" Yara asked as they walked around to the bath area.

"I think I would like that. It has been while since I have seen them."

"Good" Yara said as she helped Esther down into the pool.

Mordecai awoke with Esther on his mind. I probably should have gone to see her last night, even if it would have been for a moment, he thought to himself. "I will arrange to have breakfast with her just to make sure she is alright." As he came out of the bed chamber, the guard knocked on his door.

"Yes, what is it."

"I have a message from the Queen Sir."

"Oh, please come in."

The guard stepped inside the door and handed Mordecai the note, then closed the door behind him.

Mordecai read the note. Father, I would be pleased if you would join me for breakfast in the royal dining room. Thank you. The note was signed 'Queen Esther.'

The note was not Esther's handwriting and Mordecai's concern heightened. Putting on his royal robe and golden crown, he hurried down the hall toward Esther's personal quarters. As he reached her door, the guard opened the door to her lounge without announcing him. Mordecai looked at him and went inside without questioning his behavior. As he stepped inside, he saw Yara coming out of the bed chamber.

"Oh, good morning Sir. The Queen will be out momentarily. Would you like to have a seat while you wait?"

"Yes. Is the Queen feeling alright?" Mordecai asked calmly.

"Yes. She is feeling better."

"She was sick then?"

"She was a little sick, but she is feeling better now."

Mordecai hesitated a little. He could always tell when something was wrong with Esther. Even as a child, when she would get sick, or something was bothering her he always knew. He knew something was or had been wrong with her now.

"Yara" Mordecai said slowly. "Please tell me the truth. Has Esther been sick?"

Yara looked at Mordecai and knew that she could not withhold the truth from him. "Yes Sir. She has been sick for the past three days. I called for the doctor this morning and…"

"The doctor?" Mordecai said sitting up in his chair.

"Yes," Yara continued slowly. "I called the doctor because Esther had not been eating and was extremely sick to her stomach. He came and gave her some medicine and she is feeling better now."

As Yara finished speaking, Esther came out of the bed chamber. "Morde!" She walked over to where he was sitting and hugged him around the neck. "How good it is to see you. Will you join me for breakfast?"

Mordecai pulled Esther away from himself and searched her face. "What is wrong Esther." Tell me. Please do not hold anything from me. Are you alright?"

"Yes Morde. I am fine now. I was sick for a while, but the doctor gave me some medicine and told me that these symptoms were normal for a person in my condition and that it would pass. I am fine now."

"You look pale." Mordecai said still looking at her intently.

"That is because I am hungry! Come, we will go and eat our breakfast. I believe Ahasuerus will be joining us, yes?" Esther asked looking at Yara.

"Yes, Your Majesty, he will be joining you also."

"Good." Esther replied as the three of them left the lounge area.

Chapter Twenty-Three

ZERESH'S ATTEMPTED ESCAPE

Memucan made his way down the cobblestone street that led to the palace. With each step he took, he winced with pain. His feet and his sides were extremely sore from the night before. It even hurt to breathe. He did not understand how the peasants could walk bear footed regardless of the surface they were walking on or the temperature outside.

Admatha met him at the palace gate and laughed looking at him. "What is wrong with you Memucan? Why are you limping?"

"Come to my office" Memucan whispered "and I will tell you all about it." Admatha followed him to his office and sat waiting patiently for an explanation. Memucan hobbled around to his chair behind the desk and let his body fall into it wincing all the way down.

"What is wrong with you Memucan? What happened to you? You are all scratched up and limping. Did someone assault you?"

"No. No one assaulted me. I went out late last night looking for a place to have our meeting and fell over a hill. I am alright though. I found a good place way on the other side of the palace grounds down over the hill about two miles away."

"Yes, I know the place. There are walls left over from a fight years ago."

"That is it. That is the perfect place to meet seven days from now. Spread the word to all who need to know. I will meet you there. Until then, we should not be seen talking together. None of us should be seen talking together." Memucan deliberately left out his meeting with the three Amalekite soldiers. The less people knew about his plot, the more successful it would be, and no one could point the finger at him.

"Alright. I must leave anyway. You take care of yourself" Admatha said opening the door looking both ways making sure no one saw him. He slipped out and closed the door behind himself.

"You want how many bottles of wine?" the merchant asked.

"Ten."

"Ten? Why so many? Are you going on a journey or something? Ten bottles of wine; five bags of flower, three jars of honey, seven bundles of dried beef and three barrels of oil. Do you have enough silver to pay for this order?"

Aspatha looked over his left shoulder and noticed a palace guard watching him. He hunched his brother on his left. "Look!" he whispered. See that guard over there? He is watching us."

"I see him," his brother answered.

"Excuse me gentlemen, I asked you if you have enough silver to pay for this order? Hey, you boys are Haman's sons are you not?"

"How much is the order Sir?" Aspatha asked looking back at the guard.

"Fifty pieces of silver. Do you have that much?"

"Here…, here is 75 pieces of silver, how quickly can you pack up the order?"

"Seventy-five pieces of silver! Why, thank you gentlemen. Thank you. I, er, I can have this ready for you in ten minutes. Just wait here."

"No, ah, we, ah," Aspatha looked back again and saw another guard walk up to the first one. They began talking together looking over at Aspatha and his brother.

"Sir, please prepare the order, we have some other things we need to pick up. We will come back here in ten minutes if that is alright with you?"

"Yes, that will be fine. Anytime someone places and order this large, ah, take all the time you need. It will be ready when you return."

Aspatha grabbed his brother's arm and the two boys quickly walked in the opposite direction from the guards. The guards waited until the boys walked away then went over to the merchant.

"What kind of order did those boys place with you?" the guards asked.

"They, ah, they just bought some supplies I guess for home" the merchant replied. "Is there something wrong?"

"How much silver did they give you?"

"Ah, er, seventy-five pieces of silver. Why?"

"Is that the exact cost of the order they placed?"

"Well, ah, no. The exact cost was fifty pieces of silver. They gave me an extra twenty-five for packing up the order and having it ready for them in ten minutes. Have they done something wrong? Is it alright for me to have their order ready for them as they requested and keep the extra twenty-five shekels of silver?"

"You are fine, merchant. Go about your business, just do not mention to them that we inquired about their order. Is that understood?"

"Yes Sir, I understand fully."

"Very good," the guards said as they turned and walked away.

Aspatha and his brother walked down the alley and doubled back hiding on the other side of the merchant's tent and listened as the guards questioned him. When the guards walked away, they walked further back behind the tent.

"What should we do?" Aspatha asked his brother Parmashta.

"We will wait back here for ten minutes and then pick up the order and hurry home" Parmashta said. "We left the horse and wagon in front of the merchant's tent. When the order is filled, you go to the right side of the tent. If the guards are not around, quickly get into the wagon and meet me on the other side of the marketplace. Mama wanted me to pick up some extra blankets and pillows for the trip. Once we get all our supplies, we can head back to the house."

"I sure will be glad when we get out of here and back to mama's homeland."

"Me too" Parmashta replied. "Hurry now, we need to get this done and get back home before mama and the others get worried about us."

Aspatha embraced his brother, then ran around to the right side of the tent looking to see if any guards were around. Parmashta ran in the opposite direction down through the marketplace where the rugs, blankets and pillows were being sold.

"Hurry up, get those boxes packed and stacked in the back room. We only have six days to get out of Shushan" Zeresh shouted to her youngest son Dalphon. Dalphon heard his mother but was looking out the window at the man standing down the street. "Do you see any guards around Dalphon?" Zeresh asked as she walked back and forth taking things off the shelf and placing them in cloth sacks.

"No." Dalphon said. "I see a man standing beside the building across from where the gallows are standing."

"A man? What does he look like?"

"Just an ordinary man."

"What is he doing?"

"He is just standing there doing nothing."

Zeresh came over and looked out the window. The man saw them looking at him, so he turned his back to them and slowly walked down the road and through an alley.

"Hmmm" Zeresh said putting the curtain back in place. "Something is not right. Why would a man be standing on the street outside a building doing nothing?" They took your father's body down and took it away several weeks ago. There is no reason for anyone to be hanging around."

Dalphon watched his mother moving back and forth through the house gathering things together so they could leave Shushan.

"They did not allow us to give papa a proper burial mama."

"I know son, I know. We cannot think about that now. Help me pack these things up. Your brothers are out purchasing supplies for our trip; come and help me."

Dalphon sat at the table and continued watching his mother. Anger began to build up in him each time she walked in front of him.

"Why must we run?" he blurted out. "We could stay and fight. I have talked to several of the towns people. They are not running. They are prepared to stand and fight. This is what papa died for, for us to get rid of all those Jews!"

Zeresh slammed her hand down on the table and looked at Dalphon sternly. "Did you not hear your father tell you stories about the god these Jews worship. All the strange mystical things that have happened to our people and other people who attempted to rise up against them! Were you not paying attention! No, it is better if we get out of here now while we still have a chance. The King has ordered the soldiers to fight on the Jews' side. If we stayed and fought, we would not win! We would be killed! Is this what you want? Now, are you going to help me or not!"

"Yes, I will help you" Dalphon said getting up from the table.

"Here, this bag is full; set it over there in the corner." Zeresh said.

Taking the bag, Dalphon noticed his brothers coming carrying bags of supplies.

"Here come the boys now mama" he said as he took the bag she had given him and set it in the corner. Zeresh walked over to the door and opened it quickly so the boys could come in.

"Where are your other brothers?" she asked as the boys set their bundles on the table.

Parshandaltha, Zeresh's eldest son came in last. Setting his supplies on the table, he turned to answer his mother. "I saw Aspatha and Parmashta buying flower, wine, and the other things you had on their list. But I also saw a guard watching them too. I did not go over to them because I thought it would look suspicious to the guards. They know how to be discrete; I am sure they will be home soon."

"What did you get?" Zeresh asked looking through the supplies. "What is this?" She held up several swords and shields. "Why do we need these?"

"Mama, we will need weapons for protection along the roadways. Even though the King has patrols on duty, you never know when a bandit will jump out of nowhere and attack us. We must be prepared."

"Yes, mama," Dalphon piped in. You never know who we will have to fight."

Zeresh looked at Dalphon and Parshandaltha. "I think you boys just want to fight."

"Yes mama! Yes!" Dalphon blurted out. "They killed papa! Yes, I want to fight and so should you! We should avenge papa! Do you think we should avenge papa Parshandaltha?" Dalphon asked turning to look at him for support.

Parshandaltha pulled out a chair from under the table, sat down and put his head in his hands. "I am not sure Dalphon. I am just not sure."

"What do you mean you are not sure! They killed papa and you are not sure? What is wrong with everybody? Are all of you afraid? Is that it? You are afraid?" Dalphon was so upset that he was now screaming at his mother and his brothers.

"Calm yourself down Dalphon and sit down!" Zeresh said slapping him across the face. "Yes, we are afraid. You are too young and foolish to be afraid." Zeresh hesitated looking around at her four sons. "Sit down boys. I have something to share with you."

All four boys sat down around the table. Zeresh continued to stand but began pacing up and down beside the table again. "There is good reason that I have decided to leave Shushan before my brothers get here from Canaan and before the thirteenth of Adar. I saw one of Haman's loyal servants that worked for him in the palace four weeks ago after they hung your father. He informed me that the King gave all your father's goods, his wealth, and this house into the hands of Queen Esther, who put it into the hands of her father Mordecai, Haman's chief enemy. Any time he chooses, Mordecai could come here with Persian Soldiers and kill me as well as all of you. I am not sure why he has not done so yet, but this may be our only opportunity to escape death. If we leave before the thirteenth of Adar, we may be able to save our lives. Do you understand now Dalphon?"

Dalphon sat staring straight ahead. It was hard for him to accept what his mother was saying but he now understood the urgency of leaving Shushan before the thirteenth of Adar. "Yes mother, I understand now."

No one else spoke. They all sat there silently. In the quietness, someone began banging on the back door and everyone in the room jumped.

"Be quiet!" Parshandaltha whispered as he tiptoed to the back door. "Who is it?" he said in a low voice.

"It is me, Aspatha and Parmashta. Hurry open the door; we have supplies out here that need to be brought inside. Hurry!"

Parshandaltha quickly opened the door and called for his other brothers to come help unload the wagon. Zeresh's other four boys came running up to the back door with more supplies. In fifteen minutes, all the supplies were inside. Dalphon took the horse and buggy and put them away behind the house and then joined the others in the dining room.

With all the supplies the boys had bought in, the house was cluttered. Zeresh looked at everything, sighed and looked out the window. A man was standing beside the gallows facing their house watching them. "There he is again" Zeresh said as the boys sat down at the table.

"There who is?" Parshandaltha asked.

"Some man has been standing outside the house all day long."

"Is it the same man every time or a different man?"

"I am not sure if they all are the same" Zeresh said putting the curtain back in place. "I just see a man standing in different places watching the house. When he notices that we are looking at him, he walks away."

"There were two palace guards watching Parmashta and me when we were buying supplies at the market too" Aspatha said. "When they thought we left, they went over to the merchant and asked what we bought and how much we paid for it. Then he told the merchant not to mention to us that they were there asking questions. We are definitely being watched. Do you think the man outside the house is a plain clothes palace guard with orders to watch us?" Aspatha asked looking at Zeresh.

Zeresh shook her head and sat down at the table and began to cry. "Why has all of this happened to us? We are going to die and there is nothing any of us can do about it."

Parshandaltha went over to his mother putting his arms around her. "We will think of something mama. We will think of something to save all of our lives."

"But what?" Zeresh said through her tears. "They are already watching us. How are we going to get out of here!"

"Maybe we will have to stay and fight after all" Dalphon said. No one answered him; they all sat quietly at the dining room table.

Ahasuerus was happy to see Esther attempting to eat her breakfast. Esther was happy to see the two men in her life also and smiled as they held hands as Mordecai blessed the table.

"Did you get enough sleep last night Esther? Your father and I missed you at dinner. The servants said you were rather tired."

"Yes, I feel much, much better this morning. Thank you for asking" Esther said smiling at Ahasuerus.

"I looked in on you earlier this morning; you were fast asleep; I decided not to disturb you. I am glad to see you out and eating again."

"Me too" Mordecai said smiling reaching for Esther's hand squeezing it.

"I am sorry I was not feeling well enough to keep company with the two of you, but I feel much better now."

"Your Excellency." Abagtha interrupted.

"Yes, Abagtha, what is it?"

"Memucan and Hegai are outside with documents they said you wanted first thing this morning. Shall I show them in?"

"Ah, no Abagtha. Have them wait; I will meet with them after breakfast."

"As you wish Your Excellency."

"Your Majesty, would you care for some fruit, biscuits and broiled fish?"

Esther looked at the food and helped herself to the fruit and biscuits. "I will have the meat at my noontime meal. Thank you."

"As you wish Your Majesty."

Esther looked at her food again. Ahasuerus directed his attention to Mordecai. "Did you get enough sleep my friend? We were up late last night."

Mordecai laughed glancing nonchalantly at Esther to see if she was eating. "Yes, we did stay up late, but I thoroughly enjoyed it. I love talking about my God."

"And I enjoyed hearing about Him as well" Ahasuerus said sipping his tea still watching Esther out of the corner of his eyes. Both men had been updated about her visit with the doctor and the difficult morning she had had, but neither wanted to address it with her at breakfast.

Esther sipped her tea letting it settle in her stomach to see if it was going to stay down. To her surprise, it tasted good, and she felt fine, brave enough to take a bite of biscuit. That too tasted good and stayed down. Hmm, that herb the doctor gave me works well she thought and decided to eat the rest of her food normally.

"Mordecai, the thirteenth of Adar is next Friday, are your people ready?"

"Yes, I think they are ready as much as possible. We have done everything we can to prepare; now we will trust God to do the rest. Everything will be fine."

"Trust God to do the rest. Humph, is that the way it works? You do everything in your power to get prepared and leave the results up to God?"

"Almost."

"What do you mean? I thought all you had to do was ask God for whatever you wanted, believe that He will give you what you want, 'that faith thing,' and you will get whatever you asked for?"

"That sounds good Ahasuerus, and many people would love it to be that simple and direct. That is like having your private god that grants everything you ask, just because you asked for it. Your own personal 'gift giver.' One must first find out what God's Will would be for the situation you were asking about."

"God's Will? How does one find out what God's Will is for their life Mordecai?"

"My friend, you ask difficult questions" Mordecai said sitting back in his chair while sipping on his tea. As the two men talked, they both kept an eye on Esther. She had eaten all her biscuits, the fruit and drank two cups of tea.

"Excuse me, Abagtha, is there more fish in the back?" Esther asked.

"Yes, Your Majesty."

"Please bring me a piece of fish with more tea and biscuits and fruit."

"As you wish Your Majesty."

"It is so good to see you eating Esther" Ahasuerus said patting her hand.

"It is good to be able to eat!" Esther said and all three of them laughed.

"Continue my friend; I want to learn all I can about God."

Mordecai smiled. This was the first time Ahasuerus had referred to Him as 'God" and not 'your god.' Esther picked up on it also catching Mordecai's eyes, they both smiled. Ahasuerus went back to eating his breakfast.

"God's Will for one's life. The first thing we must understand is that God's ways are not like our ways. When a problem or situation arises, the way we would handle the problem would be totally different from the way God would handle it. For example, when Haman practiced deception against us to destroy all Jews in the entire

Persian Provinces, and when we received the decree that the massacre was to happen on the thirteenth of Adar, my human rationalization would have been to; one, prepare to fight against the Persian army, or two, to secretly make a rapid exodus out of Persian Territory."

"But you did not do either of those choices, why?"

"When your grandfather freed us from Babylonian captivity and gave us permission to settle anywhere in Persian territory and even to return to our homeland and rebuild our temple; when the temple work was stopped for a time, some of the Jewish brothers decided to come to Shushan. I was one of them. I just felt led to settle here, and bought Esther along with me, seeing that her father and mother had died in captivity. Some of my brothers who stayed in Jerusalem and continued the temple work questioned my decision to settle here. This is an example of 'God's Divine Providence' in mine and Esther's lives. We were not aware at the time we moved to Shushan, how God was going to use us in the lives of our people. I made a decision based on the strong feeling that this is what God wanted me to do, and so I did it.

Another example of God's Divine Providence was when you sent out notices to all the maidens in the Persian Province for a new Queen. Because you did not force the Jews to follow your customs and beliefs, all the Jewish maidens were exempt from competing for the Queen's position. However, when Esther received her notice from the palace, she was most upset."

Ahasuerus sat back and looked at Esther in surprise. "You were upset about receiving the decree? Why?"

"The way I was raised in Jewish customs," Esther began, "I always thought that God would grant my prayer for a Jewish husband and that I would have my own traditional Jewish family. If I competed for the Queen's position, I knew I would have to give up my purity and chastity to you and that there was no guarantee that I would be chosen Queen. If I were not chosen, my life, in my eyes, would be ruined. I would not be free to marry another, especially a Jewish man, and I would not have children of my own and be able to raise them."

All three of them were quiet as Ahasuerus took in Esther's answer waiting for him to respond; he said nothing, he was speechless. Mordecai continued the scenario.

"We, Esther, and I discussed your decree at dinner, and she expressed to me the same concerns she just stated to you. I could not put myself in her position to wholly understand how she felt, but I could see she was most unhappy."

"What did you do?" Ahasuerus asked giving Mordecai his full attention.

"We prayed about it at dinner, and I told God that whatever He wanted us to do in this situation, we would do it. That what we wanted was not important, we would do whatever He wanted us to do if he would let us know what His will was in this situation. We both said 'Amen' in agreement and began to eat our dinner in silence. Before dinner was over, I had this tremendous yearning that Esther was to fill out the application and compete for the position. I shared what was on my heart with Esther and we decided that she would compete.

I questioned my fellow Jewish brothers about submitting their daughters to compete. They were gravely against it and said I was breaking Jewish law by permitting Esther to compete. So, I went back to God and asked again if I should allow Esther to compete. I experienced the same strong impression to go ahead with what Esther and I agreed. I was ostracized by my people for participating in Persian customs. The most difficult time for me was when Esther came to the palace for her year of purification. I was alone with no fellowship with my Jewish brethren, so I came by the palace every day to see how she was doing. She appeared to be doing fine. I understand now that she was having a difficult time as well."

"Is that when your roommates turned against you and left you alone too?" Ahasuerus asked Esther who had finally finished eating.

"Yes, that was part of it. The other part was my living in luxury while Morde was living in poverty in the hut back home and my having to give up my purity not knowing what was to become of me."

"What did you do about your fears Esther?"

"When the other maidens ignored me, I spent that time in prayer with God. He gave me His peace and His strength. When I was not in class, I spent my time knitting making blankets, sweaters, and socks for Morde and my staff."

"I heard about that" Ahasuerus said smiling. "All of the other maidens were requesting makeup, gowns, and such and when I asked what you requested, they told me yarn and a spindle. I thought that was very strange. Go on Mordecai, please."

"Esther apparently became Queen and God used her to intervene and stop Haman's plot to kill all of the Jews."

"Esther," Ahasuerus asked, "why did you decide…., ah how did you decide…, ah," Ahasuerus hesitated searching for the right words to ask his questions. "Knowing Persian law, you knew that you could lose your life if you approached me without my calling for you. Were you not afraid?"

"Yes, I was very afraid. Morde told me that I had to approach you. That was the only way our people could be saved. I had to come to you and ask you to change Haman's ordinance."

"How did you know to invite Haman to a banquet to expose his plot there?"

"When Morde told me I had no choice but to come to you and petition you for our lives, I told Morde to have all the Jews to fast with me for three days and at the end of the three days, I would come to you and if it was God's will for me to perish, then I would perish. So, at the end of the three days, I came to you, and you did not kill me, so I requested that you and Haman join me for a special banquet in my personal lounge area and you agreed."

Ahasuerus was sitting on the edge of his chair with his right arm resting on the table looking Esther full in the face as he asked his next question. "Why did you have two banquets? Why not expose Haman at the first banquet?"

"At the first banquet, I became a little apprehensive and fear took over, so I requested that the two of you come back the next evening. In between the two banquets, I did more praying to God and asked Him for his strength and boldness to fulfill His will. When the two of you came back the next evening, I followed through, and Haman was exposed."

"That is another example of God's Divine Providence for His Jewish people for Esther, for me and for you." Mordecai replied.

"Me!"

"Yes, you." Mordecai said smiling. "Even though you were not aware of our God, He still moved upon your heart and placed a great love there for Esther. He moved upon your heart to grant her petitions to destroy the enemy of the Jews. The God we serve is a very, very powerful God. The one and only true God. The God of Abraham, Isaac, and Jacob. He is the God we serve."

Two hours had passed since breakfast began. Abagtha stepped into the room.

"Your Excellency."

"Yes, Abagtha."

"I am sorry to interrupt you again, but Memucan and Hegai are still waiting for you. Would you prefer to reschedule their meeting for another time?"

"No, no. Tell them I will be with them in fifteen minutes. Thank you Abagtha."

"As you wish Your Excellency."

"Mordecai, Esther, this has been a most informative breakfast." Ahasuerus turned to Esther standing as he reached for her hand. "Esther, may I walk you back to your quarters?"

"As you wish Your Excellency" she said smiling getting up from her chair. "Morde?"

Mordecai came around to Esther and embraced her. "I am so pleased that you are feeling better. I will come back and visit with you before the thirteenth. Please take good care of yourself and the baby."

"I will Morde, I will" and she kissed him on his cheek.

As he and Esther left the dining room, Ahasuerus looked back at Mordecai. "Mordecai, I will want to meet with you before the thirteenth arrives as well."

"As you wish Ahasuerus" Mordecai said smiling leaving the room another way.

"Why do you call you father 'Morde' Esther?" Ahasuerus asked.

"When I was a baby, he tried to get me to call him Mordecai because he was my cousin but all I could say was 'Morde' and he liked it and allowed me to continue calling him that instead of 'father.' He is the only father that I have known outside of my Heavenly Father."

"Heavenly Father. I like that. Heavenly Father." Ahasuerus said over and over. "I think I am going to enjoy getting to know God" he replied as they walked into the lounge.

Feeling so much better and having eaten a good breakfast, Esther realized how much she missed her husband. When the lounge door was closed, she put both arms around his neck and kissed him on the lips. Ahasuerus groaned.

"Oh, I miss you too, but I must go. I have an important meeting to attend. Do you feel up to having dinner with me tonight in my bed chamber?"

"Right now I do; I am not sure how I will feel later on" Esther said laying her head against his chest.

"Have Yara arrange it anyway and if you do not feel up to it, we can change our plans accordingly." Ahasuerus held Esther close to himself for a long time kissing her softly on the lips then gently pushed her away. "If I do not go now, I will have to reschedule my meeting. I will see you tonight. I love you Esther" and he turned and walked out the door.

Memucan had grown tired of waiting for the King in the conference room. "It has been two and a half hours now. What is taking so long?

"I am sure he will be here soon. Have some tea and biscuits; they are good" Hegai said trying to get Memucan's mind off himself. Hegai knew that Memucan had been loyal to Haman even though he disliked how Haman berated him and was elevated above him. He also knew that Memucan's loyalty to the King was now strained. Everyone could see it and wondered how long Memucan was going to stay in the position of First Prince.

"Abagtha, Abagtha!" Memucan shouted. "Did you check on the King as I requested?"

"Yes sir, I did."

"Well, what did he say?"

"He said he would be with you in fifteen minutes."

"And you did not think it important to inform me of this?"

"I was on my way here to tell you when I heard you calling may name Sir" Abagtha said looking Memucan in the eyes.

"Very well then, you may leave."

Abagtha did not comment; he just turned and left. Hegai did not comment either; he sat in his chair next to the table with his hands folded resting in his lap watching Memucan intently. It is apparent whose side he is going to fight on when the thirteenth arrives, Hegai thought to himself. I wonder if he has all his plans perfected. I will wait and see Meres in a day or so. The King would have his head if he knew that Memucan was plotting against him. Hopefully, I will be able to expose him before too long. Memucan kept pacing back and forth, back, and forth. Suddenly in mid-stream, he stopped and glared at Hegai.

"Just what are you staring at!" he screamed. "Am I amusing to you?"

"No." Hegai said slowly deciding to choose his words carefully. "I was just wondering why you are so upset. We are on the King's time schedule; I do not understand why you are so agitated."

"No, you would not understand Hegai. What are you? Oh yes, you are a eunuch. A eunuch does not have a life of his own. I, on the other hand, have a life of my own and my time is very precious to me. I do not have time to sit around all day doing nothing."

Ahasuerus had been standing in the back doorway with his two guards listening to Memucan since he started yelling at Abagtha. He and the guards were quiet; no one else knew they were there. "This will never do" he said quietly to the guards. "I am going to have to replace this prince with someone who is loyal to me."

"Would you like us to apprehend him Your Majesty?"

"No, no. I will take care of it. We will enter the conference room at the other end of the hall. Ahasuerus and the two guards walked all the way around and down the other hall and entered the room where two other guards were posted and came to attention. When he entered the room, Memucan stopped pacing, turned bowing at the waist and said in a mechanical sing song voice; "Good morning Your Excellency! How was your breakfast?"

"It was good Memucan."

"Good morning Your Excellency" Hegai said standing beside the table.

"Good morning Hegai; thank you so much for patiently waiting for me. Have a seat."

Memucan turned red in the face noticing that the King addressed Hegai differently than him. Ahasuerus took his seat at the head of the table, directed Hegai to sit to his right and Memucan to sit to his left. This too angered Memucan. In the past, his seat was always to the King's right; today, it seemed as if the King purposely selected that chair for Hegai.

"Memucan, do you have the divorce decree documents I asked for?"

"Yes, Your Excellency."

"How many are there?"

"There are fourteen Sir."

"Fourteen? Hegai is that all of the concubines that remain in the palace?"

"Yes, Your Excellency. All the others accepted your financial stipend and went back to their families three months ago."

"Of the fourteen that are left, how many are with child?"

"Six of them are still pregnant and eight children have already been born."

"How many of them want a divorce and are willing to leave their children behind?"

"Nine of them are requesting divorces and are willing to leave their children behind; five of them have not yet delivered their babies but they have informed me that they are willing to stay and live here in the palace and raise their children. They want to know if they will be permitted to help raise the children that the mothers leave behind instead of sending them to the infirmary for the wet nurses to raise" Hegai asked looking at the King.

"According to Persian law," Memucan interrupted, "all of the King's offspring must be raised and supervised by the King's staff, wet nurses and guards included."

"I see" Ahasuerus said turning his attention back to Hegai. "Hegai, inform the ladies that I will address that last issue with them later. Draw up the names of the concubines that want the divorce and give them their divorce decrees along with 100 shekels of silver a piece to help them start a new life. Tell them to take all the time they need to find a place to live. Inform them that they will have the right to come and visit their children at the palace whenever they like, just inform security so the palace security laws are not disrupted."

"Your Excellency," Memucan interrupted again, "A hundred shekels of silver a piece? Do you know how much money that is?"

"I most certainly do Memucan. Hegai, change the amount from 100 to 200 shekels. I think that is a much better sum for what they have gone through.

"As you wish Your Excellency. Shall I go and do this now?

"No, wait just a minute. Memucan, I have noticed that you have been most unhappy in your post as First Prince of Shushan."

"Me! No, ah, I am not unhappy Your Excellency! I am fine, really!"

"I have decided to send you to assist the First Prince of India with the scientific work that is being done there. You will pack your things, your family and leave tomorrow morning. I will send a letter with you to the First Prince of India explaining in detail what your duties will be."

"Tomorrow morning! Your Excellency! That is not enough time to pack up my family to move to India!"

"Take only those things you will need to make the journey. I will have your servants pack up your household and send them to you. Turn over all your books and files to Hegai. Hegai, I want you to store those files in your personal quarters until Memucan's position has been filled. Thank you again for patiently waiting for me. Oh yes, Hegai, one more thing."

"Yes, Your Excellency?"

"As you leave, send my secretary to my personal lounge to prepare the letter to be sent along with Memucan and have Abagtha inform all my lawyers, Mordecai included, that I want to meet with them tomorrow morning after breakfast.

"As you wish Your Excellency" Hegai replied standing and bowing at the waist as Ahasuerus left the room. Memucan did not stand and did not bow. The King ignored him as he left.

Memucan still sat at the table as Hegai was leaving muttering to himself. "India! He is sending me to India! I am to work under the First Prince of India!"

"Memucan" Hegai said softly as he was leaving the table, "I will be at your office to pick up the files before dinner time."

Memucan just grunted and remained seated at the table with his head in his hands groaning. "How did this happen? What are we going to do now?"

Hegai left the door to the conference room open when he left. Admatha walked by glancing in and saw Memucan sitting at the table moaning. "What is this?" he said out loud then rushed in closing the door behind him looking all around making sure no one else was in the room.

"Memucan, Memucan! What is the matter?" he whispered keeping his voice low just in case there was someone around that he did not see.

Memucan looked up. "Oh Admatha, it is you."

"Yes, what is wrong! What are you doing here by yourself like this? What is wrong? Are you still ailing from the fall last night?"

"I just had a meeting with the King; he is sending me to India! To India!"

"To India? Why? For how long?"

"I am not sure why!" Memucan said exasperated. "He said something about me not being satisfied with my position here as First Prince so he decided to send me to India to be the assistant under the First Prince of India to help with the scientific work that is going on there. I do not know anything about science! I am a lawyer!"

"When do you have to leave Memucan?"

"Tomorrow!" he said lifting his hands in desperation. "Tomorrow!"

The door opened and a servant carrying a basket hurried through. Seeing the two men, she hesitated in mid-stride. "Excuse me Sirs, I was not aware that there was a meeting going on in here" and she hurried out the other door.

"Come Memucan, we should not be talking here; someone may overhear us." Admatha walked toward the door turning to look and see if Memucan was following him. Memucan followed with his head hung low and his arms hung down by their sides. "Memucan! Straighten up! Lift your head. Do not let anyone see you looking like this, they will know something has happened! Straighten up!" Memucan lifted his head and pulled his shoulders back as he followed Admatha, but he could not erase the defeated look on his face

As they approached the door, Admatha looked out and spotted a guard walking down the hall. Turning back to Memucan he whispered, "there is a guard down the hall walking this way. I will leave and go to the right. You wait a minute or so and go to the left. I will meet you in your office in five minutes." Admatha walked down the hall as if he were on urgent business for the King. Memucan did not wait as Admatha instructed but left right after him walking the opposite way stepping out right in front of the guard. The guard slowed his stride to keep from running into him, hesitated then turned to look at Admatha walking in the opposite direction. He stopped, leaned against the wall watching the two men. Being a highly trained palace guard, he sensed something was not quite right about the two men but just made a mental note of it and let them go.

Having peace that Esther was feeling better, and the baby was fine, Mordecai walked back to his personal quarters. He had sent a message to Reelaiah to meet him for lunch in his lounge area. The breakfast with the King and Queen lasting so long that he was not hungry himself, but he would have the servants serve him tea and a little fruit. As he entered the lounge, he was surprised to find Reelaiah already seated in a chair by the fireplace.

"Oh, hello my friend!" Mordecai said walking over to him and embracing him.

"Hello Mordecai. I hope you do not mind my coming a little early."

"Not at all, not at all. Have a seat. I will have the servants bring our lunch."

"If you do not mind, I am not hungry. If we could get right into the meeting, I have some arrangements I must make for my family at home. The thirteenth is just four days away."

"Yes, I know."

"I and the others were wondering how the fight was going to take place. Now that the men are trained, they want to know what they are to do, how they are to fight?"

"I have been thinking and praying on that matter myself Reelaiah. Several weeks ago, I had messengers rush these instructions to all the Jews throughout the Persian Province. I told them that they should take their women and children to a safe place. The King has instructed the Persian soldiers and guards to participate in this fight and support all Jewish citizens; therefore, every man should stand up and guard his own home. When any Persian citizen attacks us, they must strike them down. Even though the King has given us permission to take all their spoils after we kill them, I do not believe God would be pleased with us if we did that. When they strike out against us, we are to kill them; their men, their women, their little ones, but leave their spoil."

Mordecai sat back in his chair and looked at Reelaiah. "Well, what do you think?"

"If this is what the Lord has laid on your heart Mordecai, I agree with you. We should assemble the brethren together immediately and give them these instructions."

"Good. Will you handle this?"

"Yes. I will see that everything is set in order and ready. In four days, we will avenge our enemies."

"The King has requested a meeting with me before the thirteenth. I will inform him of our plans."

"Good" Reelaiah said getting up shaking Mordecai's hand. "Will I see you before the thirteenth?"

"If you need me, you know where to find me Reelaiah. I will always be accessible to you and all my Jewish brothers."

As soon as Memucan reached his office, he sat down and wrote a note to send home to his wife and children to begin packing up supplies to go on a trip and that he would explain in more detail when he came home. Folding up the note, he walked outside his office, found a runner, and told him to rush this note to his wife at home.

Five minutes later, Admatha knocked on Memucan's door softly and quickly slipped through the door and closed it behind him.

"Did you wait for that guard to pass the door before you left?"

"What guard?" Memucan asked.

"The guard I told you about just before I left the room! Did you see each other?"

"No, no, I did not see any guard" Memucan said slumping into a chair by the fireplace.

Admatha walked over and looked down at Memucan. "Tell me again, Memucan. What did the King say?

"He told me he was sending me to India and that I was to assist the First Prince in the scientific work there. He told me to pack up my things and my family and be gone by tomorrow morning, that he would have the servants to pack up the remainder of my household and send them along later."

"You said something before about his mentioning your dissatisfaction with your position as First Prince of Shushan? What was that all about?"

"I do not know. We were discussing his concubines. He was giving instructions to Hegai about their documents of divorcement. Then he looked at me and said he had noticed that I had been extremely unhappy with my position as First Prince and decided to send me to India!"

"Something had to happen to cause him to take such drastic measures against you" Admatha said leaning against Memucan's desk. "Do you think he found out about our plans?"

"No" Memucan retorted. "We were very, very careful with our plans. There is no way he could have found out."

"Then…, what else could it be…?" Admatha became quiet deep in thought. "Memucan, what were you doing before your meeting with the King and Hegai?"

"Nothing. Last night, the King asked me to have the documents of divorcement drawn up and ready for him first thing this morning, that I was to bring the documents and Hegai with me to this meeting. He was emphatic about everything being ready first thing in the morning. So, I followed his command, had the documents ready, picked up Hegai and went to the royal dining room informing Abagtha that we were there per the King's command. The King sent word back that he would meet with us after breakfast, and we were to wait for him in the conference room. We waited, and waited, and waited. Finally, after two and a half hours of waiting, I sent Abagtha back to see if the King still wanted us to wait; maybe we could reschedule the meeting."

"What were you doing while you were waiting for the King?"

"Nothing! Just waiting."

"What did Hegai do while he was waiting for the King?"

"He drank tea and ate biscuits watching me walk back and forth waiting for the King."

"You were walking back and forth waiting for the King and Hegai was drinking tea and eating biscuits. Did you talk to Hegai?"

"We, no…, not exactly."

"Memucan, were you talking at all?"

Being a lawyer himself, Memucan knew where Admatha was going with his line of questioning and became uncomfortable. Getting up from his chair, he ran his hands through his hair, a nervous gesture he did when he was upset.

"Yes, Admatha, I was talking."

More like ranting and raving which you do when you become impatient. You were pacing back and forth, ranting, and raving, probably shouting 'where is the King!' at the top of your voice. Knowing Hegai, he sat there watching you as he drank tea and ate biscuits. Someone saw or heard you undo word Memucan! You let your temper get away from you! How long was it after you were ranting and raving that the King came in?"

Memucan thought for a second then turned toward Admatha. "Oh no!" he groaned deeply within himself. "You are right Admatha. As soon as I finished screaming at Abagtha, two to three minutes later the King walked through the door."

"What door did he enter through?"

"The main door from the hall."

"He heard you Memucan. He heard you ranting and raving. He saw your impatience in waiting for him and took it as disloyal! You should be grateful that he is only sending you and your family to India! The old Ahasuerus would have had you hung, and your family sold into slavery!"

Memucan slumped back into his chair and stared into the fire. Admatha stood there looking at him in disgust. "Now what are we going to do about the day after tomorrow? The thirteenth of Adar? Who is going to lead the people in the fight against the Jews?"

Memucan looked up at Admatha. "You will have to lead them."

"Me? No, no, no, not me! The fight is less than four days away! It would be impossible to gather all the people together to change the plans!"

"There is nothing I can do now Admatha" Memucan said walking over to his desk opening drawers and pulling files out stacking them on top of each other." I must rush home and inform my family that they must immediately begin packing and turn all my files over to Hegai, per the King's orders. If anything is to be done, you are going to have to do it. You are the only one that knows what has happened."

Admatha stood watching Memucan pack up his things then disgustingly walked out of his office slamming the door behind him.

Chapter Twenty-Four

HADASSAH

Zena lay awake in bed turning from side to side. She just could not get comfortable. The tongues of fire danced as the wood crackled in the fireplace. Watching them for a moment or two comforted her a little. Normally she would fall asleep as soon as her head it the pillows and sleep until one of the servants woke her up, usually late morning. She had not slept all night. She just tossed and turned. The baby seemed unusually quiet and still. Zena put her hand on her stomach feeling all around; there was no movement. "I am glad one of us is able to sleep" she said softly addressing the baby then turned her back to the fire. "God of Abraham, Isaac and Jacob" she prayed quietly, "my time to deliver is very near. Please make the delivery easy to bear and the baby healthy. Please bless the King's heart to grant the petitions that were submitted to him so that we can be happy with our lives and the lives of our children. Bless Arwa, Orit, and the others who are with child that their babies will be born healthy, and the deliveries be easy as well. Thank you God for hearing my prayer. Thank you for making me your child. Father, I know I have not always done what was right even though I did not know who you were, but I still knew right from wrong. Everybody does. I am not sure how it all works because people believe in many gods. But it is like Esther says, if they just look up, look out at nature, they cannot help but know who you are and that you are the great creator. Please forgive me for my selfishness and my vanity. I know I did not have the right attitude about life, please, please forgive me. Father, I surrender my life to you now. Whatever your will is for me, I accept it. Your will be done." Zena began yawning, "thank you for Esther…" she fell fast asleep.

Eight concubine mothers stood outside the infirmary door listening as their babies cried. They longed to go in, pick their child up and nurse them, but the servants banned them from the nursery. Several of them paced back and forth in front of the door trying to see in; others stood on the side crying; anyone looking at them could see that they were heartbroken. The thought of not holding their child was too much for them to bear.

Hegai stood at the end of the hall out of sight watching the women. He could feel their grief way down the hall. "These women are in anguish" he said to himself. "Why did we not see this before?" Having seen enough, he sighed and walked toward the grieving group.

"Good morning ladies. Ladies, I have good news for you. The King has granted all your petitions!"

All the ladies turn back to face Hegai with questionable looks on their faces.

"It is true!" Hegai said. "The King has granted all your petitions! You are free to go in and nurse your babies right now if you like. You can take them back to your own personal quarters. Not only that, any of you who desire to leave the palace will be given a decree of divorcement and 200 shekels of silver to help you begin a new life for yourselves. After dinner tonight, I will explain everything to you in detail. Excuse me," Hegai said clearing the women away from the door. "I will go in and inform the servants of the new orders from the King, then all of you will be free to come in and pick up your babies. I will also instruct the servants to provide all the supplies you will need to take care of your babies."

When Hegai finished speaking, he made his way into the infirmary. All eight mothers followed behind him, picked up their babies and headed back to their personal quarters.

Zena woke up yelling at the top of her lungs. "Oh! Oh! Oh! She rolled from side to side holding her stomach until the pain subsided and she could breathe normally again. Lying flat on her back, she tried to make sense of what had just happened and noticed that her night gown as well as her bed was wet. "What is this!" she screamed. The wet sticky mess was uncomfortable and cold. Zena decided to get out of bed and change her gown. Just as she rolled on her side and struggled to get up, Yara opened the door and rushed in.

"Zena! What are you doing? Here, get back in bed."

"No!" Zena screamed and began to cry. It is all wet in there. I want to take a bath and clean up. My back hurts and I had a sharp pain in the bottom of my stomach!"

Yara rushed over to her placing her hands gently on both sides of Zena's shoulders. "The baby is ready to come out Zena. It is very dangerous for you to try to get up and bathe by yourself."

Three other servants came in the door waiting for Yara to give them instructions.

"Get me two basins of water, one hot and one cold. Get me fresh clean towels and linens from the linen closet. Hurry!"

"I am afraid Yara!" Zena said through her tears.

"Yes I know Zena, but you will not be alone. Someone will be with you the whole time; everything is going to be alright."

"Will you stay with me Yara? Please do not leave me."

"Zena, you know I am the Queen's personal servant, and I must go and serve her. There are plenty of midwives here in the palace to help you and the doctor is here also."

"Please Yara, please do not leave me. Please ask Queen Esther if you can stay with me today while I have this baby. Maybe she will relieve you of your duties just this once."

Yara saw the fear in Zena's eyes. "Alright Zena. I will go and speak with the Queen. Please sit still and do not try to get up. Allow the servants to clean you up and put you back to bed. If the Queen gives me leave, I will be back shortly. If not, I will have another midwife to tend to you. That is all that I can do."

"Thank you Yara" Zena said calming down a little.

"You are welcome Zena," Yara said patting her hand as she waited for the servants to return. As they returned with the supplies she ordered, Yara turned to one of the servants named Hannah, a Jewish Servant, "Hannah, I want you to come with me to the Queen's quarters. You have worked closely with me in serving the Queen on several occasions. Maybe she will allow you to wait on her today." Turning to the other servants she commanded them to take care of Zena as she and Hannah hurried out the door to Queen Esther's quarters.

Zena sat shaking a little on the side of the bed. The pain had subsided; her back still ached but the pain was nothing compared to what she experienced earlier.

"Is this going to be a difficult delivery?" Hannah asked as they hurried down the hall.

"I am not sure. We will do our best to make it as easy for her as possible. We must hurry, I am already late. The Queen will be wondering what is keeping me." The two of them quicken their steps as they entered the Queen's courtyard.

Esther stretched her legs, yawned rolling to her side to get out of bed. She slept late again but that was normal with her these days. Looking back across the bed, Ahasuerus was not there. She appreciated him letting her sleep. They both greatly enjoyed their time together last night. Sitting on the side of the bed, she wondered why Yara had not come to her yet. The fire was almost out. "I can put a log on the fire myself. I am not helpless" she said to herself and got up from the bed. Before she could get over to the fireplace, someone knocked on the door.

"Yes, who is it?"

"It is Yara Queen Esther. I have my assistant Hannah with me. May we come in?"

"Yes, please come in" Esther said as she bent over the wood pile picking up a log and throwing it on the fire.

"Queen Esther!" Yara shouted. What are you doing?"

"The fire was just about out, and I put a log on it" Esther said a little startled at Yara's parental tone.

"Oh Queen Esther, you should not be doing this!" Yara said regaining control of her voice. If Hannah had not been with her, she would have scolded Esther more in a motherly tone even though they were close in age. "Please forgive me for being late Your Majesty. It will not happen again."

"Everything is fine Yara. I knew something important must have happened. You are very careful in fulfilling your duties to me.

"Yes Your Majesty. One of the concubines went into labor this morning and I was attending to her."

"Oh?" Esther said with interest. "Which one?"

"It is Zena Your Majesty."

"Zena! Is she alright? Esther asked sitting back down on the bed.

"She is in the beginning stages of her delivery, and she is rather frightened. She asked if I could stay with her through the delivery. I told her I would have to ask your permission first."

"Yes, of course. Go now Yara."

"Would you permit Hannah to serve you while I am away? She has assisted me in serving you many times in the past and is a very competent servant."

"Yes, yes, of course. Hannah will be fine. Tell her I will be praying for her."

"As you wish Your Majesty" Yara said bowing at the waist and rushed out the door.

When Yara reached Zena's bed chamber door, she heard Zena crying out in pain."

"Ah! Ah! Ah! Please make it stop! It hurts so much! Zena cried turning from side to side again."

Yara rushed inside, pulled up a chair beside Zena's bed grabbing her hand. "Zena! She called. Zena was in severe pain and was not aware that Yara had returned. Yara called her name again and again. "Zena! Zena! Look at me Zena!"

As the pain began to subside, Zena finally heard Yara calling her name and looked at her.

"Help me. Please help me Yara. This hurts so much! Please make the pain stop" she whimpered squeezing Yara's hand.

Yara reached for a towel, dipped it in cold water and began wiping the tears from Zena's face. Dipped the towel again in cold water and placed the cool wet towel on Zena's forehead. When Zena settled down again, Yara began talking to her softly.

"Zena, were you old enough to remember your mother giving birth to your sister, Zoe? Do you remember that?"

"I remember hearing my mother screaming if that is what you mean. I was five years old, and I thought someone was beating her. She was screaming so loud that I started to cry too. My father picked me up and took me outside for a walk. I remember we walked up and down the alley for a long, long time. Eventually he took me back to our hut and showed me that mama was alright. She was holding a little bundle in her arms and smiling.

"Childbirth is difficult and painful; but I am going to show you some little things that will help you to manage the pain. When you feel another pain coming on, I want you to blow or pant like a dog. Ha, ha, ha, or ho, ho, ho." Yara demonstrated for her. "Now you try it."

Zena imitated Yara's ha, ha, ha and ho, ho, ho. "Like that?" She asked.

"Yes, just like that."

"How long will it be before the baby comes out?" Zena asked.

"Oh, maybe three or four hours." Yara lied. She knew that Zena could be in labor a day or a day and a half with a first child, but she did not want to frighten her more that she was already. Zena's baby would be the ninth baby she delivered this year. All of them reacted the same. They were all afraid.

"Is your back hurting?" Yara asked.

"Yes it is, but not as bad as those pains."

"Can you roll over on your side? I will rub your back for you and help you to relax."

Before Zena could roll over, another sharp pain hit, and she began to scream again.

"Blow Zena, blow or pant like I showed you. Come on you can do it."

Zena just screamed. "I cannot get my breath! Help me! Help me please!"

Yara was concerned. It was too early in her labor for the pains to be coming so close together. She looked around at the servants.

"Run and get the palace doctor! Hurry!" then turned back to Zena. "Zena, I know it hurts but you must blow for me. Trust me, it will make the pain easier to bear! Come on now blow!"

Zena took a deep breath and tried to sit up bearing down on her stomach. Yara shouted, "No! Zena. No! Do not push! It is too early to push. Please just blow like I told you!" Zena kept on pushing and screaming, "I must push, it hurts, it hurts! I must push!" and screamed again.

Yara quickly got up from her chair and moved to the bottom of the bed. Lifting Zena's nightgown, she could see that the baby was coming out but bottom first instead of headfirst. Looking up at Zena who was still pushing and screaming she was not sure what to do. "Please doctor get here quick!" she said to herself. She had never delivered a breached baby before but knew if Zena did not stop pushing, she and the baby might die together. Going back to the side of the bed, she grabbed Zena's hand again and begged for her to stop pushing.

"The doctor will be here soon Zena, please try and blow like I told you! Please!"

Zena did not hear her, by this time she was delirious. She had screamed so much that she hardly had any voice left. Emotion began to take over Yara. Usually, she could remain detached from her patients, even when she lost one to death, but she had grown fond of Zena knowing that she was like Esther's sister. She did not want to lose this one.

Only one of the servants remained in the room with her and Zena.

"Go and get Zena's parents and sister. Do you know where they live?"

"Yes. My family lives down the alley from them. I will go." She passed the doctor hurrying through the door with his medical bag.

"What do we have here Yara?" he asked.

Yara met him at the bottom of the bed. "We have a breech doctor. I have seen them before, but I have never delivered one."

The doctor looked at Zena, opened his bag pulling out a folded white linen cloth and poured some liquid on it from a little bottle. Holding the cloth arms-length away from himself, he went to Zena's bedside lightly placing the cloth over her nose and mouth. Immediately Zena quieted down and went into a deep sleep. Leaving the cloth over her face he turned to Yara.

"Quickly, I need a basin of warm water" the doctor ordered. "We must work quickly!" the doctor said lifting Zena's night gown. "I must insert my hands inside her womb and turn the baby and pull him out headfirst. We only have minutes to spare. I must get that cord from around his neck; hold her legs for me."

Yara moved around and assisted the doctor. In minutes, he had the baby turned around, the cord was removed from the baby's neck, and he gently pulled until the baby slid out in his hands. It was a little girl, but she was not breathing. Yara looked up at Zena. She was still sound asleep.

Clearing the baby's eyes, nose and mouth, the doctor turned the baby over supporting her neck, face, and chest in the palm of his hand smacking the baby on the bottom. Nothing. He turned her over again and held her up by the ankles and smacked her a little harder on the bottom. This time the baby let out a loud cry.

"Good, good, good" the doctor said gently placing the baby in the warm basin of water rinsing off the blood and mucus. "Here, you finish with the baby and place her in her basket. We still must work quickly and try to stop her bleeding." The bottom of the bed was crimson red with Zena's blood and the doctor looked worried. Yara quickly rinsed the baby off, wrapped her in blankets and placed her on the soft pillow inside the basket.

"Hurry Yara and get me more towels. I have packed her with linens. Put more towels down here; hopefully the bleeding will stop." They feverishly packed her and wrapped her legs with gauze. Removing the linen from her face, they rolled her from side to side, removing the bloody bed linens and replaced them with clean ones. When they were done, the doctor pulled a chair up beside the bed, sat down wiping his face with a towel and watched Zena. She was still breathing but not as deeply as she was with the linen over her face.

"Will she be alright doctor?" Yara asked.

"If it is God's will, she will live; it is in his hands now."

Zena moved her head from side to side and began to moan a little.

"Zena, Zena. Can you hear me?" he asked.

"Yes" she whispered.

"Are you in any pain?"

"No."

"Can you open your eyes?"

Her eyelids fluttered and she went back to sleep. The doctor let go of her hand and went back to the bottom of the bed lifting the blankets. Again, the blankets were soaked with blood. Sighing deeply, the doctor turned to Yara and shock his head.

"My baby, where is my baby?" Zena said looking at Yara.

"She is here, right here" Yara turned picking up the baby and laid her on Zena's chest. Zena pulled her arms up around the baby to support her looking down at her.

"A girl! I had a little baby girl!"

"Yes you did Zena, and she is beautiful!"

"Yes she is beautiful. Yara, please, go get Esther and the King. I need to see Esther and the King. Please go and get them. And Yara."

"Yes Zena."

"Please hurry."

"I will hurry" Yara said and rushed out the door. Zena's mother, father, sister, and the servant she sent to get them were waiting in the lounge area outside of Zena's bed chamber.

"Is Zena and the baby alright? May we go in and see her?" Zena's mother asked.

"Ah, the doctor is still with her. Give him and the servants a little time to clean her up, then you may go in." Looking at the servant, she instructed her to go in and assist the doctor, then ran out the door.

Yara ran as fast as she could down the hall, around the corner, down another long hall, through both courtyards and up the steps toward the King's throne room. Stopping briefly to catch her breath, she was met by the King's guard who stepped out in front of her.

"Is there a problem?" he asked.

"Yes, I need to see Queen Esther immediately; it is a matter of life and death!"

"The Queen and King are in the royal palace. You have not been summoned by them."

"Please! I need to speak with them! I know they will want to see me. Please!"

Hearing all the commotion out in the breezeway. Ahasuerus looked over and recognized Yara talking frantically with the guard. She looked very upset, so he held out the golden scepter to her. The guard seeing the King's gesture, stepped aside letting Yara pass through.

Yara ran toward Ahasuerus and Esther, touched the golden scepter, bowed at the waist looking up at them. With tears in her eyes, she took a deep breath.

"Yara, what is the problem!" Esther asked leaning forward on her chair. Ahasuerus grabbed Esther's hand and held it tightly.

"Your Majesties, you know Zena has gone into labor this morning."

"Yes" Esther replied. "How is she? Has the baby been born already?"

"Yes the baby is born, it is a little girl, but the birth was a difficult one and…" Yara began to cry.

"Is Zena alright?" Esther asked above a whisper.

Recomposing herself, Yara looked at Esther. "She is asking that the two of you come to her. She wants to see you. Will you come?" Yara said pleadingly looking at each of them. She knew it was unorthodox for the King and Queen to be summoned to the bedside of a concubine.

Esther looked up at Ahasuerus with tears flowing down her face. "May I go? Please. She is like a sister to me."

"Esther, that is a long way to walk. I do not want you to jeopardize your own health and the health of our baby."

"We could have the servants bring a buggy around for us. We could ride around to the back of the palace; we do not have to walk. Please Ahasuerus!" Esther was crying openly now.

"Guards!" Ahasuerus shouted. "Quickly prepare the royal chariot, no, that will take too long, just provide a regular buggy for us to ride around to the concubine's quarters."

"As you wish" the guard said walking toward the door.

"Run! We are in a hurry!"

Hearing the command in the King's voice, the guard ran.

Drying her eyes Esther looked at Yara. "Thank you Yara" she said. "You may go."

"No," Ahasuerus said. "She can ride with us back to Zena's bed chamber. This is where you are going is it not?"

"Yes Your Majesty."

"Well, why should you run all the way back when we are going to the same place. Come with us." The three of them walked toward the door, down the steps and into the buggy. In minutes they entered Zena's lounge area. The doctor and the servants were sitting in the lounge area giving Zena's family time to visit with her. When he saw the King, Queen and Yara enter, he sent the servant in to have the family come out. Ahasuerus looked at the doctor questionably. The doctor slowly shook his head from side to side then looked down at the floor.

As Zena's family came out crying, Esther and Ahasuerus went in and sat down on chairs placed on both sides of the bed. Zena was still holding the baby in her arms as Esther sat down.

"Zena," Esther said softly. "I am here, and Ahasuerus is here with me. Everything is going to be fine now."

Zena looked at Esther and smiled, then looked at Ahasuerus. "Thank you for coming Your Majesty. You have a little baby girl" and she held up the baby for Ahasuerus to hold.

In all his years being King, this was the first time he had ever held one of his infant children. He was a little nervous and was not quite sure how to hold her.

"Put one hand on her bottom and support her head and neck with the other hand" Zena instructed him smiling. "That is correct." The effort it took to hand the King their baby girl completely exhausted Zena and she let her arms fall back to her sides on the bed.

Ahasuerus could not control the tears flowing down his face as he held his baby girl. He could not take his eyes off her. Zena turned her attention to Esther who picked up her hand and held it to her chest.

"Esther, I do not have much time left. I have made peace with God. I want to thank you so much for being in my life and telling me about God and His goodness. I know he loves me. I know He has forgiven me for being so vain in my youth. You were right; He is a great comfort. The last four months of my pregnancy were so peaceful and happy. I have never known such happiness." It was exhausting for Zena to talk, and she rested a bit.

"You do not have to talk Zena. Rest. I Know how you feel."

Zena shook her head no and closed her eyes her breathing slowing. Ahasuerus watched her. He knew she was dying but he also heard her reveal her relationship with God. She seemed to know God intimately, personally, just as Esther described her relationship with God to him. Even in death he saw that God loved her dearly and he was greatly moved with compassion. He was glad he allowed Esther to come to her.

"No, Esther, you do not know how I feel. I am at peace. I have joy in my heart. I am not in any pain, I am no longer afraid, just a little tired."

"If you are tired then you must rest Zena. Close your eyes now and rest. We will sit here beside you; we will not leave you."

"No, no. I want to make a request of the two of you. As my King and Queen, would the two of you raise my daughter as your own?" Zena smiled, chuckled a little. "She is half yours already! Turning to look at Ahasuerus.

Ahasuerus looked back at her through his tears. "Yes, she is" he said.

"Esther, would you do me the honor of raising my child as your own. Please do not place her in the palace nursery and let the servants raise her. Keep her with you, in your personal quarters, raise her with the child you are carrying now?"

Esther looked at Ahasuerus who nodded his head yes. "Yes Zena, we would be honored to raise your daughter as our own."

"Thank you Esther, thank you. You have been the best sister I could ever have."

"What about Zoe?"

"She is a great sister too" Zena said smiling and closed her eyes. Her breathing became more shallow as she lay there peacefully. Esther and Ahasuerus watched her closely.

"Esther?" Zena whispered now.

"Yes Zena."

"Esther, the baby's name is Hadassah. Name the baby Hadassah and teach her about God. Teach her how to live a Godly life in fear and reverence to Him. Will you do this for me?"

Esther, crying openly replied "yes, yes I will do as you say Zena. Everything you say" she said through her sobs. Hadassah was Esther's Hebrew name. "How did you know my Hebrew name Zena?" she asked. Zena did not answer. Her eyes were closed; she had gone back to be with God.

Esther laid her head down on the bed and sobbed uncontrollably until Ahasuerus came around to her putting his free arm under her arm lifting her up from the chair. Getting up, she dried her eyes, looked back at Zena one last time, then walked out of the room.

As they entered the lounge area, Zena's family stood to their feet. Zoe looked at Esther who was crying softly. Esther walked over to her and held her in her arms, and they cried together. Ahasuerus saw the grief and sadness in Zena's family and his heart was moved.

"Zena will be given a proper burial. This is your granddaughter; you are free to come and visit her at the palace as often as you like. She shall be called 'Hadassah,' which means Star."

"Thank you Your Majesty" Zena's father said bowing at the waist.

"Shall I take the baby to the nursery?" Yara asked walking up to the King.

"No. Set up a nursery in our private quarters. How soon could that be done Yara?"

"We will start working on it immediately Your Highness."

"Thank you Yara. Thank you for all that you have done for us. We appreciate your service and your loyalty."

"You are most welcome Your Majesty" Yara replied bowing to them again and backed out of the room.

Esther went over and hugged Zena's mother and father as tears continued to flow. "She was my sister" she said through her tears. "I will greatly miss her."

Her mother raised her hand to Esther's face drying her tears. Do not cry dear, she is with God now. She is in a better place. You take good care of yourself and your little one" she looked at her granddaughter and patted Esther's stomach, then stood back and let the King and Queen go.

Ahasuerus and Esther rode in the buggy to the front of the palace. As Esther held Hadassah, she cried softly looking up at Ahasuerus. "Why did God have to take Zena?"

Looking down at Esther, Ahasuerus' heart was breaking seeing his wife in so much pain. "I am not sure Esther. Your father tells me that God's ways are not our ways. I do not know why He has taken Zena, but He must have His reasons."

Ahasuerus put his arm around Esther to comfort her. She leaned her head against his chest holding the baby close to her as she dried her tears.

Chapter Twenty-Five

MEMUCAN'S TRAGIC DEMISE

Spending quiet time in his personal quarters with the Lord, Mordecai suddenly felt a deep sorrow. "Sorrow? Why would I be feeling sorrow?" he asked himself. He had just seen Esther this morning and she was fine. Where is this coming from, he thought. Everything was on schedule for the thirteenth of Adar, things were fine between me and the brothers. He could not pinpoint where the sorrow was coming from so he dismissed it and began praying again, but the sorrow would not go away. "Father, what is it? Who is in trouble?" He sat quietly and Esther's name came to his mind. "I just saw her this morning Father, but I will go to her and make sure she is alright." Getting up off his knees, he put on his royal robe and walked down the hall toward the King and Queen's personal quarters.

Esther sat in her personal quarters holding Hadassah rocking her back and forth as she lay in her arms sleeping. "Oh Father, I am sad that you have taken Zena home with you. I guess you have your reasons. Please help me to accept your decision and take this grief away from my heart and replace it with your peace." Esther began to sob again. "Please Father, take this grief away and help me to rejoice over Hadassah that Zena has entrusted to me."

"Queen Esther, your father is here to see you, may I show him in?"

"Quickly drying her eyes on the towel that was placed on her shoulder, Esther answered "yes, please show him in."

Stepping into the lounge area, Mordecai stopped short looking at Esther holding a baby. "Esther! He said walking over to her. "What…, you have not had your baby yet, it is too early!"

Esther looked up at him and the tears began to flow again. "Oh Morde!" she cried.

Mordecai sat down beside her on the couch. "Where is Ahasuerus?"

"He is making arrangements for Zena's burial with the servants."

"Zena's what?"

Wiping her eyes again Esther took a deep breath trying to regain her composure and tell Mordecai what had happened during the day. "Zena went into labor early this morning. She bore a little girl. Here she is." Esther turned the baby around so Mordecai could see her. The baby began to cry, and Esther held her close to her breast again.

Mordecai looked at Esther, then the baby. "Zena? She had her baby?"

"Yes but she died in childbirth Morde. She died!" Esther broke down again and cried. "I do not know why God allowed her to die, but I guess He had His reasons."

"Yes, yes, yes, Esther. God always has a reason why he does everything. Now you must stop crying and get yourself under control. This is not good for you or your baby. Zena has gone back to be with God, I know you understand this. Do not let this grief overcome you!"

"You are right Morde, you are right" Esther said drying her eyes again. "Before she died, Zena called for me and Ahasuerus and asked us to raise her daughter for her, not to send her to the palace nursery and to teach her about God. Ahasuerus said that he would grant her petition and that is why the baby is here with me now. Morde," Esther hesitated looking at him. "Zena named the baby 'Hadassah!'" Esther whispered. "That is my…."

"Yes I know Esther" Mordecai said tears welling up in his eyes. "I know that is your Hebrew name. What a blessing this is. Ahasuerus, does he accept all of this?"

"Yes he has" Esther said smiling. "God is good."

"Yes he is. We have so much to be thankful for. Zena is with the Lord. Let us be happy for her and surround this baby with all the love and support we can give her."

"Yes Morde" Esther said Smiling at him.

Sitting on the three crates around the campfire in the vacant area five miles from the palace, the three Amalekites talked among themselves. "It is late enough. I think we can hunt for dinner now and not be seen by anyone" the big one said. Picking up their swords and spears the three of them walked off into the shrubbery looking for food for their dinner. During the day they stayed behind the stone walls keeping out of sight of any Persian soldiers or villagers. They ate and drank sparingly from the supplies they bought with them. It had been a full day and night since Memucan had fallen into their campsite.

"Do you think that Memucan man was telling us the truth?" the little one asked.

"I do not know" the big one replied. "I do know this, if he was lying to us, he and his whole family will pay with their lives. Now be quiet so we can catch our dinner." The three of them walked quietly through the weeds.

It was late, very, very late in the evening when Memucan finally closed his office and headed down the cobblestone street toward his house. Again, he found himself out late at night without security. Once again he heard his footsteps echoing in his ears as he walked away from the palace lights into the darkness. After the events of the day, he no longer felt that sense of peace he experienced the other night and it seemed as if the darkness was enveloping him, swallowing him up. He quickened his pace to a run-walk until he reached his home out of breath.

Going into the house he found his wife and four children, two boys and two girls sitting by the table. All five of them looked up at him as he stood in the doorway. Hazilad, Memucan's wife, searched her husband's face for an explanation of the note instructing her and the children to be packed and ready to leave. He had traveled for the King on many occasions. Sometimes with no notice at all. There were situations where he would send a note home saying "pack a bag for me, the King is sending me here or there on business." This was the first time that she and the children were going along with him.

"Is everything ready to go Hazilad?" he asked ignoring the look on all their faces.

"Yes" Hazilad replied obediently. "Everything is ready, as much as we and the servants could pack. We prepared the rest of our things for storage when we return."

"Where are the servants?"

"I sent them to bed several hours ago."

"Hmmm" Memucan said looking around the room. "That is good. They have had rest then?"

"If they went directly to bed, yes."

"Have the servants get up and load the buggies and the chariot."

"All of them?" Hazilad asked. The King had assigned ten servants to live and serve each of his lawyers and their families.

"No, just three. They will be traveling with us to India."

"To India? Is that where we are going?" Hazilad asked surprised.

"Yes we all are going to India per the King's orders. I will explain why after we get on the road Hazilad. Please have the servants get up and do as I ask. I want to be on the road in 20 minutes."

Everyone began moving quickly getting the supplies ready to be loaded. Memucan's sons went out back with the servants to get the buggies and the three carriages and bought them around to the front of the house. In fifteen minutes, everything was loaded, and the little caravan began moving toward the royal road. It was the middle of the third watch as Memucan, Hazilad and their four children made themselves comfortable in the carriage while the servants controlled and steered them down the road.

Memucan held Hazilad close to him waiting for the children to go to sleep before explaining the events of the day. His children were young from 10 years to 16 years old and had established friends here in Shushan. He knew they would be extremely upset when they found out that they were moving to India permanently. Everyone was exhausted with the events of the day including the servants. No one else was on the road as the darkness surrounded the carriages. The steady clip clopping of the horses' hooves on the royal highway put the servants in a trance. All three servants, Memucan and his wife fell asleep at the same time as the children fell asleep.

As the small caravan traveled away from the palace grounds, the carriage lanterns provided only enough light to illuminate the road ten feet in front of the horses. The servants, being asleep, did not see the Amalekite soldiers. The big one was standing in the middle of the road, the other two on the sides of the road in the bushes. With his eyes accustomed to the dark, the Amalekite could see that everyone, including the servants, was asleep. He put his finger up to his mouth signaling to his brothers to be quiet. Gingerly inching his way close to the horse, he was able to stop them without causing them to panic. His other two brothers did the same with the two carriages that followed the first carriage. Tiptoeing to the side of the carriage, the big one looked inside. He recognized Memucan but not his wife and children. Making signs with his hands, the big one told his other two to dismount the servants from the carriages and subdue them. Memucan, Hazilad and the children remained fast asleep. Once the servants were bound, gagged, and placed in the weeds beside the road, the three Amalekite soldiers stood in front of the door of the carriage.

"Ah, this is the one calling himself Memucan. The one that fell into our campsite two nights ago, right boys!" he said loud enough to awake everyone in the carriage.

At hearing his name, Memucan jerked himself awake. Slowly Hazilad and the children also awoke rubbing their eyes not sure of what they were seeing. Focusing his eyes, Memucan recognized the three Amalekite soldiers and fear came over him as he looked at them. With all that had happened that day, he had forgotten his promise to meet them on the 12th of Adar and lead them to Mordecai's office so they could kill him. Panic set in on top of the fear as he recalled the big one's threat to him that if he did not show up, they would hunt him and his family down and kill all of them.

Hazilad sat up looking at Memucan. "Who are these men? Where are the servants?" What is going on Memucan?"

"Hush Hazilad! Hush" Memucan said in a quiet voice. "Be still and let me handle this." Waiving his hands in the air he began trying to explain to the soldiers. "Gentlemen! Gentlemen. Listen, this is not what it looks like."

"Oh," the big one said. It looks like you are trying to trick us. He is trying to trick us by running out of town" he said looking at his brothers standing on both side of him. "I believe this man was lying to us all along. I believe his name really is Mordecai and this is his family! They are running with him. Look boys!" He pointed to the two buggies carrying supplies, "we were having trouble hunting for food tonight. Look at all their supplies!"

"We can eat like royalty!" the little one said. "The dinner has come to us. This is great!"

"Ah, er, gentlemen, please, please let me explain. I had every intention of…"

"Yes, your explanations are nothing but lies and we will no longer listen to them." Opening the door, the big one pulled Memucan out of the carriage. "Bind all of their hands and feet and put them back in the carriage, we will take them to our campsite and deal with them there" the big one ordered.

"Please, please do not hurt the children! They have nothing to do with this. Please let them go and take my husband and me! Please!" Hazilad begged as she was dragged out of the carriage and then her children.

"I am afraid they are involved ma'am" the big one said. "Your husband, Mordecai, got you and your children involved when he broke his promise to us. Now gag her and the children so we do not have to hear their crying and pleading and throw them back into the carriage. We will avenge our brother tonight, take their supplies and head back home."

"What about Zeresh and the boys!" the little one asked.

"All we were interested in was avenging Haman. Zeresh was not aware that we were even in town. I am sure she has her plans already made. With her ten sons, she should be able to do what she needs to do. I do not think three more men will make much of a difference. Hurry, we have a lot of work to do. I want to be out of this area before the sun comes up."

After everyone was bound, gagged, and thrown back into the carriage, each of the soldiers mounted the three carriages. They left the three servants bound and gagged in the bushes on the side of the road as they made their way back to their campsite and pulled the carriages behind the walls. Jumping down from the seats, they went around to the carriage door, pulled Memucan out, standing him on the side then pulled the rest of his family out and pushed them on the ground where their campfire was smoldering. The fire had gone out but the lights on the carriages provided enough light for the three of them to see clearly.

As they went to get their swords, Memucan began to squirm trying to yell through his gag, but the men ignored him.

The big one grabbed, what looked to him to be the youngest of Memucan's children, stood her up putting his knife to the girl's throat. He looked at Memucan who was sobbing through his gag. "Mordecai!" the big one said.

Memucan was trying to yell through his gag, "I am not Mordecai! I am not Mordecai!"

The big one ignored his pleas and continued. "Because you were instrumental in having our brother Haman killed, I am going to force you to watch each one of your family members die. Your wife and your daughters are beautiful women. We have not had a woman in several months have we men?"

"No!" the other two said rubbing their hands together thinking they were going to have their way with the females before killing them.

Memucan was violently shaking his head from side to side screaming "No! No! No!" through his gag.

"I want you to know, Mordecai, that we Amalekites are not the heartless and cruel beasts you Jews make us out to be. We are not barbarians that would take your women right in front of you. We are polite. We would take them on the other side of the wall and have our way with them in private, take their gags off and let you hear their cries, right boys!"

The other two Amalekites pranced from one foot to the other looking at Hazilad and her two daughters wide-eyed rubbing their hand together. "I want that one!" the little one said as he moved next to his brother holding Memucan's youngest daughter. The big one held the girl securely allowing his brother to stroke the maiden's face while the gag remained firmly in place. He allowed his younger brother to play with her for a few minutes while they watched Memucan crying in agony.

"No Mordecai, we are not the barbarians you people make us out to be. I will show you mercy and just kill them outright without violating them! See!" he said as he slit the younger girl's throat and let her drop.

Memucan screamed as his daughter fell to the ground. Hazilad and the other children laid there terrified waiting for their turn.

The big one did not say anything else as he went about his work one at a time, slitting their throats and throwing them over one on top of the other close by where Memucan was standing. After all the children were dead, Hazilad was brought to him. He pulled the gag from her mouth and ordered to have Memucan's gag removed as well. "Mordecai, I have removed your gags to give you a chance to say your good-byes to each other. Being in shock, Hazilad stood there shaking with tears streaming down her face. Memucan, also crying whispered, "I love you; I am so sorry. Please forgive me."

As soon as Memucan uttered his last word 'me,' the big one slit Hazilad's throat and the other solder ran his sword through Memucan's back and dropped him next to his family's piled up bodies. The Amalekite soldier knew how to thrust the sword into Memucan's back in such a way to cause him to die a slow death. "I left you partially alive Mordecai. I want you to think about what you have done in having Haman Killed. While you look at your dead family, you will die a slow death. This is the price you pay when you kill an Amalekite."

The three men stood looking at the five bodies on the ground as Memucan lay moaning on his side. Satisfied with their revenge, each of the three soldiers gathered their supplies and placed them on the carriages and left the area. It was the morning of the eleventh of Adar. The three Amalekite soldiers had four hours before dawn. They drove the horses hard getting as far away from Shushan as fast as the horses could carry them.

Chapter Twenty - Six

THE ELEVENTH OF ADAR

On the morning of the eleventh of Adar, Reelaiah and Bilshan stood in front of their huts talking.

"Have all of the women and children been moved to the safe area?" Reelaiah asked looking around making sure no Persian villagers were around to hear them.

"Yes they have all been moved. All the brothers decided not to go to work today in preparation of the thirteenth. We plan to sleep as much as possible, getting up at the beginning of the second watch on the 12th ready to fight." Looking in Reelaiah's eyes, Bilshan asked, "are you afraid Reelaiah?"

"I am a little nervous. I have been spending a lot of time in prayer through. I believe God will give all of us the boldness we will need to do what we must do. Mordecai has asked that you, me, and a couple of other brothers accompany him to Haman's house to deal with his sons. Will you go with us?"

"Of course! I would be honored to fight by Mordecai's side."

"Very good. We should go and check with the other brothers to see if they need any help with anything" Reelaiah said as the two men walked down the alley.

Per the King's instructions, Hegai informed all the lawyers and Mordecai that he wanted to meet with them. Shethar, Carshena, Admatha, Tarshis, Meres and Marsena sat at the table with the King and Mordecai at the head of the table. Everyone was there except Memucan. All the men looked around looking for him except Admatha. The King did not acknowledge nor give a reason for his absence.

"Gentlemen," Ahasuerus began, "As you know tomorrow is the thirteenth of Adar. You also know that I have instructed all palace guards and Persian soldiers to participate in this fight. If you so desire, you can bring your wives and children inside of the palace walls for protection. You are welcome to come as well or to stay and fight against the Jews; it is your decision. But know this, if you should lose your life in the fight, the palace will not be responsible for the care and upkeep of your wives and children. They will have to fend for themselves."

All the lawyers squirmed in their chairs except Meres. He never had any intention of fighting against the Jews. Knowing the plans that they and Memucan had made, he quietly watched the other men digesting what the King was telling them. Admatha sat with his head hung low staring at his folded hands in his lap. Running Memucan's plot through his head, Meres wondered why he was not present in this meeting.

"Does everyone understand? Does anyone have any questions?" Ahasuerus asked.

Meres stood bowing at the waist. "Your Majesty, I was wondering where Memucan was and why he is not present at this meeting?"

"I have sent Memucan and his family to India to assist the First Prince with their scientific work. He was very unhappy in his work here in Shushan, so I provided different work for him in India. Is everyone else satisfied with their duties here in the palace?" Ahasuerus asked looking at each of his lawyers intently. All of them shook their heads yes, that they were happy in their position. "If there are no other questions, this meeting is adjourned." Ahasuerus stood and beckoned Mordecai to follow him. "I would like to speak with you privately in my lounge area. Will you come with me?"

"Of course," Mordecai answered and the two of them left the meeting together.

All the lawyers stood waiting until the two men left the conference room before anyone spoke.

"What has happened? Why did the King send Memucan away!" Carshena asked. No one answered him. Admatha kept his head bowed with his hands jammed into his pockets. "Admatha, do you know anything about this?"

Looking up at each of the men, Admatha studied each of them for a minute before speaking. "We cannot talk here. Meet me in my office in five minutes and I will tell you what I know.

Ahasuerus and Mordecai sat down in the King's lounge area.

"Is everything ready?"

"Yes it is. The brothers have moved their wives and children to a safe place and are ready to defend themselves."

"They have been moved already?"

"Yes, we thought it better to move them early and discretely so they would be safe. I plan on taking a ride through the villages later this afternoon to encourage the men.

"Make sure you take plenty of soldiers with you for security. Do not be surprised if one of the Persian citizens try to kill you first. Based on what I have learned about your God, or, ah, God, they do not know that trying to kill you would not make a difference in God's Divine Plan to protect His people."

Mordecai smiled. "You are learning well, my friend. Yes, I am aware that I have enemies that would like to end my life. Your First Prince being among them."

"You have noticed him then."

"Yes I have, and I understand his plight."

"What do you mean?"

"He has worked for you for a long, long time has he not?"

"Yes he has. He had been faithful to me for a number of years."

"Your promoting Haman over him did not make him happy and when you promoted me over him, he became even more unhappy."

"I am aware of that. That is why I shipped him and his family off to India."

"To India? What would he do there?"

"I sent a letter to the First Prince of India instructing him to have Memucan assist him with the scientific research going on there."

"Hmmm" Mordecai said with a slight smile on his face. "And he is gone already?"

"Yes he is. He and his family left early this morning. Going forward, everyone who works for me must be loyal and happy in their work. I will settle for nothing less."

Mordecai nodded his head in agreement. "When the fighting starts, I will send runners back to you intermittently giving you progress updates."

"I would appreciate that Mordecai. Changing the subject, are you aware that one of my concubines died in childbirth yesterday? Her name was Zena. She bore a little girl."

"Yes, I stopped to see Esther late last night. She informed me of Zena's death. The two of them were like sisters. She took it very hard."

"Yes I know."

"How is she today? How is the baby?"

"They both are doing well. Esther seems to have accepted God's Will in the matter. She has her sad moments but manages to bring herself out of them. Hadassah is bonding with both of us. I am enjoying having a little one around me."

"Babies are a blessing from God."

"I am beginning to see that. Would you care to have lunch with Esther and me and the baby? It may be the last time we see each other before the fighting begins."

"Yes I would love to" Mordecai said. "Where is the baby now?"

"In with Esther in her lounge. We have made a nursery out of her lounge area."

Admatha sat at his desk twiddling his thumbs as the other lawyers filtered in one at a time and took a seat around his desk. Meres was the last to come in.

Before Admatha could say anything, Carshena asked? "What is going on Admatha? Why did the King send Memucan away?"

"Memucan was foolish."

"What do you mean foolish? What did he do?"

"Remember when we were in his office discussing what we would do about Mordecai, and he began to rant and rave about the King promoting Mordecai over him like he was the only one that was offended?"

"Yes I remember that. We all told him that he was not the only one that was offended and that he should control himself and his temper."

"Yes, yes, yes" Admatha said leaning back into his chair. "Well, his temper got the better of him. He did indeed begin to think and act like his predecessor. Arrogant, full of pride and impatient. The King had called a meeting with him and the eunuch Hegai a couple of days ago. He told them to wait for him in the conference room until he finished his breakfast with the Queen and her father. While he and Hegai were waiting, Memucan started ranting and raving about how long the King was taking to come to them. He began yelling at Abagtha, sending messages to the King asking how long he was going to be. He yelled at Hegai because he was sitting their calmly eating biscuits and drinking tea. What Memucan did not know was that the King was standing in one of the doorways listening to him rant and rave, complaining about him and yelling at Abagtha. The King went around to the main hall and entered the conference room where Memucan and Hegai could see him come in. They took care of the business at hand. After the meeting was over, the King informed

Memucan that he was being transferred to India and that he and his family were to leave the very next morning."

"Oh!" Meres shouted sitting back in his chair. That is the end of that, he said to himself looking at the other men.

"What do we do now?" Carshena asked. "What about our meeting? Does anyone know where the location is that Memucan found?"

"I know where it is" Admatha said flatly. "The thirteenth is less than a day and a half away. There is no way we can organize and get everyone at the meeting place. You heard the King at the meeting. He said we could fight if we wanted to, but he sounded like he would prefer it if we did not fight against the Jews? Are all of you still planning to fight?"

Because Meres was the last man to enter Admatha's office, he sat in the back. This gave him the advantage of observing the other men without them noticing him. None of the men answered Admatha, so he asked the question again. "Are any of you still planning to fight against the Jews?"

"With all that has happened," Carshena said slowly, "if we would get killed, how will our families survive? The King said he would not take care of them. I do not see how any of us could fight against them in good conscience."

"Is that the way all of you feel?" Admatha asked looking at each man. All of them shook their heads up and down including Meres. "Well, I think we should prepare to bring our families as well as ourselves into the palace for protection. And gentlemen, going forward, are we going to become loyal to the King again?"

"With everything that has happened, beginning with Haman, if we want to keep our lives and the lives of our families, I think we should be happy with what we have. None of us should ever speak about Memucan and his plot to kill Mordecai ever again. After this fight is over, we should serve the King and Mordecai as we should" Marsena said who had been quiet throughout all that had transpired.

"I agree with Marsena" Meres said getting up from his chair walking toward the door. "If the rest of you know what is good for you, you will do the same" he said as he walked out the door closing it behind him. One by one, each of the other men left the same way without saying another word and left Admatha sitting alone in his office.

Meres quickly walked down the hall toward Hegai's office hoping he was there. He wanted to share the good news with him. Turning the corner, he and Hegai bumped into each other again.

"Oh!" Hegai said.

"I was hoping you would be in your office" Meres said looking both ways. "Come, I have a lot to share with you." The two men went into Hegai's office and sat down. Not too long ago I was in a meeting with the King, Mordecai, and all the other lawyers. Everyone except Memucan."

"He was not there" Hegai said smiling.

"How did you know?" Meres asked looking at Hegai astounded.

"I have not had a chance to tell you but yesterday, the King, Memucan and I had a meeting to talk about the concubines. While we were waiting for the King to come, Memucan was ranting and raving, complaining about having to wait so long for the King to come to the meeting. He said he had important things that he needed to do and did not have time to wait around all day doing nothing. Well, the King finally came, and we had the meeting. Just before the meeting ended, the King looked at Memucan and said he understood that Memucan was not happy in his position as First Prince of Shushan and he was transferring him to India! To India! He was sending a letter to the First Prince of India announcing Memucan. His assignment was to assist the First Prince with the scientific research going on there. Meres, I was shocked! But not as shocked as Memucan. He tried to beg to keep his position here, but the King would not hear of it."

"Well!" Meres said sitting back in his seat. "We no longer have to go to the King to let him know that his lawyers were disloyal to him. I have just come from a private meeting with the lawyers. Admatha told us that the King heard Memucan ranting and raving in the conference room and that is why he sent him to India. I told the men that after what had happened to Haman and Memucan, that they should forget any ideas of being disloyal to the King and become satisfied with their employment as it is. They all agreed."

"You did good Meres. Very good. Are any of the men going to fight against the Jews?"

"No, none. The King wisely gave them a choice. He told them that if they chose to fight against the Jews, they were free to do so. They could bring their women and children inside the palace for safety; however, if they were killed in battle, he, the King, would not be responsible for taking care of their families. The women and children would have to fend for themselves. When they heard that, none of them decided to fight."

"Our King is not as stupid as they made him out to be is he?" Hegai said laughing.

"No. He is not stupid at all. His association with Mordecai seems to be making him wiser every day."

"Tell me this Meres, are the Persian villagers still going to meet out in the fields behind the palace?"

"If they do, they will be on their own with no leadership."

Esther, Ahasuerus, and Mordecai sat around the dining room table eating lunch. Hadassah lay peacefully in her soft pillowed basket on a stand right beside Esther. Every so often, Esther placed her hand on Hadassah to let her know that she was nearby. As she reached over this time, she felt movement in her stomach. "Oh!" she said out loud. "I just felt the baby move" Esther said smiling at Ahasuerus. "Oh, there it is again!" She quickly grabbed Ahasuerus' hand placing it on her belly. Ahasuerus smiled as the baby moved under his hand.

"Oh, he has a strong kick."

"He?" Esther said smiling.

"I agree with Ahasuerus" Mordecai said. "We pray that he is a boy."

"God's will be done" Esther said as she began eating her lunch. "Morde, are you going to stay within the palace when the fighting begins?"

"No, I will be out with the brethren helping and encouraging them."

"You must be careful Mordecai" Ahasuerus said. "As we spoke earlier, you do have enemies out there."

"Yes, I am aware of that. I will not wear my royal attire when I go out so no one will know who I am. Reelaiah, Bilshan and a few other brothers will accompany me to do what I must do. I will not be out very long." Mordecai thought it best not to share all his plans with Esther and Ahasuerus. He did not want them to worry more than he knew they would.

"Your Majesty" the guard said at the door. "One of the servants is here and wishes to speak with you."

"Is it urgent?"

"He says he thinks you would want to hear this information right away."

"Have one of the guards escort him to my throne room. I will be there in a minute."

"As you wish Your Majesty."

"Please excuse me, something has come up that I must attend to immediately. You two finish your lunch; I will meet up with you later." Taking a biscuit from the plate, Ahasuerus kissed Esther on the forehead, squeezed Mordecai's shoulder as he walked by and hurried out the door.

The guards accompanied him to the throne room. After taking his seat, he held out the golden scepter to the servant as he came near the throne and touched the tip of the golden scepter and bowed at the waist.

"What is it that you have to report?" Ahasuerus questioned the servant.

"Your Excellency, a few minutes ago, I and my brother were riding our horses down over the hill behind the palace about five or six miles away where the three brick walls are standing."

"Yes, I know the place."

"We were riding by when we noticed six dead bodies on the inside of the brick walls."

"Dead bodies?"

"Yes Your Excellency."

"Did you identify them?"

"We dismounted our horses and went over to investigate. We did not recognize the woman and four children, but the man was your First Prince, Memucan. I knew who he was because I have delivered many messages for him within the palace."

Ahasuerus sat there quietly, then asked. "And you are sure it was Memucan?"

"Yes, Your Excellency. As I said, I have delivered many, many messages for him within the palace. I delivered one to his home yesterday."

"By inspecting the bodies, could you tell how they were killed?"

"The woman and the four children appeared to have had their throats slashed. It looked like whoever killed Memucan stabbed him in the back with their sword and left him there to die. His body was still warm when we came upon them. It looked like they made him watch while they killed the woman and the children, then stabbed him and left him to die a slow death."

Ahasuerus groaned within himself. He was displeased with Memucan's behavior over the past year, but he did not desire to have him killed. Especially like this. "Did you or your brother move any of the bodies?"

No Your Excellency. Once I identified Memucan, we came directly here to the palace."

"I see. You and several other servants get a wagon, go pick up the bodies and deliver them to the palace morgue. I will see that they are properly buried. Before you go, stop at Admatha's office, and have him come to me here. Thank you young man, you did well."

"Thank you Your Excellency" the servant said bowing at the waist as he backed out of the room then ran down the hall toward Admatha's office. Knocking on the door, Admatha yelled, "Yes, who is it?"

"The King has requested your presence in the throne room Sir."

"Very well, I will come immediately. You may go."

"Thank you Sir" the servant said through the door and continued running down the hall.

Admatha laid the paper down he was reading and walked down the hall toward the throne room. The guard immediately let him in.

"The King is expecting you" the guard said and stepped aside.

"Your Excellence, you called for me?"

"Yes I did Admatha. You and Memucan were pretty close friends were you not?"

"Yes, yes we are."

"I have just been given a report that Memucan, his wife and four children were found dead five miles outside of the palace grounds. Do you have any idea who could have done this?"

"Dead! They were found dead! No! I, ah, I...., I do not know of anyone who hated Memucan that much to kill him and his family! Were they not on their way to India per your instructions?"

"Yes. I told them to leave yesterday. It is too close to the palace grounds for thieves or robbers to have killed them the way they were killed."

"May I ask where and how they were killed?"

"Their bodies were found stacked on top of each other behind the three walls about five miles from the palace. Everyone had their throats slashed except Memucan; he was killed with a sword through his back."

"Oh my! Oh my!" was all that Admatha could say.

"Alright Admatha. I just wanted to know if you knew who could have done this. I will put my investigators on this right away. You may go."

Admatha bowed at the waist, backed out of the throne room running back to his office. He was about to be sick.

Ahasuerus sat on his throne trying to figure out what reason someone would have to kill Memucan and his family. He knew that in less than 24 hours, the fighting would start and any leads that may be there would be gone. Who could he get to discretely ask questions about this. Lately he had noticed Hegai, the keeper of his concubines, had carried himself very wisely in his duties. He tends to keep to himself and is very observant and astute in his duties.

"Guard."

"Yes Your Majesty."

"Have Abagtha to find Hegai and bring him to me immediately."

"As you wish Your Majesty."

Ahasuerus sat back in his chair remembering Memucan and his service to him over the years. Up until a year ago, he had been nothing but faithful to him. He had to do something outrageously wicked that would cause someone to kill him and his family that way.

"Your Majesty, Hegai is here as you ordered."

"Send him in."

Hegai stood in front of Ahasuerus bowing at the waist. "You called for me Your Majesty?"

"Yes Hegai. I just received a bit of news that upset me greatly and I was wondering if you could shed some light on it."

"Whatever I can do to assist you Your Majesty."

"A servant of mine just informed me that he and his brother found Memucan, his wife and children dead down over the hill behind the palace."

"Oh, he and his whole family!"

"Yes Hegai" Ahasuerus said watching him closely. "I was wondering if you knew anything about it."

"About his death! No! No Your Majesty! Who would kill him and his family?"

"This is what I am trying to find out Hegai. You do not know why someone would kill him, but judging by the way you answered my question, you know something about Memucan; am I right?" Ahasuerus kept a steady gaze into Hegai's eyes as he asked him questions. He could see that Hegai was becoming uncomfortable. "What do you know Hegai. Tell me and nothing will happen to you."

"Your Majesty, Memucan was very unhappy."

"Yes, I know. That is why I transferred him to India!"

"Yes, yes, ah…,"

"Hegai, would you be more comfortable talking to me in my personal lounge?"

Hegai perked up and was relieved. "Yes I would Your Majesty."

"Very well, come with me." The two men walked out of the throne room with the guards following close behind and sat down in chairs in front of the fireplace. The guards stood outside the door leaving them alone. "Now that we are alone, tell me what you know."

Hegai began telling the King of Memucan's plot to kill Mordecai, to have him ambushed when the fighting started, the secret meetings his lawyers were having behind his back and how he and Meres were monitoring those meetings to find out all the details so they could report it to him. "But when you transferred Memucan to India, we thought everything was fine. All the lawyers agreed to remain loyal to you and be satisfied with their work. None of them decided to fight against the Jews."

"That is only because I told them I would not take care of their families if they were killed in battle Hegai." Ahasuerus was quiet; his mind was racing. "You say Memucan told Admatha that he had found a place for the Persian villagers to meet to organize against the Jews and that meeting place was where Memucan and his family were killed?"

"Yes Your Majesty. In their private meeting, Carshena asked who was going to lead the Persian villagers into battle. Admatha said they would have to be on their own."

"Hegai, this is very important. Were all my lawyers involved in this plot to kill Mordecai and to fight against the Jews?"

Hegai lowered his eyes. He knew what the King was asking him and if he said yes, he would have all his lawyers put to death. However, he had to tell the King the truth. "All of them except Meres Your Majesty" he said slowly with sadness in his voice. "Meres and I did not report this because we thought everything would be find after you transferred Memucan to India. He was the ringleader and the one that was the most-unhappy and spiteful against you."

"I understand what you are saying Hegai, and I also understand what you are feeling. However, if a King is to remain strong and run a kingdom as large and successful as our Persian Kingdom is, everyone who works closely with that King must be loyal to him. The fact that all but one of my lawyers could be persuaded to turn against me poses a threat not only to me, my family, and my servants here at the palace, but every Persian citizen that lives securely within the 127 Persian Provinces. Do you understand this?"

"Yes Your Excellency. I understand" Hegai said with his head bowed. He knew that all the lawyers were going to be killed except Meres.

"Thank you for your information Hegai. In the future, if you or any of your staff become aware of anything that does not look or sound right; that looks or sounds like it would be a threat against me or the kingdom, please come to me immediately. Do not wait to find out more information. It may save someone's life."

"Yes Your Excellency. Please forgive me for my error."

"Do you still have all of Memucan's files in your possession?"

"Yes."

"Good. Keep them until I call for them. You may go Hegai and thank you for the information you provided to me. It was very helpful."

Hegai stood up bowing at the waist and backed out of Ahasuerus' lounge. Once he was outside in the hall, sadness overwhelmed him. If he and Meres had gone to the King immediately, Memucan and his family might still be alive and none of the King's lawyers would have to lose their lives. With a heavy sigh, he walked back to his personal quarters.

Ahasuerus did not move from his chair in front of the fireplace. He had no choice; he was going to have to kill five men who betrayed him. He could not allow them to live, if he did, they could and most probably would come back and try to overthrow him later. No, they all had to die as well as their families. The thought of taking all their lives grieved him to his heart. "God, I know I have never prayed to you before about anything. I do not understand these feelings I am having. As King, I must do what I must do to keep the kingdom safe. In the past, I would not have hesitated a minute to bring all my betrayers to stand in front of me and have them and their families killed while others watched to show them that this is what happens to traitors. I know that this is what must happen now, but it grieves me to take someone's life. I feel sorrow in my heart for Memucan and his family even though he betrayed me. I do not understand, please help me." Ahasuerus sat on the window ledge looking out over the palace landscape watching the sky turn to gray, then to dusk. "Guard!"

"Yes Your Majesty."

"Has all of my lawyers and their families moved into the palace for safety?"

"Yes Your Majesty."

"Take two to three guards with you and lock up all the lawyers in prison cells. Do not put them together so they can converse with each other, separate them. Do not let them see each other being taken into custody. Take them one at a time. If they are with their families, tell them the King wants to see them so their families do not get upset, then lock them up in cells. Do this with all of them except Meres. Bring Meres to me here in my lounge area."

"As you wish Your Majesty. What about the lawyers' families?"

"Have the servants wait on them; take care of them, but keep them there in a secure place. They are not to have access to any other areas of the palace or to go outside of the palace."

"Are they under arrest as well?" the guard asked.

"Yes they are. All of them except Meres' family. Provide separate quarters for them away from all the others. Do not tell the others that they are incarcerated. If they ask questions, tell them they are being secured for their own protection. Do you understand?"

"Yes, Your Majesty. I understand completely" the guard said as he closed the door.

Ahasuerus continued sitting on the window seal watching the dusk turn into night. In a matter of hours, the fighting will begin. "Father, it is my desire to do your will. Please let me know what that is."

"Your Majesty, Meres is here as you requested."

"Show him in" Ahasuerus said moving from the window back to the chair in front of the fireplace. "Come in Meres. Have a seat." As Meres sat down, Ahasuerus sat back in his chair and observed him for a minute. "Meres, I have talked with Hegai. He has informed me that you and he were aware of Memucan's plot to have Mordecai ambushed tomorrow in the fight."

Meres became nervous and Ahasuerus saw his nervousness. "There is nothing to be nervous about Meres. You are not in any trouble. Hegai explained everything to me. The only thing I would have advised both of you was to come to me earlier with what you knew. However, what you may not know is that Memucan, his wife and children were killed early this morning. I do not know who committed the killings, I am investigating that now."

The blood appeared to drain from Meres' face. He became pale listening to the King.

"Because you were the only lawyer who was not swept up in Memucan's web of deceit, I am promoting you to First Prince of Shushan. You will work directly under Mordecai. Can you handle this authority and remain loyal to me?"

"Yes Your Majesty. As you wish Your Majesty" was all Meres could say.

"Very well. Hegai has Memucan's files. After the fighting is over, I will meet with you again and give you further instruction. You and your family are within the palace walls for safety now is that correct?"

"Yes Your Majesty."

"You may obtain those files from Hegai and begin reviewing them while you are here, and I will discuss them with you later. You may go."

"As you wish Your Majesty" Meres said standing and bowing as he backed out of the room and closed the door.

Wearied with the events of the day, Ahasuerus met Esther and the baby in his personal quarters sitting by the fire. It warmed his heart seeing his family waiting for him. He spent the rest of the evening with the two of them by the fire. Esther ordered dinner to be served in their personal quarters.

Chapter Twenty-Seven

HAMAN'S SONS ARRESTED

The lights were out in the room as Dalphon watched out the front window facing the street. He was looking to see if anyone was watching their house. His brothers were out back loading the wagons. His mother was in the other room trying to rest up for their escape in a couple of hours. It was the second watch in the evening. No one was out in the streets. Good, he thought to himself. They have finally given up watching us. Satisfied that there was no activity on the streets, he replaced the curtain in front of the window, walked over to the table and poured himself a cup of tea.

Six men dressed in black moved into position behind pillars, stone walls, anything they could hide behind to shield them from the view of the window and anyone else in the house. Two of the men went around the back of the house out of sight of the brothers loading the wagons. Their surveillance positions were in place; they settled in and waited until the wagons were loaded and Zeresh and her sons were aboard ready to pull out before ambushing them.

Holding his cup of tea in his hand, Dalphon went back to the window and continued looking out.

"What do you see?" Zeresh asked coming out of the room rubbing her eyes.

"Oh, mamma, did you get enough rest?"

"No, I am too worked up to sleep. I came to get some tea. Is there any left?"

"Yes, there is plenty. The streets are very quiet. I do not see anyone, not even any villagers. This is very unusual."

"Everyone is probably staying in-doors until the battle is over."

"You are probably right."

"I am going to see if they have finished loading the wagons. If they have, we should leave immediately while no one is out in the streets."

Parshandaltha and his eight brothers filtered back into the room breathing heavily.

"Mama, everything is loaded. We can leave whenever you like. No one is on the streets. If we leave now, we probably could be well out of Shushan when it becomes daylight."

"Good," Zeresh said. "I see no reason why we should wait, come, let us go." All of them followed Zeresh toward the back door, picked up their wraps, wrapping them around their shoulders and walked out. They had five wagons full of supplies. Zeresh sat in the second wagon with Dalphon. Parshandaltha headed out the caravan sitting in the first wagon with two of his brothers. He pulled out around to the front of their house and stopped. Three men dressed in black with their swords drawn stood in front of the horses pulling Parshandaltha's carriage. Three Persian soldiers equipped with swords, spears, helmets, and shields stood behind them. Three men in black with swords and soldiers behind them surrounded the sides and the back of the five carriages.

"What is the meaning of this!" Parshandaltha yelled trying to sound authoritative.

"The King has enforced a curfew for all Shushan. No one is permitted to come in or to leave until the 20th of Adar. That includes you, and your family. Now dismount and go back inside!"

Parshandaltha heard his mother cry out "Oh no, we are too late!" He climbed down out of his carriage, went back to his mother picked her up in his arms and carried her back into the house. All his brothers followed them. Once everyone was back inside, they sat down at the table.

"Here mama, drink some tea. It will calm you down. I do not want you to worry, we will just have to fight like all the other Persian villagers. That is why I made sure we bought enough supplies so we could fight and defend ourselves. Dalphon, you and the other boys go out to the buggies and bring our weapons back inside" Parshandaltha ordered.

Dalphon and the others went outside as instructed. As they opened the door to go out, all five carriages with all their supplies were gone.

"No! No! No! Dalphon screamed.

Parshandaltha came running out to see what was going on.

"They have taken all of our weapons and all of our supplies!" Dalphon screamed. "We have nothing to fight with! Nothing!"

Hearing what her son had said, Zeresh fainted and fell off the chair onto the floor.

As the hours lagged on, everything was quiet inside and outside of the palace. Everyone seemed to be holding their breath, waiting for the fighting to begin. No one was on the streets. The marketplace was shut down; everything was secured and locked down.

Ahasuerus spent the entire day in his personal quarters with Esther and Hadassah. He did not tell Esther nor Mordecai what had transpired the day before; Memucan's death, the plot against him by his own lawyers nor the fact that he was going to have to kill five men and their entire families. He tried to put it out of his mind as he watched Esther taking care of and playing with Hadassah. He had to do everything in his power to keep them safe. That had to include killing any traitors within his kingdom. He knew he would not want to live if anything had happened to Esther, Hadassah, or any of his other children. He would keep them safe at all cost.

Mordecai was in his personal quarters walking back in forth in front of his fireplace praying to God quietly, thanking Him and praising Him for all He was about to do.

"Your Majesty, your brothers are here to see you. Shall I show them in?" the guard asked.

"Yes, please" Mordecai said standing facing the door. "Gentlemen, come in, have a seat." Reelaiah, Bilshan and three other Jewish men equipped with swords, knives, helmets, shields, and spears came in.

"Are you ready Mordecai?" Reelaiah asked.

"Yes. How are the women and children?"

"They are fine. They have decided to fast and pray for us while the fighting is going on."

"Good" Mordecai said. Come, let us go and get this done." All the men left the palace and walked down the cobblestone street toward Haman's house. No one was out on the streets. The clip clop of the men's boots on the street echoed in their ears as they made their way. None of the men spoke. As they approached the house, the men stopped. Mordecai noticed several men, some dressed in black and some he recognized as the palace guards. They had been patrolling Haman's house out in the open since they tried to escape.

All the men standing guard nodded their heads for Mordecai and the others to proceed. Even though Mordecai was not dressed in his royal attire, the guards recognized him and did not hinder him or the men that were with him. Walking up to the door, Reelaiah kicked it open. Zeresh and her ten sons backed up against the wall. Zeresh fell on her knees and began to beg for mercy.

"Please, please, please, Mordecai, please have mercy on our souls. Please do not kill us! Send us away! Please spare our lives!

Mordecai looked down on Zeresh. "Guards!" he called. The guards came running into the house.

"Yes Your Majesty."

"Take all ten of Haman's sons and put them in prison cells within the palace."

"As you wish Your Majesty." All the other guards, including the ones dressed in black bound Haman's ten sons and marched them back toward the palace. Zeresh lay on the floor moaning and sobbing.

"What shall we do with her?" one of the guards asked.

"Nothing" Mordecai said sadness suddenly flooding his heart. "Let her lay there" he said as he and the other men left the house. As they went back into the street, several Persian villagers rushed toward them with their swords drawn screaming "Die! Die! Die! You dirty Jews! Get out of our country!"

Mordecai and the others stepped back, drew their swords slicing man after man in the stomach, cutting off their heads and pushing their bodies down on the ground. The six men fought with their backs toward each other working their way up the hill back toward the palace gate. Mordecai stabbed a man in the stomach two to three times before he fell to the ground. After the man fell, up popped a boy that looked to be nine or ten years old with a knife in his hand. Mordecai hesitated for a brief second not really wanting to kill the boy, but the hatred and rage he saw in the boy's eyes saddened him. He was just a boy. A boy full of hatred for a people he knew nothing about, only what the adults told him. Mordecai stepped back again hesitating. "Oh God!" Mordecai cried. I am going to have to kill this boy!" Stepping back again, Mordecai yelled at the boy, "go on home to your mamma boy! What are you doing out here?" That seemed to infuriate the boy. He screamed and advanced toward him with all his might. Mordecai knew he had to defend himself. Quickly he kicked the boy to the ground with his foot and ran his sword through the boy's chest, stepped over him and continued fighting.

The men worked quickly as they made their way toward the palace leaving a pile of dead bodies on the street behind them. People were out fighting throughout the streets and alleyways in Shushan. Mordecai and Reelaiah fought side by side.

"Mordecai!" Reelaiah yelled as he stabbed a man's chest. "Do you feel tired?"

"No!" Mordecai yelled back. "I have never felt strength like this before!"

Ahasuerus, Esther, and the baby sat in front of the fireplace watching the fire. They could hear the fighting going on outside of their window. Hundreds of guards were posted inside and outside of the palace grounds. The King ordered that the guards were to kill anyone who dared enter the King's palace or the palace grounds. As night turned into day and day turned back into night, the fighting continued.

"Your Majesty! Mordecai sent me to give you a report on the fighting."

"Yes, give your report" Ahasuerus said.

"He has reported that five hundred men have been slain around the palace and in all Shushan! He had the guards to arrest Haman's ten sons and placed them in palace prison cells."

"Very good. Tell him I received his report."

"As you wish Your Majesty."

"Where is Mordecai now?"

"He is down in the village on the other side of the marketplace."

"Very well, you may go."

With the runner gone, Ahasuerus attempted to get up and go back to his personal quarters with Esther and the baby when the guard interrupted him.

"Your Majesty, a couple of guards have asked permission to see you."

Ahasuerus stopped, eyed the guard that addressed him closely. "Do you know these guards personally?"

"Yes Your Majesty; I know them. They have information regarding Memucan."

"Memucan?"

"Yes Your Majesty."

"Instruct them to leave their weapons outside in the hall and show them in." Ahasuerus stepped back up and sat down on his throne and the three guards came, bowing in front of him.

"What is the information you have regarding Memucan?"

"Your Majesty, the three of us were out patrolling the palace grounds. Our orders were to patrol the area within a five-mile radius of the palace. Walking down the royal road on the west side, we saw three men bound, gagged, and thrown in the bushes. We untied them, took the gags out of their mouth giving them water. When they came to themselves, they told us that three large Amalekite soldiers ambushed them as they were driving Memucan and his family to India. They heard the soldiers call Memucan, Mordecai! They said that he lied to them to save his own life and that his real name was Mordecai, and he was responsible for their brother's death. They pulled Memucan and his family out of the carriage, bound them, gagged them, and threw them back into the carriage and drove off."

"Where are Memucan's three servants?"

"They are in the hall Your Majesty."

"Bring them in."

The three servants were bought before Ahasuerus. Their clothes were dirty, packed with mud and smelled of urine. They looked and smelled like they had been out in the wilderness for two to three days without food or water.

"Take them out, wash them, feed them. Take care of any wounds they may have and bring them back to me."

"As you wish Your Majesty" the guard said leading them away."

Hegai and Meres were correct, Ahasuerus thought leaning back in his chair. Memucan was extremely unfaithful. He conspired with Amalekite soldiers to have Mordecai killed and it backfired on him, and he lost his own life. God watches over Mordecai and eliminates his enemies even when he is not aware of them, and He is giving him the victory over the enemy he is fighting now. Everything Mordecai and Esther have told me about you Father is true! You are the one and only true God, and I will worship you also. There it was again, that peace he experienced a few days ago. He sat there for a long-time cherishing God's peace and His presence. Eventually, he got up and walked back to his personal quarters where Esther and Hadassah were.

"I have just had a report from one of your father's runners. He told me that five hundred men have been slain. He has Haman's sons locked up in prison cells within the palace."

Esther placed Hadassah on her shoulder and patted her back lightly. She was pleased with the report. Ahasuerus came and sat down next to them on the couch. "Esther, is there anything more that you would have me do regarding your people? Ask and it shall be done."

"Yes Ahasuerus. If it seems good to you, could you have Haman's sons hung on the gallows and continue to allow the Jews to fight one more day."

"As you wish my Queen" Ahasuerus said as he went back and sat on his throne.

"Guards!"

"Yes Your Majesty."

"Spread the word that the fighting is to go on for one more day. Have the guards to build gallows equipped to hang all ten of Haman's sons all at the same time."

"Where would you like to have the gallows built Your Majesty?

"Tear down the gallows that was built in front of Haman's house and build a larger one in the same spot, capable of hanging all ten of Haman's sons at once."

"As you wish Your Majesty" the guard said as he turned to leave.

Mordecai and Reelaiah fought all the way back to the village where Reelaiah's hut was. They had fought all day and all night up until midnight. "Would you like to rest here for a few hours Mordecai or would you prefer to go back to the palace?"

"Hmmm. I sent a runner back to the palace to report the status of the fight to the King. I do not see any harm in my sleeping here at your house Reelaiah. Thank you for your hospitality."

"I do not know how hospitable it is going to be. All we have to eat are biscuits and dried fish that Tamara left for me."

"Do you have any tea?" Mordecai asked.

"Yes I do."

"Well, that will be fine."

The two men sat eating, drinking, and talking about the fight and then fell asleep sitting up against the wall. Two Jewish brothers guarded the front and back of the hut making sure no one barged in on them.

Mordecai and Reelaiah did not know how long they had slept. They awoke to the sounds of fighting outside of Reelaiah's hut. Jumping up, they grabbed their weapons and rushed outside. Several Persian men had challenged the two Jewish men guarding the hut. Mordecai and Reelaiah quickly jumped in and fought until the men were killed, then made their way toward the back allies of Shushan. The strength they felt surging through their bodies was just as strong as they were the day before.

All the Jews in all the 127 Persian Provinces were fighting and subduing their enemies. At the end of the second day, over seventy-five thousand Jewish enemies were slain, but none of them took any of the spoils of their enemies and the fighting stopped just as quickly as it started.

Mordecai, Reelaiah and all the other Jews stood looking all around at the dead lying on the streets and alleyways of Shushan. Satisfied, they retrieved their wives and children and returned to their homes praising and rejoicing in the Lord.

"Well my friend" Mordecai said turning and embracing Reelaiah, "God has been faithful to his children once again."

"Yes He has," Reelaiah said. "Yes He has."

"I am going back to the palace. I told Esther that I would not be out long. I have been gone for two days. She is bound to be worried.

"I understand. Tamara too must be worried. I will see you later my friend. God be with you."

"God be with you as well Reelaiah" Mordecai said as the two men turned stepping over the dead and went their separate ways.

Chapter Twenty-Eight

JEWISH ENEMIES DEFEATED

ight from the full moon lit the pathway and kept Mordecai from tripping over the dead bodies that lay in the streets as he made his way back to the palace. "Thank you for the victory! Thank you for the victory!" he said over and over with each step he took. Suddenly his body was overcome with fatigue, and he could not wait to shed the stench and blood-stained clothes that stuck to his skin. Getting closer to the palace gate, he could see guards and servants picking up the dead bodies, throwing them on carts and hauling them away.

"Good evening Your Majesty!" the gate keeper said as he bowed before Mordecai while opening the gate to him.

Mordecai just stood there. He did not go through the gate. As tired as he was, he looked at the gate keeper in a bowed stance. "Stand up!" Mordecai commanded with a little more force than he intended. Hearing the authority in Mordecai's voice, the porter stood up and became uneasy not looking Mordecai in the eyes. "Look at me" Mordecai ordered. The porter reluctantly looked at him. Looking deep into the porter's eyes, Mordecai remembered his incident with Haman, the honor Haman tried to demand from him. "I am a man just as you are and do not require you or any other human being to bow down and worship me. The only thing I require of you is respect. Is that understood?"

"Ah, yes Your Majesty."

"Also, it is not necessary for you to address me as 'Your Majesty,' Sir is all I require."

"Yes Sir" the porter replied opening the gate.

Mordecai went through the gate, up the stairs and down the hall toward his personal quarters. Turning the corner, he spotted his servant Zethaiah waiting for him beside the bathing pool. "Zethaiah! It is good to see you."

"It is good to see you as well, sir" Zethaiah said directing Mordecai toward the pool. "Here, let me help you get these off" he said as he took hold of his sword, shield, and helmet. Pulling a chair beside the pool, he had Mordecai to sit down, pulled off his boots and began to take his clothes off. Mordecai was too exhausted to object to Zethaiah removing his clothes and did as he instructed him. In minutes, he was in the warm water up to his neck with his back resting against the back of the pool wall. Mordecai relaxed and closed his eyes allowing every muscle in his body to relax. Zethaiah sat on the chair watching him. He let him lay there for a while with his eyes closed but kept watching him to make sure he did not fall asleep and his head slip under the water. After fifteen minutes, one of the other servants stepped inside the pool area.

"Zethaiah, do you require any help?"

"Yes, Yes I do. He is very, very tired. I need help to wash and clothe him." The two servants washed Mordecai and put his night clothes on him, then put him to bed.

Mordecai stretched his body and rolled over on his side facing the fireplace. Opening his eyes, instead of seeing the fire in the fireplace, he saw Esther sitting on a chair beside his bed.

"Esther! What are you doing here? What time is it?"

Esther smiled. Morde, I came to see about you. Your servant, Zethaiah sent a message to me. He was worried."

"Worried? About what?"

"Morde, you have been sleeping for two days now."

"Two days!"

"Yes. Two days straight. We had the palace doctor look at you. He said you were just plain exhausted and needed to sleep. So we let you sleep. I just wanted to come and check on you myself. I have been sitting here for about an hour or so. I am glad to see you awake."

Mordecai pulled himself up into a sitting position in the bed and groaned. "I am so sore."

"You should not be surprised at being sore. You were fighting for two straight days Morde" Esther said watching him. "You told me you would only be out for a little while, remember?"

"Yes, I remember" Mordecai said looking down at his blankets.

"I was worried Morde."

"It was not necessary for you to worry Esther. You knew I was in God's hands. You knew He would take care of me and all the other brothers. I know you prayed for all of us."

"Yes, of course I did."

"You say I have slept for two days?"

"Yes."

"It has been two days since the fighting has stopped?"

"Yes."

"What time of day is it?"

"It is almost time for dinner. Would you care to have dinner with us?"

"Yes, of course. I will meet you in the dining room in about an hour."

"Is there anything special you would like to eat Morde?" Esther asked pulling herself up from the chair. The baby inside her had grown causing her to find unique ways to move her body around.

"Yes. Food!" Mordecai said watching Esther struggling to get up from her chair. "How are you and the babies doing?"

"Oh, we are doing fine. Just fine" Esther said letting out a big sigh after standing. I will see you in about an hour then" she said going out the door and closing it behind her

Things had quieted down in and around the palace. Everything was almost back to normal, whatever normal was now Ahasuerus thought. Two days had gone by since the fighting had stopped. Sitting on his throne, he was waiting for the casualty reports to come in from all 127 Persian Provinces. After interrogating Memucan's three servants, he finally understood why he and his entire family were killed. He still had the task of executing five of his top lawyers and their families. They had been incarcerated a day before the fighting started. The lawyers' wives and children were beginning to ask the guards questions about being kept inside the palace walls now that the fighting was over. Knowing the order for all their deaths had to be given, he had spent the last two days in prayer asking God if there were any other way to handle the situation. As far as he could tell, he had heard nothing from God either way. Maybe Mordecai would be able to help me with this, Ahasuerus thought. He did not mention and had not planned to mention any of this to Esther. She was preoccupied with her pregnancy, Hadassah, the other palace children, and her regular Queenly duties. Now that the fighting was over, all the concubines that remained in the palace had their personal quarters turned into nurseries. It seemed that they and the staff were very happy about the changes that had been made. "No, I will not mention any of this to Esther" he said to himself softly. "I will wait for Mordecai."

"Guard."

"Yes Your Majesty."

"Check on Mordecai. See if he is awake. If he is, ask him to join the Queen and me for dinner in the royal dining room, then send a messenger to the Queen as well. I will wait for them in the dining room."

"As you wish Your Majesty." Ahasuerus left his throne and walked down the hall with the remaining guard to the dining room.

Admatha paced back and forth inside the small cell he had been incarcerated for the past four days. The only details the guards provided to him when they came and took him away from his family was that the King wanted to see him. But instead of taking him to see the King, they put him in this cell. They did not give him an explanation. They did not talk to him at all. They gave him food and water to drink, but no explanation. He was in this dark cold cell all by himself with no other prisoners around; there was no one to talk to. He wondered what had happened to his wife and children?

Tired of pacing, he walked over to the pile of straw heaped up in the corner and shuddered at the thought of sitting or lying down on it. The guards gave him one blanket to wrap himself. Three days of being incarcerated he thought he would have become accustomed to sleeping on straw with the water bugs, spiders and rats running around his head and feet. He could not get warm. The dampness from water seeping through the bricks below the ground caused a continual chill to run down his spine. To keep the insects, rodents, and chill away, he jumped up and down, ran back and forth from one side of the cell to the other until he wore himself out to exhaustion; then fell on the pile of straw and slept. He stuck to this routine for the four days he was jailed. "I wonder if Tarshish, Meres and the other lawyers are incarcerated as well" he said to himself through chattering lips.

In the distance, he heard a loud clang than footsteps on the stone floors. Standing up, he wrapped his hands around the iron bars poking his head as far as he could through the bars to see who was coming. Two guards came walking toward his cell, the same two guards that came everyday about this time. One carried a tray of food, the other carried a large ring of keys that swung back and forth making a clanging noise against each other as he walked. They stopped when they reached his cell. The one opened the lock and told Admatha to stand back against the back wall. When his back touched the back wall, the other guard put the tray of food down on the floor and slid it over to the center of the small cell.

Admatha watched the two men and tears welled up in his eyes. "Please Sir. Please, can you tell me why I am here? What did I do?"

The guard that had the keys turned to the other guard. "Oh, he is not demanding anymore, and he called us 'Sir!' did you hear him?"

"Yes I did" the other guard replied. "That is a first for me. I am a 'Sir' now" he said laughing as the two men began to walk away.

"Wait! Wait! Please wait!" Admatha cried falling on his knees.

Both guards turned and looked at him. "We can do nothing for you or your situation. We must follow the orders that were given to us."

"Will you summon the King for me and ask him why I am here? This must be a mistake! Please," he begged, "summon him, ask him, please!" Admatha cried.

"Do you know what happens to a person who summons the King without him calling for him? They die!" the guard said. "The King will have them put to death! I do not know what you have done Admatha. You must have done something dreadfully and wickedly wrong to end up here in this dungeon. Think about it. Think about all that you have done in the past few days, the past few weeks as well as the past few months. If you think hard enough, I am sure you will be able to figure out why you are here. You are, or were a lawyer were you not?"

"Yes" Admatha whispered. I am a lawyer."

"Use your legal skills. You should be able to figure it out for yourself" the guard said as the two of them turned and walked away leaving Admatha in his lonely cell with one dull torch on the side of the wall, the bugs, and the rats.

Ahasuerus sat in the chair watching the fire in the fireplace as he waited for Mordecai and Esther to join him in the royal dining room. Hearing the door open, he turned in his chair and stood when he saw Esther and Yara enter the room. Yara was carrying Hadassah in her arms. Yara's assistant Hannah followed behind carrying the baby basket and stand.

"Esther" Ahasuerus said walking over to them. "How are you?" he asked bending down kissing her on the forehead.

Esther looked up at him smiling and kissed him on his cheek. "I am fine" she said moving over to the table to sit down. "I went to see Morde earlier. He is finally awake and will be joining us any minute now."

"Good" Ahasuerus said sitting down in his usual seat at the table. Yara laid Hadassah in Esther's arms and set up the basket beside Esther, bowed and left the two of them together. Ahasuerus sat back and looked at Esther. She was glowing. She was beautiful sitting there holding the baby and carrying one in her stomach. "Esther, has Hegai reported to you on the status of the concubines that stayed here in the palace with the children?"

"Yes he has dear. He tells me that those that remained are very, very happy. Their children, ah, your children are all doing well. The servants have set up a large spacious area where the children and their mothers come every day to sit and visit with each other. I have gone to see it; it is beautiful Ahasuerus. Thank you."

Ahasuerus smiled as Mordecai entered the room. "Good evening my friend!" he said walking over to shake his hand. "Did you get enough rest?"

"After two days, I think so" Mordecai said laughing. "I am rested and ready for dinner" he said taking his seat. They held hands as he blessed the table.

"You may begin to serve" Ahasuerus said clapping his hands. "Everything has quieted down and almost back to normal since the fighting stopped."

"Almost normal?" Mordecai asked looking at Ahasuerus.

"Yes. Some things have happened before the fighting began. I will discuss them with you after dinner. I would like your input. I am waiting for the final report from all 127 Provinces regarding the fighting. I should hear something in a week or two."

"God has come through and protected His people once again" Mordecai said smiling at Esther. "We should make this day a national holiday for the Jews to always remember how God protected us from our enemies, make it a day of rest and feasting. With your permission Ahasuerus, I will send out a decree to all the 127 Provinces that the 15th day of Adar be declared a holiday with resting, feasting, and sending presents to each other acknowledging how God defeated our enemy, Haman. These days will be called 'Purim' meaning lot because Haman had the impudence to gamble for the day he planned to exterminate God's people. Does this meet with your approval Ahasuerus?"

"As you have said it, so it shall be written" Ahasuerus replied reaching for Esther's hand and squeezing it.

The three of them ate their dinner talking about how good God was. After dinner, Esther excused herself. "I am rather tired" she said to both Ahasuerus and Mordecai. "Hadassah and I will retire to our personal quarters" she said standing up. Yara, standing in the doorway, saw Esther get up and came over to assist her and the baby. Ahasuerus and Mordecai both embraced Esther and stood as the women left the room.

"Mordecai, would you please join me in my lounge area? I have a few things I would like to discuss with you."

"Guard, please have the servants prepare wine for us in my personal lounge."

"As you wish Your Majesty" the guard replied opening the door of the lounge for the two men, then disappeared down the hall.

They took seats in front of the fireplace and settled in. "A lot has happened since the fighting began. Things that are most troubling for me."

"Oh?" Mordecai said raising his eyebrows.

"Yes" Ahasuerus said. "On the 12th of Adar, I found out that my entire staff of lawyers, except for one, was involved in a plot to kill you."

"Me!" Mordecai said sitting up in his chair.

"Your Majesty" the guard called through the door. "The servants are here with the wine."

"Show them in" Ahasuerus said. Both men discontinued talking until the servants poured the wine and left.

"Why were your lawyers plotting to take my life?" Mordecai asked.

"It started with Memucan. We discussed Memucan's dissatisfaction and my sending him to India. He was more dissatisfied than we both realized. He and the other lawyers had been having secret meetings for months now plotting to have you ambushed on the 12th of Adar. Memucan met with three Amalekite soldiers who turned out to be Haman's brothers from Canaan. It is my understanding from Memucan's three servants who were accompanying them on their journey to India that the three soldiers ambushed them on the royal road early in the morning. They pulled the servants off the wagons, bound, and gagged them and threw them over in the bushes on the side of the road; then bound and gagged Memucan and his family, took them back to their campsite and killed the whole family."

"Why! Why did they kill Memucan and his family?"

"The servants told me the soldiers kept calling Memucan by your name. They believed he was trying to run out of town before the 12th because on the 12th, Memucan promised them that he would lead them to your personal quarters to kill you for having their brother Haman killed. Memucan told them you were responsible for his death. They told him that if he did not keep his word, that if he did not show up on the 12th, they would find him and kill him and his whole family. The Amalekites found Memucan and his family on the royal road on their way to India and thought he had double crossed them, so they killed them all. His evil deeds caught up to him."

Mordecai sat staring straight ahead into the fireplace. "God protected me through all of this, and I did not know! Our God is an awesome God!" Mordecai whispered.

"That he is" Ahasuerus responded. "I have had an opportunity to spend some time with God over the past five days. I took your suggestion and got up early in the morning and prayed, talked to Him as you instructed."

"And," Mordecai said smiling.

"Well…., I believe, Mordecai. I really believe He is the one true God. It is hard for me to explain…."

"I understand. You do not have to try and explain. You experienced God's peace and presence, am I right?" Mordecai asked smiling.

"Yes! Yes, that is exactly right! But there is more Mordecai. With all that has happened, my finding out that my top lawyers were traitors, I now must kill them as well as their families. In the past," Ahasuerus settled back in his chair looking into the fire, "I would not have hesitated to kill the men, women, and children out in the open for all to see. To show everyone what happens to those who betray the King. As King of Persia, it is my duty to keep the kingdom safe, I know that all five of those lawyers must be killed along with their wives and children. If I permit any of them to live, they will pose a threat to the kingdom at some future time. I cannot allow that to happen. I am just surprised by the grief I am experiencing over having to perform this duty."

"I see" Mordecai said sitting back in his chair. "You no longer enjoy taking another human being's life."

"Yes, exactly. Did you have a problem killing your enemies over the past three days?"

"You know, there was a young boy around nine or ten years of age who charged me after I cut down a man in front of him. I hesitated a few seconds looking at the boy. I yelled at him to go home to his mamma and prayed, 'Father, he is just a boy! I do not want to kill him.' The Lord told me to look into his eyes. The hatred that I saw in his eyes changed my mind and I killed him and stepped over his body. I did what I had to do. Did I enjoy doing it? No. Sometimes you just must do what you have to do."

"I think I understand" Ahasuerus said standing up walking around sitting on one of couches. "I am going to have to kill all those people, Haman's sons as well. I do not have to enjoy it; I can perform my duties as humanely as possible."

"Hmmm" Mordecai said still sitting where he was. "How were you thinking of killing your lawyer's families?"

"After giving it a great deal of thought, I decided to give them a fair well dinner. I have talked with the palace doctor. He has informed me that there is an herb that can be mixed with food that causes the one eating the food to become extremely sleepy and die in their sleep. It is not painful and takes affect 30 minutes after the dinner is eaten. I thought that was appropriate for the wives and children and would be done before killing the men."

"Hmmm" Mordecai said again still not moving. "What about your lawyers?"

"Esther has requested that Haman's ten sons be hung from the gallows. After their deaths, I thought it appropriate that the lawyers be hung after them, that statements be posted for the reason for their executions. That a procession of drummers proceed before them as they walk to the gallows. This should dissuade anyone else from entertaining any future ideas of committing treason against Persia."

"Where are your lawyers being held?"

"They are isolated in private prison cells in the palace dungeon."

"Do they know why they are there?"

"I have not spoken to any of them, except Admatha when I questioned him about Memucan. The guards secured them one at a time, they do not know why they are being held."

"And they have been incarcerated for how long?"

"Since the 12th of Adar."

Mordecai got up from his chair and sat down on the couch beside Ahasuerus. "Are you planning on telling them why they have to die?"

"I do owe them that much."

"Yes" Mordecai said still watching Ahasuerus. "You seem to have made up your mind."

"Yes I have. Thank you for listening Mordecai. It has been a big help."

"When are you planning on carrying the executions out?"

Ahasuerus sat thinking for a long time. Mordecai sat with him and waited while he thought on the matter. Turning to face Mordecai, Ahasuerus began speaking slowly, "I have decided to address all the lawyers together tonight. I will tell them what I have learned about them, that it grieves me to have to execute them, but that they, as lawyers, know the law and this is the price that must be paid for committing treason against the Persian Government. That they will be hung by the neck until they are dead at dawn tomorrow morning. They must know that their actions have caused the lives of the wives and children to be taken as well; however, their deaths will be handled very humanely, in their sleep."

"Would you like me to accompany you when you hand down your sentences?"

"I could use your support."

"As you wish my friend. As you wish."

"Guard!" Ahasuerus called.

"Yes Your Majesty?"

"Take five other guards and bring Shethar, Carshena, Admatha, Tarshis and Marsena who are being held in the palace dungeon. Stand them before me in the throne room immediately. I will meet you there."

"As you wish Your Majesty."

Ahasuerus and Mordecai walked quietly down the hall, entered the throne room sitting down; Ahasuerus on his thrown, Mordecai pulled a chair up beside him on a lower platform but close enough to him to be able to reach out and touch him and speak to him quietly without anyone else hearing. Moments later all five lawyers stood in front of the King and Mordecai each with a guard standing behind them.

All five men still wore the same raiment they had on four days ago. None of the men looked into the King's eyes.

"Do any of you know why you were jailed?" Ahasuerus asked looking at each of them.

Admatha fell on his knees and began to cry out to the King pleading for his life. "Your Majesty, Your Majesty, please forgive me. I made a horrible mistake. It was Memucan's idea, not mine! Please…." He begged.

The guard grabbed Admatha by the scrub of his neck and stood him upright on his feet again and yelled at him, "You approach the King again without his permission and I will kill you right where you stand!" Admatha stood up his head bowed sobbing and his whole body shaking. None of the other men said a word as Ahasuerus read their crime and the price they were going to pay, but they all began to cry out and moan when they heard that their wives and children would also have to pay with their lives. "Take them away" Ahasuerus said in a sadden voice. "They shall be executed at dawn tomorrow morning."

Both Mordecai and Ahasuerus sat quietly for a long time after the men and the guards left the throne room. "Well, it is done" Ahasuerus said. "I am very tired."

"Yes, so am I" Mordecai said standing up. "I will see you at dawn. Try and have a good night's sleep my friend. After tomorrow, everything will be done, and we can go on with our lives as God orders it."

Ahasuerus embraced Mordecai, shook his hand with tears in his eyes. "Thank you Mordecai. Thank you."

Chapter Twenty-Nine

THE EXECUTIONS

Zeresh lay on the hard cold marbled floor in a fetal position in the same room where the soldiers had taken her ten sons three days ago. All the screaming and crying took all her strength away and she lay there moaning and crying until she fell into an exhaustive sleep. None of her neighbors came to check on her for fear of the Jew's retaliation against the Haman family. After the fight, all Persian citizens kept to themselves and stayed inside their own homes out of fear.

The fire had gone out in the fireplace three days ago, Zeresh shivered wrapping her arms around her body trying to warm herself. Opening her eyes, grief enveloped her again as she remembered all that had taken place over the past several months; the execution of her husband, the surveillance of her home preventing her family from escaping Shushan and Mordecai taking her sons away. She was dry inside. There were no more tears she could shed, only raspy moans that hurt her throat and chest as she tried to breath. Nothing came out. She laid there shivering, twitching thinking of all that had happened to her and her family.

Hearing a strange sound, she quieted herself trying to listen to make out what it was. There…., there it was again. What is that sound? she wondered. She could not make it out. It was getting closer. "Rump., rump., rump, rump, rump. Rump., rump., rump, rump, rump." It seemed as though it was coming in her direction. Mixed in with the rumpling sounds were footsteps. She lay still and continued to listen. Now she heard "Rump! Stump, Rump! Stump, Rump, rump, rump! Stump." Somewhere deep inside of herself, she gathered enough strength and pulled herself up and sat on a chair by the table. The sounds were getting louder and stronger. Using her arms on the sides of the table, she stood up, her legs wobbling and shaking, she made her way to the window and looked out. Pulling back the curtain she saw a large gallows that had been built right in front of her house. She had never seen such a large contraption. "When did they build this one!" She whispered to herself. The gallows were so large that it filled the entire length of the road in front of her house with several stations lit with torches. "Just how many stations were there?" She whispered to herself and began to count them. "One, two, three, four, five, six, seven, eight, nine, ten! Ten! Ten! Oh no! Please no!" She cried. The sounds were loud now. Looking past the gallows, she saw lights bobbing up and down on the sides of the street and rows of Persian Drum Soldiers playing the rhythmic patterns and marching in time. Behind the drumline was the King in his royal chariot with several people following. "What is this? What is going on now!" Zeresh bellowed through her raspy throat. As the mob got closer and closer, she could clearly see the King and Mordecai sitting in his chariot. They pulled over to the side of the road in clear view of the gallows. The drummers kept drumming and marched to the other side of the gallows. Ten soldiers each escorting a man led them up the steps to the top of the gallows. All the men had their heads down toward the ground and she could not see their faces at first. Zeresh kept her gaze focused on the ten men. Suddenly one of them lifted his head and looked in the direction of the house making eye contact with her through the window. "Dalphon! Dalphon!" Zeresh stumbled groping the wall to help support herself and made her way out the door falling on the ground. Seeing her fall, one of the soldiers standing close to her house picked her up. Another soldier went inside of her house, pulled out a chair and gently lowered her on to it facing the gallows.

It was early dawn. The sun had not risen yet, but the neighborhood people began coming out of their homes to see what was going on and the streets began to fill up and encircle the gallows.

Zeresh sat there looking at each of her sons from the youngest to the eldest; Parshandaltha, Dalphon, Aspatha, Poratha, Adalia, Aridatha, Parmashta, Arisai, Aridal and Vajezatha. She looked at each of their faces in horror. All of them were crying softly as they watched her sitting outside of their house. With no more tears in her, no more voice to cry or moan, Zeresh wrapped her arms around herself and rocked back and forth sitting on the chair. She watched as they hung her husband, Haman, now she had to watch as they hung her ten sons. She could not bear it. Two guards stood on each side of her looking straight ahead watching the execution. With her head down, she eyed a long sheath hanging from the soldier's belt to her right. Taking a deep breath, Zeresh stood up and snatched the sheath from the soldier's belt at the same time. Before the soldier could stop her, Zeresh rammed the sheath into her stomach and fell to the ground. All ten of her sons let out a horrific cry as they watched their mother fall to her death. There was nothing they could do; their hands were tied behind their backs as they stood on the gallows platform

The crowd gasped as they witnessed Zeresh's actions, but no one ran to help her. Not even the guards standing beside her bent down to assist her in any way, they let her lay where she fell.

Ahasuerus and Mordecai sat in the chariot in clear view of Zeresh, her house and her ten sons standing on the platform gallows. "Mordecai" Ahasuerus whispered as he watched Zeresh dying on the ground.

"Yes, I know, this is very hard."

"Yes it is. Yes, it is. Do you think men really know and understand how their actions, the choices that they make in their lives; do you think they understand how many people around them suffer if they make the wrong choices? Look at all the people who have had to die because of one man's insecurity and greed."

"I believe every man, every woman, even every child has some sense of right and wrong Ahasuerus. I believe that God has placed moral ethics in all of us. Even the animals know right and wrong. They know how to take care of their young. They do not kill haphazardly. They do not offend haphazardly, only for survival. But man, if you watch and study man, he is greedy, selfish, and corrupt if left to his own devices. If he does not look and recognize God and submit himself to the one true God, he becomes worse than the animals in the wilderness."

Ahasuerus sat quietly watching until Zeresh died. "Guard! Go check on Zeresh. See if she is dead. Take the sheath out of her, place her on a wagon and take her to the palace morgue."

"As you wish Your Majesty" the guard replied and ran over to where Zeresh lay.

Meres stood beside the royal chariot. Ahasuerus looked down at him. "Do you have the decree that is to be read for Haman's sons?"

"Yes Your Majesty."

"Stand in front of the gallows and read it loud enough for everyone to hear."

"As you wish Your Majesty" Meres replied stepping away from the chariot and to the front center of the gallows. Meres looked over at the drummers, held up his hand for them to stop drumming. When all was quiet, he began to read.

"Hear ye, hear ye, hear ye! These men are the sons of Haman, who conspired to have all the Jews throughout the 127 Persian Provinces exterminated. As a result, these ten sons of Haman must also pay with their lives. Parshandaltha; Dalphon, Aspatha, Poratha, Adalia, Aridatha, Parmashta, Aridal, Adalia and Vajezatha, each of you will be hung by the neck until you are dead. Let the executions begin!" Meres dropped his head, walked back standing beside the royal chariot. The drummers began drumming their death drum roll as the guards placed black hoods over each of the men's heads, then slipped the rope over the hoods and tightened them snug around each man's neck. Once everything was in place, the ten guards stepped back onto the solid section of the platform. As the guards stepped back, the guard responsible for pulling the main rope walked across and inspected each man's hood and rope making sure it was securely positioned around their necks, that their hands were securely tied behind their backs. Once he was satisfied, he walked back to his station and pulled the main rope. The trap door opened with a loud clank as it hit against the back structure. The drummers stopped drumming. The ten men fell through the floor and swung back and forth with their feet jerking in the air. The crowd was quiet. The guards were quiet. Ahasuerus and Mordecai sat in the chariot with their head bowed and their hands folded in their laps. Meres stood beside the chariot with his head bowed.

No one anywhere said anything. All was quiet for fifteen minutes. The sun began to rise out of the east and cast a sun ray across the gallows where the ten men swung. Ahasuerus looked up at the sun ray and sighed. "Guard!"

"Yes, Your Majesty."

"Have the palace doctor inspect each of the bodies making sure they are dead. Once the pronouncements are made, remove the bodies, and place them in the wagons then prepare the gallows for the second round of executions."

"As you wish Your Majesty."

"Your lawyers?" Mordecai asked quietly.

"Yes" Ahasuerus replied.

"What about their families? You said you were going to have them killed first."

"Yes and I kept my word. I could not sleep last night so I ordered the guards to awake the families and tell them they were going home this morning. They were to pack their things, set them by the door and the palace servants would deliver them to their homes. Once everything was packed up, the guards were to escort them to the dining room for breakfast, after which, they would be escorted to their homes; the wives to be reunited with their husbands and the children with their fathers. This was done at the beginning of the first watch. I have already received the final report from the palace doctors that the poison has taken effect. All of them are dead. The guards reported that all of them were happy to be going home and was not aware of anything. They were told that their husbands and fathers would be waiting for them at home."

It was completely daylight when the guards escorted Shethar, Carshena, Admatha, Tarshish and Marsena to the front of the gallows facing Ahasuerus and Mordecai in the royal chariot.

"Please have mercy Your Majesty, please" Admatha cried. Seeing Meres standing beside the King's chariot, Admatha pleated with him, "Meres, please tell the King we made a mistake, we changed our minds, we are loyal to him! Please tell him Meres!"

Meres did not look or respond to Admatha or any of his other colleagues. He kept his head down.

Neither Ahasuerus nor Mordecai looked at the men standing in front of them.

"Guards! Carry on!" Ahasuerus shouted.

The drummers began drumming as the guards led the five men up to the top of the gallows positioning them in the center stations and placed the hoods and ropes around their necks.

"Your Majesty, would you like me to read their sentences?" Meres asked.

"No. Post them so the villagers can read their crimes, then execute them quickly."

Meres fastened the decree to one of the gallows post, looked at the guard who had already completed his inspection of the men and returned to his station. With a nod of his head, the guard pulled the rope, the five men fell through the floor as the drummers stopped drumming.

Ahasuerus did not wait for fifteen minutes for the doctor to give his report that the men were dead. "Meres, you stay here and verify that the men are dead. Have their bodies removed and order the guards to destroy these gallows as well as Haman's house. When all of this has been accomplished, come and report to me."

"As you wish Your Majesty" Meres replied bowing at the waist.

Ahasuerus ordered his driver to return he and Mordecai back to the palace. The two men rode back in silence.

After returning to the palace, both men parted and went to their personal quarters. Mordecai stood looking out his bedroom window over the palace grounds rehearsing in his mind all that had happened to him, Esther, and Ahasuerus in the past eighteen months. He marveled at the ways of the Lord, how He elevates one man and demotes another; how He pours out His love to those who seek Him and pours out his wrath on those that hate him. His Divine Providence in the lives of men is wondrous and awesome. "One thing is certain," Mordecai said to himself as he walked over to his couch and sat down in front of the fire, "His ways are definitely not like our ways." Mordecai sat watching the fire for a long time, then fell asleep.

Ahasuerus walked back to his personal lounge and sat down in front of the fire. "God" he prayed, "Have I done everything according to your will?" That familiar peace and presence of the Lord that he experienced a week or two ago enveloped him. He raised his hands in surrender to God as the tears flowed down his face releasing the stress of carrying out his Kingly duties. After several minutes, he too lowered his hands, stared into the fire falling asleep on the couch.

Four months have passed since the Jews fought against and subdued their enemies. Peace was finally restored inside and outside of the palace. Esther delivered a healthy baby boy just as Mordecai and Ahasuerus had prayed for. God's Divine Providence, Mordecai thought as he held his grandson in his arms. How great is our God and his Divine Providence in the lives of his people? Who would have believed that God could use a lowly porter, a gate keeper if you will, and his young Jewish daughter to save the lives of his chosen people? It seems that God delights in using the lowly, the destitute, the weak and the simple to do his bidding, to do great and might things.

All praise be to the God of Abraham, Isaac, and Jacob.

Amen.

THE END

GOD'S DIVINE PROVIDENCE

God's Divine Providence can be seen through the entire Bible. Before I delve into examples of God's Divine Providence, I have outlined a brief word study for "Providence and Divine."

Providence:

Webster's Seventh New Collegiate Dictionary defines "Providence" as:

1. a. Divine guidance of care
    b. God conceived as the power sustaining and guiding human destiny
2. The quality or state of being provident

Provident:

1. Making provision for the future: Prudent
2. Frugal, saving

Divine:

Webster's Seventh New Collegiate Dictionary defines "Divine" as:

1. a. of relating to, or proceeding directly from deity, the right of kings
    b. being deity
    c. directed by deity
2. a. supremely good: superb
    b. Godlike, Heavenly, divinely

God's Divine Providence: His divine guidance, care and provision was in existence before He created the heavens and the earth and all that is in the earth.

"The Lord hath prepared his throne in the heavens; and his kingdom ruleth overall." Psalm 103: 19

From Genesis to Revelation, God demonstrates his Divine Providence in providing a people for himself from the very beginning with the first man Adam in the Old Testament and the prophets of old, all the way through to the New Testament with the second Adam, Jesus Christ. The story of Esther is just one example of how God preserved His people from being extinguished.

Another example is detailed in Geneses 45: 5 – 8; the story of Joseph, (Jacob's or Israel's son) who was sold into Egyptian slavery by his jealous brothers. His brothers thought to do evil to Joseph; God used their evil deed to provide for Jacob's family when a drought spread throughout the land. As a result, Jacob's people were provided for, and Israel became a mighty people. Joseph's brothers had to go down to Egypt to get food to survive only to find they had to go through their brother Joseph who they sold into slavery. When they found out that the official in charge of the food was their brother, they were afraid, but Joseph consoled them.

> "Now therefore be not grieved, nor angry with yourselves, that you sold me hither: for God did send me before you to preserve life. For these two years hath the famine been in the land: and yet there are five years, in the which there shall neither be earing nor harvest. And God sent me before you to preserve you a posterity in the earth, and to save your lives by a great deliverance. <u>So now it was not you that sent me hither, but God: and he hath made me a father to Pharaoh, and lord of all his house and a ruler throughout all the land of Egypt.</u>" Gen. 45: 5 – 8

GOD'S DIVINE PROVIDENCE IN THE BELIEVER TODAY

Does God use His Divine Providence in the lives of His people today? He most certainly does. He is continually preparing a people for Himself through His Son, Jesus Christ. (See John 3:16; Romans 10:9; and Revelation 3:20) These scriptural references are salvation scriptures outlining God's plan of salvation for man so man can have direct communication with Him through Jesus Christ. I like to say, "God's Providential Plan of Salvation."

Once you accept God's gift of salvation through His Son, Jesus Christ; begin reading and studying the Bible. Become obedient to His Word, accept, and implement Biblical instruction into your daily life. You can then begin to stand on God's promises and see His Divine Providence active in your personal life.

> "Trust in the Lord with all thine heart; and lean not unto thine own understanding. In all thy ways acknowledge him, and he shall direct thy paths."
> Proverbs 3: 5,6

GOD'S PLAN OF SALVATION

<u>How do you accept Jesus Christ as your personal Savior? Through belief in His Son, Jesus Christ.</u>

"For God so loved the world, that he gave his only begotten Son, that whosoever believeth in him should not perish, but have everlasting life. For God sent not his Son into the world to condemn the world: but that the world through him might be saved. He that believeth on him is not condemned; but he that believeth not is condemned already, because he hath not believed in the name of the only begotten Son of God." John 3: 16 – 18

"That if thou shalt confess with thy mouth the Lord Jesus, and shalt believe in thine heart that God hath raised him from the dead, thou shalt be saved. For with the heart man believeth unto righteousness; and with the mouth confession is made unto salvation. For the scripture saith, WHOSOEVER BELIEVETH ON HIM SHALL NOT BE ASHAMED. For there is no difference between the Jew and the Greek: for the same Lord over all is rich unto all that call upon him. For WHOSOEVER SHALL CALL UPON THE NAME OF THE LORD SHALL BE SAVED." Romans 10: 9 – 13

"Behold, I stand at the door and knock: if any man hear my voice, and open the door, I will come in to him, and will sup with him, and he with me." Revelation 3:20

BIBLIOGRAPHY

The New Open Bible – Study Edition, in the King James Version;
Thomas Nelson publishers, Nashville, TN, Copyright 1975

The New Open Bible – Study Edition, in the King James Version;
Thomas Nelson publishers, Nashville, TN

Casting of Lots, Page 196
The Historical Books, Page 523
Israel and the Persians, Page 548
Persian Customs in the Book of Esther, Page 591
Israel and the Babylonians, Page 898

Matthew Henry's Commentary on the Whole Bible; Hendrickson
Publishers, Copyright 1991, Book of Esther, page 643

Webster's Seventh New Collegiate Dictionary.
A Merriam-Webster, from G & C Merriam Company, Publishers,
Springfield, Massachusetts, U.S.A.

BIBLICAL CHARACTORS

Abagtha -	One of Ahasuerus' officials; Esther 1:10
Abihail -	Son of Kish – Esther's father; Geneses 2:15
Adalia -	One of Haman's sons; Esther 9:7-10
Admatha -	One of Ahasuerus' Wiseman or lawyer Esther 1:13, 14
Aridal -	One of Haman's sons; Esther 9:7-10
Aridatha -	One of Haman's sons; Esther 9:7-10
Arisai -	One of Haman's sons; Esther 9:7-10
Aspatha -	One of Haman's sons; Esther 9:7-10
Ahasuerus -	King of Persia ruling 127 Provinces from India to Ethiopia; Esther, 1:1
Bigtha -	One of Ahasuerus' Guards who attempted to kill him; Esther 1:21
Biztha -	One of Ahasuerus' officials; Esther 1:10
Bigthan -	Conspired against Ahasuerus; Esther 2:21; 6:2
Carshena	One Ahasuerus' Wiseman or lawyer Esther 1:13, 14
Carcas -	One of Ahasuerus' officials; Esther 1:10
Darius -	Persian King before King Ahasuerus; Ezra 6:1
Dalphon -	One of Haman's sons; Esther 9:7-10
Esther -	Jewish Maiden made Queen of Persia; Esther 2:15-20
Hadassah -	Esther's Hebrew name; Esther 1:7
Haman -	Son of Hammedatha the Agagite, plotted to kill the Jews; Esther 3:1
Harbona -	One of the Ahasuerus' Chamberlains; Esther 7:9
Hatach -	One of Queen Esther's attendants; Esther 4:5-10
Hegai -	King Ahasuerus' Chamberlain Keeper of the Women; Esther 2:15
Kish -	Esther's Grandfather; Esther 2:5

Marsena -	One of Ahasuerus' Wiseman or Lawyer; Esther 1:13, 14
Mehuman -	One of Ahasuerus' Officials; Esther 1:10
Memucan -	One of Ahasuerus' Wiseman or Lawyer; Esther 1:13, 14
Meres -	One of Ahasuerus' Wiseman or Lawyer; Esther 1:13,
Mordecai -	Esther's Cousin and adoptive father; Esther 2:7-15
Parmashta -	One of Haman's sons; Esther 9:7-10
Parshandaltha	One of Haman's sons; Esther 9:7-10
Poratha	One of Haman's sons; Esther 9:7-10
Sanballat -	Hindered Nehemiah in rebuilding Temple; Nehemiah 4: 6,7
Shethar -	One of Ahasuerus' Wiseman or Lawyer; Esther 1:13, 14
Tarshish -	One of Ahasuerus' Wiseman or Lawyer; Esther 1:13, 14
Tatnai -	Persian Governor opposing the Jews; Ezra 5:36
Teresh -	One of Ahasuerus' Guards who attempted to kill him; Esther 1:21
Tobiah -	Hindered Nehemiah in rebuilding Temple; Nehemiah 4: 6, 7
Vajezatha -	One of Haman's sons; Esther 9:7-10
Zeresh -	Haman's Wife; Esther 5:10

FICTIONAL CHARACTORS

Aisha -	Reelaiah and Tamara's Daughter
Ardist -	King's Concubine
Arwa -	King's Concubine
Asha -	King's Concubine
Baylacka -	Soothsayer
Bilshan -	Jewish Neighbor

Dr. Kazim -   Indian Medical Doctor

Eunida -   Jewish Neighbor

Hazilad -   Memucan's Wife

Milshan -   Jewish Neighbor

Motaiah -   Jewish Neighbor

Orit -   King's Concubine

Reelaiah -   Mordecai's Neighbor and friend

Sotaiah -   One of the servants

Shakera -   Reelaiah and Tamara's Daughter

Tamara -   Reelaiah's Wife

Taziah -   Jewish Neighbor

Yara -   Esther's personal servant

Zelda -   Palace Servant

Zena -   Esther's best friend and King's Concubine

JEWISH TIMES

First Watch   Sunset to 9 pm

Second Watch   9 pm to midnight

Third Watch   Midnight to 3 am

Fourth Watch   3 pm to sunrise

First Hour   Sunrise to 9 am

Third Hour   9 am to noon

Sixth Hour   Noon to 3 pm

Nineth Hour   3 pm to sunset

AUTHOR'S BIO

I was born child number 11 in a family of 12 children to Reverend James A Terry II and Thelma Bailey Terry. My mother formed the 12 of us kids into a choir. I began to sing when I was old enough to stand up and take instruction from my parents at the age of three. My mom accompanied and instructed us on piano; my dad directed the choir at times as well as pastored at various Methodist Conference

Churches. As a result, singing influenced my whole life and was the driving force that got me through my childhood; young adult and adult years. All I ever wanted to do and be was a professional singer. God had other plans.

Due to several childhood illnesses, I failed to achieve rudimentary elementary education. I was never able to catch up with my fellow classmates and was held back in the third grade. The embarrassment and stigma of having to repeat the third grade caused me to give up on education; however, I still had to go to school. It was the law of the land. Music got me through grade school, junior high and high school. I sang when I was happy, sad, sorrowful, lonely, angry and disgusted. Singing became my god and God permitted it to be so but, only for a season.

At the age of 10, I accept Jesus Christ as my Savior at an Oliver B. Green tent meeting. He was a fire and brimstone preacher and said if I did not accept Jesus Christ now, I would wake up in hell and the only thing I would remember were the red and green metal posts that held the tent up. I looked up at those red and green metal posts and studied them as he continued preaching. When he gave the altar call, I ran down to the front and accepted Jesus Christ as my Savior.

Scholastic achievement continued to be very weak in my junior and senior high school years. Nothing interested me except singing. To become a teacher of anything required higher education and musical performance was not a reliable occupation. Subsequently, I signed up for clerical courses as my only other option. After graduation, I enrolled in business school receiving an 18 month certificate which provided an opportunity to secure a clerical position within the University of Pittsburgh.

Age 18 was a major turning point in my life. Church life was dull, boring and lifeless to me. I asked my mother how long I was required to attend church. Her response was "When you turn 18, you can make your own decisions." Little did I know that in leaving the church, I was also leaving the protective spiritual covering from my parents as well as the church. For the next seven years, I went out into the world and Satan's territory. Somehow I knew God still heard the prayers of my parents; those prayers kept me alive until I came back to my senses and God delivered me out of Satan's hands.

It was a major struggle to become free from the world's influence and Satan's strongholds. But I learned, and am still learning that nothing is impossible with God. As I struggled for freedom, God began showing me who I was, who I belonged to, and what His plans were for my life. I had no idea what His plans were. I now know that I do not belong to myself.

I married William Charles Mills (W. C. Mills) late in life. Bill was an accomplished musician, piano teacher, professional keyboard and organ player. Even though we performed in some of the same nightclubs in the Pittsburgh area; we were never booked at the same clubs at the same time. I never met nor heard of W.C. Mills in my very, very short nightclub career. I do know that if we had met at that time, we would have never married; neither of us was compatible in those days. Nonetheless, In the fullness of God's time, we did meet and marry. The marriage lasted until God called Bill home 34 years later.

To my surprise, marriage brought compromise! Being single for the first 36 years of my life, I was not familiar with compromise and was shocked to learn I was no longer permitted to sing the way I desired! I prayed and prayed to the Lord about this dilemma only to be instructed to set my singing goals aside for a season and to trust God. To have faith in Him that He would give the music gift back to me in His time. In the interim, and through my husband's love, patience, and tenacity, I learned:

1. God's ways are not like man's ways
2. Submission to my husband
3. Submission to the will and authority of God
4. I learn how to become a piano teacher
5. I became co-author and author of several books:

- *Music Ministry Training Program Beginner Primary Piano Curriculum*
- *M.M.T.P. Coloring & Music Workbook*
- *Adventures In Music Land*
- *The Esther Project*

My Future Goals:

To witness for the Lord
To sing for the Lord
To learn what other plans God has for my life